P9-BBT-820

C.J. CHERRYH
LEGIONS OF HELL

LEGIONS OF HELL

Copyright © 1987 by C.J. Cherryh

All rights reserved, including the right to reproduce this book or portions thereof in any form.

A Baen Books Original

Baen Publishing Enterprises
260 Fifth Avenue
New York, N.Y. 10001

First Baen printing, July 1987

ISBN: 0-671-65653-8

Cover art by David Mattingly

Printed in the United States of America

Distributed by
SIMON & SCHUSTER
1230 Avenue of the Americas
New York, N.Y. 10020

Author's Note

Portions of *Legions of Hell* first appeared in the following short stories: "The Prince" from *Heroes in Hell*; "Knight's Move" from *Kings in Hell*; "Monday Morning" and "Marking Time" from *Rebels in Hell*; "Sharper than a Serpent's Tooth" from *Crusaders in Hell*; and "Meetings" from *The Gates of Hell*.

Because certain events in these stories are essential to what follows within this book, the author took the liberty of extracting scenes where needed, to maintain the integrity of the narrative, rather than relating them in summary; which the author hopes the reader will find more satisfactory than oblique references to these stories; and the editors have most graciously agreed to this.

Special thanks also to Janet Morris for permission to give the other side of Caesar's interview with Welch, as seen in her story "Graveyard Shift" from *Rebels in Hell*.

Also, for the reader's information and because such persons as Caesarion and Mouse and Scaevola did truly live, the author has included a glossary of historical figures and place names, as well as definitions of the more commonly used foreign words.

Book One

The Prince

1

The foundations shook. The lights went out. The computer went down.

"Dannazione—!"

Lights went up again. The monitor came up on a blank screen and the disk drive hummed away, hunting idiotically for vanished instructions.

Dante Alighieri was already on his way down the hall, down the stairs, through the grand hall, and into the First Citizen's glassed-in garden portico. *"I scellerati! I maledetti—!"*

"Sivis, sivis Graece modum, Dantille." Augustus waggled fingers, waved a hand, and anxious sycophants shied aside as he swung his feet over the side of the couch. *"Noli tant' versari—"*

"Gone!" Dante waved a fistful of papers. "Gone!" The steam seemed to go out of him. He drew one breath and another and gasped after a third. "I had it. I *had* it—"

"Indubitably," Niccolo drawled from a chair to the side.

Dante's dark eyes went wide. White showed around his nostrils and along the line of his lips. Then the eyes suffused with tears and the lips parted in a sob after breath. "If I could remember—if I could only remember—but that machine, but this place, but those lunatics, *ma questi*—"

"I know, I know, my dear boy." Augustus put out his hand and patted the poet's hand, which was clenched white-knuckled on his knee opposite him. "You have to be patient, you know. You have to expect these things."

"It is," said Niccolo, extending his feet before him, ankles crossed, "the nature of this place."

Dante bowed his head into his hands. "The damned lights fail, this insane power that comes and goes—" He looked up again, at Augustus' face, at the half-dozen sycophants. At Niccolo and Kleopatra and the visitor-youth who stared wide-eyed at the mad poet. "I was so close. They *know*, don't you think they know? And the lines are gone, *two hundred lines*—"

"You'll remember them again. I'm sure you will."

"If it made any difference," said Niccolo.

"Damn you!" The poet leaped up and for a moment violence trembled in his hands, his whole body. Then his countenance collapsed, the tears fell, and Dante Alighieri turned and ran from the room.

"Do you know," Niccolo said to no one in particular, "I did once admire the man."

"Shut up, Niccolo," Augustus said.

Niccolo Machiavelli stretched his feet the further and made a little wave of his hand. *"Dimittemi."*

"Sorry won't mend it. Dammit, Niccolo, do you have to bait him?"

"The man's dangerous. I tell you, *Auguste,* you ought to have him out of the house. Visit him on Louis. *Two* madmen ought to get on well together. They can plot strategies together."

"Be still, I say!"

A second flourish of the hand. "You always had a fondness for the arts. It served you well. This man will not."

"Niccolo—"

A third lift of the hand, this time in surrender.

"*Signore.*"

"Out!" That was for the sycophants, the collection that hovered and darted like gnats throughout the Villa. Petty functionaries and bureaucrats in life, they haunted the place and came and went in perpetual facelessness, trying for points. One scurried up with papers, a pen.

"If the Imperator would—"

"*Out!*"

The sycophant fled. The newly arrived youth, who had come wandering into the downstairs hall with some sort of petition, gathered himself to his feet and tried for the door.

"*You,*" Augustus said, and transfixed the fugitive in midstep. "*What's your name?*"

"B-B-B-Brutus, if it please you, sir."

"*Di immortales.* Which?"

"W-W-W-Which?"

"Lucius, Decimus, or the Assassin?"

"A-A-A-Assass-in?"

"S-S-S-Sounds like the First Lucius," Niccolo said.

"Shut up, dammit, Niccolo. *Which are you, boy? Uterque?*"

"M-Marcus. Marcus Junius Brutus."

"Ye gods." Kleopatra got off her couch, on the other side. Niccolo sat stiff and with his hand quite surreptitiously on the dagger at the back of his belt. And the Akkadian got up with his hand on his sword.

"What's wrong?" young Brutus asked, all wide-eyed. "What's the matter?"

"You just got here, did you?"

"I—don't know." Wide eyes blinked. "I—just g-g-got this notice—" Brutus reached into his robe and Sargon's sword grated in its sheath. Brutus stopped cold, a terrified look on his face. "Did I do something?"

"Never mind the paper," Augustus said. "I've seen them. Official directive. An assignment of zone. Where have you been all this time, boy? Downstairs?"

"I—don't know. I—I think I'm d-d-d-dead—"

"How?"

"I don't know!"

"The Administration has a sense of humor."

"Quid dicis?"

"Never mind." The house shook. The lights blinked again. Augustus raised his eyes ceilingward as the lights swayed. A wild sob drifted down the corridors. *Damn!* —from far up the hall.

"Viet Cong," Niccolo explained. Young Brutus looked pathetically confused. "The park. *Viet Cong*. They make overshots. Plays merry hob with the power lines— You don't know about that either."

A slow shake of the head. A steady gaze of quiet, helpless eyes.

"Sometimes," Niccolo said, "you really know it's Hell."

"The man who lost something," Brutus said over lunch in the garden court. "What did he lose?"

Niccolo blinked, looked at the boy across the wire and glass table—Kleopatra had joined them, demure and dainty in a 1930's cloche and black veil. And Hatshepsut. It was an unlikely association, the Greek with the Egyptian, the Egyptian in a lavender 2090's bodysuit and with a most distressing armament about her person. But they were all a little anxious lately. Niccolo kept to his dagger: and a tiny 25th-century disruptor, when armament seemed necessary.

"Dantillus," Brutus said.

"Dante. Dante Alighieri. Born long after your time." Niccolo sipped his wine, waved off a hovering sycophant who proffered more. The sycophant persisted, sycophant-like. Niccolo turned a withering look on the fool, who ebbed away. "Never trust them," he muttered. "Always ask for the whole bottle."

"Check the cork," said Kleopatra, and Brutus' wide eyes looked astonished.

"But what did he lose?"

"Oh," said Hatshepsut, "*ka* and *ba,* I think."

"*He psuche,*" said Kleopatra. "*Kai to pneuma.*"

"*Animus et anima,*" Niccolo said with a twist of his mouth, and smiled. "His soul. At least that's what he calls it. — *Dammit,* man!" He rescued his glass from a sycophant who oozed up to the table so subtly it almost succeeded in pouring.

"More wine," said Hatshepsut. "The whole bottle."

The sycophant was gone on the breath.

"You see," said Niccolo, "Dante Alighieri was very devout. He's sure it was a mistake that sent him here." He laughed, with a second bitter twist of his mouth. "Isn't it always? That rascal Cesare Borgia made it upstairs—his father was a pope. And here I sit, because I wrote a book."

"You think that's why," said Kleopatra, sipping wine. Her eyes were enormous through the veil. A diamond glittered on her cheek, beside a perfect nose. "I daresay that's what drives poor Dante mad—*thinking,* you understand. He was quite unreasonable from the beginning—began writing out all his works by hand, absolutely certain that he had offended—*ummn*—the Celestial—by some passage of his work. And he went to the computer to speed his reconstruction. Now *that's* become an obsession. Dante and that machine, hour after hour. Checking and checking. Redoing all his work. He gets terribly confused. Then the computer goes down. Poof! One has to feel sorry for him."

"I don't," said Hatshepsut. She leaned elbows on the table. "The man was a fool. *La divina Beatrice.* To put divinity on a lover—*that's* a mistake! I had a lover try to take it once; chiseled his way into my monuments— Ssst! Let me tell you, I was a god. So was my friend here—well, god*dess;* times change. Augustus was, of course, but the silly Romans only did it after they were dead. I was a real god, beard, *atef,* crook, and flail, the whole thing; I held my power and I died old. Now I know why I'm here. Politics. Niccolo's here on politics.

So's Augustus. And if Dante's here, it's still politics. Nothing else."

"Dante's become quite a nervous man," said Niccolo. "He's certain he's wronged someone important." He shrugged. "On the other hand— Perhaps he *doesn't* belong here. I'd truly watch what I told him."

"You think I belong here?" Brutus asked in dismay.

"But you have a paper," Niccolo said softly. "It says you do. Just don't trust Dante. The man was brilliant. Never mistake that. But he's not able to accept this. Some never seem to. Not to accept where one is— that's quite mad."

The sycophant arrived with the wine, another with glasses. Niccolo turned and took them, slapped an intrusive hand.

"—As for instance, I survived where others did not. I survive here. I keep company with gods. And a surfeit of sycophantic fools." He waved off a corkscrew and supplied his own from his wallet. "You never know. Poor Cl-Cl-Claudius was deified with a dish of mushrooms. Cesare Borgia had a certain touch." He inserted the prongs and pulled the cork. "Most anything can be deadly. Poison on the glass rim. On one side of a knife both parties share. One has to trust someone sometime." He poured a glass and handed it toward the youth. "As for instance, now."

"He *what?*" Julius Caesar swung down out of his jeep in the driveway, swept off his camouflage helmet, and dusted a hand on his fatigues. "I don't believe it."

"Nevertheless," said Sargon. The Akkadian leaned on the fender while the khaki-clad driver got out and stood staring. "Marcus Junius Brutus."

"There were seven hundred years of Marcus Junius Brutuses."

"The last. Augustus said to tell you." Sargon set his jaw and his ringleted beard and hair shadowed his sloe-eyed face in angular extremes. "He's seventeen."

Julius looked at his driver. Decius Mus gnawed at his lip, took the rifles out, and slung them over his shoulder as if he had heard nothing at all.

"Dammit, Mouse—"

"He doesn't remember," Sargon said. "I told you: he's seventeen."

"Oh, *hell*."

"Yeah," Sargon said.

Octavianus Augustus paced to the window and gazed outward where the Hall of Injustice towered up into Hell's forever burning clouds. Looked back at Julius, who sat in a spindly chair, booted feet crossed. Mud was on the boots, flecks of mud spattered Julius' patrician face. Julius always brought a bit of reality with him; and when he was under the roof Augustus felt like Octavianus again; felt like plain Octavius, jug-eared adolescent scholar.

Get out of Rome, Julius had advised his widowed niece Atia once upon a time, a dangerous time of civil unrest; and sent her whole family to obscurity in Greece. But there had been letters from Julius. There had been the long understanding: careful tutelage of her son Octavius, the pretenses, the cultivation of this and that faction—not least of them the army. To meet with Julius under these circumstances, in the quiet of his private apartments—it brought back the old days; brought back secrecy; and hiding; and as always when uncle Julius talked business, Augustus, *Pater Patriae*, First Citizen, felt his ears a bit too large, his shoulders a bit thin, felt his own intellect no match for the raw scheming charisma that was Julius.

Augustus was a god, posthumously. Julius sneered at gods and worshiped luck. His own. Julius deliberately created his own legends. Even in Hell. And Augustus felt helplessly antiquated, in his light robes, his Romanesque villa, before this man who took to modernity like a fish to water—

Julius spurned the *most* modern weapons. Not to be thought ambitious. Of course.

"It's us they're aiming at," Augustus said finally. "This little gift comes from high Authority. The refinement, the subtlety of it: that argues for—" Augustus' eyes shifted toward the skyscraper that towered at the end of Decentral Park. And meant His Infernal Highness. The Exec.

"Well, whoever set this little joke up has certainly bided his time," Julius said. "If it was planned this way from the start, that lets Hadrian out as originator—Brutus was in storage a damn long while before he got here. Has to be someone who predated us."

"I've wondered—" Augustus' voice sank away. He came back and sat down, hands clasped between his knees, in a chair opposite his great-uncle. A boy again. "How high up—and how far back—do the Dissidents go?"

"Making the boy a catspaw for that lot?" Julius rubbed the back of his head where a little baldness was; it was a defensive habit, a nervous habit, quietly pursued. "Damn, I'd like to know how long he's been held in reserve and where he's been."

"No way to find that out without getting into Records."

"And deal with the fiends. No. That's vulnerability. Open ourselves up to his royal asininity—"

Hadrian, Julius meant. Supreme Commander. Lately kidnapped by the Dissidents. So much for High Command efficacy. Augustus flinched at the epithet. "He's in favor—"

"Asses are always in fashion. They make other asses feel so safe."

"*Absit mi!* For the gods' own sake, Gaius—"

"Isn't it the way of empires? You set one up, then you have to let the damn bureaucrats have it. Only thing that saved Rome, all those secretaries, with all those papers—no one after us ever did run the government. Couldn't find the damn right papers without the secretaries. The thing got too big to attack. Even from the inside. It just tottered on over the corpse of every ass who thought he could shift it left or right. Same thing going on down at the Pentagram right now. The Dissidents work for the government. They don't know it; but they do. Whole thing runs like a machine." Julius ticked his hand back and forth. "Pendulum. It gets the great fools and the efficient with alternate strokes. Now here's Hadrian gone missing—you think the government's really going to miss Hadrian? Not before snowfall. You think it cares, except for the encouragement it affords fools? His *secretaries* know where all the damn papers are. The Exec'll put some other ass in if they lose him. If they get him back they'll let him serve a while before they advise him to retire— he's lost prestige, hasn't he? But appoint me in his place? Not a chance in Hell. They'll pick some damn book-following fool like Rameses."

"You think all of this is interconnected."

"You miss my point. *Chaos* is the hierarchy's medium. They don't plan a damn thing. Half the chaos comes from the merest chance some insider with a capital S has a coherent plan. The rest of it comes of every damn nut outside the system who thinks he's just figured it out. The waves of the bureaucracy will roll over it all eventually. But you have to think of that chance: that very briefly, someone in a Position wants to neutralize us. Beware the bureaucrats. Beware the secretaries."

"*Prodi*. You escaped them."

"Oh, no, no, no, *Augustulle*. What do you think, that geniuses masterminded my demise? It was the bureaucrats. The fools. And who survived it all? You killed the conspirators and inherited all the secretaries. And where are those same secretaries?" Julius waved a hand toward the wall, the window, the Skyscraper. "Still at it. All those damn little offices. You wonder why I stay out in the field? The army's the only bureaucracy you can't sit on. I *really* don't want to find his imperial asininity. I'd *like* the damn Dissidents to send Hadrian's head in. That'd take him out of circulation a while. I'm terribly afraid they won't. But someone in those offices is either afraid I'll take out the Dissidents—or thinks I might use this operation to gather troops for myself—"

"Of course you're not doing that."

"Frankly I'm not. I always preferred Gaul. It was much safer than Rome. Wasn't it?"

"You never were a politician."

"Never."

"Niccolo says kill him."

"Pah. Kill him! What would that stop? I tell you: what they've done in sending this boy is damned effective. I'd rather face a regiment."

"Than kill him? *Pro di*, when the State's at risk, one life—*any* life—"

"Now that's Niccolo talking. No. I'll tell you another thing. I have a soft spot." Julius picked up his helmet. Looked at it and fingered a dent ruefully as if it held an answer. "Maybe it's my head, what do you think?"

"I think he's a problem you want to ignore." Augustus got to his own feet with a profound sigh. "I'll tell you where the soft spot is. It's age that gets to you. It's battering down the fools time after time and finding they're endless. It's getting tired of treachery. There's a point past which Niccolo's advice has no meaning. There's this terrible lassitude—"

Julius looked up at him, a stare from deep in those black eyes, and Augustus/Octavius flinched. "Do you think they know that—the secretaries?"

"Like rats know blood when they draw it. They're playing a joke."

"Does it occur to you that they're playing it on him as well—on Brutus? Maybe he's offended someone."

"Dante."

"Offended *Dante*?"

"No. *Offended someone*. That's how they manage us, you know. There's always that nagging worry. Who it could offend. Who might know. How far the ripples might go. Dante's obsessed with it. It's a disease. It's the chief malady in Hell. I have it. You have it. We're all vulnerable. *Prodi, win* the damned war!

Julius smiled that quirkish smile of his. "I do. By continuing to fight it."

"Damn, as soon argue with Mouse!"

"No one argues with Mouse. He doesn't *want* anything. He knows this is Hell. You and I keep forgetting it, that's our trouble. They make it too comfortable for us long-dead. And then they do something—"

"Like this."

"They find something you want. It doesn't take a great mind to do that. A fool can do it. What they can't see is where it leads. And how it leads back to them. Mouse teaches me patience, *Augustulle*. A man who *chose* this place of his own volition has nothing they can hold him by. I have no intention of winning my war. Or of killing this boy. Now I know about him what I should have known all those years ago."

"That he's your son?"

"That, I knew. No. *Now* I know how to hold him."

"Like Antonius. Like Antonius, brooding over there with Tiberius and his damned—"

Julius quirked an eyebrow. "You were my trouble with Antonius, *Augustulle*. You still are. Antonius refuses to come where you are. And my only Roman son knew I couldn't acknowledge him. For my reputation's sake. For that bitch Rome. I'll tell you another secret. I never expected to live as long as I did. It's the women; the Julian women—gods, if we could persuade my aunt in here. Old aunt Julia pushed and shoved Marius; did the same to me; and trained my sister, who taught your mother, who trained you. Brutus didn't have a Julia, that was what. Just the little society-minded fool I got him on. I turned him away. And lo, in fate's obscure humor, he turns out to be the only *Roman* son I ever sired. I always thought I had time. You, off in Greece—you were insurance."

"You'd have killed me if you and Calpurnia—"

"*Prodi*, no. What was Alexander's will? *To the strongest?* I knew which that was. You don't hold a grudge, do you? *Don't* create me another Antonius, nephew. Brutus, I can handle."

Augustus opened his mouth, trying to find something to say to that. But Julius turned and left, closing the door gently behind him.

The floor shook to a distant explosion. The lights dimmed and brightened again.

Julius never paused in his course down the hall. The troops had the Cong baffled. The Cong made periodic tries on the villa. It was perpetual stalemate.

It was a *raison d'etre*. And a power base.

He snapped his fingers and a half a dozen sycophants heard the sound and converged beside him as he walked along. No sycophant ever resisted such a summons.

"I want," he said, "the young visitor: in the library."

He walked on. There were other orders to pass. Some of them were for Mouse.

"He's out of his mind," said Sargon.

"His son," Kleopatra said, drifting on her back. The pool was Olympic-sized, blue-tiled. Kleopatra righted herself and trod water while Sargon sat on the rim and dangled his feet in. "Son, son, son, dammit." She swam off toward the other end, neat quick strokes, and Niccolo, standing chest deep, wiped his hair back and gazed after her.

"Ummnn," Niccolo said. While Kleopatra seized the baroque steel ladder and climbed out, black and white striped 1980's swimsuit and very little of it. "Doesn't *look* like a mother, does she?"

"Caesarion."

"Very touchy. *Very* touchy." Niccolo waited till the diminutive figure had walked away toward the dressing rooms, lips pursed. Then: "Half a dozen children and estranged from all of them."

"This damned boy is setting the house on its ear."

"He'll do more than that. It's a master stroke. Marcus Junius Brutus. Julius' natural son. Augustus had more than one reason to kill him, didn't he? Brutus couldn't have *claimed* his paternity and built on Julius' without acknowledging himself a parricide. But Augustus could take no chances. Brutus murders Julius; Augustus takes out Brutus—Kleopatra's brats all side with their dear papa Antonius, completely his. Even Julius' other son, the noble Caesarion. Dear, *ambitious* Caesarion; Augustus killed both of Julius' natural sons, you know. So in Hell Julius sides with his heir Augustus; Kleopatra sides with Julius, completely ignoring Augustus' little peccadillo in murdering one of her children—Isn't love marvelous? While Marcus Antonius sulks in Tiberius' merry little retinue, drinking himself stuporous. *There's* the man who handed Julius his soul to keep; and Julius just used it and tossed it. Do you know the worst irony? Antonius still loves him. He loves Kleopatra. And those kids. And his sister and *her* little crew of murderers and lunatics. Antonius loves everyone but Augustus, who destroyed him. And lo! Brutus—who always was the greatest threat Antonius understood. This just might bring the poor fellow back."

"Neutralize Caesar."

"Someone in the Exec's service planned this one. Someone *Roman*. Someone who understands enough to know where the threads of this run."

"Tiberius?"

"Tiberius was never subtle. Try Tigellinus. Try Livia. Try Hadrian himself."

"Before he was kidnapped?"

"If he was kidnapped. What if he ran the Dissidents?"

"You dream!"

"I put nothing beyond possibility. I'm surprised by nothing."

"Brutus certainly surprised you."

"Only in his youth. He would arrive someday. That he hadn't only meant that he would. It was irresistible to someone."

"Maybe he just served out his time in the Pit, eh?"

Niccolo leaned his arms back on the rim of the pool. His eyes half-lidded. "The Pit is a myth. I doubt its literal existence."

"Then where do they go? Where *are* the ones we miss?"

"In torment, of course. Wondering when *we're* going to show up. And when it palls, when at long last it palls and we all stop worrying—" Niccolo made a small move of a scarred hand. "*Eccolo*. Here they are."

Sargon's hands tensed on the pool rim. He slid into the water and glared.

"There are people we *all* worry about finding," Niccolo said. "Look what they've done to Brutus. *Innocence*. *Ignorance*. Whips and chains are a laugh, Majesty. It's our *mistakes* that get us. The Pit is here. We're in it."

"You have a filthy imagination!"

"Intelligence is my curse. I am a Cassandra. That is *my* hell, Majesty. No one listens *all* the time. Always at the worst moment they fail to heed my advice." Niccolo rolled his eyes about the luxurious ceiling, the goldwork, the sybaritic splendor. "I will not even solicit you. I *know*, you see, that if I gain you, you will fail *me*, Majesty, Lion of Akkad. That is the worm that gnaws me."

"Insolence ill becomes you. *You* are the worm that gnaws this house. Sometimes I suspect *you*—"

Niccolo's dark brows lifted. "*Me*. You flatter my capabilities. I have no power."

"Remember you're in Hell, little Niccolo. Remember that everything you do is bound to fail. *That* is the worm that gnaws you. Power will always elude you."

"I adopt Julius' philosophy. Cooperate in everything. And *do* what I choose. Which is little. Fools are their own punishment and they are ours."

"Fools are in *charge* down here!"

"That's why they suffer least. Are you content, Lion? Does nothing gnaw at *you*? No. Of course not. You're like poor Saint Mouse. The one virtuous man in Hell. The one incorruptible soul. He had no hope. But you do. Why else do you live in this house? You were no client king. You ruled the known world."

"Flatterer. I also adopt Julius' philosophy. And you will not stir me, little vulture. No more you stir *him*." Sargon leaned into the water and swam lazily on his back. "I am immune." His voice echoed off the high ceiling and off the water. "Better a foreign roof than Assurbanipal's court. If you want intrigue, little vulture, try your hand there. My own ten wives are *all* there. Not to mention the heirs. Why do you think I'm *here*? Not mentioning all the other kings, and all the other queens and concubines. Don't teach *me* intrigue, little vulture. Take notes."

He reached the ladder. He climbed up to the side, water streaming from dark curling hair and beard and chest. And Niccolo smiled lazily, not from the eyes.

"I am writing a new book," Niccolo said. "Dante inspires me. I am writing it on the administration of Hell."

"Who will read it, little vulture?"

"Oh. There will be interest. In many quarters."

Sargon scratched his belly and wiped his hand there. "Damn, little vulture. They'll have you in thumbscrews if you go poking around Administration."

"For instance, do you know that Julius exchanges letters with Antonius?"

Sargon stopped all motion.

"Mouse takes them." Niccolo turned and heaved himself up onto the rim of the pool, turned on his hands and sat, one knee up and hands locked about it. "I wonder what he's going to write today. He *will* write. Mark me that he will." He smiled, not with the eyes. "He'll have to tell Antonius that Brutus has come,

you know. Antonius would never forgive him if he
didn't. And never's such a damned long time down
here."

"Damn your impertinence to the Pit. I had a wife
like you. I strangled her. With my own hands."

Niccolo spread wide his arms. "I could never equal
your strength, Lion. I should never hope to try."

Sargon glared a moment. Then he seized up a towel
and wiped his hair and beard with it. Hung it about his
neck with both hands, and there was a glint in his
almond eyes. "Come along, little vulture. I have uses
for you. How many others do? Hatshepsut? Augustus?
—Hadrian?"

"How should I betray a confidence? Lion, do you
attempt to corrupt me?"

"Impossible."

The lights flickered. A screen went dark, and Dante
leaped from his chair. "Ha!" he cried, "*ha!* I got you,
you thrice-damned sneak!" With a note of hysteria
crackling in his voice and a maniacal stare, man at
cyclopic machine. "Thought you got me! I had it saved!
Saved, do you hear me?" He jerked the recorded disk
from the drive and waved it in front of the monitor.
"*Right here!*"

"Do you really think they hear you?"

He dropped the disk and spun about, hair stringing
into his eyes. He wiped it back, blinked at something
that did not, for a change, glow monitor-green; and
straightened a spine grown cramped with myopic peering
at minuscule rippling letters. That something which
did not glow was a man in 20th-century battledress.
Was the owner of a pair of combat boots that flaked
mud onto his Persian carpet. Of a large black gun at his
hip, a brass cartridge belt, brass on his shirt, a black
head of hair, and a face that belonged on coinage.

"Caesar."

"Marvelous machines." The Imperator-deified walked

over to the computer which had come up with *READY*, and picked up the disk.

"Don't—d-don't." Dante Alighieri perspired visibly. Knotted his large, fine hands.

"Oh?" Julius tapped a few keys. *DRIVE?* the monitor asked. "Wondrous," Julius said. "Do you know, I need one of these." He looked the disk over, one side and the other. Slipped it into the drive. Called up *MENU*.

"Please—"

"I did quite a bit of writing myself, you know. I still keep notes and memoirs. Old habits. You're sweating, man. You really oughtn't to work so hard."

"Please." Dante flipped the drive drawer, ejected the disk into his hands. "Please. I'd hate to lose it."

"The great epic? Or your little list of numbers?"

"I—" Dante's mouth opened and shut.

"Never trust the sycophants. I'll *give* you a number, scribbler. I want to run with it. I understand you're quite talented."

"*Io non mai—*"

"Of course you do." Julius reached out and gathered a handful of the poet's shirt. "*Prodi*, you do it all the time, *mastigia*. With our equipment, on our lines, with our reputation. Let's play a little game. You like numbers? Let me give you the one for the War Department."

"I—I—I—"

"It even works."

Brutus paced the library, paced and paced the marble patterns, up and down in front of the tall cases of books and scrolls. He waited. That was what the message had told him to do. He paced and he worried, recalling innuendo, Niccolo's small barbs, and the brittle wrath in Kleopatra's eyes. He had amused the Egyptian: Hatshepsut. There had been mockery in the way she looked at him. There had been invitation.

And he was very far from wanting *that* bed or another

bottle of wine with Niccolo Machiavelli or another of
those looks from Octavianus Augustus *ne* Octavius,
plebeian—who regarded him as if he had coils and
scales and still dealt with him in meticulous courtesy—
wise, he thought of Octavianus; *wise man*—with instinc-
tive judgment. And he could not give a copper for his
life or his safety with the others without whatever
restraint Gaius Octavianus Augustus provided—but he
did not know how long that might last.

Did he order me to wait here? Brutus wondered in
confusion. *He knows me. I don't remember him. With
the adoption suffix on his name. I didn't catch the new
clan. And gods, what clan has Augustus for a cognomen?
No, it's got to be a title. Imperator, they called him. A
war hero. And a god, prodi! And goddesses. And Dantillus
and Niccolo— Are they serious?*

*They're laughing at me, that's what. They hate me. I
threaten them. Why?*

What am I to wait for here?

He found the wine uneasy at his stomach, and his
skin uneasy in the chill air, in this awful half familiarity
with things-as-they-were. He did not like to look out
the window, where a building towered precariously
skyward, vanishing into red, roiling cloud. The sight
made him nauseated. It would fall. It would *sway* in
the winds. What skill could make such a thing?

*Is it like this, to be dead? What happened to the
world, that books are mostly codices and lights come on
and off by touching and how do I know these things
and why do these people I never met in my life all know
me?*

Is this what it is, to be dead? Are these shades and
shadows?

Is this man Niccolo one of us?

Is he a god like Hatshepsut?

Am *I*?

What did I die of? Why can't I remember?

The door opened. A man in clean, crisp khaki walked

in, a handsome man of thirty with dark hair and lazy amusement in his eyes.

"Is it you?" Brutus asked—for he doubted everything around him. "O gods, is it *you?*"

"*Et tu,*" Julius said, and closed the door behind him. "My son."

Brutus drew a gulp of air. Stared, helplessly.

"We've had this interview once before," Julius said. "Or *have* we? Massilia?" Julius walked toward him, stopped with head cocked to one side and hands in his belt. "You surely remember."

"I remember."

"Well, gods, sit down. It's been too long." Brutus retreated to the reading table and propped himself against the edge with both hands, trembling.

"My mother—told me—"

"So you said in Massilia."

"But—when did I die? You *know,* don't you? Everyone knows something I don't— *Prodi,* can't someone be honest with me?"

Julius gave him that long, heavy-lidded stare of his. The mouth quirked up at the side the way it would and the lock that fell across his brow the way it would. This was the Caius Julius Caesar who had gone over the wall in Asia; made scandal of the king of Bithynia; set the Senate on its ear.

Are all those things gone, above?

"So," Julius said. "Honest with you. You stand here less than twenty. And you don't remember anything."

"*Me di—*"

"That might be a benefit."

"Why? What happened? Where did I—?"

"—die? That's a potent question. What if I asked you not to ask yet?"

"I—"

"Yes," Julius said. "*Hell* of a question to hold in check, isn't it? Hell is doubt, boy, and self-doubt is the worst. Doubt of my motives—well, you must have made

some sort of mistake up there, mustn't you? Or here.
You can die in Hell too, you die down here and you can
come back right away or a *long* time later. When do
you think you came?"

Brutus stood away from the table edge, waved a
helpless hand at sunlight no longer there. "I was riding
along a road, there by Baiae, just a little country track,
it was just—an hour or two— Then—I woke up—*di me
iuvent!*—on a table—this—this unspeakable old man—"

"The Undertaker. Yes. I do well imagine."

"Did I fall? Did my horse throw me?"

"You weren't to ask, remember. For a while."

"It was something awful! It was something—"

"Can't let go of it, can you? Especially self-doubt. I
tell you that's the worst for you. Be confident—look me
in the eyes, there. See? Better already. Straighten the
back. Fear, fear's the killer. Kills you a thousand times.
Somebody put that in my mouth. *Nice* writer. There
now—" Julius came close and adjusted a wrinkle in
Brutus' tunic. "You just take what comes. You and
I—well, there're worse places. Assuredly."

"Is my mother here?"

"I really don't think she wants to see me. I don't hear
from her. Never have. One thing you learn down here,
boy, is not to rake up old coals. People you think you
might want to see—well, time doesn't exactly pass down
here. Oh, there are hours in the day—eventually.
Sometimes you know it's years. Sometimes you don't.
Whatever time it's been, you're not the boy who was
riding down that road outside Baiae, now, are you?
Death is a profoundly lonely experience. It changes
everyone. But— You don't have that, do you?"

"I *don't!* I *haven't,* I can't *remember*—"

"Without that perspective. Gods. Poor boy, you can't
well understand, can you? You just—"

"—blinked. I blinked and I was *here*, on that table,
with that nasty old man, that—*creature*. I—"

"Can you trust me?"

Brutus took in a breath, his mouth still open. His eyes flickered with the cold slap of that question.

"Can you trust me?" Julius asked again. "Here you are. You never liked me much. I've told you that the dead change. You don't know what direction I've changed. You came to me at Massilia and I never did figure out exactly what you expected of me. We talked. You remember that. You asked were you truly my son and I said—"

"—only my mother knew. *Pro di immortales*, was that a thing to say to me?"

"But *true*, boy. Only she does know. I had to tell the truth with you, the absolute truth: it was all I could give you. Self-knowledge. I had to make you know your situation. And what certain actions could cost. Protect your mother; protect your father's name—the name you carry; protect myself—yes; from making the feud with the Junii worse than it was. Politically I didn't need it. Maybe it was misguided mercy that I was as easy on you as I was. It was a hard trip for a boy to make. It alienated your father's family, humiliated your mother; and if it weren't for your mother's relatives and that little military appointment you got after that interview, the scandal would have broken wide open. It was a damned stupid thing you did, coming to me. Too public. Too obviously confrontation. And you're still the boy who made that trip, aren't you? I see it in your eyes. All hurt, all seventeen, all vulnerable and full of righteousness and doubt. And you needing so badly to trust me. Have you an answer yet?"

"Damn you!"

"You said that then too. Well, here we are, both of us. Damned and dead. Can you trust me? Can you trust life and death made me wiser, better? I know you. You're a boy looking for his father. And you've found him. You've got all this baggage you've brought to lay at his feet and ask him to do something magical to make you not a bastard and *not* whispered about in your family and not at odds with your relatives, and not, not, not every damn thing that was wrong with your existence when you rode to Massilia. A lot of problems for a seventeen year old. You think I could have solved them with a stroke."

"You could have done something."

"Well, you're a *few* months older, at least. In Massilia that winter you wanted everything. Let me give you the perspective of my dying, since you lack your own: everything and anything I did with you that day was doomed to fail. You were the only one in that room who had the power to do anything. Do you know—you still are?"

"Dammit, don't play games with me!"

"Not a game. You're seventeen. It's the summer after. You haven't figured it out *yet*. I failed to handle your existence. Your mother failed. Your father of record failed. They found a compromise that let you live ignorant until he died and you were old enough to pick up on the gossip. Then it started, right? Must've been hell, you and the Junius family gods. Manhood rites. *That* must have been full of little hypocrisies. February rites: praying to Junius ancestors, not that they heard it. Hell on earth. All your seventeen years. And I regret that, boy. But what could I do that late? Make it a public scandal instead of a private one?"

"Was I a *suicide*?"

"There you are, back to that question. So you considered suicide after talking to me. Maybe you considered killing yourself all that long ride home. Am I right?"

"Yes." A small voice. Brutus rolled his eyes aside, at the wall, at anything. "I *didn't* kill myself. Not on that road, that summer. I'm sure of that, at least. I was happy—I loved a girl—"

"Good for you. So you did find an answer of sorts. I told you, it had to be your own answer. Your existence was centerless as long as you looked to me to justify

you; as long as you looked to your mother or to Junius.
You were your own answer, the only possible answer.
Do you understand me now?"

"I was the only one who cared."

"Not the only one who *cared*, son. The only one who
could *do* anything. You could have killed yourself. Or
me. Which would have been even worse for you. Or
you could go back to Rome, go out to Baiae and be
seventeen and in love. How was she?"

"*Dammit*, do you have to put your lecherous hand on
everything?"

Julius made a shrug, hands in the back of his belt. "It
probably made a difference in your life—one way or the
other. *Prodi*, you were so vulnerable."

"Was she. *Was* she. *Is! Is! Dammit*—"

"You're dead. I assure you, you're dead and so is
she. Whoever she was. And remember what I said about
the dead changing. You're late. I've been waiting for
you—thousands of years. Now do you see what you're
into?"

"*Di me iuvent.*"

"You're a lost soul, son. One of the long wanderers,
maybe. This is Hell. Not Elysium. Not Tartarus. Just—
Hell. And it rarely makes any sense. Do you trust me
yet?"

Brutus stared at him in horror. "How can I?"

"That's always the question. Here you are. Here
you'll remain. I offer you what I couldn't in life. But the
problem of your existence is your problem. You want
me to embrace you like a father? I can. I can't say I'll
feel what you want me to feel. I know you won't.
Remember that you're a long time ago for me. And
you're a long way from Massilia."

"*Gods!*" Brutus sobbed. And Julius obligingly opened
his arms, invitation posed. "*Gods!*" Brutus fled there,
hurled himself against the khaki shirt, put his arms
about his father, wept till tears soaked the khaki and his
belly was sore. And Julius held him gently, stroked his

hair, patted his back till the spasms ebbed down to exhaustion.

"There," Julius said, rocking him on his feet, back and forth. "There, boy—does it help?"

"No," Brutus said finally, from against his chest. "I'm scared, I'm *scared*."

"You're shivering. It was awful, I know, the Undertaker and all."

"It's not that."

"Me? Am I what you're afraid of? A lot of us are to be afraid of. Marcus Antonius, for instance. But he's not in this house. I warn you about him simply in case. You want a commission, dear lad? I can manage that. I'll show you the best side of this place. Gaius doesn't bite—I adopted him. You see? I *needed* a son. It came down to my niece's son, finally. Caius Julius Caesar Octavianus Augustus—nephew of mine's got so damn many names and titles I can't keep up with them myself. And Mouse. You'll like Mouse. He lived a long time before us. Vowed himself to Hell to save the country— charged Rome's enemies singlehanded—"

"Decius Mus!" Brutus raised a tear-streaked face and looked Julius in the eyes. "*That* Mouse!"

"Damn good driver. Not much scares him. I told you you can get killed down here. It still hurts. I really appreciate a man with good nerves. Got a lot of good men. Mettius Curtius. Scaevola."

"Marius?"

"Poor uncle Marius got blown to local glory. Haven't found him since. Little fracas with Hannibal—gods, two hundred years ago as the world counts it. Mines. You know mines? Of course not. A little like *liliae*. Worse. Hell, they invented a lot of ways to kill a man up there." He slapped Brutus' shoulder. "You want to dry that face? You want to stay here by yourself and rest a while, or do you want to take a tour around with me? Mouse has got the jeep, but he'll be back. You know cars? Did you walk here?"

"I—I—" Brutus made a helpless gesture at the view out the library window. "I thought this was another part of the building where I woke up. But I don't know. I walked down a hall—"

"Well, things like that happen here. Don't try to figure them. You've figured out the lights, the plumbing's fancier, but ours *worked*. You can ride wherever you like, horses we've got—but you'll want to learn to drive. Augustus isn't much on modernity, but he makes up for it on quality. He has an excellent staff, never mind the sycophants—"

Something roared overhead. Low. Brutus flinched and ran to the window. Julius stayed where he was. "They *fly* here, too. I don't advise taking that up. Awfully chancy." There was a boom from the other side of the house, a series of pops. "Fool's overflown the Park. The Cong take real exception to that."

"I'm going mad!"

"No, no, no, it's just change. Novelty. I tell you, it's attitude. Doubt's your enemy. Disbelief is another. Believe in airplanes. Believe in yourself. Believe in visiting the moon and you extend yourself. I believe it happened. There's a limit to what I believe—I just like to have a *little* touch with the ground, you know; like feeling the mud under my feet, like the smell of gasoline—"

"What's gasoline?"

"It runs jeeps. Come along, come along, boy. *Gods*, there's so much to catch you up on—"

11

"What in the name of reason is he up to?" Kleopatra cried. A sycophant bobbled her nail polish and she shoved the creature down the chaise lounge with her foot, sent a bright trail flying over the salon tiles in the sycophant's wake. Ten more took that one's place, mopping polish, seeking after the gesticulating hand, in a surration of dismay and self-abasement, while the stricken sister wailed and snuffled, hardly audible. *"O fool, fool—!"*

"They'll never improve," said Hatshepsut. She lay belly-down on a marble slab while a masseur worked slowly on her back.

"I don't mean her! It! I mean *him!* O, damn! I don't believe it. He can't. He *hasn't* acknowledged that boy."

"It hardly makes any difference, does it? *Everyone* knows. Ummmm. Do that again. You're better than my architect."

"Dammit, he can't, he can't, I won't have it!" Kleopatra fisted a freshly lacquered hand and pounded the cushion. "He—" Her eyes fixed beyond, incredulously. Hatshepsut rose up on her elbows, looking toward the window, where a jeep pulled into the drive, and her mouth flew open as wide as Kleopatra's, whose lacquer-besmirched hand was instantly enveloped by frenetic sycophants.

"Ohmygods."

28

*   *   *

"*Who?*" Augustus cried. "*Who?* I'll have his—"

"Not publicly," Niccolo drawled, and carefully drew back the curtain, peering down onto the drive as Mouse got out one side and a stocky, curly headed man in tennis shorts bailed out the other. "Look at that. Even Mouse looks perplexed."

"The hell he does." Augustus came and took a look of his own out past the curtain. The handsome, lop-eared face showed a hectic flush. "What in the name of reason is he thinking of?"

"Antonius?"

"My uncle, dammit!"

"Ah." Niccolo smiled, a fleeting cat smile, long-lashed eyes lowered in contemplation of the scene on the driveway. "On that man I take notes. I never presume to guess him."

"*Antonius?*"

"Your uncle."

"That little bastard downstairs got him once. That *ass* out there tried to get *me*— He's got Kleopatra's brats over at that pervert Tiberius'— *Prodi!* He's got *Caesarion* in his camp!"

"Whom you murdered."

"A lie."

"*Auguste*, all statecraft is a lie and lies are statecraft, but split no hairs with me. This earless ass in your driveway is a schism in your house and a damned uneasy pack animal. I don't think he'll bear patiently at all. And I wonder what he'll do to young Brutus."

"Wine," said Sargon from the far side of the room. "It worked with my ass of a predecessor. Of course—I could just shoot him."

Niccolo turned and lifted a brow. "Like Sulla?"

"Not on my doorstep." Augustus turned from the curtain and snapped his fingers. A horde of sycophants appeared, saucer-eyed. "Get me a Scotch. Where's Caesar?"

Some sped on the first order. A few lingered, feral grins lighting their eyes. These had more imagination. Not much more. "Dante," the whisper came back. "Brutus," came another.

"Mouse went to Antony," said a third, not too bright.

"Out!"

It wailed and departed.

"Be civil," Niccolo said, "my prince. Learn from your uncle. Aren't we still guessing what *he's* up to? Welcome your enemy. Forgive him. If the divine Julius wants a minefield walked, why, he sends for Antonius." Niccolo tweaked the curtain further aside and stared down his elegant nose at the drive. "Ah, there, now, one question answered. There comes Julius and young Brutus. Now, there— They meet. How touching. Father with son on his arm. Antonius' gut must be full of glass. He *counts* on Caesarion. He's been trying to seduce Caesar and Kleopatra out of here for *so* long, and he so hopes Caesarion will prove the irresistible attraction— Look. An embrace, a reconciliation, Julius with Antonius."

"Watch for knives."

Niccolo grinned. "None *yet*. Antonius is too devoted, Julius too convolute, the boy too innocent. And look— now the divine Julius draws Antonius aside, now he speaks to him while Mouse holds young Brutus diverted with the jeep and the gadgetry and the guns— O fie! Fie, Saint Mouse, where is your virtue? Adoration, positive adoration shines in young Brutus' face—boy meets the hero of his youth. Meanwhile the divine Julius is whispering apace to mere mortal ass— Antonius glowers, he glares, he swallows his wrath—oh, where are sycophants when they might be useful?"

Something whistled, distantly. Boomed. Power dimmed. "*Maledetto!*" wailed from down the hall.

"Got him again," Sargon said.

"I can't!" Kleopatra said, and fidgeted as a sycophant buttoned her silk shell blouse. Another fastened her pearls, a third adjusted the pleats of her couturier skirt. "I *can't* face him."

"Yes, you will." Hatshepsut shut her eyes and, leaning forward, submitted a bland, smooth face to the ministrations of clouds of sycophants armed with kohl pots and brushes. The sable eyes lengthened, took on mauve and lavender tint about the lids that accorded well with the mylar glittersuit. Fuchsia beads hung in her elaborate Egyptian coiffure. Some of them winked on and off. So did the diode on the star-pin she wore. And the ring on her hand. And the circlet crown, which swept a trail of winking lights coyly over one strong cheekbone and back beneath the wig, and into her ear where it whispered with static and occasional voices in soldierly Latin. "Ssss. Aren't they friendly? Talk about the weather, talk about the house, talk about the boy—all banal as hell."

Kleopatra rolled her eyes. "O *gods*. How can I put up with this?"

"They're coming this way."

Kleopatra's red lips made a small and determined moue. Her tiny fists clenched. Hatshepsut took an easy posture, arms folded, as a half-dozen sycophants suddenly deserted them to dither this way and that around the door.

It opened. Sycophants on the other side beat them to it while the sycophants inside were undecided. A trio of men who knew better stood behind a boy who knew not a thing.

"How nice," Kleopatra said with ice tinkling on every word. "A whole clutch of bastards."

"Klea!" Julius said.

"Do come in. I was just leaving."

"Maybe—" Brutus said, stammered, his young face blanched. "Maybe we ought—"

"Not likely," Julius said. "I want you upstairs, Klea. Both of you."

"Klea." The man in tennis shorts looked soul-in-eyes

at her, advanced holding out his hands. "I've come to make peace. You, me. Augustus. Brutus."

She looked past him to Julius, whose face carefully said nothing.

"And to what do we owe this?"

"She's difficult," Julius said. "She's always difficult." He put his hand on Brutus' shoulder. "Klea, this is a boy. This is a nice boy. *Don't* be difficult."

"I—" Brutus said. And shut up.

Kleopatra cast a look Hatshepsut's direction. Hatshepsut lowered elaborate eyelids, lifted them again in a sidelong glance, and Kleopatra walked deliberately past Julius with a shrug of silken shoulders. There was a sudden and total absence of sycophants. "Well, well, well. Tell me, *mi care luli*—just what *did* bring you back from the field?"

Julius' brows lifted. Kleopatra walked on, sharp echo of stiletto heels on tile, sway of petite hips and pleated skirt. "Come now," she said, snagged Brutus by the elbow, hugged it to her and drew him a little apart, conspiratorially. "These are my husbands. My second and third. How do you like the villa?"

"I—" Brutus cast a desperate look over his shoulder to Julius and Antonius and Decius.

"He doesn't have the perspective," Julius said. "He remembers a road outside Baiae. He was on vacation. Two blinks later he's here. *Think* about it, Klea."

Kleopatra froze a moment. Took her hands carefully from Brutus' arm.

Brutus looked from one to the next to the next. Last and pleadingly, at Decius Mus.

"Come here, boy," the hero said. Held out his hand. Brutus retreated there, to the firm grip of Mouse's hands on his shoulders. "Let's talk reason," Julius said. "Upstairs. The plain fact is, Klea, we're under attack."

"Brilliant," Niccolo said, ear inclined to the library doors as he leaned there with his shoulders. He rolled his head back to face Sargon, who stood with arms folded, sandaled feet square, and a keen curiosity on his dark-bearded face. "Brilliant. Julius has Brutus in there as hostage. Augustus, Kleopatra, Antonius—all sit there on best behavior, knowing full well that any one of them could blurt out something that might jog Brutus the innocent right over the edge— And Hatshepsut sits silent as the sphinx—the cooling influence: he has her there, an outsider-witness to keep this loving family from too much frankness; while the silent, the redoubtable Mouse is a damper on everyone. No one bares his weaknesses to that iceberg."

"It's not only his own life Julius's gambling in there," Sargon muttered. "Someone'll have to kill that boy if he's not careful. And is Mouse incorruptible? Beware a man of extremes, little vulture. Mouse is a passionate man. Ask his enemies."

Niccolo looked back and raised a brow, turned his ear to the door again. "More of family matters. The politeness in that room is thick enough to stop a man's breath. Antonius vows selflessness, with tears in his voice he swears he's changed profoundly; Augustus swears he wishes to sweep all complications away—as he has come to love, he says, Kleopatra as his sister—as he will regard Antonius as his friend and this engaging young stranger as his younger brother—oh, and Augustus means it, Lion, he always means such things. And will mean them to the day some offense inflames him—then, *then*, he strikes without a qualm. There is no liar, Lion, like a sincere and reasoning man."

"A plague on his reason. What's the old fox got in his mouth?"

"Julius won't be hurried. That's a certainty. He's ranked his pieces, made his move— You ought to have taken this invitation to conference, Lion."

"I? I'll be waiting when the sun comes up on these oaths and protestations. They'll come to one who wasn't witness to their oaths, when they want to break them."

Niccolo made a grimace of a smile. "Ah, well, to *you*, Lion, they come for moral advice; but to *me* they come only when they've set their course. And come they will, to us both—to me when they wish to be rid of this young leopard. To you when they wish to justify it. Even in Hell we must have our morality."

Sargon chuckled softly. "What's the boy doing?"

"Silence, of course, silence—a *tabula rasa*, blank and oh, so frightened. Julius plies him with such a wealth of trust as would daze any prodigal son—and the leopard cub yet is leopard enough to look for blood on the old leopard's whiskers. But being cub, being cub quite lost and desperate, he nuzzles up to any warmth—if *Hatshepsut* clasped him to her bosom he would call her mother and weep for joy."

"He'd be far safer."

Niccolo laughed, merest breath. "Oh, with either of *us* he'd be safer, Lion, at least his life would be. Ah! now, now, we get to business! Attack, says Julius: he names enemies—"

Sargon stepped closer, applied his own ear to the door, royal dignity cast aside.

". . . an executive-level operation," Julius was saying. "We've got the fool Commander in Dissident hands; and what put him there was a ragtag nothing having a chance dropped into their laps—administrative blundering or a leak in the Pentagram; or you can draw other conclusions. *Hadrian*, son. Publius Aelius Hadrianus, so damned modernized he's forgotten his own name. Supreme Commander of Hell's Legions. Remember you're thousands of years late. Hadrian ruled Rome— *Ruled*. Exactly so. He was— Never mind what he was. There's a group of rebels—just think of the civil war and you've got it. The rebels grabbed Hadrian while he was gadding about on another of his damn tours; the headquarters is in its usual mess; you walked into a situation, boy. The Administration's embarrassed; the Dissidents have scored a big one. And you can count on

an embarrassed Administration to make some moves to
distract *anyone* they don't trust. That's one level of
thinking. There are others. There's one level that says
we may have personal enemies that want to take
advantage of the chaos and the Administration's lack of
attention. You want to ask a question, son?"

"I—"

"It's a confusing place. Seventeen and you don't know
any real facts about how your own country ran, you
didn't understand why Rome tore its own guts out—"

"I know about Marius. And Sulla."

"Well, think of it like that, then. Gods help you,
we're thousands of years old; you're seventeen. You
wonder what you're doing in this room? You have to
learn. You're going to learn." The sound of footsteps
crossing stone. "There's something in the wind. *Antoni*,
tell them what you told me."

"Rumors," Antonius' voice said. "That's all I can call
it. Talk. The Dissidents—they're laying plans for some
kind of strike— Klea—Klea, forgive me— Caesarion—"

"What? What about Caesarion?"

"He's left, Klea, he's—gone. He's joined them."

"Oh, my GODS! Joined the Dissidents?"

"I didn't want to tell you, I wanted to tell you—
down there—I—"

"Do something!" The sharp impact of stiletto heels on
the stone. "Zeus! You're his father! DO SOMETHING!"

"That," said Julius' low voice, "is why I think we're in
trouble. From both sides of this affair. Caesarion moves
to the Dissidents. And—"

Upstairs a door opened and closed. Footsteps pelted
down the hall upstairs and down the steps— Niccolo
heard it coming, turned in utmost vexation and Sargon
hardly a moment slower, as a disheveled black-clad
figure came bounding down toward them and the door,
papers in fist, trailed by a chattering horde of sycophants.
"L'ho fatto! L'ho fatto! Scusi, prego, prego, scusi—" as
he came barreling up to the doors. "Here, is he here?"

Yes-yes-yes, hissed the sycophants, fawning and whisking right on through the closed door so brusquely Niccolo sucked in his gut in reflex. Sargon retreated in dismay as Dante shoved the doors open and charged on, papers in hand. Sargon's mouth stayed open, his feet planted. But Niccolo Machiavelli strolled on through the doors as smoothly as if he had been following Dante Alighieri from as far as upstairs, right into the library and the conference.

Dante never stopped. He walked right up to Julius and waved a paper in Julius' vision. "There, there—it's *here*—"

It evidently had import. Niccolo's brows both lifted as Julius took the paper in his own hand and read it carefully, as Julius listened to the poet chatter computerese at him and jab with a pencil here and here and here at the selfsame paper. And the people in the room had risen from their chairs, Sargon had trailed through the door, everything had come to a thorough stop.

"Out!" Julius snapped suddenly; but that was for the sycophants, who went skittering and wailing and tumbling over one another in panic flight from the room. No one else budged, except Dante Alighieri, who ventured another poke with the indicating pencil at the paper that trembled in Julius' fist. A quick whispered: "There, *signore*, there, I'm quite sure—"

Julius flicked pencil and hand away with a lift of his hand. "We've found who sent you here," he said, looking straight at Brutus. "How's your current events, son? Six eighty-five from the founding of the City. Your year. Who's the man to fear—in all the world: who's worst?"

Hesitation. Brutus stared at Julius like a bird before the serpent.

You, that look said. It was painfully evident. Then: "In Asia. Mithridates."

"The butcher of Asia," Julius said. "*Mithridates* is one of our problems—he's the one who plotted this little surprise, holding you out of time. And if he's sprung it—" Julius gave a sweeping glance to all of them. "If he's spent this valuable coin, its for no small stakes." Julius shook the paper, as if it were legible. "Rameses has moved up to acting commander."

"Ummmm," said Sargon.

"Ummm, indeed," Julius said. "We've got imminent—"

Something whistled over the roof, whumped in a great shattering of glass that rocked the floor and sent shards of the great library window flying in a dreadful glitter of inward-bound fragments in the same instant that everyone dived for cover; everyone except the poet—Niccolo grabbed him on his way down, landed on him, and lay in the shower of glass nose to nose with Dante Alighieri, in utmost shock at the reflex that had betrayed him to heroism.

"Prodi," Augustus murmured from under a table. Another strike whumped down. "Efficiency. What's Hell coming to?"

"Pol! Iactum habent isti canifornicatores ter quaterque matrifoedantes Cong!" Julius scrambled up in the glass shards, hardly quicker than Mouse and Sargon and Antonius, with Brutus and Hatshepsut a close third. Augustus elbowed a glass-hazarded way out from under his table and Kleopatra staggered up on tottering heels, smudges all over her haute couture. Niccolo delayed, mesmerized by his own stupidity and the utter shock in Dante's eyes. *"Agite!"* Julius was shouting. "Up and out! *Move!"* And Sargon's hand landed on Niccolo's collar and hauled him up by one hand, shaking him.

"Out!" Sargon yelled. "Julius is right, they've got the range—*move*, man!"

Niccolo spun loose and ran when the rest started to run. From somewhere Hatshepsut had gotten a deadly little pistol, Julius was waving them out of the imperiled room, which swirled with smoke and windborne dust—

Julius passed him then, headed down the hall through which sycophants rushed and screamed in terror. He overtook Antonius, grabbed Antonius' arm and shouted at him: *"Get over that hill, get that brood of yours moving—* Take the Ferrari! Klea, have you got the keys?"

Kleopatra stopped against the wall, rummaged in her black handbag. Came up with keys. Antonius snatched them and ran, as the house quaked to another explosion and Augustus stopped and looked in anguish at a crack sifting dust from the hall ceiling. Mouse tore by him and hit the stairs downbound, while Sargon and Hatshepsut hit the same set going up.

Niccolo opted for the latter, grabbed the banister, and ran the steps two at a time.

Weapons, that was what the others were after. Their private arsenals.

He had another concern that sent him flying up that stairway like a bat out of hell—

He reached his own apartment, thrust the key in the lock as the floor shook to another shell somewhere in the rose garden. He ran inside, fumbled after more keys, unlocked one desk drawer and drew out the disruptor, unlocked another and snatched up a notebook which he thrust into his shirt.

Then he ran, as another impact shook the villa, somewhere in the vicinity of the swimming pool. Down the hall, Sargon and Hatshepsut were headed for the stairs, Hatshepsut with a laser rifle, Brutus with an M-1 in his hand and a 1990s flex-armor vest above his kilt.

Niccolo overtook them on the second turn, as plaster sifted from the ceiling and the chandelier swayed to another hit.

The Ferrari shot out of the garage in a squeal of tires on gravel; slewed as the man in the tennis shorts spun the wheel and hit the gas. Dirt rained down, and bits of sod.

"He's clear!" Kleopatra cried, and got her head down behind the driveway wall again as dirt and clods and rosebush fragments pelted their position. "You damn

dogs!" Her face was smudged and white when she lifted
it, and she had a .32 automatic braced in her hand as
she peered over the rim of the driveway's bricks. "Let
me try," Brutus was saying, while Mouse backed the
jeep around and Augustus and Julius swung the rear-
mounted launcher into action.

"Don't fire!" Julius yelled at Kleopatra. "Get down,
you'll draw attention."

She ducked. "Shells," she told a gibbering sycophant
which turned up next to her. "In my bedroom in the
top of the closet, in the shoebox—go, fool!"

It gibbered, and whether that was where it was going
was anyone's guess. It yelped as it reached the stairs
and Sargon and Hatshepsut and Niccolo Machiavelli
came tearing out. It scuttled.

"All of you," Julius yelled, "get the hell out of the
driveway! Sargon, take left flank round back! Klea,
Brutus, get to cover! Mouse, get back inside, take that
second-story center window, and save it till we've got
targets. And get the hell back down here if they get you
spotted!" He dropped a shell into the launcher and it
whooshed off in an arcing streak toward Decentral Park,
over a rhododendron hedge, a stand of oaks, kicking up a
cloud by the time Julius swung the mount over a degree
and Augustus popped another one in, laying stitches
down a line.

Kleopatra ran low, barefooted over the grass, and
scuttled in behind ornamental rock and an aged stand of
pine. Brutus hit the ground by her side, eyes wide,
about the time a shell landed in the front of the drive
and blasted gravel and shrapnel that tore through the
thicket, ricocheted off the ornamental boulders, and
shredded bark off the pine. A barrage of shells left the
jeep-launcher.

"Pro di, pro di," Brutus mumbled in a state of shock.
His face was ashen. *"Di—O Iuppiter fulminator maxime
potens—"*

"Catapults," Kleopatra said. *"Keep down, boy!"*

Another shell hit. The jeep-launcher returned fire in a steady stream as fast as Julius and Augustus could drop rounds in. Kleopatra risked a look up, just as a cloud of fire erupted in the smoke beyond the park oaks.

"Got the bastards!" she yelled, and remembered to her embarrassment who was beside her, as somewhere a motor began to grind toward them and an incredible long snout poked through the rhododendrons across the street, with crunching and cracking of branches: a Sherman tank, lurching and crashing its way up to street level.

Brutus gave a moan and froze like a rabbit as black-clad Cong followed that juggernaut, attackers pouring out of that gap in the rhododendrons, around either side of the tank. Kleopatra took aim, both hands braced on the rocks, and sent rounds into the oncoming horde. Bullets spanged back, and she ducked and Brutus yelped and ducked as the tank ground on across the pavement toward the lawn.

The ground exploded massively as the treads crunched the curb and hit the grass.

"Mine," Kleopatra gasped, huddling with her arms over the shuddering teenager. "Ours."

Brutus just gulped and tried to keep his lunch down.

Another tank broke through.

Hatshepsut steadied the laser on the rim of the flowerbed and took cool aim at the tank as Sargon blasted away at the black-pajamaed horde that tried to storm their position. Steady fire came from Mouse's position up in the second-floor window.

Niccolo took aim of his own: no good on heavy iron atoms, his little pistol, but effective enough against water-containing flesh. Cong dropped and writhed.

Then a Fokker roared over, and a screaming whine ended in a whump and a deluge of rosebushes and rhododendron.

"Damn!" Sargon yelled, and Hatshepsut rolled over and got a shot off after the plane as it headed for a turn. "Range," she complained. "Damn scatter— Where's the Legion, dammit? Where's Scaevola? Asleep?"

"I imagine," Niccolo said, picking off one and the next targets, "the Cong have *them* pinned. Air support. This is a—"

A shell hit the front porch.

"Mouse!" Brutus cried. *"Down!"* Kleopatra snapped, and fired off a series of shots, paused and had to reload. Not hide or wisp of the sycophant with the shells. The box she had picked up in the garage was near empty now.

Cong poured through the bushes, and the plane came around for another pass as Julius and Augustus sent missile after missile on as short a trajectory as they could: "We've got to pull it back," Julius yelled and scrambled over the seat, got the jeep into motion backward and then in a gravel-spitting turn around and over the lawn, headed behind Kleopatra's position and the cover of the pines and rocks.

About this time an incoming round hit the retaining wall of the driveway and sprayed the front ranks of the Cong breakthrough with brick, geraniums, and shrapnel.

"Fall back!" Kleopatra yelled, elbowing Brutus into motion ahead of her. *"Get to the jeep—we're getting out of here!"*

The boy moved, got to his feet, and ran for his life. Kleopatra sprinted after him, low as she could, while Augustus got the launcher swiveled round again and sent a ranging shot over their heads into the park.

A returning shell hit the pines—hit the gravel nearby, and Kleopatra went skidding, blinked in astonishment at pain in her back and at the wild-eyed boy who had staggered to one knee, blood starting from half a dozen wounds as he scrambled up and ran back for her.

"Dammit!" she yelled. She had died the focus of
heroic fools. She had no more appetite for futilities.
She thrust herself up to her knees, grabbed her gun
and got that far before the boy got to her, snatched her
into his arms and swung into a lumbering run with
shots kicking up the pine needles and the fragments
everywhere around him.

"*Age! Agite!*" Julius yelled at them, while Augustus
lobbed another shell overhead. Julius flung himself into
the driver's seat, put the jeep's flank between them and
the Cong. Augustus abandoned the launcher to haul
Kleopatra up and over the side into the floor of the
jeep. "Get in!" Julius yelled at Brutus, while shots
spanged off the body-work and the launcher. Augustus
came up with a grenade and threw it as Brutus clawed
his bloody way into the passenger seat: then the jeep
cut tracks out of the lawn as Julius hit the gas and
turned. Shots whined past their ears and Brutus took a
wild look back over the seat rim at a wave of Cong
running past the pines.

Then the sky went up in a sheet of flame and the
whole of Hell lurched. Julius swerved the jeep wildly
out of control and stabilized it again as the air shock
rolled over them and bits of trees and rhododendron
and worse stuff began to rain down.

"Ran into their own fire!"Augustus was screaming.
"*They blew up!*"

In truth there was a billowing cloud where the pines
had been, and that group of Cong was a scattered few
survivors staggering about in the smoke. Julius swerved
and blasted the horn, taking the jeep across behind the
house, jouncing and bumping across flowerbeds and the
remnants of the rose garden, dodging shellholes. And
Sargon and Niccolo and Hatshepsut came straggling
disheveled and dusty from the portico of the east wing,
firing back as they ran.

Another huge impact rocked the park beyond the

house, blew out a last corner of glass from the second story and toppled a cascade of roof tiles.

Then a gathering babble howled beyond the house, as the Cong regrouped their forces.

A second bedraggled pair came staggering out the back door, through the patio. Mouse and Dante Alighieri—holding each other up.

"He got into Pentagram communications," Mouse gasped as they and Sargon's company reached the side of the jeep. "He fed in attack instructions on the Cong's coordinates and the Pentagram zeroed in a couple of *their* rounds right into them. There may be more rounds incoming—"

"Get in!" Julius said. They were already climbing; Sargon boosted Niccolo and Hatshepsut up to hand on over the fenders, scrambled up himself and turned the M-1 behind. The overloaded jeep bounced and wove its way around the craters in the lawn, headed away at speed as Cong poured in a black wave around either side of the house and Sargon, Niccolo, and Hatshepsut sprayed fire across their ranks.

That was when Antonius and Agrippa showed up over the hill in front of them and Mettius Curtius and the First Cav came rumbling over the rise of the west, with Scaevola and the 10th Legion hard behind.

The harried Cong veered north, toward open parkland and the urban outskirts.

About this time Attila's division arrived over that hill, on the bizarrest instructions from the Pentagram he had ever gotten.

"Prosit heroibus nostris omnibus!"

"Quite," said Kleopatra, lifting her glass with her left hand. She was in a rose satin dressing-gown, all in flounces, her right arm in a tasteful beige silk sling. "To our heroes!" Inside the villa a plank fell. Saws buzzed. Glass tinkled.

And Kleopatra included Marcus Junius Brutus in that

sweep of her glass, so that Brutus hesitated with his
own drink in hand, his young face aflame and his eyes
filled with a new worship.

Dante Alighieri stood up and stammered out a
"*Grazie.*" Mouse, accustomed to honors, simply gave a
bland nod of his head. And Sargon stood up and raised a
fragile wine glass in Herculean fist.

"To us!" Sargon said with royal modesty, and Hatshepsut added, lifting hers: "To all us heroes!"

"*Prosit,*" said Julius, and drank that one too. And
laughed.

But Niccolo Machiavelli walked away from that
gathering with a troubled heart, in the mortifying
recollection of Dante Alighieri's face nose to nose with
him on the library floor.

He had betrayed himself, the most consummately
rational man in Hell, as a fool among the shrewd and
the calculating—all of whom had advantage to gain from
their actions; but he had had none, had absolutely no
ulterior motive in that leap which had preserved Dante
Alighieri (and gotten him painful slivers of glass in
several sensitive portions of his anatomy). He glanced
back, at the poet and the boy-assassin basking in the
warmth of praise from the powerful; and flinched and
walked away in the ruin of all his self-estimation.

111

Clang! and clang! and thump! —as steel hit steel and shield hit shield; and thump again, as Brutus went down on his backside in the dirt and the sword went flying.

"Cover!" Sargon yelled, and Brutus jerked his shield-arm over his body, desperate effort, as a blow crashed down that numbed his arm, deafened him, and all but brought the shield down on his face.

"Take his footing!" a new voice shouted, and Brutus was not sure whether it was encouragement to Sargon or to himself. *"Dagger!"*

He groped after his belt. A second blow and a third came down on his shield. It hurt. It hurt again. He was deaf and blind, but his fingers found the hilt. He tried to lift the shield enough to cover himself and strike, rolling to slash at Sargon's feet.

Something else hit his shield this time, and this time held him under it, staring up at a hell-lit sword point and the ruddy sky, at Sargon, who pinned him with a foot on his shield and the sword in front of his face.

"Cover!" Sargon yelled at him.

He tried to use the dagger. The king of Akkad was out of his reach. The shield itself blocked his arm and held him flat.

45

"Now what are you going to do?" Sargon asked.

He thought about it. He tested his aching muscles against Sargon's weight. The sword-tip touched right between his eyes, so that he looked up at it somewhat cross-eyed.

"I don't know," he said miserably. "I'm sorry."

"You lost your sword. If you have to let go something, lad, *don't* let go the sword. If you're going to fall, you fall, you cover, you *use the damned sword you didn't have!*"

"Yes, sir." It was hard to keep one's wits with a sword-point cutting into the flesh between one's eyes and Sargon's considerable weight bearing down on one's arms and chest. "I'm sorry."

Sargon was angry with him. Justifiably, he thought. He tried not to breathe hard. It hurt. He lay there and listened, in his humiliation, as the second person walked around into his view; and then he truly wished to sink into the ground.

It was Scaevola, Mucius Scaevola himself, backlit by the sky of Hell—the hero who had defied the Etruscans and burned off his own hand to shame their king.

"Bad position," Scaevola said thoughtfully. "Damn near impossible once you lost the sword. If you try to use the shield you expose your head or your gut. Damned dangerous to move it."

"Yes, sir," Brutus said. He thought his face must be red. Sargon still stood on him. The point was still between his eyes. "Please, majesty, that's cutting."

"Damned Roman shields," Sargon said. Not to him. To Scaevola. "Admit it. *You* couldn't have gotten out of that one."

"First," Scaevola said, "take it for granted I wouldn't have leaned backward. That was the lad's first mistake. Second—" He bent down and took hold of the shield edge. Sargon took his foot back and withdrew his blade and Brutus, lying on his back, lifted his battered arm and let Scaevola pull the shield free.

"All right," Sargon said, backing off.

Brutus levered himself up and massaged an aching shoulder, watching as Mucius Scaevola heaved the shield up and thrust the stump of his right wrist through the straps—not a moment's delay for accommodation, the one-handed soldier hardly more than twenty, to look at him, light of limb, even slender in his khaki uniform. He picked up the fallen sword left-handed and saluted the king, then came on guard so smoothly, so gracefully perfect in his stance, that Brutus stared at him and stared at Sargon in despair.

Clang!-clang! and thump! —attacks that came fast and furious from either side, a patterned clash of steel and resounding wood, and a shield-edge thrust that could have broken Sargon's jaw, except the king leapt back and forward again with a bash of shield against shield that staggered Scaevola.

But Scaevola did not fall. He recovered and circled, and Sargon backed up fast, still on guard.

"Again!" Scaevola panted. "*This* time I'll fall, hey?"

"Liar!"

"My word." Pant. "Come ahead."

Brutus found his own breath coming hard. He scrambled up onto his haunches in the dust, the armor cutting into him till he shifted onto his knees.

Bang! thump-clang! *Thump!*

Scaevola went down, flinging the sword aside, and Sargon came on hard, crash! onto the shield, once, twice—

He has no dagger! Brutus realized in a panic. *It's his bad arm*—

Scaevola crashed the shield-edge into Sargon's armored shin, brought his head up, shield tilted, and with a strength incredible in a slender frame, crashed his shield onto Sargon's as Sargon brought his shield-edge into Scaevola's.

"Stop it!" Brutus cried, scrambling up. "*Stop it!*"

A third crash of shields and the king of Akkad went

skipping back out of contact. Scaevola planted his shield on the ground and sprang to his feet.

Then Scaevola gave a great breath.

"Still had you," the Lion of Akkad said.

"Damned difficult position," Scaevola said, and straightened and held out the shield. "Here, lad. *Don't* yell out like that."

Brutus took the shield off the handless arm, clasping it to him, mortified. "I'm s-s-sorry, s-s-sir—"

"Good lad." The hero of the Etruscan Wars clapped him on the shoulder and shook at him. "Good eye for trouble, all the same."

"*Which* you were in," Sargon gibed.

"If your majesty says."

"Damn it, don't 'majesty says' *me*. That's a position can't be gotten out of."

"I *was* out of it. —Majesty."

Brutus stood and stared, while the argument went on, the fight replayed itself in demonstration and re-demonstration, and a khaki-clad Mucius Scaevola shouted into the face of yet another king, albeit not of Etruria; and that king shouted back—not enemies: Brutus understood that, finally. He stood and hugged the shield against him, and stood there forlornly while the pair began to walk off, still shouting at each other.

Then: "Boy," Sargon said, stopping and turning. "Come on."

He grabbed the shield up by a strap and ran, breathless and bruised, taken, *O Iuppiter*, into men's company, at least as far as the villa steps. A king taught him arms. A hero intervened to advise him; and both of them, when they had gotten to the villa, invited him into the huge baths, and into the steam room, where sycophants wrapped them in towels.

There they sat and steamed the aches away.

Himself, and a king and a hero, the latter of whom sat with his arms across his knees and laughed, now the shouting was done, with a humor that Brutus found

obscurely shocking—as if Mouse had laughed; but this
man would, this grim and dusty figure out of legend
turned out to be hardly older than himself, and with
faded-blue eyes that danced and flickered with lively
humor—Sargon a grim bull of a man, from curling
black hair to breadth of frame; and Scaevola terribly
scarred besides his hand, but blithe and cheerful, and
willing, for a moment, to include him in the conversation
as if he were an equal.

"There's a limit to what we can pull up from the
armory," Scaevola said. "Guns—are the answer to that
problem. But guns can't always be had. Swords—damn,
sticks, if we had to—*anything's* a weapon to a good
sword-and-shield man."

"Sword never jams," Sargon said. "And it's quiet."

Brutus looked from one to the other of them, swallowed
hard, and ventured the nagging question. "Who are my
father's enemies?"

It was as if a door shut. Both king and hero straightened
back; their faces went carefully blank.

Then: "Those who have reason to fear him," Scaevola
said.

"Why—" Brutus asked carefully, "—why did Caesarion
run away? Why did he join my father's enemies? —When
was he born, and why did my father have a son with the
queen of Egypt?"

There was long silence, in the haze of steam clouds.
He watched two men, his father's friends, look at each
other for a long, mutually distressed moment.

"Ask your father," Sargon said, in such a way he
managed to make the question sound dishonorable for a
boy to ask at all. And Brutus felt a pang of disquiet and
embarrassment: it was a situation he well knew—being
bastard-born in the Junius clan, and having sat through
numerous such silences in the family, while grown men
and women looked at each other and tried to think of
graceful answers.

It made him feel ungraceful and ungracious in his

person. It made him feel awkward in his very existence, and from a moment ago that he had felt accepted—he was suddenly the bastard again, and heart-sore and body-sore and tired enough for tears.

Fortunately they looked like sweat.

"Say that the world was wider when your father died," Scaevola said, not unkindly. "And Rome had changed."

"He can't have lived—more than—gods, forty years past me."

"But Rome changed. War—changes a city."

This, from a man who died hundreds of years before him. And who *remembered* what had happened. When *he* did not. Panic rose around him like a tide. He shivered, and clamped his hands on his knees to make it less evident; but his teeth were about to chatter.

And Sargon reached out a great paw of a hand and clenched it on his, shaking at him. "Hard, isn't it, boy? It'll make sense someday."

"What *is* this p-p-place? What *is* th-th-the Exec? Wh-Why—*why* does he s-s-say Mithri-Mithridates—h-held me out of t-t-time? Wh-wh-where have I b-b-b—"

"Easy." Sargon's hand crushed his. "Easy, lad. We're friends here, all friends."

"You don't belong to Mithridates," Scaevola said. "We won't let him use you. We. All of us in the Household. We'll take care of you. Your father will. He's taking steps to deal with this. Don't let it worry you."

I'm afraid was not a thing he could admit before these men—least of all before Scaevola, who had held his own hand in the fire to prove that he was not.

But he was afraid, terribly. *What* is *Hell?* he asked people who would talk to him, because he could not really understand where he was, or where home was, or what had happened to cast him here, so late, so ignorant.

He had been afraid of dying, being bastard-born, not

sure where his ancestor-soul would have a home, whether among Junian or Julian spirits, or whether anyone would give him grave-gifts in Februarys, and whether ancestor-spirits of either house would have him.

Certainly, he thought, *King Sargon of Akkad is no spirit of my house, of either house, gods save us— Scaevola is clan Mucia, he has no ties to clan Iunia or Iulia—and Klea! and Dantillus! and Niccolo— Gods, whatever gods are really mine, whatever this insane place is, or what fate has linked us, or damned us—*

What am I? What power sent me here?

They were afraid of me when I came. They thought I was their enemy. Now they treat me as Caesar's son. Now I have a home, and I never truly had, even in my father's house.

But why did Mithridates free me and send me to my father?

For a gift?

Why did my father guess it was his enemy had had me and his enemy had sent me? Why, why, why did he think so without surprise?

There were a thousand questions. He chipped away at them, even when he did not want the answers, even when each one he gained terrified him, and every new piece of information led to other questions more frightening. Like Scaevola, he held his hand in the enemy's fire, and gritted his teeth and kept it there, because there was no other thing to do.

He was too wary to pour out all the questions in a sequence that would bring his father's friends rushing to his father with a warning: your son knows too much, your son is asking questions we dare not answer, what will we do about this boy? No. That was the quickest way to find himself cut off from information, and in his father's displeasure.

Do not ask, his father had told him. Any order else that Julius had given him he would obey with religious devotion. But not one to be ignorant. Not one which might bring him and his father into an enemy's hands. He was *not* a fool. When Julius knew that his son could be trusted, surely he would tell him these things. But Julius did not know to what depth he loved him; and not knowing, held things from him; and ordered his friends not to talk to him in certain matters: he was sure of it by the looks that went past him among Julius' friends.

And until the day that he *did* win that trust, he was vulnerable, and knew it; and his father was, and defended him, he was sure of it.

As he was sure of these men—of Sargon the Lion, of Mucius Scaevola and Mouse and all the rest. There was love in this house in Hell. He felt it, and he felt the threat all about them, in the sky and in the towers of New Hell and even slinking through the rhododendrons of the Park across the street, a threat which wanted to take this house down; and he would not permit it, not if it killed him all over again.

So he took a deep breath and stopped shivering and basked in the comradeship of adult men who tried to help him and to teach him self-defense: the best, he thought, the very best teachers; he could never have imagined such masters of arms as he had in this house; or such co-residents.

They taught him tactics. He listened with all his concentration, never daring let fall a word. They were too precious to him. They were the means to survive and protect this place which protected him, and they were the good will of his father's friends: therefore everything they bade him do he meant to do, with all his heart.

"Don't worry," Sargon told him. "Your father has been handling this longer than you imagine. He'll manage."

"Is he looking for my b-brother?" It was a hard word, when he was thinking about it, an unfamiliar word.

"Yes," Scaevola said firmly. "And for his friends."

"But you," Sargon said, "stay out of it."

*   *   *

The household was in turmoil, secret conferences proliferating between Julius and Kleopatra and Augustus; Julius and Sargon; Niccolo and the furtive and nervous Dante Alighieri; and Niccolo and Sargon, Niccolo and Kleopatra, and even (there was strong reason to suspect) Niccolo and Antonius (not a friendly pair), *the* Marcus Antonius, *magister equitum, dux et triumvir,* who lived over the hill and past the tennis courts and a great deal of manicured meadow, in crazy Tiberius' villa. Such intrigue was ordinarily meat and drink to Hatshepsut.

But not to be on the inside of it, to be, in fact, systematically excluded from such conferences, *that* was insupportable.

"Madam." A youthful voice overtook her on one sullen stalk down the stairs. "Hatshepsut." She stopped. And in a patter of rubber-shod feet a teenager overtook her—Marcus Brutus in tennis shoes, tee shirt and faded denims. It was uncommon attire for Augustus' villa. But so were boys uncommon. "*Prodi,* let the boy wear what he likes," Augustus had said, when the sycophants filled Brutus' closet with 1970's denims. And: "*Perdio,*" Niccolo had aped that statement, with a little flourish of the wrist, "the divine Julius would just as soon pry the lad out of old Rome, wouldn't he rather? I *wonder* where the sycophants got the notion."

The house's private timebomb, young and full of innocence, black-haired and with exquisite dark eyes ("If I ever hear," Julius had said directly to Hatshepsut, "that you've been at him—") arrived on the steps beside her, all earnestness. "Hatshepsut, *what* are they doing up there? What are they talking about, *tanks* and *launchers* and that?"

"Large ears indeed, kitten." Hatshepsut had taken particular pains with her appearance: her pink 25th-century jumpsuit glittered and flashed, tight and virtually transparent in interesting places. The boy struggled to look instead at her face, which was itself a marvel, glowpaint on the eyelids, the left eye having a series of dots over to the rather remarkable magenta-tinted plastic of the device that swept up over her sleek black bob and incidentally insinuated a little magenta tendril into her ear, where it whispered at will with others' voices; and another tendril against her skull, where it picked up her voice and carried it elsewhere. She was virtually unarmed, in the casual peace of her own home, only a little gray box clipped to her left boot and a lovely ring that Niccolo had given her, one of her only antiques.

"Is it the Cong again?"

"No," she said, and started off down the steps again, Brutus trailing. He overtook her again at the bottom. "Listen, kit." She turned and he stopped short. "Do you talk to people?"

"Talk to—"

"Do you know how to keep a secret? Do you *want* a secret?"

He had his mouth open. He shut it and gulped, and she put her fingertips gently under that clamped jaw.

"There's a bright lad. No, a boy in this house doesn't *want* secrets, not the sort that might put him at cross-purposes with people who know far more secrets. That's always your danger, isn't it? Don't take Niko's path; don't take Dante's either. Be your charming, naive self."

"I'm not—"

She let fall the hand. "You're exquisite, but Julius would have my head, kitten. You are naive. No boy ever wants to think so, but a smart boy who wants to learn had better know that about himself first and foremost. Now I want you to do a thing for me, just carry a message."

"I'm not sure I want to." His face had a charming blush. His nostrils flared with outrage and confusion. "I'm sorry I—"

"Kit, kit, kit, just go to your papa and tell him something from me."

"What?" *Father* was a trigger-word with this boy. He adored Julius, feared him, and worshipped him with a fervor which had nothing to do with godhood.

"Just tell him I've overheard a magic word. And I really want to talk to him. There's a dear lad. Go. Go."

He fled, poor young Republican. Royalty daunted him. His father daunted him. So did most everything in the house, when it came to that, even Dante Alighieri, with his cylopic machine and his arcane wizardries; and Dante flourished in that respect. Brutus was still new, at his mere seventeen. He did not remember why he was famous; he did not know that he *was* famous. His worldly life had ended on that road in Italy, in his seventeenth summer—or at least his memory ended there.

Now he was running up the stairs to do what Hatshepsut asked him to do.

And Hatshepsut went off her own way. Wispy sycophants whisked out of her path, and made themselves invisible, which they ordinarily were: flunkies and lackeys in life, their existence somehow worked on points—and points were in decided jeopardy when Hatshepsut had that look on her face.

"He *won't?*" Hatshepsut asked, in due course.

"No," Brutus said, hands behind him, feeling after the wall as he backed up. "He said not. He said—" He met the wall and edged along it. "He said—just no."

"You don't have to be afraid of me, kitten." Hatshepsut edged to stop him, so that he stopped along the wall. "What, precisely, did Julius say?"

"That. Just that."

"You wouldn't lie to me, would you, kitten?"

"No." An emphatic shake of his head. And in a rush: "I think *you* ought to talk to him."

"Don't fret. I never killed the messenger for the message. It's very bad manners,." She patted his shoulder and smiled at him. Patted his shoulder again, because he looked so distressed. "Dear kitten."

"Is it dangerous, what he's doing? Is it—something—dangerous?"

"Don't worry yourself with it." But the boy looked outright scared.

"It is," he said. "I know it is!"

"Never you fear." She was disturbed. The boy's naivete persisted, in this house, gods, of all houses. He was *good*, not hardened like Mouse, whom the Romans called holy: she had never seen such goodness in the world alive. Some power hostile to Julius had detained Marcus Brutus thousands of years out of time, then returned this bastard son of Caesar's youth not the embittered man he had died, but well before the hour that had led to that end. This boy was pure and he was vulnerable, waiting the one who would corrupt him. And she did not wish to be the fool who did such a thing. She had hung men and old friends screaming from hooks on the walls of Men-nophren; but the tremor of distress in this boy's voice engaged her pity. And frightened her. "Never fear," she said again, "*I'll* see to him. Nothing will happen. Only—" Pity was a narrow and specific emotion with Hatshepsut: and right in its hollow heart an idea took root that bared her teeth in a small, false smile. "I have to be with him to do that."

"You can't—"

"Welcome to reality, kitten. This isn't your City or anything you know. And we Old Dead control as much of the new technology as we can believe in. Your father believes in it right down to the day they landed on the moon."

"They? Who? On the moon?"

"Julius and I were quite different, you know. Both of us were explorers in our way: he opened up his north. He had a vision, a great vision, what that territory would mean to him: if Rome thrust him out he would open a new world and rule it, shape it—" She ceased. The boy was Roman, and Republican Roman at that: one had to be so careful with his sensibilities. "For the sake of the peace," she amended it. "But myself, kitten, *I* was a reigning pharaoh who sponsored explorations for exploration's sake, up the Nile, around the coasts, wherever I could. If I had known then the moon was a world I would have tried for that."

"The moon's a *world?*"

She had not had much experience with newcomers of late, and Brutus was a special case, far out of his own time. She saw terror in his face. "Dear kitten, so are some of the stars. And I'd have gone for those, if I'd had then what I have now. Julius' vision is different than mine. He's a homebody at heart. Italia, Italia is all he yearns for. He makes everywhere Rome. And I, I, kitten, sat on a very hard-seated throne, surrounded by very tedious priests, and held an empire together from the center; but the world was strange and wild in those days, and I wanted to know all of it, I had a vision—" It was too hard to speak of. Of a sudden her throat tightened as it had not done in ages, and there was a stinging behind her eyes and a pain in her heart. The emotion shocked her profoundly; the fact that she stood here in a hallway pouring out her soul to a teenaged and uncomprehending boy amazed her, the more so because she had begun with devious purpose. His innocence was a rock around which all currents had to flow. And she cursed herself for a fool and a sentimental fool at that, all the while touched inside by his evident struggle to understand. No one understood. No one of her age had ever understood. She did not expect it in this place, among the Old Dead. And if she were not Hatshepsut the pharaoh, she might blurt out, simply, with tears: *I want to go,* the way she had ached when her explorers had come back to her and told of great waterfalls and strange tribes and unknown coasts and vast seas. *I want to go,* because she had ruled two thirds of the known world and had no freedom ever to see those things, she could only send others, and learn

about them with a longing that had been dead in this
privileged section of Hell—so very long.

The boy could not know. He only stared at her with
his own vulnerability, seeming to know the subject had
turned off into dark territory where he no longer knew
what they were talking about: where there were
frightening motives and where it involved his father's
safety; that was all he could understand. He talked
about his father and she talked about the moon and her
throat froze shut on her, so that they stood there trapped
and staring at one another.

"I'll talk to him again," he said finally.

"No," she snapped. "No." And regained her direction,
straight for the opening he offered. "But you have to
help me."

"How?"

There were deeds that blackened the heart and
weighted it like lead; and if somehow she had passed
the river and the Judge (she conceived it rather as a
downward journey, and sometimes as the elevator in
the Hall of Injustice, and the Judge of the Dead as a
withered and foul-breathed old man who had terrified
her with the thought that she had come alive into the
House of the Dead, among the embalmers with their
little hooks for the brain, which they drew out the
nose—but however she had come here, so very long
ago, it had been the Judge and not the embalmers; and
she had answered the right answers to the great Monsters
and the Guardians and the Judges)—if somehow, then,
she had passed these things, still the thought niggled at
her that there were indeed the lower hells that Sargon
named, and that there were ways to go there even
having been judged once blameless.

And she named Marcus Brutus certain steps he would
take—for reasons of his father's safety, how he would
keep a constant eye on his father and tell her instantly if
Julius intended to leave the villa.

It was surely why Caesar's enemies had sent this

boy . . . not that Brutus was himself and presently a
danger to Caesar, but that someone of Caesar's friends
or Caesar himself would someday make him so.

It was the whole house this boy was intended to
destroy.

She feared it altogether, the appearance of the boy,
and other moves within the powers of Hell. She saw
foundations crumbling, and everything they had known
in jeopardy.

Most of all she saw Julius taking the offensive. He
was never wont to defend. She had studied his methods
and the methods of generals like Alexander and others
uncounted. She saw patterns.

"Fools," she muttered when she had left young Brutus
in the hall, his instructions specific; and she struck out
at a luckless sycophant who chanced into her path.

The soldiers came and went in unusual numbers, and
Brutus kept his vigil faithfully on the back steps that
overlooked the driveway and the guardpost and small
parking area they had put in since the Cong attack.
Caesar's whereabouts and intent was not something he
dared ask the sycophants. They would tell his father.
And his father, being clever, would then find a way to
escape him. The pharaoh of Egypt had told him so, and
he believed it, because she had said it was to protect
him that Julius would try to slip away.

He did not go in for lunch. He dared not call a
sycophant even to bring him a glass of water. He stayed
by his post and he watched and he listened to every
sound in the house; and then, eventually, Dante came
in from the refurbished rose-garden and informed him
it was dinner:

"I'm not hungry," he said; and *magister* Dantillus
went on past him in that absent-minded way of his,
then looked up, worry furrowing his brow.

"A boy isn't hungry?"

"No, sir."

Dante gave him one of those looks a mother might give an oddly behaving son, and raked a hand through his hair. Not a word did he say—unlike a mother. He only turned and went a few more steps up, and looked back, and went on to the landing.

"*Magister*," Brutus said. "Where is Niccolo?"

A third halt. A worried look. "I'm sure I don't know. I wouldn't know. No one tells me anything."

And the *magus* scurried up the stairs.

An engine purred to life down by the side of the house. Brutus looked up, listening, heart pounding. And sure enough, there came the Ferrari around the bend of the drive, down by the re-planted pines, with Machiavelli at the wheel and Horatius beside him. They reached the street and turned left, toward the city. He thought that might be what he was looking for; and he was tempted to leave his post and go find Hatshepsut.

But he thought then if he were his father trying to escape he would have a diversion; and he would dress himself as a soldier and he would go out in one of the jeeps, just like all the soldiers that came and went.

And he would *not* speak to his son, to even him. So he stationed himself where he could see everything, there by the garage steps.

Then: "*Boy*," a sycophant whispered, close by his ear, so close he jumped in fright. "Your father wants you."

"Where?" he asked, jolted breathless.

Follow-follow-follow, it said, and he got up and hurried after the whisper in the air.

He heard a truck starting up, of the several that were parked in the gravel lot where the soldiers came and went.

And sure enough it was here that the sycophant led him. *Julius will take me with him*, he thought with a pounding heart. *He needs me. That is why Sargon's been so hard on me—because my father needs me to go with the army— That's what all this is about—and I won't tell the queen, then, I won't—*

He saw Mouse standing by one of the trucks, Julius' shadow. He hurried that way, out of breath, daunted by Mouse's presence. But Mouse said something to the truck's interior, and turned and gave Brutus a nod that said he should climb up.

There were iron rungs at the back. He set his foot into them. Mouse boosted him ignominiously from behind, and propelled him up and into the shadow, and into a shadowy presence.

"F-father?" Oh, damn, he had to stammer. He did not want to do that.

"Son," Julius said in Latin, softly, quietly. "I have a job for you."

"Sir?" His heart leapt up. He did not stammer at all, he was so elated.

"I'm leaving for a while. Military maneuvers. I want you to go to Octavius and keep yourself at his orders. Hear? We're going to be short of men in the villa, men that can use weapons. And we have enemies. You know that."

His elation went on a long, slow slide, a degree with every word. It was what Hatshepsut had called the cover, which meant it was a lie. And his father told it to him with so straight a face and so simple a delivery a judge could not have doubted it.

"Y-yes, sir," he murmured, and tears stung his eyes. A knot was in his throat.

"Don't look like that." Julius sat in the dark, on the benches along the side of the truck; he himself stood in the edge of the daylight, where a gap in the canvas threw light up off the metal floor plates. "I'll be back soon enough."

"Yes, sir," he whispered. And, lifting his face and setting his jaw: "Is it the Cong?"

There was long silence. "Maneuvers," his father said patiently, instead of the blow he thought he might have gotten for that impertinence. Julius moved, a shifting of cloth in the dark; and he braced himself as Julius got up, he set his chin firmly and expected chastisement. Junius would have hit him, beyond doubt.

But Julius laid a gentle hand on his shoulder. "Don't be impatient. When you're a target, son, you don't stand up. I want you at the villa. I want you safe, under cover. Just trust the old man knows what he's doing, hey?"

"Is it M-M-Mithri—"

"Don't name names." Julius' strong fingers pressed his shoulder hard. "Not open warfare. No. He's not ready for that. Neither, truthfully, are we. I want all my soldiers where I station them. Hear? And your place is in this house. You have a good arm. You're learning. You'll be with Sargon, with Hatshepsut, with Dante and Augustus. Your studies go on. You do what your tutors tell you. *That's* the thing you can do for me. Promise that."

"Yes, sir."

Julius drew him into a close embrace, patted his back, gripped his arms and looked at him, in that treacherous, reflected light.

"Stay safe," Julius bade him. "And get back in the house."

"Yes, sir." Brutus turned and felt his way through the curtains at the rear, and jumped down to the ground, though it hurt. A great deal did. He went past Mouse without looking at him, sent away like a child, all muddled up with Julius' affection and his dashed hopes. . . .

And the recollection of Hatshepsut. *No matter what he tells you, he is in danger. He is in deadly danger. My weapons can protect him. But I have to be with him to help him. Do you understand me?*

He still felt the pressure of his father's arms about him. He still saw that last look of his.

And he went to find Hatshepsut in her rooms, and to tell her the meager little that he had learned, that Julius *was* with the group that was going out openly from the villa, and that he was taking most of the household with him. . . .

"Under Administration's nose," Hatshepsut said. "*Damn*, straight down the field for once and not off the flank. You're sure."

"He could have lied to me," Brutus said, in Hatshepsut's starkly graceful quarters, which smelled like incense and like perfumes and made him thoroughly uncomfortable, like a rabbit in a fox's den. He thought how that had sounded. "—To keep me here. He s-said you were st-staying. With S-sargon."

"The hell I am," Hatshepsut said, and went to a drawer in a spindly chest and took out a dangerous-looking thing she clipped to her belt; and went to the closet and took out a khaki pack, which she carried in one hand as she waved him toward the door. Outside, the trucks were moving out. He heard them.

"You have to h-hurry," he said, "m-majesty."

"In my own time, kitten. In my own time. The divine Julius wants noise. Noise he will have. *Pretty* kitten." She touched him under the chin, and he flinched, terrified, sensing she was mocking him—and not; and he did not know what to do about it. She was not a Roman girl from Baiae. The hand that touched him and withdrew carried a ring and a bracelet that danced with lights and might be a weapon. The eyes that stared into his were painted and foreign and full of thoughts he did not know how to understand.

He doubted, for one terrible moment, that he had loosed a friend to help his father.

But she patted his arm then and swayed off through the door with a movement that—he could not help it—drew his eye.

And he knew—knew for certain that there was no member of the house that was not dangerous and more than dangerous, if he saw them unveiled—as the queen of Egypt had dealt with him, foreign that she was, and of a mind that frightened him. The *numen* in her was ancient; was the Great Mother; the prophetess; a queen— the ancient serpent-queen and the blood of the sun— Helios, Apollo—Ra, she said. Revealer of truths and mother of mysteries.

That was something with which no man ought to trifle. That was what had turned his blood cold.

But without Her in one of Her aspects, and without the God, no enterprise might succeed. Rome had always known that. Serpent-queen or she-wolf—the unnameable Divine Twins were still Hers, in whatever guise.

He signed himself against the Eye, and shivered, and left Hatshepsut's room and closed the door.

It was rare, that one of the House left a room undefended. But the door had latched. He felt it when he closed it behind him, and tested the lock.

The Pharaoh, the Lord of the Two Lands, whose person, Sargon had explained, was so sacred that hordes of nobles used to attend her rising and her sleeping, vanished down the stairs with a sway of glittering hips and a positively cheerful anticipation in her going.

And his chin where she had touched him still felt the coolth of her fingers.

Klea! he thought. Klea was not one Julius had named to stay with the house and take Augustus' orders.

Nor was Machiavelli. And to know that that dark man was on Julius' side—was a matter of uncertain comfort.

IV

The house was all too quiet since Julius had gone away. Brutus lounged in his room, played his records, did his studies (Augustus was merciless), swam in the pool, and did his fencing practice alone, partnerless, because Sargon was busy, had been busy, continued to be busy; and Dante Alighieri was no fun at all, locked in his room with his computers.

Mostly Brutus pitied himself. His father Julius had gone away with Mouse and Hatshepsut and Kleopatra (the *women* had gone off on some great and dangerous adventure and he, seventeen, almost a man, languished on his bed, chin on arms) and Antonius and mysterious and foreign Germans and even Niccolo, of the stinging wit and the frightening stares—Brutus even missed Niccolo Machiavelli, and sighed and sighed and sulked even to the point of tears because he had lost the world all on a summer's day near Baiae—he never even remembered dying; and he had found Julius here in Hell and gotten Julius to say what he had known, oh, for at least two years, that he was Julius' son. Better, Julius had taken him, the bastard, into his arms and hugged him and *called* him son in a way that made up for all the whispers (almost) and all the misery of a boy about whom there had been plenty of whispering in his life.

His fierce, his handsome, his clever father had acknowledged him and shown him wonders like jeeps and
telephones and installed him in this gloriously beautiful
villa where Augustus claimed to be Commandant of all
Roman Territories or something like that . . . the world
had certainly gotten very strange just after his little
span of life, and something had changed the Rome he
knew, but he did not know what. And did not presently
care. He had spent all his life treading around the
mystery of his own existence with his mother wincing
and looking terrified at this remark and that (oh, a boy
could pick up such subtle things that his elders never
knew he saw or sensed) and living in general with a
nagging pain like glass in his gut—just so he sensed
another pit which might swallow him and spoil all this
wonderful life: and his father stood on the edge of it and
Augustus in the midst of it, so he did not ask, not at all,
he was good at not asking things. He only wanted Julius
to love him and call him son as his father Junius had
never been able to do . . . *boy* and *lad* and *youngster*
and every endearment but son.

So now Julius was off in some danger with the women
and he was too much the baby to be with his father. He
struck chips out of the practice pole, he begged to be
allowed onto the firing range, he was afire to get his
hands on weapons and prove himself a marksman and a
fencer to be reckoned with, to show such brilliance that
Sargon would be awed (if Sargon ever came near him, if
Sargon ever had the time) and would go off with him to
join Julius and show him what a man his son had
become and what a mistake it had been for Julius to go
off without him.

Julius would be in some great danger with hordes
of barbarians pouring down on him and Mouse and
the others and he, Brutus, would come roaring over the
hill with Sargon driving the jeep, firing as they came;
the barbarians would all run in terror and Julius would

jump down from his jeep and stand there looking so proud of his son—

Brutus sniffed and wiped his eyes and his nose and wished he had something to eat, because his stomach hurt, and he was tired of the stupid records. "Off," he said. And a sycophant materialized far enough to cut the stereo off. "Food," he said. "I want a sandwich." He was not supposed to use the sycophants like that. *Don't get lazy*, Augustus would say. *Do it yourself.* But no one knew and no one cared. Sniff. "Ham and cheese. Glass of milk." The Emperor himself had food brought in when he was busy. So he was entitled. It was a mansion, after all. They were rich. There were no slaves, Julius and Augustus both hated them, so they had to use the sycophants you could never look at and never talk to (some of the slaves he had liked, at home, and some were kind to him and stole him tidbits out of the kitchen when his father sent him to his room without supper, which was what this felt like. And old Melanippe had told him stories while she would sit and peel apples. But the sycophants had no such stories.) Sniff. Sargon had, and even Augustus, and Dante wrote them even, but none of them had time for him.

He could run away and join the army. Julius would be in dire trouble and he would spot the enemy sneaking up on him and slip through enemy lines and warn Julius, rescuing the whole Roman army and becoming a hero. Even Mouse would be impressed. Fathers were easier, having an investment at stake.

A door closed in the hall. His ears pricked up. Sniff. Someone was up here? He had lost track of Dante, then. He had thought Dante was in his office with his damned old computer. That was who it had to be.

But he heard no footsteps, just a moving out there. Stealthy-like. And someone brushed heavily against the wall.

Brutus' heart began to pound, as if somehow he had gotten across that line from his vivid imaginings to

something wrong in the house that was not exciting and
interesting, it was scary, and he was seventeen and not
up to the kind of trouble that tended to come down on
this house.

Viet Cong? He wondered, had some Cong assassin
gotten in an upstairs window or something and was there
some barefoot black-clad man going down the hall with
a machine-gun, ready to mow them all down? He
gathered himself up off the bed, careful not to make a
sound, his tennies silent as he could make them on the
floor as he cast about him desperately hunting a weapon,
any weapon, and finding only the *rudus*, his stick-
sword, there in the corner.

Pssst! he said, and quietly snapped his fingers, hoping
for a sycophant; but they were *never* there when trouble
came, and that desertion made him sure that it was real
trouble, there was danger, o gods, and he was all alone
up here, the Cong might murder them all and it was all
his fault if they got to Dante and to the downstairs.

He gathered up the foil and slipped to the door,
listened at it, tried to nerve himself to yell out and raise
the house and not be a fool and not open that door at
all, but just to yell and hide under the bed the way a
boy ought with a hall full of machine-gun-wielding Viet
Cong outside and Sargon of Akkad downstairs—Sargon
would come charging up there with his gun and mow
them all down—

—Sargon would come rushing up into their fire and
get killed and they would all be butchered by hordes of
Cong, even poor scholarly Dante, slain like Archimedes
at his papers—

"*Haaaiiii!*" Brutus yelled, and jerked the door open,
and rushed out to kill the intruders one and all, and
frighten them down to Sargon and ambush if he could.

But it was a lone and naked man out there, who
turned round and stared at him in shock—a one-handed
man—Mucius Scaevola, who had gone off with Julius,
who stared at him now as if he had seen the most

bewildering sight in his life, and who then lost his balance and staggered and went down on his side in a heap.

"*Sargon!*" Brutus cried. Of all his seniors in the house, it seemed more Sargon's department than anyone else's, that one of the bravest soldiers of Caesar's army turned up stark naked in the upstairs hall and fainted on the floor.

"*Sargon!*"

Brutus had no experience dealing with unconscious people or dying ones. He hesitated in that doubt, afraid of touching Scaevola, afraid of moving him and hurting him and almost as vividly . . . of being a fool and wrong and deserving blame for stupidity; but it was a cold floor and hard and no one ought to lie there with a fool staring at him. "*Sargon!*" Down the hall Dante's door opened. And Brutus came and got down on his knees and tried to pick up Scaevola's head and shoulders, finding out how heavy a dead weight was. He gave a great heave and got his knees under, and saw Dante hurrying down the hall. "He's hurt!" he yelled at the poet. "Dante, get Sargon!"

A glass of milk and a ham and cheese sandwich materialized and fell and shattered.

"Fool!" Brutus yelled, cradling Scaevola against his own warmth; Dante had run, the sycophant had fled, leaving the mess behind. He was terrified. He felt Scaevola breathing, he patted the man's face and gathered up his limp left hand and shook at him. "Please, *Muci,* please wake up, please, please, please, come on, wake up."

A racket in the downstairs hall now, Dante yelling after help, and sycophants chittering about. "Get a blanket!" Brutus snapped at the servant-ghosts. "Find Augustus!" Because everything was sliding into chaos and the Emperor could make them all do what they ought. He felt a stir in the body he was holding, felt

Scaevola draw a little gasp of a breath, and he patted at Scaevola's cheek again. "Oh, please."

Scaevola's eyes opened, blue eyes, faded blue, a little slit of color in a white face. Brutus could see it, felt the sudden difference in Scaevola's body as muscle came back to life, so slight a change, but over the edge toward living. Scaevola's eyes wandered in that half-open state, opened further, as if he did not know where he was, or did not recognize Brutus upside down.

"It's me," Brutus said, trying to twist round so that Scaevola could see him more rightside up. "It's Brutus."

"Am I home?" Scaevola's lips trembled. O gods, Brutus thought, a grown man was going to cry, he had thought a man must never cry, and he had never dealt with a situation like this, which terrified him as much as death did, that Scaevola was going to embarrass them both forever. Tears ran a crooked trail down Scaevola's face when he blinked, his eyes rolled glistening and desperate, but he got his mouth to a hard line and got several large breaths. There was more noise belowstairs; heavy sandals were headed up, Sargon was on his way, and likely Augustus, and Scaevola was trying to hold it. Brutus took his fingers and swiped the tears off Scaevola's cheek, and looked up at arriving help with a defiant scowl, for both their sakes.

"Dammit," he said to Sargon, and the Emperor of Rome and the poet Dante, "I've been yelling half an hour! He's hurt—" He caught his breath, held tight to the young soldier who seemed hardly older than himself. Such a hero as this could never give way, Brutus would not permit it. "He's all right, I think, he's going to be all right, he's freezing to death and I can't get the damn sycophants to get a blanket!"

One settled out of midair and floated down over Scaevola soft as a wish. A baby blue one.

"Here." Sargon, Lion of Akkad, squatted down and shifted his sword out of the way. His huge arms gathered Scaevola up blanket and all, and got him to help himself a little; Sargon stood up, and Brutus did, trying to help and knowing he was in the way now.

"I died," Scaevola murmured. "Trouble—trouble down there." His head came up, nodding with weakness, and his eyes wandered as if they still saw something terrible. "O gods. Lion—"

"*Were you with Julius?*" the Emperor demanded, and Scaevola turned his face that way, leaning heavily against Sargon's support.

"I was just with him—" Scaevola blinked and tried again to focus. "Mycenae. It's Mycenae. The damned Trojan war—"

"Get him downstairs, get him a robe," Augustus shouted at Sargon and the air about them, which was suddenly thick with nervous sycophants all chittering and anxious to please.

Sargon drew Scaevola toward the stairs. Brutus hesitated, then hurried and got up against Scaevola's other side, holding onto his handless right arm, as Scaevola tried the stairs and worked his way down them, step by difficult step.

"Get me a drink," Scaevola muttered under his breath. And managed to walk, with their help, all the way to the bottom.

In a warm robe and sitting in a big easy chair in Augustus' own study, Scaevola was a little steadier. A sycophant showed up with a bottle of wine, the First Citizen's best chilled white, and when Sargon had opened it and poured, Scaevola took the longed-for drink, incredible luxury, when for the last terrible night he had been fighting a losing battle for his life and the lives of the men with him, first on ground he knew and then in a surreal stairwell full of fire and smoke and endless enemies. And finally bleeding to death of a careless step, that had let a fallen enemy thrust his blade up under his armor—

He shuddered and took another drink, washing the

dust and the taste of the Undertaker's antiseptics down, and drew a panting breath, looking at Augustus and Sargon and Julius' newly-found son, and the poet Dante Alighieri, who stood and sat in a solemn half-ring, waiting and staring at him in a way that made him altogether nervous, and sent his mind scattering this way and that with worry for the men in his command who were *not* with him—and those who had been, and those—

—but he had left them in Caesar's charge, Julius would see to them, he would not have left them in any peril on that hill.

It was mad. Julius was in Mycenae. Which was also Troy. Scaevola raved and fretted, and Sargon was off and Dante was busy with his machines and Augustus stayed mostly in his office. . . .

"Take care of him," the First Citizen had asked, personally; and Sargon had patted Brutus on the shoulder and entrusted him with the same.

"But—" Brutus had said in dismay.

"Keep the sycophants in order," Sargon had said. "They'll manage."

"But," Brutus said, "but—" —*I don't know what to do,* was what he intended to say in both cases, but no adults were listening lately.

So he sat by Scaevola's bed the night long, and could not ask him more questions because it was not right, Scaevola being as weak as he was, and so tired, to badger him; Scaevola slept a great deal, and sometimes his face twitched as if he were having bad dreams.

Suddenly he cried out, this man who had braved the Etruscans and their fire, and died twice at last, once on Earth and once in Hell; and he fought the bedclothes and reached wildly about him.

Brutus guessed well enough what for, and having trained with this man, yelled: "It's me, it's Marcus!" —and dived behind an overstuffed chair in the half-dark. "Scaevola, it's Marcus Junius—*di omnipotentes, Scaevola! Amicus sum! Socius!*"

The mattress creaked under a sudden and substantial weight. Brutus put his head up. Scaevola was sitting on the edge of the bed in the disarray of the bedclothes, his face glistening with sweat.

"*Vales?*" Brutus asked tentatively.

Scaevola's chest heaved to a deep breath. He ran his one hand through his hair and drew another breath, and Brutus levered himself up on his arms against the chair and stood there, prudently staying on the other side of it.

"Are you all right?"

"I'm awake," Scaevola said, and jerked the sheet off the bed and flung it around his right shoulder and his left. "Uniform."

"I'm supposed to take care of you. I'm not supposed to—"

"Who's the duty officer?" Scaevola asked, all quiet and businesslike, and impatient under the surface.

"Arrius. But—"

"I have to get back. Hear me, *Marce Iuni?*"

"Yes, sir." *Danger* ran under that tone. Danger to Julius. To all of them. Of a sudden they were co-conspirators. Brutus obediently went to the closet and snatched up Scaevola's clothing, rummaged drawers for socks and underclothes, and brought them to him as Scaevola, quick and deft with his one hand, dressed in the nightlight. And a sycophant materialized, despite the stealth they used.

"Pretend you weren't here," Brutus hissed at it. "*You weren't here!* Or you'll regret it! This is Caesar's business!"

It gibbered and vanished.

"It will go straight to Augustus," Scaevola said, grim-faced. "We have to hurry. Help with the damned belt and buttons, lad, they're hell."

"Yes, sir." Gingerly Brutus took the starched khaki

and buttoned it up; and fastened the belt which Scaevola
could do for himself well enough; but not the way his
hand was shaking, not the way the sweat was broken
out on his face. "I'm going with you."

"No. Absolutely not."

"I'm not a kid, dammit! If my father's in trouble—"

"—he doesn't need his son to worry about along with
everything else. He's all right. I know he's all right.
There was never a question of it. It's his route home we
have to worry for. He's deep—deep in Hell; and there's
no damn map to go by. It's the return I'm worried
about. I've got to get his line of retreat open again—"

"He's not losing!"

"He's not losing, *prodi*, but he's got to divide forces
to get the damn supply lines open, and that costs lives
and it sends us past the Undertaker—" Scaevola gave a
little shiver. "And interrogation. Before they send us
out again. *If* they send us out, or out to our own. How I
got back—I don't know. And we can't lose him; we
can't let *him* go that route. Not if it sends all of us on
the Trip. Do you understand—how important he *is?*"

Brutus swallowed hard. He did not understand. "He's
my father."

"He's the linchpin that holds the Roman west together.
Ancient *and* modern. Without him—chaos. The east in
the ascendency. And we can't risk him. Octavianus'
damn caution—can't rule without him. There. That's
treason. But it's truth. The Empire rests on the Republic.
And Caesar is the turning-point. *Wait*, Octavianus says.
That's *always* his advice. Wait on what, I'd like to
know." Scaevola bent and stepped into one boot and
Brutus dropped hastily to his knees to help him with
the other. "He's got some damn notion to send a courier,
let him send one. I'm not going to wait on it."

"Take me with you!"

"It's no damn place for a kid."

"I'm seventeen." Brutus leapt to his feet. "You can't
have been much older when you—"

Scaevola looked at him with the planes of his face gone all to stone in the dim light. "Say I aged. I was a damn fool kid and Porsena wrapped me up in a sheet and bundled me home out of pity. And I'm a hell of a lot older since. You stay here. You be damned glad you're staying here."

Brutus said not a word. It hurt, the slight and the bitter tone both, from a man who had never used either with him. He stood there, wounded, and Scaevola reached out and clasped him by the shoulder.

"My father," Brutus said, reminding him: family matter. *Julian* matter.

"Your father's orders." Scaevola threw it right back in his lap. "If I brought you with me I'd have to fall on my sword, and damn, I've had enough of the Undertaker." Scaevola shook at him gently. "Hear me?"

"*T'audio, legate.*" He heard, in a numb-surfaced panic. He knew right when it was thrust up to him. He knew he was a fool and that there were grown men and more experienced ones—and Hatshepsut and her deadly weapons—to take care of his father. But, gods, gods, it was hard.

"Good lad." Scaevola dragged him close and embraced him like kin, and pushed him toward the door. "See if the way is clear. Get me to Arrius. I can reason with him."

"You can't do anything if Augustus—"

"—sends orders to prevent me; but he won't. I want a head start to the armory. That's all I need. I don't need a damn committee to study it and I don't want to wait to explain it. He'll accept what's in motion."

"*Yes*, sir." That was logic he understood. He had learned Augustus' ways for himself. He headed for the hall with a will.

And quickly enough, a jeep was pulling out of the villa's driveway on a night run to the Armory, a courier, Arrius said dourly—no unusual matter: the legate was going to the Armory, the legate could carry a message, quite well, thank you, sir: do it several times a night and a day, the phones being suspect.

There was cause to worry about Scaevola on that street: there was always the chance, Brutus thought, of the Cong, whose territory paralleled that route along Decentral Park to the New East Armory—

But a man who had determined to assault the deeper hells a second time—was not likely to fall to the Cong. Brutus watched the tail-lights vanish and hugged himself and shivered.

"You're not alone," Scaevola had said to him. "Julius has friends. They're watching you. Never doubt it. Do what you're told and don't rush out into trouble the next time. No knowing what I might have been, out in that hall. And where it comes to politics—trust Octavianus knows damn well what he's doing. That's why he's here. Now he'll know he has to move, now he's lost me."

He thought about that now.

Liches, Scaevola had described to them. The walking dead.

Or Cong.

Or Mithridates' soldiers—Asians and Hittites and no knowing what else.

Has Julius found my brother down there? he had almost asked. But Scaevola had told him so little. And questions on that topic almost always brought an end of all questions. Nothing he had learned of Scaevola, nothing of the truths Scaevola had poured at him, would he have learned, if he had asked that question.

And Scaevola had told him more than he would have told a child. Scaevola had spoken to him as Caesar's son. As Caesar's son of his own persuasion—Octavianus Augustus notwithstanding; and told him things which were dangerous to have said—being Scaevola, and a great man, for all he looked hardly older than himself.

Twenty-five centuries older, in Hell.

And trusting a boy of seventeen brief real years—for

reasons which Brutus suddenly apprehended as complex and desperate and utterly beyond his understanding. Trust Augustus and don't trust him; rely on him and doubt him; most of all—*push* him into motion.

And Julius—the rock on which all their safety rested. *Do you understand how important he* is?

"Go in, boy," Arrius said.

"My name is Junius, sir." Respectfully, but with a straightening of his back and a hardening of his jaw. His pride had borne a great deal.

"Inside," the duty officer said, refusing to be impressed.

He retreated, up to the floor where his room was, and where Scaevola's had been.

Then it occurred to him that he would have to answer where Scaevola had gone. Then his hands began to sweat and his heart to beat hard—not that he had been brave. He simply had not thought of the fact, until then, that he had disobeyed Augustus' direct orders.

Perhaps the First Citizen would have him punished. He would try to be brave in that case, even if it were harsh. A beating was within Augustus' rights, as his commander. *Death* was.

But most likely, he thought, Augustus, who was his adopted brother, and his elder by survival, would only withdraw all trust of him, as Augustus already regarded him with misgivings that might be resentment for his turning up: he sensed it in the air every time he was near the First Citizen. It would take so little for Augustus to hate him; there was so much reason. Augustus would cast the worst light on it when Julius got home. Augustus would never trust him. And never, in Hell—had no earthly measure about it, and reached into spans no one could imagine.

He was not wise in a great many things; but when it came to resentments in a household, he had lived through his own hell on earth, and this one had little to teach him except degree.

He wiped his eyes and, ignominiously, his nose; and

shut the door and flung himself down on his bed, to bury his face in his arms and wait for morning.

But in a little time a step approached the door; and a hand tried the latch. And rapped, loudly.

"*Brute. Aperi.*"

He shivered then, being no hero. It was Augustus' voice.

He got up and went and opened it, blinking in the strong light and trying not to look up, because his eyes were wet and red, and there was no hiding it.

"Where is Scaevola?" Augustus asked.

"I don't know, *princeps.*"

"Don't split hairs with me. Did I say watch him?"

"My father—"

"*Our* father. Do you forget that?"

"Scaevola belongs to *him,*" Brutus said. "Sir. He said he had to. I take it for Julius' order. And that takes precedence."

He stood there a long time, remembering that this brother-by-adoption could have him arrested. He tried not to shiver, or to let his chin tremble.

"*Two* of us have concern for him," Augustus said. "And more than two. Think of that."

And the door shut.

He stood facing that blankness, stunned that it had been that short and taken that bent; and still not knowing his adopted brother's mind.

In the morning he half expected the door to be locked, but it was not.

Then he repented his distrust of his adopted sib, his cousin-by-bastardy, in some remote and shameful fashion too difficult to reason out. He walked the halls, he sought after Sargon, who was out, he went to the sanctum sanctorum and tried to talk to Dante Alighieri, since he reckoned that Dante was wisest, in his own befogged way.

But Dante shooed him out. "No time," the *magus* said. "No time, no time."

The next day came, and the next, and a weight seemed to settle on him—it was guilt, he thought, for what he did not know, since he certainly would have helped Scaevola again, in the next moment, without reservation, and rising whatever punishment he must. But it seemed to him things had not gone right, and he wished that Augustus would have shouted at him, or cursed him, or hit him.

His father Junius Brutus—would have struck him. *Had* struck him, for far less.

And in the third restless evening he knew that that was the guilt—that he did not believe that Scaevola was wrong; and he believed everything about the First Citizen was true; but the First Citizen had been wise enough to have seen everything, all their little treason, and come to him with it, and walked away and left him with the burden of it.

"Sir," Brutus said when he had gotten a come-ahead from behind Augustus' study door; and walked into that untidy place where Augustus worked and ate and worked—the desk had dirty dishes no sycophant entered this room to remove, mingled with papers which were soldiers' lives, and their safety in this house.

And Augustus' eyes looked at him with ineffable pain, bruised and weary in a freckled face that matched the statues, but somehow looked less like a god and more like someone's next-door neighbor—a little absent-minded, like Dante; a little world-weary, like Mouse.

"What is it?" Augustus asked him after a moment, in that dreadful, dreadful silence, in which Brutus stood with his hands locked behind him and his heart hammering and hurting all at the same time.

"I came to beg your pardon," he said. He could not force his voice much above a whisper. But he did not, thank the gods, stammer it.

"What have you done?"

"F-for Sc-scaevola." Oh, damn, he was muddled now.

He was cold and his teeth were all but chattering. "I d-don't s-say. I w-w-w-*wouldn't* have done it—b-but I'm s-s-*sorry* I d-disobeyed your orders."

Augustus' weary eyes blinked, several times, and looked—not angry, but sorrowful and interested at the same time. "Thank you," he said distinctly, softly, "*Marce Iuni.*"

There was prolonged silence. "May I g-go?" Brutus asked, in what dignity he could muster, under that long, long stare.

The First Citizen nodded, curt inclination of his head. And was still staring at him when Brutus turned his back and quietly opened the door and left.

He felt better, anyway. He felt he had done the right thing. Maybe he had mended something that he had broken. That Augustus had not warmed to him did not truly surprise him, though it left him feeling less than whole: Augustus had, perhaps, resented him all his earthly life, even if he had never known Augustus existed: Augustus' jealousy of Julius' natural son—was not unnatural. And perhaps the right thing to do was to walk softly with Octavianus Augustus, and show him the respect he ought to have as house-head, and—

—Gods, there was no honor he could gain by Julius' acknowledging him that did not in some manner take away from Augustus his heir—himself being firstborn. Augustus had been no friend to Caesarion. He had gathered that much. Augustus was a jealous man in that way, if nothing else. Brutus was resolved not to provoke him more than he must.

And behind closed doors Augustus shoved closed the drawer he had opened, where the little pistol lay, and rested his eyes against the heels of his hands.

One more thing, one more damnable mess he did not need.

He longed for Machiavelli's counsel at the moment—if he could reach Machiavelli, which he could not,

Machiavelli being on campaign with Julius—and he earnestly hoped Scaevola had gotten through. For all the mistaken signals that were always between himself and that impulsive legate, he earnestly hoped *not* to have Scaevola in the upstairs hall again—or worse, lost to them.

Scaevola gone, and no debriefing, beyond what they had gotten him in the first hour. The man had been through the Undertaker's hands, in Administration, and Dante's little maneuver that had somehow gotten Arrivals to print out upstairs, in a way that could look like a software glitch—Dante talked in such arcane terms— had at least let Dante intervene in Reassignments, enough to turn up the old assignment, Dante had said, that would bounce Scaevola straight to the villa. They *owed* the poet—owed him considerably for this one.

But gods knew what Scaevola might have spilled. Thanks to a well-meaning boy and a conniving, hard-headed legion officer, *they* did not know.

Julius might rely on luck, but Gaius Julius Octavianus Caesar Augustus had no such faith in the commodity: he had had damned little of it in his life, and carved his way through the enemies Julius himself had spared, or there would be no Rome.

Mithridates sent them a Marcus Brutus remembering only his youth, not knowing that he had been one of Julius' murders. Not knowing that Augustus and Antonius had killed *him*, that was the second irony: the boy came to apologize, so nobly and so politely that Augustus was genuinely moved. Had it been any other seventeen-year-old penitent, Augustus would have answered his heart and gotten up and hugged the boy and made them friends.

But it was just damned hard—to embrace the man who had killed Julius, whom he had faced on the battlefield, and whom he had hounded to his death by suicide.

He had tried it once with Caesarion, and gotten

nothing but bitter contempt. Caesarion *remembered* his death, though he had been older than the seventeen Hell had made him.

Brutus might someday remember.

Seventeen. Seventeen. A number evidently ominous among Julius' irregular sons. Perhaps not even of Hell's choosing.

But of someone's choosing—who had something in mind.

Augustus disliked precipitate moves. He disliked operating out of a corner, where he was—or as a decoy and target, which Julius had made him.

But it was time to do *something*. Scaevola had made that necessary.

V

"But who is he?" Brutus asked, lifting the shade ever so little at the stairwell window, and the sycophant at his elbow whispered: *Napoleon*.

"A friend of my father's?" Brutus wondered. "Is he Old Dead?"

Yes-yes-yes, the air said, and: *No-no-no, New*.

Brutus stared. New Dead were a novelty in Augustus' house. Not unknown, but a great novelty. Many were very tall. This one was not. This departing visitor was, at least, not Viet Cong, nor, he supposed, anyone associated with them, and perhaps he was one of that group of soldiers who somehow kept an eye to things about the house and grounds and made him think that his father Julius was somehow watching over them all at distance.

The Viet Cong were skulking about the park again, a determined and long surveillance could spot them, now and again; and Brutus existed in an agony of worry. He stood now watching from the lower hall till Horatius and the stranger Bonaparte and the other soldiers had gotten into the jeep and gone off out of the driveway, then he turned and went up the stairs, a spatter of tennis shoes on the terrazzo: T-shirts and jeans were all the sycophants provided him, which he was doubtful of

83

at first, and he still tripped a bit over his own feet, but such clothes were Modern, and Julius had taken to modern things, so Brutus took to them with a vengeance. He studied, in these terrible, lonely days. He tried to do everything that would please Julius when he asked, on his return, what his newest son had been up to.

Up the stairs and down the hall to the end where Dante had his rooms—he knocked ever so gingerly, and knocked again.

"Who?" the voice came through the door. "Who is it?" And perhaps, inside, a sycophant answered; for: "*Scelerato!*" the voice raged. "Out, out of here!" As the door opened and Dante Alighieri stared at him all exhausted-looking and with his long hair frizzed and disordered. "Busy," Dante said. "I'm busy, doesn't anyone care?"

"Dante, there was a New Dead here. Napoleon Bonaparte. Is that a friend?"

Dante took in his breath and leaned in the doorway, his pale, large-knuckled hand gripping the frame. "Buonaparte, you say." His eyes were large. "With whom?"

"With Augustus, I think. Horatius brought him. The sycophants said he was a friend."

"Buonaparte," Dante murmured, and wandered into the maze of books and papers that was his room. The Machine glowed there, its monitor screen alight, dominating a littered desk. The heavy velvet curtain was drawn, making the room far too dark for comfort. Dante ran a hand through his hair, faced about again. "With Augustus." Dante often repeated things. Being a wizard of sorts, a *magus* and a *grammaticus* and continually communing with his machines as he did, he seemed to find talking with actual people a confusion to him. But he would talk, when there was something like this afoot; and no one *else* would tell a boy anything.

"What is it?" Brutus asked. "Is he dangerous?"

"Dangerous," Dante said, and raked his hand through

his hair a second time. "The whole situation is *dangerous,* young man."

"Is he a friend?"

"Of Julius', once, yes. But resigned, *resigned,* you understand, nothing could get him back here. How did he look?"

"Worried."

"Augustus sent for him. Augustus has sent for him or he has come to Augustus."

"Is there something wrong out there?" Brutus went and looked at the arcane numbers on the screen in hopes of reading something, anything, of that tenuous connection with the Armory which might have connections to Julius.

"Is my father all right?"

"I don't like this," Dante said, and paced and wrung his hands. "Oh, damn, *damn.*"

"What are you talking about? *Magister,* what have I told you?"

"Where is Sargon?"

"I haven't seen him. Not since—since—" He felt a little chill, realizing it. "Yesterday. *Magister Dantille,* where is he?"

"I'm asking you."

"I don't know—but—but a lot of people have come and gone—"

"A snake," Dante said, wiping his hair back with both hands. "A snake with huge coils—" Sometimes Dante declaimed poetry. Sometimes he looked frighteningly mad. He did now, his hair fallen wildly about his face, his eyes large and white around the edges. "We can't see them all, it's far too large, large as the hills. Buonaparte is here. And he would never come here."

"Enemies, you mean." Brutus grasped after meanings like a suppliant after a sibyl's utterances. "You mean it's enemies, *old* enemies."

"Old enemies, yes. And new. Go, go, out, I'm busy here, very busy—"

"But who?" Brutus asked, being shoved at the door. He dared not affront the man. "What enemies? The Cong?" That they had come slinking back to the Park seemed a sinister thing, full of omen. Perhaps, he thought, Mithridates had sent them. "What is my father doing? When is he going to come home? What is he *doing* out there?"

"Saving us all. Like the emperor. Saving us all. Don't spy. It isn't polite."

Brutus found himself outside the door. And the door shut. The lock snicked.

Inside, Dante Alighieri took another harried swipe at his hair. He was trembling. The boy was part of it. The boy was *their* piece, and did not know it. That was the terrible thing. One was so tempted to forget that, and see only the boy.

He went back to his console and sat down and called up the latest reports. Nothing informative. Julius kept in contact, that was all. Mettius Curtius and his communications tests bleeped and blipped at appropriate intervals and, once, reported liches. With Scaevola, the Armory had lost contact entirely: and that boded no good at all.

Augustus was moving on his own initiative. Dangerously. Strategy was Julius' forte, never Augustus'; and the very worst of Dante's nightmares was actuality. Augustus was taking matters into his own hands, *having* to move, without any of the assistance he was accustomed to rely on, except only Sargon and Horatius and the remaining cohorts of the 10th. There were other legions to call on. But to move them would cause ripples.

And Augustus always came to Dante when he wanted something done with the records—would not understand, did not want to hear, how repeated delvings into Pentagram computers were more and more difficult, how they must not do this recklessly: Julius would understand. Machiavelli would understand. Augustus refused to understand, and sought miracles to save them from consequences.

Dante was running out of magic numbers.

Publius Aelius Hadrianus Caesar blinked and blinked again at the sound that disturbed his night; and lay in his bed in a moil of uncertainties till the sycophant (there were so few of them lately, and so few the aides that remained on-staff) told him there were visitors.

"Who?" he asked it.

Romans, it said. *Your aides are refusing to let them in. The visitors insist.*

The sycophant almost had a voice. Almost he knew it. It had been with him so long. He was abjectly grateful. He feared the others as he feared the aides. He had so many enemies. Like Caesar. Like Rameses. Like Augustus and Tiberius and Tigellinus and Lawrence and gods knew, the Parthians and the Germans and the Egyptians who smiled like crocodiles and supplanted him. His staff had deserted him. His servants had fled. His lover had vanished. Whether they had killed him he had no idea. He asked few questions in his misery. He did not want the answers, he, Hadrian, once supreme commander over the legions of Hell. When a man fell this far, he had no friends.

It was not the Undertaker he feared, though that was horrible. It was existence. It was living, knowing that everyone around him was shifting, seeking some new loyalty, that the staff that stayed with him was likely Rameses' staff, or worse, Mithridates' or Tigellinus'. That the servants spied on him. The sycophants deserted him. Only the one stayed, the one so near to reality, the one which for centuries had pinned its reality to his and, poor creature, so close to its goal, too close to start over, knew that it served a declining influence. It alone had reason to be loyal. No one else. If there were Romans outside, they had come to harm him, though what form that harm might be when Reassignments seemed so doggedly determined to return him to New Hell, he could not imagine. Kill him again and again and again? And each time Reassignments would put him back. They surely knew that.

But his Roman kindred had come to him and his traitor staff, hand-picked by his successor, had determined to block them, because they wanted him alive and in their hands.

Two sets of his enemies fought over the corpse, that was what. He lay here in bed, weak and hallucinating of crocodiles, and his enemies tore at his flesh and bartered away the scraps of his souls, such as he had left.

He could not decide what to do. He could not decide anything any more. He did not want to decide. But he hated the traitors with a personal spite. And that alone brought him out of bed, brought him staggering to the door and wrapping about him togalike the sheet the lone sycophant had brought for his dignity.

He clung to the stair-rail and walked the few steps down to the hall and to the door of his apartment, where by the entry desk he saw two of his staff arguing with someone on the intercom at the door.

"Open the door," he said, and his staffers turned around, whey-faced and furtive. "Open it." In his old voice of command, such as he could muster. They had drugged him. He knew that they did. All the room swam. He staggered forward and reeled against the wall where two gilt swords and a funerary shield made a display. Ripped a sword down and staggered their way. *"Open it."*

The lock clicked. The door swung open. It was the sycophant which obeyed him, not his fish-mouthed aides.

Beyond that door, framed in the tasteful, civilized apartment corridor, Atilius Regulus stood in city-dress khakis and backed by half a dozen of the legion in the same. There were Uzis in their hands. Hadrian stared at them and the aides stared and melted away out of the line of fire.

Hadrian made a small, a desperate gesture. "Welcome," he said in Greek, it was so ingrained in him; and saw them frown in offense, though they understood that tongue. He knew that Regulus did. An old Roman; a name for honor; but it was a bloody-minded kind. Tears suffused Hadrian's eyes, a profound longing for these countrymen who despised him and had come to do him more hurt; but with them it was at least a personal hate. "*Salvete*," he said. "Come in. Or do you do your business from that doorway?"

"Octavianus sends you his affections," Regulus said, clipped and measured. Augustus. The *emperor* Augustus, he meant. This was a Republican Roman: no titles, no bending of the head, no respecting of majesty in that stare. Not even for the majesty he served. *Affections*. Hadrian did not miss the irony in the voice or in Regulus' basilisk stare and sphinxish smile. "Majesty. He asks after your health."

"How will it be?" Hadrian asked. His voice was faint, but it was assuredly the sphinx who had come to catechize him, assuredly the ancient, ritual riddling game. He gave it smile for smile, weary though he was. "You will have to tell me, *Atili*."

Regulus waved his hand. The legionaries moved inside and shut the door. One immediately stared through the staff desk. Another picked up the phone.

"Here," an aide objected. And fell quickly silent as he received too much of their attention. All the aides were silent. The legionary began unscrewing the receiver of the entry hall phone. Another, beyond the arch, took a small detector the sweep of the living room, with particular attention to the van Gogh.

Hadrian watched, dully. Turned his eyes then back to Regulus. "What does he want?"

"Your well-being," Regulus said in soft and modulated tones, with just the least edge of Republican scorn. "Majesty. You are in *our* keeping now. You may find your lot improved, —majesty."

*   *   *

Sargon came in at dawn. In military khaki. That was not unusual, but the hour was. Brutus watched from the stairs, now the king of Akkad slipped in; and he guessed that Sargon had no wish to talk to a boy just now. A woman, he imagined. The kind of mystery that men pursued and he had only longed after in his life. And ordinary things *did* go on, while the extraordinary ones worked themselves out. Like a soldier going Downtown for—what soldiers went there for. He had heard a car come in, a car, not one of the jeeps.

In fact it was a long time before Sargon showed himself in the main wing of the house: he was swimming, the sycophants said, and steaming, and swimming again, and when Brutus, chafing in idleness, thought to go downstairs to ask the king for his lessons:

The Lion wants to be alone, a sycophant whispered; and added, for sycophants always had to fear displeasure: *Please*.

Brutus sighed, and slouched down the stairs, small dispirited skips of rubber-shod feet. He could take the whole stairs on his heels. Most everyone would think it impudent. It was hard to be his father's son, and to have to live up to that.

He hoped for Augustus, at least. But: *Hush, hush*, a sycophant said, before he could touch the office door. *The emperor is having a nap*.

He went and sat on the steps, elbows on knees, and hands between ankles, and sighed again, and a third time.

He understood too much and too little. And his father was in danger and everyone cared about Julius, but no one remembered *his* pain. That was all right, as long as they took care for his father. He would allow them that. He could take the slights and the snubs and being shoved aside, the way his father's soldiers took other wounds, for his sake, if that was what he had to do.

But it would cost them so little to give him just a word.

He moped.

He skipped his lunch in the forlorn hope that someone would notice.

No one did.

By the number of soldiers coming and going there was *something* going on, and he queried sycophants and even (once and in fear) listened at the library door, where Augustus was closeted with Sargon, and hung about listening near the garage where the off-duty soldiers tended to gather for smokes and gossip.

"Got that damn snake," he heard one man say.

"Friendly fire," another chuckled. He did not know how fire could be friendly; but someone was dead, and it pleased the troops. All the same it upset his stomach, because he was not sure, even yet, who all their friends and enemies were.

He moped and spied such as he could.

And once Augustus caught him in the hall as Augustus and Regulus came out of the library; he got as far away from the door as he could, but maybe it was the look on his face. Augustus stopped cold and looked at him a moment that he thought his heart would stop; a look that peeled him away in layers like an onion and said that Augustus was not at all deceived and not at all pleased at being spied on.

The other man was Atilius Regulus, who had died at Carthaginian hands—surrendered to the enemy to die with his men, after he had told Rome: *No ransom*. That was the kind of man Regulus was. They had killed him in a barrel studded with knives. And crucified his men. And Regulus was not a pleasant man to have giving you the same sort of look—like you were something objectionable that had turned up in his path. Regulus and compromise did not belong in the same breath.

They ignored him then. Brutus took the chance and slipped away, and sat down by the rose garden, in

solitude. There was nowhere else he could go in the
villa that did not look as if he might be spying on
someone. Intrigue was that thick about the house.

He had his supper in his room. And no one noticed.
Sycophants were hard to summon and deserted him
after they had brought his milk, and his sandwich,
which came with mayonnaise, which he hated; and they
forgot the potato chips. They abhorred a soul in despair.

He ate it down in small bites, because there was a
lump in his throat that had been there for days.

He heard someone coming down the hall—Dante, he
thought, whose room was in that direction. But it was
two someones. He had not been asleep. He had not
heard anyone *going* that way.

He froze, with the half-eaten sandwich in hand. He
swallowed what he had in his mouth in one great gulp,
so as not to miss hearing anything.

He heard Dante's voice, and almost thought it was all
right and ordinary.

Then he heard one he had not heard in very long—it
was Niccolo Machiavelli's. Niccolo was back.

From Julius.

The phones rang off the wall, and every light in the
villa was on, sycophants rushing to and fro with such
energy they made colored streaks in the air and came
and went with little pops; and Brutus could hardly hold
himself in restraint.

Julius was back. Julius was safe. The whole convoy
had turned up at the Armory without anyone sighting
them and after they had been out of radio contact for
much too long, and soldiers were going around with
smiles on their faces and cursing to all the gods and
yelling at each other, jeeps and trucks were growling
and backing here and there, the gunners on the roof
were ordered to keep strict attention and *not* let their
attention lapse, and there was activity in the kitchens,
and in every apartment of the returning family—as

sycophants hastily mended all their neglect, polished and cleaned there and in the hallways so that one could hardly dodge the solid traffic without getting a yelp from a trod-upon sycophant arranging a vase or dusting a table.

"When is he coming?" Brutus asked of Sargon, as the king of Akkad passed him in haste. "Majesty—is he coming back tonight?"

Sargon stopped. "On his way," Sargon said. "Pentagram doesn't even know yet. And we aren't telling them."

Sargon grinned at him, who had not smiled in days, and turned with a half-skip and hurried on his way to meet Horatius, whose eye-patch and lean, lank figure made him recognizable in the far distance.

And Brutus went outside the house and back in hunting rumors, and out again, till he realized he had collected a little sycophant of his own, that wistfully followed him, a little green-glowing dot which he could only see when he was out in the dark

Not much of a sycophant, to be sure. But one of them seemed to have suddenly found him and tagged him.

Caesar was back. And all the sycophants scurried to realign themselves at points of advantage.

There were headlights coming. A jeep pulled into the driveway and Brutus thought for an instant that it might be Julius, but it was only one of the couriers coming in, swinging into the parking area they had made on the lawn.

He went back into the house in dejection. There had been too many such false hopes in an hour. He went into the downstairs hall to see if he could learn anything—

—about the time that the doors opened upstairs and Augustus and Horatius and a horde of staff officers started down in haste, with a sudden noise of engines coming up the street outside.

"Is it Julius?" he asked, dodging out of the way of important men. "Is it Julius?"

He followed them, as everyone in the house seemed to want into the same doorway at once, and onto the steps that led down toward the drive and the guard station—

Jeeps and trucks turned in at the drive and lights blinded them, so that it was all a confusion of glare and black figures running.

He heard Kleopatra's voice, high and clear above the rest. He jumped off the side of the porch and ran out among the rest, to the foremost jeep, where he was sure his father would be. A truck nearly hit him in the confusion. He dodged, heart pounding, and recovered his balance. *Careful-careful,* his little sycophant shrilled in its faint voice.

He hesitated there on the grassy margin, with lights and vehicles more and more confused, until he saw not Julius, but Mouse walking across the grass with a kind of traveling case in his hand, and a rifle slung from his shoulder, and an amazing array of equipment about his person. "My father," he cried. *"Ubi'est pater, Deci?"*

Mouse hitched up a strap and pointed, toward the other side of the road; and Brutus turned and hurried, where he saw a group headed toward Augustus and Sargon and the others, where Hatshepsut and tall pale-haired barbarians walked, and Julius! Julius himself, not the tallest of that crowd, but he saw the brass glitter on a collar, and saw his father's distinctive bearing—

—and he nearly got himself hit by a backing jeep as he dived across the grassy strip between.

"Father!"

Julius turned at the sound of his voice, as he came running up and discovered at the last moment that he could not do what he had wanted to do, what he had wished until now to do: he could not throw his arms about him here, in front of all these men and these strangers.

"Sir," he said when he reached Julius' side, among the others.

Julius reached out and gripped his shoulder, briefly, a quick and cursory attention. "Lad." And the hand dropped, and men got between with a deluge of questions and answers. "Later," Julius said saying; and: "Not out here. Staff meeting."

The house steps got in the way. Augustus and Horatius and Julius and the returning heroes and the soldiers went up them, and Brutus stood out at the side of them, jostled out of the way.

He only stood there a moment, till Julius and the others had gone inside. There was a painful lump in his throat.

Well, he told himself, his father was a great man, and he was still a boy in their eyes, and there was probably something dire and dreadful going on, some danger that they had to talk about; they were all in danger, that was it, and he had no right to have come up to his father like that. He had made a mistake again, he had been awkward; they were probably all in fearful danger; and it was stupid and selfish to have a knot in his throat and to think about himself.

Mouse passed him, Mouse with his load of weapons and cases; and he jumped up onto the steps to intercept him. "Can I help?"

"Here." Mouse slipped a strap and gave him a case to carry.

Only like a fool he started crying before they got down the hall, and when Mouse passed his gear to a centurion of the 10th and turned around to get what Brutus was carrying, Brutus had to stand there with his eyes brimming.

Grim, dour Mouse, of all people, reached out and put his arm around him for an instant. And being Mouse, said never a word. Mouse walked on, then, and he did not know where to go.

Or if they had found Caesarion. Or what had happened.

Until he found Mettius Curtius trailing in late. "Did they find my brother?" he asked, thrusting himself in the path of the cavalry commander. "Is Caesarion with them?"

Curtius looked exhausted and bewildered. He only stood there and looked him over as if he had seen a ghost. "Caesarion," he said. "—No. No. No, we didn't find him."

And brushed past him.

He looked after Curtius in despair. He waited.

And sat down on a fragile bench outside the library and waited. And waited.

And fell asleep there.

"*Veni*," a voice said to him in his dream, "*mi fili*." And he blinked himself awake, because it was Julius' voice, and someone was pulling him upright. *Come on, son*.

A shadow was over him, and it had his father's voice, his father's outline against the blurry light. He blinked and it was Julius leaning over him, gathering him up with an arm under his shoulders, pulling him to his feet.

"Come on," Julius said, and steered him along the hall, and up the stairs in this mazelike villa that was so full of levels and turns.

He went, walking on his own, but with his father's hand on his shoulder. "I was worried," he murmured. "When Scaevola came back—"

"Not here," Julius said, and: "*Exite!*" dismissing a persistent clutter of sycophants. Julius brought him to his room, and tried the latch. Brutus fumbled after the key.

"They said I should always lock it."

"You should. Never trust the sycophants."

He got the key in and opened the door; and turned on the light.

Julius closed the door behind them; and of a sudden, unwarrantably, Brutus felt his heart speed, all the reactions of terror, which he ought not to feel—except it was truth he faced, the one man at least who knew all the truth, and kept it from him.

"Have you found C-Caesarion?"

"I know where he is." Julius grasped him by the shoulders and faced him toward the bed, sending him that way with a push. "Not tonight, son. For godssake, not tonight, the old man's had a lousy day. Go to bed."

"Is everything all right?" He faced Julius again. He could not sleep without knowing that.

"For Hell, things are perfectly fine. *Bed,* lad. I'm out on my feet."

Brutus sat down on the bedside and pushed off his tee-shirt, started to fling it on the floor, then remembered there were no sycophants at hand and hung it on the bedpost, to be neat, because Julius was there. "M-Mithridates?"

"Say he's damned uncomfortable. *Not* going to be happy." A light danced in Julius' eyes despite the lines of fatigue. Julius slipped his hands into his belt and stood easy. "I had a good report on you."

Brutus drew a long breath and ran that through his head several times to savor it. He pried off the tennies with one foot and the other and let them fall. "I wish I'd gone with you."

"I'm damned glad you didn't."

"Is everyone all right? What was Troy like? What—?"

"Wait till morning. I'll tell you about it." Julius put his hand on the latch.

Brutus got up out of respect. "Yes, sir," he said, aching inside, remembering at least his father had put his arm about him, had found a moment to talk to him.

But it was an earthly lifetime he had to make up—in which Junius Brutus had never done the one thing, and rarely done the latter, and even then avoided his eyes. And he wanted—so much—

"Something wrong, son?"

"I—" He was going to cry like a baby. He drew a deep, fast breath. "I'm g-g—" *Oh, damn!* "—glad you're back."

"That's two of us." Julius walked back to him and

took him in his arms and hugged him, and Brutus hugged his father hard and tried not to cry; which he did not, except several short, desperate gasps of which his father had to be aware. Julius patted his back and just stood there a while, rocking him, which he never wanted to stop; but it had to. "Damned tired," Julius said, setting him back. "There's a lad. Go to bed. Everything's all right. Trust me."

VI

Mithridates walked gingerly down the polished hall, in that restricted area of Pentagram corridors which gave protected access to inmost offices. Cleanliness and order and quiet were a balm to the king of Pontus: he had had a hot bath, soothing massage, and his hair was ringleted and banded with gold about the brow, his tunic and breeches glittered with silver and bronze medallions. In fact he looked tolerably well for a man lately dead, but one felt it in the joints, in the creak of stiff ribs and soreness of the gut, and in the lingering stink of cold and formaldehyde, a combination of sense and smell of that peculiarly nightmarish sort that persisted past perfumes and oils and the ordinary office smells which cut through it without dispelling it. It was the odor of humility, the chill of the grave, and the memory of defeat.

More than that it was the smell of a Roman agent in the works, and Mithridates had an abiding, burning hatred of the breed.

It had the smell of a Pentagram leak, *something* having poured out a chink somewhere, and he was on the hunt for it this morning like a hound to the track— albeit a slow-moving one and a stiff and a cursed sore one.

Dying *hurt*, dammit. And when it was a damned screw-up it hurt doubly. The stuff started coming in, and by the time they had it pegged that it was *not* an attack by Dissidents who had stumbled onto the base of operations . . . that it was, in fact, friendly fire, there had been no damned choice but to tough it through.

Now, there was the small matter of courtesies, a *necessary* courtesy; and when he had passed the guards with a sullenly returned salute and a glower for whatever thoughts passed behind their eyes . . . Egyptians of Ptah Regiment, gold-belted and kilted and watching him with dark, long eyes behind his back: he felt the stares as he passed—Egyptian guards, at doors which opened onto a carpeted foyer, and the splendid mahogany doors beyond, with the brass insignia of the vulture and the snake—

Modest, considering the occupant. There were more guards. There were damned fools who insisted on ablutions and passed him through a room of reeking incense that made his stomach heave.

And behind that last door, a bald, stoop-shouldered man in khaki; a man of elegant, Egyptian profile, who wore a pair of wire-rimmed glasses perched on his arched nose, who looked up from his reading with a blink of slightly magnified eyes. "Eh. Oh. Indeed. Back again."

"Back, yes." The rage in Mithridates seethed up to the surface and threatened to break out in shouting. He drew instead a quiet, a very quiet breath, and smiled as if he were strangling. One *needed* this man, this delver into books, this womanizer, this . . . *fool*: Rameses II, who gave them the might of Egypt.

"It was a great misfortune. We are making inquiries."

We are making inquiries, we are making inquiries. Mithridates caught his breath and clenched his hands. "We were targeted, do you understand?"

"We understand it was a very extensive mistake. We do *not* understand how this arose. We do not understand why you did not use radio to advise these attackers to cease. They *were* our forces, were they not? Friendly fire. *We do not understand why we are subject to these mistakes, king of Pontus!"*

Because you are an ass, king of Egypt.

But aloud: "Because we have traitors among us, because we have damned traitors and we do not make examples, Pharaoh."

"Why did you not use the radio?"

"Because—" Infinite patience. A tilt of the head, metallic precision to the voice. "Because, Pharaoh, light of the Two Lands—we were blown. How were we to explain to our own forces *why* we had a base in Dissident territory, or what I was doing there? Or should we prolong the skirmish, let the fire draw other attention, and bring down the whole damned countryside? Eliminating our witnesses or getting ourselves out of there, light of Egypt: those were the choices, and they were damned well set when they opened up, they had position on us."

Pharaoh slid the wire-rimmed glasses down and peered over them. "But how did they find you, king of Pontus? How did this happen?"

"I am investigating." All but a whisper. "Believe me, Pharaoh, I will find out. We will bring them through Reassignments."

"As you did Maccabee—"

"Tsssss. Not without its value."

"Not with full value either, as we understand it. We do not know Hadrian's whereabouts, Kadashman-Enlil is in our displeasure, our severe displeasure—"

"Look to Tigellinus and his staff! I warn you, Pharaoh, I have warned you that *there* are our leaks. Confide in Stalin if you must, but Romans are poison. Romans have relatives, information spreads from household to household like plague, and Tigellinus' patron is a lunatic with ties to Julius Caesar. I warn you. I do earnestly warn you."

Pharaoh blinked, replaced the glasses and stared at him with the minutest alarm, not of common sense, to be sure, but because Mithridates was rarely so blunt with him; and he was offended.

"Light of the Two Lands," Mithridates said, out of breath, for breath seemed thin in him this morning, and his voice hoarse and strained of a sudden, the words difficult as he tried *not* to say things that would make this man hard to manage . . . this man more interested in his papers than in the real events those papers represented. "I am going to my office. I am going to inquire into this."

"We will want a report." In a brittle, precise tone. Pharaoh adjusted the glasses. "We are not convinced of this strategy. We do not trust these elements. We were faced with a rabble ill-officered and ill-equipped. So we give the Dissidents both superior officers and more modern equipment? This seems to us a curious economy, king of Pontus."

"It worked for Stalin." Mithridates found a convenient chair back and clenched his hands upon it, leaning there to keep his balance as vertigo and rage chased each other round and round in his brain. "First, Luminance, you infiltrate, then you divert, then you control their movements and their policies. Except we have lost our field office, Luminance Arising, which is a damned great nuisance, but not a fatal one, except to the one responsible for this, when I find him, and when I find out whose staff blundered, Pharaoh, at which time I assure you I will be back to you."

"We distrust temper. We distrust precipitate acts and staff quarrels. Most of all we dislike commotion, king of Pontus. We truly abhor it. This is precisely what we warned you, that rabble in our pay for whatever reason, will generate disorders in our organization—"

"This was friendly fire, dammit. This was our own damned *orderly* forces."

"Nevertheless. Disorder is generated by the very

existence of rebels. Confusion and chaos. Sloppy accounting." Rameses picked up a sheaf of papers and waved it.
"We have no notion where funds are going. We have
equipment unaccounted for. All for Stalin's clandestine
operations and this buying of the very rebels we fight.
We do not trust accounting like this!"

The air grew thinner and thinner and the red rage
more difficult to master. One had to remember the
value of this man, who had infinite skill in putting a
wall of forms and bureaucracy between themselves and
Administration, who was successful in his maddening,
meticulous way, at diverting and soothing and screening
in ways bureaucracies trusted and went to like pigs to
swill. It was Rameses who stroked Administration and
kept them well-disposed.

"I will provide you a list," Mithridates said.

At which point the red phone rang, and made a
silence in the room.

Rameses picked up the receiver. Listened a time
with a frown making a seam between his brows and the
corners of his mouth turning down further and further.

"Yes," Rameses said. And: "Yes." And: "Thank you."
Precisely. From a man to whom *thank you* was a foreign
idea, professionally practiced. "Quite. We are very glad."
Rameses was never *I*, even in bed, one suspected . . .
damn him, damn him, what is *it?*

Rameses set the receiver in its cradle. "So. Well."

"What?"

"Caesar is back."

"Back?" Mithridates' voice cracked, as it was not
wont to do. Air failed him for the moment. His heart
sped and lurched against the counsel of his body, which
lagged behind the rage and the will to do something,
anything. "Back where? Doing what?"

"A routine equipment check-in, as it seems. It will
not be advisable to move now, let us have no precipitate
actions. We will scrutinize his list and his reports, of
course, but bearing in mind, bearing in mind, king of

Pontus, we do not invade administrative levels, we do not wish to take rash actions or place ourselves in absolute positions, king of Pontus, in places without retreat. We do not know who may have backed him in this venture, and until we know we do not pull threads at random. Do not raise your voice with us, we are not at fault."

"Of course not." Mithridates drew in a lungful of incense-tainted air, and brought himself to shuddering calm. "Of course not, Luminance." He gave a precise, courteous nod. He managed even to edge backwards to the door, in that way Pharaoh found courteous, and to go out without slamming it.

He wanted weapons in hand. He wanted the field. He wanted Caesar in his sights. Wanted, as a Roman emperor had expressed it, the whole lot of his enemies with a single neck so that he could lop it. Repeatedly.

In Hell there was no end to enemies. They came back. A man who hated, could never get rid of his hate, or of those he hated: but he could take from them what they loved; but he could work revenge without end; but he could, if he were willing, consume an eternity in that revenge.

He was a dedicated man. A man with a cause. The kind of man the Pentagram never let to the top; but the kind that would not be prevented, either, because to him everything was expendable, except his hate and his vengeance. In that much he was pure and without taint: that he truly believed in something, and counted it holy.

It was much as Brutus had thought the next day— having learned what it meant, when there was trouble about the house: *everyone* disappeared into conferences, *no one* wanted to talk to a teenaged boy, and there were soldiers everywhere.

He sat disconsolate, and finally went down to the garage with the wicked thought of talking his way into one of the soldiers' dice games.

But: "Sorry," the legionaries said. "Sorry, your father'd have our guts on a plate." And they picked up themselves and their dice and their illicit smokes and went away, that was all, so he had spoiled their good time and gotten himself nothing.

He went and hacked chips out of the post in the practice yard, and had a swim in the pool, and lay on the poolside in the altogether—gods knew there were no women around to be offended; there were no men around either, just the great, empty pool—while the sycophants which had reappeared in such numbers massaged his tense muscles and chittered information at him like: "Julius is still in the library." "Mouse has gone to the armory." And other things which told him nothing he did not know.

He had them shave the little down he imagined into a stubble. He had them bring him a good pullover and a good pair of slacks and a belt.

Maybe, he thought, he should dress up. Maybe people would take him seriously then.

People turned around and looked at him, and the duty officer quirked an eyebrow at him when he passed the doors. So did Machiavelli. And from Hatshepsut, who was in some hurry, it got both brows lifted and a pursing of lips: "Well, well, *well*, kitten, what's the occasion?"

"I just felt like it," he said, and kept his distance, while the Pharaoh looked him up and down in rapid transit and over her shoulder.

At least she did not chuck him under the chin. And *that*, he thought, was an improvement. He thought. Perhaps a man would think differently. He was not sure. He was not sure of anything where it regarded Hatshepsut, except—except if he got into her bed he would not know what to do with her and he was sure she would do things he did not know how to react to, and laugh about it and humiliate him.

Gods knew, everyone else did.

She was laughing at him already, he thought; and he wanted to slink back to his room and change his clothes, except it was an admission of defeat. So he went about with his hands in his pockets—a decided convenience, he thought, pockets.

He walked down to the rose garden and looked out over the lawn where the trucks and jeeps had far exceeded the parking lot. And was impressed and chilled at once, because a lot of them had dents and bashes, and fire-scorch on their camouflage paint.

A green dot popped up in front of his eyes, glowing even in daylight. "Caesar wants!" it said. "His office!"

He started out to walk, dignified and adult. But that was too slow. He ran as far as the doors, and then tried to catch his breath and look as if he had done the whole thing at a brisk walk.

"Here," Julius said, and handed him a glass of whiskey. "Careful with this stuff. It's watered but it's not wine."

He sampled it. It was awful at first sip, but Julius had a glass, and he was determined to like it. He sat in a leather chair in the conference area of Julius' office, and Julius sat down with his drink in the chair the other side of the low table.

"Home," Julius said, "feels good."

"Yes, sir."

"You've been doing all right?"

"Oh, yes, sir. Fine." He thought about the Scaevola affair and reckoned that Julius had to know about it, and he earnestly wished that Julius would get to that matter and get it over with.

Julius took a drink. He did.

"Everyone gave a good report of you," Julius said. "But I'd expected that."

"Augustus didn't say—"

"What?"

Now he wished he had *not* brought it up. "About Scaevola. About—" *Oh, gods, fool! you've gotten Scaevola in trouble. Augustus hadn't said anything. Now what have you done?*

"What about it?"

Brutus shifted his weight uncomfortably and looked at Julius as straight-on as he could—not easy. His father had that kind of stare. "I—guess I—" *It's your fault; your blame; so take it, that's all.* "I didn't tell Scaevola he was supposed to wait. So he left. Augustus wasn't very happy with me."

"Not the story I heard from Scaevola."

Brutus found a place somewhere on the floor to occupy his attention.

"*Prodi,* you've got to be a better liar, son, to get along in Hell. I heard it from Augustus, heard it from Scaevola. Both sides. What's yours?"

"Scaevola was yours. Not his. He said he had to get back."

"With a lot of help, as it turned out. Damn. You know, Augustus *was* right, as far as it went; so was Scaevola. We needed help, and we needed it fast. There's two kind of decisions you make, son. One's with the head, one's from the gut. Two kind of thinkers. Either one can be right. But there's a whole lot you don't know. A whole lot. It's dangerous for you to take wide actions—you understand me?"

"Yes, sir. Truly I do."

"Good." A smile quirked Julius' mouth. "If Scaevola had had to, he'd have knocked you cold. And *that* would have been on his head. Not yours."

Perhaps Julius was laughing at him. He was not sure. But Julius' smile grew gentler.

"Son, I've been taking care of myself in Hell for a while now. And we have allies."

"Napoleon Bonaparte."

Julius' brows lifted. "Ran into him, did you?"

"I *saw* him; I don't know who he is."

"Damn fine general. Old friend. You could trust him if you had to. But best you trust the ones in this house.

As you have. You want to know where we were and why. Mithridates. Mithridates set up that little fracas, I'm damned well sure of it. And it didn't go well for him. We're pushing him hard right now. That's why I won't be having much spare time, understand."

"Tell me something."

"What?"

Brutus found his mouth dry. He took a sip of the drink because that was what there was, and swallowed with a gulp and looked at Julius straight on. "Klea— Klea is Caesarion's mother. How does she feel—about me being in the house?"

"You saved her life."

A second swallow. He clenched the glass in his hand; and his head was buzzing. "My father—Junius—and I—got along. I don't say he didn't like me sometimes. Sometimes. But it wasn't always." His knees wanted to shake, even while he was sitting down. "Are you— hunting Caesarion?"

"I told you. I know where he is."

"Does *she*?"

Julius' face went hard. Brutus gave him stare for stare, clenching his toes hard to try to keep himself from shivering, and the cold glass did not help.

"In general," Julius said. "Yes. She does. But Klea likes you. Caesarion's—a complicated question. Don't get into it."

"Where did—?"

"Don't get into it."

"I—"

"Don't."

He drew a quick breath. "I can't do anything if I don't know anything, isn't that what you told me? And you don't want me to ask about Klea and you don't want me to ask about Caesarion and no one will talk to me—" He drew a second breath, seeing his father's face hard as stone. He was on the edge. He knew he was.

He tried to divert the question, to make peace. "Can you tell me—at least about where you were?"

Julius drew a breath of his own, and stretched out his legs in front of him, letting out a sigh. "Troy." His eyes grew distant. "*Two* Alexanders. Agamemnon and Priam."

Julius sipped his whiskey. He talked about cities that shifted and things that seemed half mad; and how Scaevola had died, and about liches and tanks and the river of fire. He was a story-teller, Brutus realized. He was a poet himself, like Dante. Among the other things he was.

He realized how much he did not know about his father, how many things still surprised him.

He shivered to the tale of chariots and the caves and Scamander and the Styx.

And grew quite drunk, while his father, who told these impossible things, seemed sober as could be. He put down the second glass with his fingers gone numb. He refused when his father would have poured him another one, and Julius tipped his chin up and looked him in the face and said:

"A little hazed?"

"I think I am."

Julius ruffled his hair and smiled at him in a way that seemed strangely dangerous. "Been up to no mischief, have you, while I was gone?"

"No, sir— No." He was numb in various places and the room was spinning. He recollected what Niccolo had said—about glasses and corks. And his heart began to hammer. "I swear—I haven't."

"I didn't figure you would. I'll tell you—there were questions when you came. You know that there were."

"M-M-Mithridates." He was drunk or he was drugged. He was not sure which. He stared up into his father's face and felt the sweat running on his face, felt his father's fingers stroke his temple. He had gathered all the questions he wanted, in all these days. He had enough collected, that no one else would answer. *Ask your father. Ask your father.* He asked his father. "Wh-wh-*why*—dammit—why did he h-hold me b-b-back? To h-hurt *you?*"

"What if it were the truth?"

He swallowed hard. "I w-w-would b-b-be s-s-*sorry*—dammit, I c-c-can't t-t-t-*talk*—"

"Calm down. Calm down, son." Julius' hand slid to his shoulder and squeezed, and Julius walked around behind him and massaged his shoulders and the back of his neck a moment. Then around to the other side of the chair. "What do *you* think?"

"I think I—m-m-maybe you w-w-wished I h-hadn't died. And you g-got Caesarion with Kl-Klea and n-now he's h-heard ab-b-bout me and run off—" Oh, damn, no one could make sense who had to choose his words around ones he would stammer on. "I th-think I'm h-here to make t-t-t-*trouble* in the h-h-—house."

"Damn good guess." Julius patted him on the arm. "You may have been the reason Caesarion ran. But Caesarion's Caesarion, all on his own. Not your fault. And Klea knows it. She's no fool. You may have noticed that. Neither am I. Mithridates tried to use you. It didn't work. *You* stopped him. Stopped him cold. You've made Klea like you. You've made me wish—gods, that I'd found some way—in Massilia that day— But there wasn't one. There wasn't one—that wouldn't have cost your mother—cost Junius—cost you and me— What could I have done?"

"Said you loved me." Drink made him foolish. And prone to weep. "You could have said you loved me."

"I didn't know you. You didn't know me. What could I do?"

"You could still say it."

"Come here." Julius pulled him out of his chair, and dragged him into his arms and held him, a long time, as he had the night before. "You think you're sober enough to walk down to dinner?"

"I think so." He was dreadfully embarrassed. And

not sure that he could stand up or walk without staggering. And he was content where he was. Finally.

"Come on." Julius turned him for the door, and kept an arm around him, and steered him out and to the hall. The cooler air out there helped. "Both of us are a little drunk. That's all right. Man deserves it sometimes."

Julius never had said the words he wanted. But some people never could. He was old enough to know that. Sometimes, in some men and some women, action had to suffice.

VII

As days went in Hell, it was not one of the good ones. Sycophants flitted up and down the halls of Augustus' villa like gulls before a storm, carrying this, bringing that, delivering messages in small quavering voices . . . Augustus had said, Sargon had reported, no, there was no news of the missing Caesarion, none, sorry, sorry, sorry. . . .

As weeks went in Hell, it had already been a bad one, and the black vintage phone in Julius Caesar's sometime office had already borne a considerable traffic of calls— from Scaevola, in the field; from Mouse, at the armory; and from Kleopatra, whose banal chatter delivered information from Machiavelli that could damn them all to a deeper, bleaker Hell.

"You must not compromise yourself," Augustus said— Octavianus Augustus, *pater patriae*, First Citizen and *tribunus plebis in perpetum*. He paced, that was the state Augustus was in, and Julius watched the thin figure with the toga flapping about him as Augustus went the course past his desk from the bookshelf to the windows, from the windows to the bookshelf, back again to the windows, beyond which the Hall of Injustice towered up to meet the clouds of Hell, and just out of view of which the Pentagram itself squatted in obdurate

112

hostility, in the hands of Rameses II, the genius of Kadesh, who had lost Egypt Asia Minor; and Rameses' conniving ally Mithridates the butcher.

Julius rested his head against the heels of his hands. "Compromise myself. *Di immortales*, if I had Mithridates in my reach—"

"You would lose yourself and destroy us. No, *Cai Iuli*. Let Caesarion go. Let him be."

Julius fixed his nephew/adopted son with a dark and ominous stare, which recalled very thoroughly who had murdered Caesarion in life, and who had most reason to dread any rapprochement between himself and his disaffected son. That Augustus did not flinch indicated the depth of his disturbance in the matter.

"You're on thin ice," Julius said, "*son*."

Augustus looked like a thirty-year-old, ears that stuck out, a dusting of freckles, an angularity of nose and jaw which looked younger still, and an Adam's apple that jutted and worked when he was distressed. He had died an old man and he had not lost those years, inside, no more than had Julius, who was a vital thirty-odd, black of hair, trim and hard in 20th-century military khaki, and at the moment with his sleeves rolled up and ink-stains on his fingers.

"I know," Augustus said. "But for love of you, *father*, I will say it: you are rarely a fool."

"Are you calling me a fool?"

"I am," said Augustus the First Citizen, "saying that no one profits by this preoccupation of yours except our enemies. If the boy wanted to be found, he would be found. What has this searching gained us? We've turned over every verminous rock in New Hell, we've disturbed situations far better let rest, we've jeopardized alliances and called in debts we had far rather leave for more profitable ventures, cards which we can only play once. And for what? For a boy who wants to kill you."

"And you, of course."

"*Prodi*, you're not listening—"

The phone rang. "I'm listening. I'm just not pleasing you." Julius picked up the receiver. *"Caesar adsum, quid est?"*

"This Julius?" the American voice said.

"What in hell are you doing on this line?"

"I have my ways," Welch said. *"Let me give it to you short and sweet."*

"I've got to talk to you," Julius said; and Brutus closed the study door behind him with a quick look to either side of the room to see whether they were alone or whether it involved someone else.

They were alone.

"Sir?" he asked; because his father had a look that did not bode anything good; and he sorted in panic through everything he had done and every fault he might have committed. He could not think of anything. Not one.

"There's a man coming here. Welch. The American. You remember I told you about him. He was with us in Troy."

"Y-yes, sir."

"Remember I told you I know where Caesarion is."

"Y-yes, sir."

"Well, he's in trouble. Bad trouble." Julius sat down on the edge of his desk and folded his arms. "He's with the Dissident camp—which is about to go the Trip—*die*, you understand me. And we could lose him once for all—or at least find him out of reach. Welch can get him out—he says. He says he wants *you*."

"Me?" It was one thing to daydream heroics. It was another thing to stand face to face with Julius saying a foreign man from the future wanted help from a seventeen-year-old boy. "Why?"

"Says those are the conditions." Julius' mouth made a hard line. "He wants you with him. Says you can talk to Caesarion. Damned sure Caesarion *might* show if he thought you were there, but talk might not be what he had in mind. Mostly I think Welch knows enough about us to know he doesn't know enough—he's New Dead, and American; and Americans don't understand anyone who won't compromise and they don't understand blood-feud, and they damn sure don't understand the House-hold— I think Welch feels lost without a Roman to deal with Caesarion, never mind Caesarion's a Greek Egyptian on the other side of the blanket. Just thank gods he didn't ask for Klea. You do this, you keep your distance from Caesarion unless you're damned sure he hasn't got a weapon, and you say yessir to Welch and get home in one piece. All right?"

Not—will you? Do you agree? Just—all right?

"Yes, sir," he said, and did not stammer, for which he thanked the gods.

"Welch is a good officer," Julius said. "Damned good. You do what he tells you and you duck when he says duck, you don't even think about it."

"Yes, sir." He was scared stiff. And very proud, in what measure he was not confused. His father protected him from everything—and then sent him out on this. It did not make sense to him.

It did not make sense when he was standing, in camouflage and parachute, wind-deafened in the doorway of a plane, looking down at the landscape of Hell, and remembering Welch's instructions to the letter—

He jumped and counted, with his hand on the ring he was supposed to pull: *"Un-um, du-o, tres, quat-tuor, quin-que, sex, sep-tem—"*

The ground came up frighteningly fast.

"—eight-nine-ten," he finished, desperate, and pulled the cord.

Book Two

The Brothers

1

The boy still slept, in that twilight world where he had rested much of the time since his return, in the broad bed, in the room with the record player and the rock and roll posters and the magazines and the pictures of green earthly fields and horses. A little bit of a mustache and a touch of beard was on his face, shadow of a manhood he might never reach, in Hell—a down of beard which the sycophants zealously shaved away, as they tended him in these several days and nights; but they did not disturb his rest. Locks of black hair fell on his brow, about his ears; one well-muscled young arm lay across his chest, picked out like marble in the single stripe of light which came in from the door. His father stood looking down on him, and at last, carefully, settled on the bedside.

Brutus did not stir at that shifting of the mattress, and Julius reached out ever so gently and touched the boy's face, back of his forefinger tracing a line of bone which he saw in the mirror daily. It was a theft, that touch, stolen from time and Hell—a moment he had never managed to steal from life; and his hand trembled now, which had not trembled at many things on earth—not out of fear: it took more than an assassin to daunt him—but out of the enormity of what he stole from the

Devil and from his enemies, and out of the sense of
vulnerability he found in himself. The Devil had a
hostage—here, in this bed. And he, Julius, veteran of
plots and counterplots through centuries in Hell,
possessor of vast power—risked everything in that touch.

"This isn't about Caesarion at all," Welch had said,
that day in Julius' office—when Julius' second son had
proven twice the fool and threatened Hell to pay if
Julius did not retrieve him quickly from the allies he
had chosen. Welch, the American, was an expensive
man—unbuyable in coin. And from that moment and
that observation Julius had looked on this American
recruit with doubt.

"It is," Julius had assured Welch, playing out the
role, "most especially about Caesarion. My son the fool.
My *son* who runs off to the Dissidents. Who compromises
my interest."

"So make up your own family quarrels," Welch had
said. "Put your own people on it."

*Is that what they want? Is that the name of the
game—bring my resources out of hiding? Who are you
working for, Americane? It was Mithridates sent me
Brutus. I know that. Sent me my bastard son—my
assassin, stripped of memory, Marcus Junius Brutus,
thinking he died on the Baiae road, all of seventeen . . .
because it's as far as his recollection goes. Mithridates,
in the Pentagram, the power who pulls Rameses' strings,
keeps my murderer out of time, lo, all these centuries,
and delivers him to me an innocent. The Dissidents take
out Hadrian, the Supreme Commander who was,
whatever his failings, Roman—and in comes Rameses
and the East. Arrives Brutus, helpless and seventeen,
on my doorstep. Exit Caesarion the rebel, from that
lecher Tiberius' den—to join Dissidents we know
damned well are a front for Mithridates and the Eastern
faction.*

And: Put my own people on it, this American says.

Was it Mithridates sent you last time, Welch, to work your way into my regard like this bastard son of mine?
And have I made a fatal mistake?

"Augustus will kill the boy if he finds him," Julius had said, dour-faced. It was plausible enough. Augustus had indeed done it once and long ago. "Then no matter what strings you think Niccolo can pull, we may lose him forever." This, with Machiavelli in the room, discreetly withdrawn from the negotiations.

"So." The American locked his hands behind him and paced a bit, looked at him with a curious turn of his head. "And you can't stop that? You got a real houseful here. Another son, what I hear. *Besides* Augustus. Rumor was true, was it? You. Brutus' mother."

Too many questions, Americane. *Far too many questions*. "Brutus was—is—a seventeen-year-old boy. Do you understand what that means? We just got him back. We don't know from where." *But we guess, don't we?* "He doesn't remember anything. You, of all men, ought to sympathize with that—"

—knowing that Welch himself alleged gaps in his memory. If it were so. If anything regarding this American was credible, this should be.

"Fine," Welch had said then, "I'll take Brutus with me—I need someone Caesarion can relate to, somebody he'll trust. Another one of your sons ought to do the trick."

That he had not expected; Julius had been, for once, caught facing the wrong flank. *Not* information. A challenge and a trap. "He . . . Brutus doesn't know Caesarion; they've never met here. Anyone but Brutus, Welch. Anything but that." And that was wrong to have said. Once into it, there was no way out but forward. He foreknew that little look of satisfaction on Welch's face, foreknew the demand, foreknew that he was compelled then, trapped, to make a play within a play, feigning Caesar feigning grief, which in fact was true, but he made his face hard and shot a calculating look which he well intended Welch to see—

If you are Mithridates' man; and Mithridates sent Brutus—

Beyond the play, beneath the double-layered grief and harshness, snake swallowing tail, that thought had come up like a foul bubble out of the dark. *If you ask for Brutus, if you seek him out—is it not that Mithridates thinks it time to throw the dice? Bring me back Caesarion, will you? And what do you bring back in Brutus? Trojan horse, my Greek-loving American?*

But I dare not call a bluff—not of those that may pull your strings.

No, you will not lose them. You will not fail me. Not fail Mithridates, who will bring Brutus back himself— how could he fail a revenge he's planned . . . all these centuries? If Brutus should die there—Mithridates himself would bring him back. He has planned too long for this.

"Yes," he had said to Welch. And thought: *I will have both of them returned. And you, too,* Americane, *into my hands. A man who can surprise me is too clever to leave to my enemies.*

But it had been one of the hardest actions of his life, to deliver the news to Brutus, and to turn him, coldly official, over to the American.

The boy shifted, a turn of his head against the pillows, a movement of his hand, and an opening of confused eyes. Julius took back his hand, as Brutus started upright, eyes wide and his face a mask of terror in the stripe of light from the door. "Ah!" he cried.

Do you know that I know? Julius wondered. It was fate he tempted, sitting here within reach. Or it was his enemies.

"Father?" Brutus said then, a shaken whisper. "Father?" Desperately, the way a frightened boy might ask; the way a guilty boy could not ask, not with that tone of vulnerabilty.

Then Julius drew a whole breath, and rested his hands on his khaki-clad knees as he sat there on the bedside. *Not corrupted, then. Innocent.* But he distrusted what was so attractive to believe; and hardened his heart against that frightened face that peered at him out of drugs and the dark. "Who else?" he asked. "I didn't mean to wake you."

"I'm s-s-sorry—"

"Sorry? What for, boy?"

"I d-d-don't know."

"Don't stammer." He reached and patted the side of Brutus' arm, fatherly reproof. "Feeling better, are you?"

"I—"

"Thought it was best to let you sleep."

Brutus heaved himself further upright in bed, swung his feet for the side and caught himself suddenly against his arms. "Uhhh!"

"Dizzy."

"Di 'mortales." Brutus' head hung. He shook it and groped after balance, looking up, shadow-faced ghost, the light falling across taut muscle of shoulder and side. "I'm weak."

"It's the medicines."

"I flew—"

So the memory was intact. The Lethe-water which Machiavelli had provided had confused it, dimmed all recent recollection, but it had not uprooted the event itself. Rope-burns on his arms. A fear of falling. Damned American had parachuted the boy out of a plane, during which Brutus, who had never seen a plane close-up, much less contemplated jumping out of one, had managed to stay sane. And then the damned American snagged him while he was still shaken—perhaps *because* he was shaken—and tied him to a tree—when Brutus had thought he had come along to help.

So he had understood then, surely, that his father had turned him over to an enemy.

"I had to do it," Julius said. And then, cruelly, because he was old in Hell, far older than Brutus, in the way Hell's time ran—and knew how to manipulate: "I knew you could do it. I knew you were man enough."

A shudder ran through the waxen body. "I fell. I jumped like he told me to—Welch. He said I had to find my b-brother. He said th-th—"

"Don't stammer."

"Th-that he was your enemy."

"He. Welch?"

"Caesarion. My—*b-b-brother.*"

Julius drew in his breath. Truth, from Welch to Brutus? A warning? That fell out of the stack, untidy, distressing in implications of miscalculation about the American.

"He's K-Klea's s-son. I know th-that. Is he *m-my* enemy all along? Or y-yours?"

Too much bewilderment. Too many changes. There was no chance that it was an act . . . unless one of Hell's friends had made a switch, and bedded down in Brutus' stead.

"Both, maybe," Julius said.

The face that stared back at him—gods, out of a mirror, so many, many years ago. A little of him. A little of the woman he had loved—in his own callow youth. The boy was terrified. Starkly terrified.

"What are the D-Dissidents?"

Clever lad. Right to the mechanics of the thing. Not a shallow question: Brutus knew *what* the Dissidents were; they were Hell's recent difficulty, and the stated reason for Julius' treks into the field—which was a lie, but never mind; most of Hell accepted it. Except, perhaps, Brutus, who had seen Scaevola raving about the towers of Ilium.

Well . . .

"Which answer do you want, boy? What they've got to do with Caesarion?"

"That. First."

"You know Augustus is my son too. Great-nephew. Adopted." Gods knew what the dose of Lethe-water had obliterated. The most recent events were the memories it ought to take: it had been a light dose—Niccolo swore. But all sorts of things could muddle.

Brutus nodded, impatient, and again he was relieved.

"Well, I married Klea. Egyptian law. Never mind that I had a wife in Rome—" Julius made a face. "It was legal—in Egypt. And null and void in Rome. Smart man, eh? But Klea turned up pregnant. Gave me a son and a tangle . . . because he was the only damned in-wedlock son I'd gotten. But he was half Ptolemiades and half Julian; half foreign and half Roman; and illegitimate in Rome but heir to Egypt. Klea's little maneuvering. My softheadedness. That was Caesarion. I'll tell you something. When you're old, and I was old, yes, and that was my last chance at a son—"

"And I was long gone."

Julius did not let the wincing show. "It was long past that summer in Baiae. My last chance, I say. I didn't live to see him grown. I knew—" *Knew about the conspiracy, son, that I wouldn't last the week; I knew Rome couldn't survive with Caesarion, and Caesarion couldn't survive, not a boy made heir to an unwilling Rome. So I kept my will—adopting my nephew. Gods, how that galled Antonius!* "—Knew I had so little time. Augustus succeeded me in Rome. But it was Antonius who brought up Caesarion in Alexandria. He married Klea then. *And* Augustus' sister in Rome. Damned mess. Eventually Rome went to war—again. Antonius died in it. So did Caesarion. And Klea." He rested his hand on the sheet where it covered Brutus' ankle, gently, ever so gently and matter-of-factly. "Caesarion was a rebel even then. He threatened Rome. I don't say Augustus was right to kill him. It was a hard thing to do. But the whole damned East could have peeled away from Rome. Lives lost. Wars upon wars. In fact it was a soldier killed Caesarion, for Augustus' sake because that soldier understood the way it was; did it in the heat of things and then knew that Augustus might kill him, you understand; but he did it partly for Rome and partly because he was Roman and Rome hated Caesarion. I'm telling you all the truth now. It was an ugly business. Augustus could have executed that soldier and kept his hands clean: but so many died, it was so quiet, you understand. It was just too easy to say nothing at all. And if the rumor got out, well, that was Augustus' style: no official statement. Just regrets. And Rome, you see, Rome wanted to take it at that, didn't want the blood on its hands; was glad Caesarion was gone. Was guilty to be glad. So they took the regrets and made up rumors. Maybe Caesarion walked off into the desert. Maybe he was still alive. Who knew? So many did and so many died. Do you understand? Do you understand why Caesarion doesn't forgive me?"

Brutus only stared, his mouth slightly open.

"And why he hates you?" Julius asked.

Brutus gave his head a little shake, as if any movement was too much. Julius closed his hand down hard on the ankle.

"Politics, son. It's politics the way it was played in those days. And look now: Klea's here, under Augustus' roof. They understand. They're fond of each other. Share a little wine. Talk about old times." He shook at Brutus' leg. "Perspective, son. Klea's my wife. She's Antonius' wife too. My wife, my adopted son, my old friend. They don't live the past over and over. I don't. Only Caesarion is stuck at seventeen. Never gets older. Never any wiser. Seventeen is all his understanding, just those years he had and who killed him."

"I'm s-s-seventeen."

"Don't stammer. There's a lad. Irony, yes." Marcus Junius Brutus, assassin—without the later, more tangled truth, nothing of politics, and civil war and himself grown to a disillusioned, hurting man who had committed patricide. *For hate of Caesarion? I never got to ask you. Never could ask you why you killed me. Surprised hell out of me, son, seeing you with the assassins. Hurt like hell, too. Damn, where you hit. Did you aim? Or was it a flinch on your part?* "You're shivering, boy."

"C-Cold." Brutus drew his foot up, pulled the sheets up to his chin as he sat there in the shaft of light. "I j-jumped out of that plane. W-Welch said I should j-just fall out and c-count."

"Brave lad. I'm sure I wouldn't have had it in me. Seriously. Airplanes are bad enough. Jumping out of them—I wouldn't like that."

"You s-sent me with him."

There. The accusation. The hurt. "Do you want the truth?" The lure and the bait. Brutus stared at him with glistening eyes and a mouth clamped tight. And nodded then, shortly, defensively.

"I had no choice," Julius said. "I trusted Welch. Welch didn't trust me. I knew he'd get you out. Caesarion was the one at risk. Caesarion—was the one who could lose himself to my enemies. I trusted *you*. I thought—one of my sons could reach him. I didn't know that Welch would be a fool. I didn't know that he'd throw away the chance he had. You could have helped. You truly might have made a difference. You never got a chance."

It was a lie, of course. It aimed at a boy's self-confidence in his father's sight, at a consuming desire for love. It burned in him. It knotted up the muscles of his shoulders and made him shiver again.

"Is C-Caesarion—h-here?"

"He's in our hands. He's safe. It all worked out. Most of all I'm worried for you. It was a damned mess. I'll have Welch's guts for what he did."

A stare. A small, desperate shake of the head. "He d-d-didn't hurt me. Don't."

"Let me judge that."

"No." A second shake of the head, eyes despairing.

Brutus' mouth firmed in a convulsive effort. "I'm all r-right. He didn't d-do anything." Through chattering teeth. It was stark terror.

Of what? Of me? Of death and hell? Why—plead for Welch?

"You can get anything out of me," Julius said softly. "You know that."

A softening, then, a relaxation of the mouth, the eyes, till defenses crumbled and there was only vulnerability. "You won't, then."

"I won't. Are you all right?"

"I'm all r-right. . . ."

Julius opened his arms. It was due. He had calculated it to exactitude, what was needful with the boy, if it was Brutus, if Hell had not deceived him. He took a chance. And the boy took his, cast himself into that absolving embrace, a chilled, taut body trembling against him till he locked his arms the tighter and felt Brutus steady.

Gods, it felt too good—to have a son, to have one son who loved him, after all eternity. He patted Brutus' shoulder, stroked his hair, turned his head to lean against Brutus' head, knowing all the while that he was holding the enemy's weapon, that even as much truth as he had told was a seed that would grow in Brutus' mind, and that even Lethe-water could not hold back the truth forever. There was no weapon he had in this private war but love. To turn the blade barehanded—he had tried that, the day they had killed him. It had not worked then.

At the end, Brutus had died a suicide. But it was Augustus and Antonius who had driven him to it. It was all they had left him. They were all Julians, even Antonius, in his grandfather's blood. Augustus, Antonius, Caesarion and Brutus and himself. All Julians, all damned, and Brutus the patricide damned the most of all—whose hell was innocence.

*   *   *

"He's still in there," Klea said, taking a careful and worried look around the corner of the upstairs hall, and with rare familiarity Niccolo Machiavelli seized her petite pale hand in his and drew her back again to prudence.

"Caesar will handle it," Niccolo said softly. "*Prego*, do not hasten things. It is very delicate."

Kleopatra gazed up at him, piquant face and short blonde curls and dark eyes, *dio!* which could have launched armadas— Which had, in point of fact, launched two, though the little queen had led one of them herself. She was dressed in black pleated skirt, 1930's mode; in a creme silk blouse; in black heels which did little to bring her up to Niccolo's lank height. And he, creature of habit, wore scholar's black, a doublet of fine, even elegant cut, a little accent of white here, of red at the shoulders. He had so recently come from things less elegant and less comfortable than Augustus' sprawling villa. He so dreaded a mistake or miscue that might send him out again; and he found the chance of that in the lovely Ptolemiades' distress over her own son, imprisoned below, and over Julius, who lingered tonight with young Brutus.

Julius had said—that he would speak to the boy. And Julius had also said to keep an eye on Klea, which, gratifying task that it was, made Niccolo very nervous. He had run afoul of Julius' well-known temper in matters not minor at all. And doubled as he was between Julius and Administration, Niccolo Machiavelli felt the heat indeed.

"He never should have let the boy go!" Klea cried softly. "Niccolo, I am going to see my son. Whatever he says, I'm going to talk to him—"

Niccolo caught a pair of shapely, silk-clad shoulders and faced the pharaoh of latter Egypt toward him again . . . huge eyes, dark with indignation, mouth open to protest this violence. He laid a cautioning finger on his own lips. "*Prego, prego, signora*, not now. Later."

"Later, when Julius—!"

"*Bellissima signora.*" He took firm hold of her shoulders and kept his voice very low. "At least, at least wait. I beg you. Do not put me in a position. *Ecco*, I will help you, majesty, but be calm, do nothing rash. We are all in sympathy. Believe me."

"Believe *you!*"

It stung, it truly did. Niccolo straightened somewhat with a little gesture at his heart and a lifting of his head. "*Madonna*, your servant. One who has your interests and Julius' at heart."

"One who has his precious hide at heart."

"One and the same, *madonna*. Come, come, let us go." Against her fury he made his voice soothing, his manner quiet and reasoning. "I cannot leave you."

"What, is it my bed next?"

"*Madonna*, I should perish of such a favor. In the meantime, I cannot permit, cannot—do you understand? Come. Come, let us go downstairs together, let us talk among friends. Please! I assure your majesty—we are all concerned."

"*Because my son is in chains in the basement!*"

"An exaggeration. I assure your majesty. Please."

She spun on a neat French heel and started walking, back the way she had come, determined sway of hips and black pleats, squared resolution of silk-clad shoulders. The vanishing perspective was enchanting, and not lost on Niccolo Machiavelli, amid a relief in one direction, that she had not made a try at Brutus, and alarm in the other, that those stairs for which the little Ptolemy was headed led equally well to Caesarion's makeshift cell in the storerooms. He hastened, then, waved his hand at a sycophant which had picked up his distress. It wailed and trailed its substance out of his path. Damned creature.

Then: "Find Hatshepsut," he said on inspiration. "Quickly. Quickly."

The creature fled. It had a mission. It might find favor. It fairly glowed in the air as it streamed for the floor and through it, under Niccolo's hurrying footsteps.

*   *   *

He was only a legionary, dodging in and out the slow
movement of supply vans and trucks and jeeps, in the
sodium-lit darkness of the East New Hell Armory . . . a
great deal of grumbling of motors, slamming of doors,
squealing of brakes as a third-line centurion walked up
and down the rows checking off one truck and another.
The convoy was headed out for the patrols that kept the
hills clear, the villas and New Hell itself free of attack.
Some of the 10th was out there, and the 12th . . . so
he had heard. He did not ask. He had not asked for this
summons that involved driving his car out to a certain
dirt road in the woods near the armory and transferring
to the hands of legionaries who dressed him in a khaki
uniform and dumped him yonder, from a troop truck,
to make his way through this maze with a notebook in
hand—a notebook, that badge of men entitled to go
crosswise through the chaos of a moving unit, and right
up the steps of the armory itself.

Down an unremarkable hall, the ordinary plasterboard
and paint of 20th-century architecture. He found his
door, showed a pass to the rifle-carrying guards who
stood there, and walked on with one of them for escort,
measured tread of boots on cheap green tiles in a nasty
green hallway, but one which had real light fixtures,
government issue, and the smell of recent paint in a
wing which he had never, in all his career, visited.

More doors, double, this time; windowless, painted
steel, that gave back on a dim room in which metal
glittered all about the walls, bowed, rectangular shields,
staffs, bannered and not, staffs that bore golden hands,
and circles in various arrangement, all massed at the
end of the hall, where fire burned. And among them,
taller standards, winged and gold and sending a chill
through the blood, a gathering of Eagles that flung their
winged shadows about the room. About the walls,
rectangular shields, legion shields worked not in leather
but in gold, hung one after the other in their preced-

ences, the thunderbolt of the 10th, the Jupiter and
Bolts of the 12th Fulminata centermost to the Eagles
and the standards. A single space was vacant. A set of
standards and an Eagle would be with it: Victoria Victrix,
it might be, which was on duty on the southern coast.

Napoleon Bonaparte knew what it was he saw, to
which outsiders were not admitted; and the Emperor of
France felt his shoulders tighten as the legionary-guide
brought his rifle to rest with an echoing rattle of modern
weapons. *Why am I here?* he started to ask; and heard
the second set of footsteps clicking from behind those
sounds, saw the officer advance down the hall from
which they had come—a man he would see in the
legions as identical to a dozen others, as Roman, as stern
and hawk-nosed and lean as a wolf in winter.

No display of brass, no panache at all. But when that
man walked in, the guard braced up stiff; and when that
man lifted his hand that guard brought his rifle up and
took himself outside, closing the doors behind him. At
this range Napoleon knew him very well indeed.

"Decius Mus," the Roman said.

The redoubtable Mouse. Caesar's personal shadow.

"Napoleon," Napoleon said, for courtesy's sake.
"Bonaparte. To old times, is it?"

Mouse's face hardly varied. But he walked further
into the room, so that it was the legion shrine which
backed him, and the fires that leapt and flared on gold
did the same about Mouse's figure. This was a Roman
older than Caesar. This was the man who had volunteered
for Hell, and *chose* to be here, having sent a good part
of an enemy army ahead of him. This was the man—
they said—to kill whom was worth a deeper hell than
this, and Napoleon thought of this as he looked into
that old-young face, among the fires.

"Caesar sent me," Mouse said. "I speak for him." It
was English the Roman spoke, with an Italian accent.

"I don't doubt," Napoleon murmured, and there was
the most terrible feeling of a call-to-arms, that summons

which he had most zealously avoided. "But I have expressed to your emperor that I am retired, that I remain most ardently retired, *m'sieur le souris*, and a man who bumps my car in traffic and murmurs assignation and gives me rings with his apologies is not the way I prefer my mail, *m'sieur*, which you may tell to Julius, with my profound regards. How am I to know who asks me out on a deserted road, how am I to know *whose* Romans they are who expect me to get out and undress in the dark?"

The least humor touched the hawk-nosed face. "The ring, *m'sieur*. Julius does not often part with it."

Napoleon scowled and slid the heavy gold signet from his last finger. Easy done. His ring size was smaller. Mouse slipped it on. Figure of Venus intaglio on that ring, Venus Genetrix, patron of clan Julia. God knew he had seen that ring and its impressions through the centuries. And there was no question, no question that he had to come, or *why* he had come on this fool's venture, alone, on this outer edge of town, beyond which was wilderness and worse.

"Retired," he said.

"There was a set-to in the hills," Mouse said, "very recently. Che Guevara has taken the Trip."

"Good riddance."

"Louis XIV is planning an event. A grand ball, you would say. A very elaborate affair."

"A damned—" *Tedious* stuck in his throat. Tedious, looking into the Roman's implacable face, did not seem the probable word.

"Exactly your *consocii*. Your associates."

"I have nothing, *nothing*, in common with that crowd. I maintain no contacts, none whatsoever—"

"You will receive an invitation. Accept it. You will not be compromised."

"Not be compromised."

The Roman walked a pace or two and looked at him again, faceless against the light and the glitter of ancient gold. "There is a delicate situation. Say that a well-placed source is in possession of papers. He wishes to change allegiances, East to West, shall we say?"

"Then, dammit, let him bang my car and pass the damned paper!"

The shadow bent its head. Locked its hands behind it. "*M'sieur,* I would much prefer it. But this is a very well-placed source. This is a very cautious source, with a great deal to lose. He wants to do this very indirectly. A third party to our third party. He has known Julius. He wants to be courted."

"Well-placed."

"One name is Tigellinus."

"*Mon dieu!* Nero's pet!" Napoleon flung up his hands. "I refuse. The man is filth, is—!"

"—is doubled. Considerably. He may achieve cabinet rank. He's presently up for appointment. Do you see? Tigellinus is the key Mithridates is using to Tiberius' villa; he already has agents in the ministries. The murderer of Romans is courting certain Romans, is establishing ties within Tiberius' household—"

"I don't want the names!"

"—and in Louis' society. Very close to home. But the debacle in the hills has left a certain paper—fallout, I believe is the expression. Certain papers are in the hands of a very disillusioned man. Whose agents will find you there, to pass you a certain original document. Suffice it to say, Tigellinus will not want that to come to light."

"I don't want to know these things."

"Without these things you will be vulnerable. Be assured: Caesar is detaching Attila to your assistance."

"*Dieu en ciel.*" There was a sinking feeling at Napoleons's stomach. A small lurch of panic.

"The contact will come. You have only to receive the paper and take your leave, all very smooth. You'll have a string on you all the way. No problems. You'll find your drop where your car is now. And you will have done Caesar a great favor."

Napoleon clenched his fists. But the damned arrogant Roman turned his back and walked away, to stand before the standards, shadow still. As Mouse's speech went, it had been a major oration. And now Mouse was done. Stood there, facing the Eagles, leaving the emperor of France to find his way from the room.

"I take it you are done with courtesies."

"Caesar has done you a favor." Not a twitch. Not an inflection. This *servant* of Caesar's had delivered his speech and was out of courtesies. Republican Roman, Caesar had warned him about Mouse. Not tolerant of outsiders. Nor of emperors. "Attila will contact you."

"*Mon dieu,* the man *has* no discretion!"

"More than you would imagine, *m'sieur l'empereur.* But you do not need to know that part of our operations. I would not advise it."

Shadow before the fires, broad-shouldered and modern in its outlines, against the shields and the standards. Devotions? Napoleon wondered. But this was a man who had delivered himself to Hell, a willing sacrifice to the darkest of his gods.

Napoleon drew in a sharp and furious breath, and turned and strode out; but he was glad to be back in the light, back in modern surroundings, more akin to his age than what lay behind those doors. He rubbed his finger from which something only moderately ancient had parted. Something which belonged to a man he had thought he knew. He had thought all these years that he had known.

But the smell of fire and antiquity stayed with him, out the doors and into the keen night air.

"There, there," Hatshepsut said, leaning across the glass and wire table to pat Klea's hand. The interception, for which Niccolo was profoundly grateful, had been swift and sure, and the distraught latter-age pharaoh sat with a glass of excellent Piesporter before her, the stem in one listless hand, the strong, darker hand of Hatshep-

sut holding the fingers of the other. Sargon had come.
The short, stocky Akkadian had a beer in hand, his
broad face all frown: an ancient of the ancients, bare-
chested, kilted and with a dagger at his belt, while
Hatshepsut of Egypt wore a silver jumpsuit, *most*
distractingly transparent here and there in shifting
patterns as the light hit it. Gold and brass and silver
adorned her wrist and circleted her black, bobbed hair,
uraeus-like, but the serpent wound its tail right round
beneath that coiffure and into her ear—not engaged,
now, Niccolo thought: mere decoration. But one never
knew.

"Don't give me advice," Klea said. "I know, I know
all Julius' reasons. Does it mean that he's *right?* Because
Julius wants it, is it always *right?*"

"Listen to me, kit."

"Don't take that tone with me!" Klea snatched her
hand back, and the wine sloshed perilously in the glass.
Her eyes, suffused with tears, turned to Sargon, turned
to Niccolo. "You said you'd help. Who's on watch down
there?"

"Regulus' guard. Not bribable, *signora*. But if you
want me to reconnoiter, I will. I will try to carry a
message. Understand—" Niccolo cleared his throat.
"Cesare has *me* under surveillance. This will not be
without personal hazard. But if you will write this out—if
you can be clever about it—I believe I can persuade
Cesare himself to permit it."

"Damn you, you have an opinion of yourself."

"Tssss," said Sargon. "Niccolo is *not* the boy's mother.
He has far more chance of reasoning with Julius."

Kleopatra took up the wine glass and took a healthy
slug of it. Moisture threatened her makeup. "Paper,"
she said. "Pen." There was a chittering in the air, a
rushing here and there among the insubstantial servants.
Hands materialized to dab at a little spilled wine, to fill
the glass again, but Niccolo swatted at the latter—
"*Vatene*, let the bottle alone." He topped off the glass

himself, spilling not a drop, while the requested paper and pen materialized and flurried across the room to arrange themselves in front of the little Ptolemy.

Kleopatra seized up the pen and set it to the paper, lifted it without a mark and bit anxiously at the cap as her brow furrowed in thought.

"A sentiment," Niccolo said, "that will be easiest to get through. An expression of concern. *Your mother is here.* I can persuade Julius that *that* has value."

"Of course he knows I'm here! That's the problem, dammit!" Klea lifted the glass and drank. Her hand shook and spilled a straw-colored drop on the paper. "Damn!" A fierce brush then at the moisture.

"Maternal tears," Niccolo murmured. "Very effective."

Kleopatra glared at him, then set pen to paper, hesitated, wrote, and hesitated again, wiping her cheek with a pale hand. The hand when she set it back to paper, trembled violently, her frail shoulders hunched, and her head lifted with a wide-eyed, open-mouthed stare at Niccolo.

"Oh, damn you, damn you—"

"Don't just sit there," Hatshepsut said, thrusting back her chair, a scrape of metal on terrazzo. She took Klea by the shoulders; and Sargon was hardly slower, taking the pen from Klea's unresisting fingers, supporting her drooping head as she slumped against the table.

"A fine help you are," Hatshepsut snapped at Niccolo.

"They always blame me," Niccolo said in genuine offense. "Why do they always look at *me?*"

11

It was a narrow hallway, down among the storerooms. In fact the room had seen such use before, was a prison with all the plumbing, inescapable, for Caesarion had tried the door, probed the windowless walls, had examined the cot for materials for weapons and paced and paced till he knew it was useless and until the anxious sycophants that came and went through the walls of the place began to crowd upon him with chittering admonitions to be still, to give in, a hundred whispering voices, touching hands, contacts which brushed against him until he flung his arms about and yelled at them for silence.

It only diminished the volume of it. The voices maintained a continual susurrus, *give up, give in, hush, you'll only harm yourself* . . . till Caesarion tucked himself up in a corner of his cot against the wall and held his hands over his ears, breathing in great gasps. Still the touches came at his body. He flailed at them and screamed aloud, great inarticulate screams of outrage.

Then, quietly, huddled amid the blankets in a fetal knot: *Mother*. But that was only in his mind, because he had had his tutelage in the courts of Egypt, and the hall of mad Tiberius on the lake, where sycophants were ordinary and betrayal was matter of course; and where only great fools opened up their hearts in a matter of sentiment. There was no one, finally. His half-sister Selene and his half-brothers Alexander and Ptolemaios, Antonius' Eastern brood, had made their accommodations with their destiny—Selene and Alexander Helios at Assurbanipal's court, Ptolemaios at Tiberius' court, lost in his library and his pretensions—oh, and there were the Romans: half-sister Julia, who was lost, he had never met; Antonius' daughter Antonia and her mother Octavia were Augustus' kin, and lived in retirement, in decent shame, it might be. His nymphomaniac remote *cousin* Julia was in and out of Tiberius' court, off lately with her darling daughter Agrippina, in Tiberius' disfavor (in this case tasteful) of Caligula and all his hangers-on—Zeus and Bastet! it was a household. But he would rather the devils he knew than face the ones here, in this house, his father, and his two damned brothers, the one who had murdered him and the one who had murdered his father.

He clenched his hands against his eyes and gritted his teeth and tried not to hear the voices counseling surrender. He hid his face in the blankets and turned over finally, scanning the ceiling for convenient places for a rope made of bedding— There were none. And there were the sycophants, who would bring alarm, who would—

He relaxed, sprawled wide on the bed, staring and thinking of that, that there was one way out and past the guards.

What are you doing? the voices wondered as he rolled out of bed and applied his teeth to start a tear in the sheet. He grinned at them, tucked up barefoot as they had left him—barefoot and beltless and without his jacket, just a tee shirt and pair of jeans, well-searched. He ripped another strip and began to tear a third.

Sycophants were not an intelligent breed, but they smelled disaster. They began to tug at the sheet. Voices reached a whispering crescendo as they tore at the strips in his hands, pulled with less success at him, and sycophants by the hundreds began swirling about and through the walls— *Help, Help!* they cried; and: *Not our fault!*

It took about a quarter of a minute to have a key turning in the lock and that steel door opening; and Ptolemy XV Caesarion launched himself with a drive of his heels, knocked a startled legionary into the door frame, and used karate on a second as he barreled toward the last guard who, he was betting, dared not shoot him.

"Halt!" the man yelled, and swung a rifle butt at him, but Caesarion sucked his gut out of the way and slid past, pelting for the door at the end.

Which was locked.

"Oh, shit!" Caesarion moaned, and turned back to face three irritated and oversized legionaries in a hall with one exit only.

One legionary crooked his finger at him.

Then: *No, no, no,* a lone sycophant wailed, materializing between. *Caesar wants! Caesar wants!*

The magic word. The legionaries glared and Caesarion, feeling his knees weak, slumped back against the door.

"It was stupid," Julius said. "I don't say it wasn't a good try."

"You want to take the cuffs off, —*Father?*"

Sullen look from under too-long black hair. Cheekbones and coloring his; the mouth Klea's, full and giving Caesarion a girlish handsomeness. Gods *knew* what Tiberius' house had taught the boy. Not that swagger, not that dark glare from under the brows: that did not go well with courtiers. Julius watched his youngest son walk over and drop himself, hands chained behind him, into a slouch in a fragile chair, curl the toes of his bare feet under him like a small boy and stare at him with the surliness of a defeated general.

"No," Julius answered, regarding the chains, "I don't, particularly."

"I'm a Roman citizen."

"Fine. That entitles you to one appeal and a beheading. *Venus cloacina, quoadmodum insaniam petisti? Nonne Antonius te meliores instruxit?*"

"Sure, he taught me a lot of things. Taught me everything an old sot could. Tiberius too."

Julius stopped his hand, not before Caesarion flinched and shut his eyes. *Damn, that's what he's after, that's what he wants, that's what he believes in.* He turned it into a gentler gesture, patted Caesarion on the shoulder. Caesarion jerked the shoulder aside, and glared through a fall of black hair. Klea's mouth, set in fury.

"Look." Julius put a few paces between them, sat down on the desk edge. "You could have come here any time. Nothing ever stopped you."

"Sure."

"*Quid petis?*"

"Enough with the Latin. It's not *my* language."

"You're a spoiled brat. Damn, you're spoiled."

"Sure. Coddled half to death."

"You're damned lazy! You don't think! How far in Hell did you think you were going to get till you found a door?"

Shift feet and hit him with a specific off the flank. Caesarion's mouth, open to shout, shut while he regrouped.

"How far in Hell," Julius threw after that, "did you think you were going to get with the losers you were running around the hills with? Peace and justice? Overthrow the Administration? I know. It's Satan's place you're after."

"I'm looking at him."

"I *have* looked at him, which is a damn sight more than my fool youngest son can say. I've worked in the Pentagram, which is a damn sight more experience than you have, son, and if you think that was an army you were with, if you think that was the grand army going to liberate Hell and take on Paradise, you are a damned shortsighted fool! Look at yourself!"

"You killed them." The chin, firm till now, quivered. "Men, women, kids, you blew them all away. No, they didn't have a chance. No more than me."

"*Than I*, dammit, you grew up illiterate to boot."

"Split grammars with me. Is that all it means?"

"*Means*. My gods, *means*. We're at that age, are we? The meaning of life. Look at Curtius, he died young, but he *changes*, for godsakes! Man looks eighteen and thinks like three thousand. Put him in the field, you know he'll do his job, he'll think it through. Damn, you're a thundering disappointment."

"Then fuck you."

"What did you say?"

"Fuck—"

This time Julius came off the desk and the hand did not stop. It cracked, ring and all, backhand across Caesarion's cheekbone; and the chair rocked. Caesarion's head went over, his body did, and it was a moment before he lifted his head, with a welt started white and red, and the mark of the signet a split in the skin. His brain was rattled. It could not but be. And the front was gone. The bluff was called and the boy did not want to be here now, in this situation, facing more of the same with his wits addled.

"Boy," Julius said, pulling Caesarion's chin up. "You don't insult a man from that position. That's real stupid. That's what I'm talking about. You don't expect real consequences, you don't live in a real world, you go and do things you're bright enough to know won't work, but you're not living, you're writing little plays that don't come out that way in real life, son, and they get people killed, the same way Che Guevara got all his people killed, the same way lousy tacticians all over Hell get their followers sent back to the Undertaker like cordwood, and the same way they'll always find sheep to bleat after their causes and pigs to swallow the swill they put out. You want to say that again, son?"

Caesarion's face was set in fury, red except for the white mark on his cheek; the eyes ran tears and his whole body quivered. But very judiciously he tipped his chin up in the old Med *no*.

"That's a hell of a lot better," Julius said. "Hell of a lot. I'm relieved. I thought I'd sired a fool."

"You'll find not. Sir."

Hate. Outright hate. But much better control.

"That's fine," Julius said. "Next time you break for a door, I hope to hell you counted 'em on the way in."

Caesarion's eyes flickered. It was genuine embarrassment.

"Damn," Julius said, "there's so much you could learn."

"I'm not your son! I never had a chance to be. I never knew you. And I'm not Roman."

"Doesn't matter. Sorry about getting assassinated. I didn't plan that, you know."

"Then *you* made a mistake, didn't you?"

"Son, I do occasionally make them. I'm generally good at fixing them."

"Except me."

"Your mother wrote you a note. I didn't want her down there." Julius picked up the wine-stained paper. Held it out as if he had forgotten about the cuffs, then fished the key out of his pocket. "Here, well. Let's be rid of those."

Caesarion turned in the chair, offered his hands meekly enough, rubbed at his shoulders when he was free and then took the offered paper.

Your mother is here, Klea had written. *I love you*.

Caesarion's hand trembled. He wadded up the paper and clenched it in his fist. "Touching. Where is she?"

"You'll see her when you manage that mouth of yours. *That* may take some time."

"I'm not staying here."

Julius shook his head wearily. "Son, if you're going to escape, *don't* announce it."

"Damn you!" Caesarion came out of the chair.

Julius blocked the blow left-handed. His right sent Caesarion back into the chair and the chair screeching back against the wall.

"You're no better with your hands free," Julius said.

Caesarion put his hand up to his jaw and looked toward nothing at all.

"Going to be a fool all your life?" Julius asked him. "My gods, boy, you've got a brain. Are we playing games, or are you here, in my study, with my guards out there, and the damned Dissident army funded and run by the Pentagram—"

Dark eyes came up to his, wide and angry.

"Run by the Pentagram," Julius said. "Officers installed. Paid for. Guevara's betrayed. It's a damned *front* for a Pentagram split, son, your great revolutionary leader is either in their pay or he isn't, and if he isn't, he's been had. If he is, he's had you. Which will you bet?"

"It's a lie."

"It's a lie. Of course it's a lie. Guevara's brilliant. There aren't any mercs coming into the cause. Just all purity of purpose. *Di immortales*, boy, Guevara's taken the Trip so often he just waits for the next, comes out like a puppet and staggers through the motions and damned lunatics follow him. You think the Pentagram couldn't crush that headless snake? It's damned useful having it thrash about, lets them maneuver where they want, crush their real enemies—"

Caesarion's eyes were still wide. But the anger began to lack conviction. "Meaning you."

"Mithridates is running it, son. Your precious Dissidents didn't capture Hadrianus, the fool was set up by his own staff, was *thrown* into their hands. You're playing Mithridates' game. Never mind Rameses. He doesn't know what goes on. I pulled you in here because I didn't want you into Reassignments. Die out there and gods know where you'll end up. Or in whose hands. Mithridates', for one. With your mind laundered. Is your English up to that? Do you follow me?"

Long silence.

"Do you follow me?"

"Not that far." Caesarion rubbed his jaw and shook his head. "Wasn't it not to be a fool you were teaching me?"

"Hell, you still haven't got it."

"You've got a mouth your—" Caesarion started off hot; and with a nervous flicker of his eyes upward, swallowed it, frozen like a bird before a snake.

"Right." Julius folded his arms and contemplated his youngest.

"Tiberius failed," Caesarion sneered. "He tried to break me too."

"There you go again. For godsakes I've got men could peel you like an onion. Let's don't lay bets. There's nothing you've got that I'm after. It's yourself I wanted back. For your mother's sake. For mine. Dammit, I've *been* your route. I hoped time would cure it. But this last I can't tolerate. Attach yourself to a ragtag like that, a fool like Guevara—you're too damn smart to believe that crap they hand out. It's my name you're after. To make me any damn trouble you can, and you were so damn smug you walked right into a trap two thousand years in the making."

"What are you talking about?"

"One foot in Roman territory, one in the East—oh, they do want you. Freedom isn't what you're bargaining for. Look at it. You wonder what you'll be worth to them—if ever you get out of line. Where's your independence then?"

Caesarion thrust himself to his bare feet. Tee shirt and jeans, like his other son, but darker. And the flush still showed on the left side of his face. "So what place have I got?"

"That's negotiable." It was as much as could be gotten. "Depends on how convinced I am. But that's your job." Julius walked to the door, shot the inner bolt back and opened the latch. Two legionaries waited outside. "Mind your manners."

"Back to that place."

"Son, we just haven't got a lot of secure accommodations here."

Caesarion straightened his shoulders. "Sir," he said. And walked out, quietly between his guards.

Stopped then, dead in his tracks, at sight of the toga-clad, freckled man who stood across the hall. One half heartbeat.

Then Caesarion ran, broke from his guards and pelted down the hall as the legionaries reached for guns.

"Damn!" Julius hit the first-drawn pistol aside and blocked the second, shoving the legionaries into motion. "No! Catch him!" As Augustus himself hesitated and fleet bare feet headed around a corner. The legionaries ran after the boy; Julius sprinted for the stairs to head the boy off from the downstairs main hall.

Down and down, his boots less sure on the marble than bare feet would be. Down into the main hall and around the turning as he saw Caesarion coming down the hall between him with the two legionaries in hot pursuit.

A door opened midway down the hall. Dante Alighieri stared in profoundest shock as he stepped out carrying a sandwich and a glass of milk.

"For the gods' sake—" Julius yelled, but Caesarion bowled the Italian aside on his way out the offered door to the kitchens, and Julius hit the poet from the other side, rattling the French doors and leaving a second crash of glassware—legion oaths then, as the GIs followed, on a crescendo of Italian imprecation. But with the lead he had gained Caesarion sped ahead, down another, darkened corridor toward the dining rooms, toward the turn that led round again by a row of windows. He snatched up a bronze bust off a bureau one-handed and sent it through the window in a shower of glass and wood, himself leaping after it without ever, the thought came to Julius in a fit of frustrated rage, ever knowing what damned floor he was on.

Julius got that far, leapt up with his foot on the ledge to try the eight foot drop to the flower garden, before the legionaries grabbed his arms and pulled him back, risking that jump themselves, one and the other landing in the bushes and staggering across dark bark chips where glass shone.

There was one thing in which a fit seventeen-year-old, even barefoot, had the advantage of a pack of thirty year olds. Caesarion was on his feet in the halflight of Hell's night, running like a deer across the lawn and toward the hedges—gods knew how cut, or bleeding. But the legionaries with their gear and their guns could not catch him. "Track him!" Julius yelled into the dark, and at the flicker of a sycophant that came to the broken glass: "APB," he said. "Get Horatius."

Horatius, Horatius, Horatius—the creature whispered, and went for the security chief.

Damned little chance, he thought, seething. And heard the agitated apologies of the poet down the hallways, protestations of innocence . . . Dante had heard the commotion, had come out in all good faith to see what the trouble was. . . . Augustus' voice then, no little agitated on its own. Julius looked, hearing footsteps, and found Augustus coming toward him in haste down the hall.

"I'm sorry," Augustus said. *"Pro di,* I'm sorry."

Julius stared at his adopted son. The Emperor, who after effecting Antonius' and Klea's earthly deaths, had lured Caesarion and his tutor to Alexandria and into his keeping, from which neither had come alive.

"Sorry for which?" Julius asked. "Then or now?"

Augustus said not a word.

111

Brutus leaned from the upstairs window in the general tumult and rubbed his eyes. The house had gone crazy, with legionaries leaping from the windows, running across the immaculate lawn, with lights sweeping the dark and the bushes, and people shouting and yelling from the windows. He had waked to the sound of glass breaking, of—he thought—his father's voice raised in anger: he had leapt from bed trailing bedclothes, his head reeling with sleep and the dread that enemies were in the house—his father *had* enemies, very many enemies—he knew, but he did not know what enemies were on them, or who had most reason to attack—

—Flash of a landscape spread out like a blanket; huts and tents; brown, impoverished desolation, as a god would see it—men made tiny and antlike—

—Blaze of fire and clouds of smoke rising above it. Black clouds staining the ruddy sky, above a tilted horizon, in a hell of noise and wind—

A motor coughed to life in the dark around by the villa's garage and more lights speared into the bushes, bouncing and growing as a jeep came roaring across the lawn and kept going right through the rose garden. Soldiers shouted and waved at it and gave harried chase, but there was never gunfire, just the shouting and the racket as the jeep picked up a trio of legionaries and veered off right through the ornamental hedge.

Brutus' mouth opened. He leaned there out the window to the waist and looked from the vanishing lights of the jeep to the window below and down at the end of the wing, where most of the commotion was, and where legionaries were going about the flowerbeds with flashlights as if someone had lost something.

Things all piled up together, the American Welch, who had taken him to find his brother and shown him how to fly like a god (except the landing), and tied him to a tree and told him his brother was his enemy—

—and the dazed, drugged ride back in a tilting machine, his brother lying drugged and bound beside him— For Caesar, the American had said: a present.

—Drink this, he remembered his father telling him, after which things became decidedly unclear and memory became untrustworthy. He thought that this was after they had come to the house again—

Now the soldiers were chasing someone and something dreadful had happened, he knew that it had. He pulled his head back inside the windowframe, and shut and locked the window with trembling hands—Sargon and Mouse had dinned that into him with certainty: *secure perimeters*, they called it— Augustus' villa, for all its light airiness, was a citadel as strong and as watchful as the Capitoline, and far better armed.

He staggered from the sill in the dark room, grabbed up his practice sword that he kept by the nightstand, and headed for the door, tangling a foot in the sheet that lay in the floor.

On a second thought he grabbed up the sheet, but he did not stop to wind it around him till he had gotten into the lighted hall and well down toward the stairs, his head spinning, the whole world seeming to go and come in waves of haze and clarity.

"Where is my father?" he asked the empty air.

"Brother, brother, brother," the air said, the chittering

voice of a sycophant, but it whisked away, terrified. "Escaped."

"My father!" he shouted at it, surmising terrible things. He had memory of his half-brother as a prisoner, struggling in Welch's grip, the same as himself— He won't hurt you, he had said to Caesarion, trying, in his shame, while Welch cut him free from the ignominious tree, to reassure this angry and frightened sib of his— and Caesarion had twisted around to look at him and cursed him in obscenities that first stunned him and then left him shaking with anger and outrage, that a son of his father and kin of his could shame them all—

But Welch had shoved them both along, and had help—the memory flashed back to him suddenly, of Caesarion struggling all the way to the copter and screaming curses on all of them and on their father—

There were soldiers everywhere in the lower hall, khaki-clad men of the 10th rushing in and out the doors on what missions he did not know. He spatted barefoot off the stairs in heart-thumping panic and found Dante Alighieri, in nightrobe and slippers with his hair standing in frizzy spikes and his eyes darting fearfully about the traffic that passed him.

"Where is my father?" Brutus asked. "*Magister*, where is—?"

This shouting from inside the dining room answered that question. Dante indicated as much with a shift of his eyes. "I would not," Dante said. "I assure you, young gentleman, I would not— "

But Brutus was already running, dodging harried legionaries and their guns.

He got as far as the closed doors of the dining room before he ran into two who did not clear his path—who stood, tall as mountains, in front of the doors, and barred his way.

He stopped then, backed up a pace or two, and took sober account of the situation, himself in his sheet and clutching the wooden *rundus* which was the only weapon he was allowed to have, facing two dour-faced and obdurate soldiers with rifles and, doubtless, orders.

Orders, he respected. One got nowhere in Augustus' house without authorizations. That fact of life, *everyone* had taught him.

"Tell my father I'm here," he said reasonably, respectfully, paying no mind to the approach of heavy footsteps behind him, except to think if someone was coming who *could* get in, that door would open, and if that door opened, he would have a chance to shout through it.

Except the Someones behind him seized his arms with a force that meant business.

"Take him back to his rooms," the right-hand sentry said.

"I'm Marcus Brutus!" he cried as they pulled him backward. "My f-f-*father* is in there! Tell my father I'm here! Tell him I want to talk to him!"

"Sorry," one said. "Your father's orders."

His sheet began to come unwound. He made a desperate effort to save it, but they had his hands. He tripped on it. "Stop, stop!" he cried. And: *"Father! Father!"*

No one paid any attention, except a soldier picked up his sheet and they threw it around him.

"Father!"

They hailed him along the hallway, up the stairs—another calamity of the sheet; and along the hall upstairs to his room.

"Stay there," one said, thrusting him inside. He came back, barring the closure of the door with his body.

"Is my father safe? Is he—"

"Your father is attending to one son. His orders are to keep you in your rooms, lad, and out of trouble. Out of trouble you will be. Back!"

"Tell him I want to see him! Tell him—!"

The other pushed him back and pulled the door shut, leaving him in the dark.

"*Mastigia!*" he shouted at the blank door. His mother would have been aghast. He jerked it open again.

The two soldiers confronted him, shadows in the light of the hall. "We'll *be* here," the larger one said. "We'll stay here. *Sorry* about that, lad."

He shut the door again and slammed his fist against it, threatened with unmanly tears.

He was terrified. His memory was in pieces. He had done something, that was all he could think of. He had *done* something in that time he could not remember.

His father had come to him, had talked to him, and hugged him and held him as if everything was well.

But Caesarion had said—had said—

He saw Caesarion's face in memory—darkly handsome, his brother, except the features were twisted with hate, the mouth moving and saying something which had no sound at all, there on that desolate plain, where the American had held them both prisoner, where the metal bird had come beating down from the sky and lifted them away.

Why Welch had held him prisoner like Caesarion, he did not know. What he had to do with this other son he did not know.

Now something was amiss with Caesarion, and his father's soldiers handled him like an enemy.

He wrapped the sheet about himself and went over to the window and looked out on the floodlit lawn, where legionaries stood guard.

His teeth began to chatter. He hugged the sheet tight, leaned his elbows against the sill and shivered.

"Cesare," Niccolo said carefully—very carefully, for Julius had that look on his face which no one in his right mind would brave. "I have sent discreet inquiries—" He coughed, breaking off at a quirk of Julius' brow. That marvelous, wide-browed face could be expressive. It was not, at the moment. Just the lifting of the eyebrow, and the stare of eyes dark and ominous—and Niccolo had second thoughts about duplicity.

"Yes," Julius said. And there was long silence after, only that long, long look which made Niccolo reflect on the state of his bartered soul. "No one's *fault*," Julius said, in a dead deathly tone. "No one's fault, except old faults, and old mistakes, in multiple. I want him back, Nikos. I want him back—I want this business settled. You enjoy the hospitality of this house. You share our table. You find some advantage here. I trust this is the case."

"*Si, signore.*" Niccolo all but whispered it. It was a measure of his distress that he slipped into his native tongue, mentally as well as physically. It was honesty, as best he could offer it. He balanced his various loyalties. And presently this house was in grave jeopardy.

"Then I do not need to explain our problem," Julius said.

"*No, signore.*"

"Is there anything you ought to tell me?"

"*Prego, signore, si io—*"

"Anything."

"Nothing," Niccolo said, and caught his breath. "I swear. I swear, Cesare. I will learn what I can."

"Do this for me," Julius said softly, ever so softly, "and I will forget certain things, Niccolo." It was terrible, that voice. It was so full of patience and restraint. "This is the important time. This is the time that our lives are truly in danger. More than our lives. Our existence as a house. I want to know about Mithridates. I want to know where Caesarion is, and who his contacts are. You understand all these things. I will not detail them. There will be no holding back, do you understand? Use every access you have."

"*Si, signore.*"

"As if I were the Devil himself."

"*Si,—signore.*"

"Go," Julius said. "Find him."

                    *   *   *

The house grew quieter finally. The light died away
from the lawn, the tumult and the traffic of people
coming and going—ceased.

The room was very quiet, the rufous light of hell-
night falling slantwise through the window, a small
patch of light in which Brutus worked feverishly.

He had seen this on the television. He worked and
he wiped at his eyes, muffling the sound of tearing
sheets with his fists, for fear the legionaries outside
would hear and open the door. He dared not bring the
bed over to the window. He tied his bath towels onto
the sheets to make his rope longer and tied it all onto
the bedpost. His heart was beating fit to burst as he
gathered up his little packet of belongings and crawled
astride the sill.

He let the sheets down. Now he must go. There was
no choice. The guards might see him. Someone might
see the sheets past the downstairs window.

And the makeshift rope did not reach as far down as
he had hoped.

But he safety-pinned his little packet of belongings to
the belt-loop of his jeans, hugged the sheet-rope up in
his arms and his fists and crawled out onto the sill and
over with the same heart-thudding terror that he had
felt in his jump with the parachute: and his muscles—o
gods—still hurt from the thump he had gotten meeting
the ground.

They hurt worse on the way down, his arms and his
ribs hurt, and when he ran out of sheet and had to
drop, he landed hard in the bark-chips and sprawled
flat and hit his head like the last time, enough to hurt,
everywhere.

Up, he thought, up! He imagined Sargon's voice—
Sargon who was his fencing-master, and Mouse who
taught him other things, and his father: Go! Bullets
don't think and you haven't got time, son!

He rolled over and scrambled up and ran, over the

lawn and toward the hedges the jeep had smashed, and along the tire ruts the jeep had made. If Caesarion had fled and the jeep had gone on his track, then the jeep must be his guide; and he followed it . . . not beyond the tennis courts toward Tiberius' villa, but down the hedge in the other direction and out toward the sidewalk.

That brought him out facing Decentral Park, where regrown rhododendrons screened the tree-grown green and the brushy mazes where the Viet Cong waged a continual and sinister warfare, and from which they had launched the memorable attack on the villa.

His half-brother could not, Brutus thought, have dared venture *that* hazardous ground. It was only a question then whether Caesarion had doubled back toward the villas and toward the armory in the one direction, eventually to escape toward open land and the dread rivers of Hell; or whether he had gone toward the topless towers of New Hell itself, which beckoned with lights and rose up and up into the rolling clouds that forever hid the firmament, such as it might be here.

Toward the armory was toward Julius' own territory, and Brutus did not think—his memory was still full of holes that came and went—that his escaped half-brother would have gone that way, which was so thoroughly unfriendly. It could not have been toward the Cong, who were given to noisy barrages at all hours, and who would have heralded any intrusion with a thunder of guns.

Caesarion would not go to Tiberius' house—one teenaged runaway knew another's thinking. Caesarion, fugitive from one father, would not go to the other, to that place he had run away from in the first place, escaping from his stepfather Antonius—a boy did not want to admit he had been a fool; and assuredly he would not go there.

Not while there was a choice.

New Hell. By process of elimination, that was where.

He struck out running till he was far beyond the hedges and well up across the greenbelt that divided the villas from New Hell's outlying districts. He ran until the pain in his side made him slow down, and he limped along within the trees and beside the hedges and took to the road only when he must, imagining tracking dogs, imagining—what the television had showed him—of barbed wire and guard towers and searchlights—

One thing was real as the other in Hell—a box that showed him pictures and told him stories about America and Mars—or this night in which once and twice and three times jeeps with searchlights came along the lane and swept the bushes.

He was escaping from the Reich.

Or the FBI. He could not sort it out. Better to think of that, of the pictures in the box, than to think it was his father out there with the jeeps and the guns, among the soldiers—that it truly *was* his father orders which had had the soldiers drag him bodily to his room and lock him inside.

Or gave him to an American who said that—

—said that—

Drink this, someone had said; and Niccolo leaned across the table with a wineglass in his hand and said: "You have to trust someone sometime."

He sat shivering in a thicket of rhododendrons while the lights went back and forth over his head, and wished that he knew now what to do, or that he had dared ask *magister* Dantillus, who was a wise man (though he gained little respect for it in the house) or that he could have found Sargon, on whose judgement and honesty he would have cast himself without hesitation.

Kitten, Hatshepsut would have said, *come here.* And taken him to her glittering bosom and protected him against any comers. He did not know why he trusted this strange, mad woman, with whom he knew his young virtue was not at all safe; but his life and his freedom was—she was mad enough to be honorable, fixed as the pole star, and if she had been there, not Julius himself would have prevailed to hand him to the American.

Go! she would say to him. *Go, kitten, run for it! Don't surrender, don't stop! Keep running! End of the world, kitten—go, go, go!*

And Scaevola: *Use your wits, boy, and stay out of the open!*

Run, and walk, and run again, till he was beyond pain, and the running was a drug potent as that Julius (or was it Niccolo?) had made him drink.

But there was a nightmare in his skull that would not go away, a memory of the interior of the chopper—*chopper*, Welch had called it—and of the boy lying beside him, who looked at him and said things that, try as he would, he could not recall—except they were about their mutual father; except they regarded *him*, and murder, and stupid as it was, he knew that there was a curse on him and Caesarion had put it there— Caesarion his brother, Caesarion Klea's son, Caesarion the Egyptian—for the Egyptians were *magi*, some of them: were magicians, and witches, even perhaps, Klea; and most especially Hatshepsut, whose reliance might be on machines, but she had other resources, one felt it, one heard the slither of the snake and felt the wind out of the dark when she had the *numen* of her god about her.

In his delirium he saw Caesarion's dark eyes staring into him and felt truth slipping from beneath his feet, danger to himself, danger to their father, intimation that *he*, Brutus, was the ultimate threat, the snake in the dark, the death without a name—and that that situation well pleased Caesarion.

His mouth tasted of copper, and of blood. He dodged the searchers and knew that if they took him back he would be helpless, a hostage a second time to his father's enemies, be they outside or inside the house. He did not know now whom he could trust, if his father delivered

him over to the lies of Welch and drugged him and
held him in prison: if Julius held him to blame for some
nameless reason, he dared not fling himself on Niccolo's
mercy, or presume on Klea's, who was Caesarion's
mother as Julius was his father—

Hell was not a place of reason. He had learned that
much. Men flew and died and came back again, and
fathers turned on the sons they loved and pursued
them with jeeps and guns and searchlights.

But he could find his way back again, he believed it
because he had to believe—if he could find out what he
was guilty of, and why his heart ached and why he
broke out in sweat over things he could not remember.

Caesarion knew. He was sure that Caesarion understood; as he was sure that he had to get to his brother
first and learn the truth, or the unreason would drink
him down and separate him from everything he loved.

*"Di inferni et nefandi, quonam fugit? Quomodo puer
vos delusit?"*

The soldiers in question had no better idea than the
ones who had let Brutus escape in the first place: jeep
met jeep in the lanes and byways that crossed the hills
between the villa and New Hell; and Julius gripped the
rim of the windshield and controlled his temper, seeing
pale, set faces in the glare of lights.

They were good men. They did not deserve the
blame he flung at them. He saw the desperation in
their faces—men of the 10th; men who had braved the
nether hells for him, fought on Scamander's banks—for
the sake of the City which did not exist in Hell, but
which maintained one powerful citadel, the villa; and
one base of power, the Armory; and who served both
with the devotion the City had once claimed—on leave,
some of them, from Pompeii, from lost Cenabum, from
enclaves throughout Hell, even from the North Shore,
in the hill territories, where a large number of the
women stayed, attending business that kept the Roman

west operating, noncombatants who lived in a military zone quite different from the airy grace of the villa in New Hell's suburbs. The legionaries were all too conscious of the fragility of the *pax Romana* at this end of Hell—and how the Powers of Hell waged war in subtle ways to dislodge them, not least of all, though Julius had never fully explained the matter to the legions, in the matter of Julius' sons—war by proxy, war on small scale, war between offices and officials—because all of them could lose too much and draw down the Devil's attention if they took to full-scale war.

The legionaries did not know all of it, but they knew that losing one of Julius' sons was bad and losing both of them was reason to contemplate ritual suicide, if it would not land them in worse than they left—on the Undertaker's table, spilling everything they knew to Pentagram interrogators. Romans lately tried damned hard not to die, even when it was easier.

Now the legionaries in question looked desperate and overwhelmed with their failure, and Julius, who loved these men with an honest affection, felt sick at his stomach and stopped yelling at them because it hurt too much.

Whereupon the men in question looked utterly despairing.

"Get over to the villa," Julius said then. "Make another pass. He's smart. He had good teachers. Search the bushes. He might have laid low early. For godssake, don't threaten him. He's a scared kid. Don't hurt him."

"Yes, sir," the squad leader said soberly, "no, sir. Everyone understands that."

"Go to it." Julius sank back into the seat and let go his breath. Mouse, at the wheel, waited, while the other jeep rumbled off into the dark; and Julius sensed Mouse's silent look his way. "Tiberius," Julius said.

Mouse looked at him in profound disturbance, his lean face lit by light flung back from the hedge. Without a word, Mouse put the jeep in gear—thinking, Julius reckoned, what armament they had aboard and what it might take to get them out in one piece.

So did he. Thank the gods there were a few items they had "lost" on the last campaign. Or misfiled as "expended."

IV

Night was not the best time to approach the villa on the north shore—that hulked on its cliff overlooking the Lake, black structure between the rufous night sky of Hell, and the sky-reflecting water. "Damn place ought to have bats," Julius said as Mouse pulled up in the drive and parked. "Fits the architecture. You—" he said as Mouse reached for the gun and prepared to get out. "Stay here."

They were faceless in shadow. "I ask you—" Mouse said.

"*Someone* out here with a gun is better than two of us in there," Julius said. "Hold here. I want you on the outside—if I have to come out of there in a hurry."

"Half an hour," Mouse said.

"Half an hour," Julius said.

And from the driveway and up the nightbound steps of this place that looked like some monstrous toad crouched on the mountainside, Julius thought of the automatic weapons the guards had in this place. *He* had, back in the jeep; but being here was provocation enough to the lascivious old sot who ruled here, and he limited himself to what would fit his pockets.

Enemy headquarters, for all practical purposes.

The westernmost base for Mithridates' sympathizers,

if Tiberius ever came out of his fog long enough to realize it.

He climbed the steps. He snapped his fingers, summoning one of the sycophants who clustered invisibly about the grounds—and got half a dozen, blobs glowing wanly blue in the reddish night, bobbing and circling like marshfire.

Caesar, he heard whisper, *Caesar, Caesar—*

"Damn right," he said. "*Don't* wake your master. Where's Antonius? Tell him I want him."

Tiberiusssss—one hissed. *Forbidssssss.*

"There are ways," Julius said, and that bobbing light retreated, while the others swirled indecisively.

But one fled, one flitted up and through the iron doors, and Julius walked on, one hand on the Beretta in his pocket, one hand for the doors at the top of the step.

One would feel more comfortable, he thought, if the doors of a paranoid's palace were *locked.* They were not. Perhaps the sycophant had undone them. Perhaps someone was forgetful.

He doubted it.

He pushed gently on the cold iron, and it swung inward with a soft groan of hinges.

Eyes glared at him, out of the firelit dark inside— eyes in a bronze face, a heroic statue of a seated man, among erotic, lifesized statuary, alternate with the grim, deep-lined faces of the Claudian ancestors, grim as fiends.

The eyes of the bronze statue glowed white and sullen red. They blinked, mechanical as the mouth which parted lips and spoke.

"*I was murdered,*" it thundered. And: *murdered-murdered-murdered,* the walls and the ceiling echoed.

Drusus. Tiberius' brother.

"*Augustus killed me. Cold, cold, the way from Gaul, colder still the grave. Food of worms. Food of worms. That is the end of man.*"

"Damn well may be *your* end," Julius muttered, and walked carefully into the hall, still in reach of the doors. It might be Tiberius, playing games with the thing; it might be some recorded voice. Sometimes, he had heard, it was one and sometimes the other, and no one in the house was forewarned.

He stood there, thinking of traps in the floor, of poisoned darts and plain bullets and gods knew what his enemies might use.

And no knowing where the sycophants had gone—in a house which was crawling with enemies.

Footsteps whispered in the hall beyond this atrium, this hall smoked with incense and lit with brazier-fire and the uncanny lamps of the statue's eyes.

And a man in unbelted *tunica* and nothing more came padding barefoot out into that light, sword in hand.

"*Antoni,*" Julius called softly.

"*Di omnes—quam insaniam petis?*"

"Caesarion's run," Julius said. "Brutus went after him. We've got a problem, *Antoni.*"

Antonius' sword-hand fell. He stood staring.

"*Death and blood,*" the statue said.

"He's not here," Julius said.

"He wouldn't come here," Antonius said. "Damn, no—not now. Not after—" He did not finish: *after what Rome's done for him;* or anything so graceless. He staggered over. He had a wine-smell at this range. "You've got to get out of here. Modern weapons—in this house—"

"*My name was Drusus. Augustus is a fool.*"

"Get dressed. I need you. Find Caesarion and we can trace Brutus. Hear me?"

"*The way from Gaul is rain and mud.
The way to the throne is death and blood.*"

"I'm coming, I'm coming— Go, get out of here—fast. For the gods' sake, *Cai,* go!"

—*"You drive away my guests,"* a rusty voice said, not the statue. A living voice, phlegmy and rough. "Treason, treason. The god Julius comes to see his brother god—and you drive him away. Shame and treason."

Brutus sprawled, flat in the leaves, in a ravine in the greenbelt, and dared not move, dared not breathe, except to wriggle behind a hillock and try, after that, to make no sound.

Damn useless to hide in bushes, Sargon had said, *if modern stuff is on your track. It can see your heat. It can see your breath. It can hear you breathing.*

He tried not to shiver. He hoped it was not New Dead. He knew that Augustus had connections. He had seen them. He knew that Julius had, Julius had Welch—and Welch surely had American friends who would bring these machines to hunt him and hunt his brother, that was the way the world had gone.

He pressed his face against the ground and heard the jeep go on, finally, its slow way through the lanes and back roads of the rolling parkland.

He saw a green dot then, just in front of his eyes. And blinked.

It was his sycophant.

"Where's my brother?" he asked it, desperate. "Have they found him?"

It retreated. It meant him, he thought then, to follow it.

Julius took a deliberately easy stance, hands in pockets, facing Augustus' successor. "Hello—grandson." They were, by two adoptions, kin, he and Tiberius Caesar; damn well none at all, by blood. And while he was a black-haired and vital thirty, Tiberius was a raddled, wrinkled and syphilitic wreck of a tough old soldier. Drugs and embittered self-indulgence had taken their toll in life, and hate took its toll in death.

He had not been on the grounds of this place since the

night it had appeared a couple of millennia ago, like a poisonous mushroom sprung up on the shores of the Lake, and all Roman Hell knew that *something* powerful had arrived, something powerful and wicked, establishing its domicile in Hell, its earthly course done and something launched in the affairs of Men so fateful that it *merited* a Seat of Power.

One knew, when the damn place had decor like this, it did not represent one of Earth's happier episodes.

"Grandson, grandson," the old soldier chuckled. "*Caesar* comes sneaking into my house—looking for what? Antonius? Assignation? —Assignation with Antonius? Caesar the god. *I'm* a god. The Senate voted it."

"Deserved, I'm sure. Come on, *Antoni*."

"Not so fast." Tiberius snapped his fingers and the door, when Julius pushed against it, was locked.

He turned around slowly, his back to the door, Antonius to the left. Tiberius had acquired a cloud of sycophants, glowing variously blue and green and gold in the dim hall.

> "*Murder the friend, the guest, the brother—*
> "*Power is law and there is no other.*"

"Open the damn door, *Tiberi*. You won't like me when I'm angry."

Tiberius gave a lascivious chuckle and leaned against a piece of statuary that would have brought a blush to de Sade. His fingers stroked the marble of a faun's skin. "Have a drink. Share a drink with me, *Cai Iuli*. Visitors of quality are so few. Tell me your troubles. One god can help another, after all. Tell me, do you still sleep with Egypt?"

Antonius was there. The old devil damned well did not ask that by accident.

"Open the door, *Tiberi*. I'm not in the mood for this. *Neighbors* should avoid quarrels."

"I'm a very good neighbor. —Aren't I?"

A hundred sycophants whispered: *Yesyes*. It amounted to a gentle breath of a sound.

"You're just fine," Julius said carefully. "Meanwhile we've got a problem Antonius and I have to take care of—"

"Egypt."

Nearer night than you think, old man. And aloud: "A son of mine. Open the door."

"Drink." Tiberius snapped his fingers and a glass of wine appeared. He lifted it out of midair. Another one appeared near Julius. *"Drink with me!"*

Julius took it and shot a glance to Antonius, who made a desperate face, averted from Tiberius. *Don't.*

He took it all the same. And held it, while Tiberius tipped his up. It refilled as he held it, and the blocky, countryman's face licked its sore-pocked lips and grimaced at him.

"Drink, drink."

"There's a conspiracy," Antonius said desperately. "Julius is here to protect you, Imperator. Legions of troops are ready to protect you. It's the damned Egyptians! They seduced Caesarion away and now they're ready to invade this house!"

"Conspiracy!" Spittle flew. Tiberius drained the next glass; again it refilled. "Conspiracy! Where's my guard? *Where's my German guard, where's my Germans, hey? Egypt suborned 'em! Cowardice joined 'em! Beware this man*, Cai Iuli, *beware Antonius, beware Egypt, beware Augustus*—" He hooked an arm around the satyr's leg and swung half-round, hanging there, facing Julius; and said, confidentially: "Augustus was wrong. We never should have pushed into the north. I told him that. He made me marry that damn Julia."

"I'll tell him," Julius said reasonably. "But I'd beware of Egyptians, *Tiberi Claudi*. I'd beware of the East."

"Where's my Germans? Where's my German Guard? *Where's my German Guard?*"

"Guarding the West, *Tiberi*."

"Egypt promised. *He* promised—" Tiberius made a sloshing jab of the wineglass toward Antonius. "—he'd find my brother. *Liar! Liar! Liar!*"

"*Murder, murder, murder,*" the statue of Drusus thundered. "*Death and blood.*"

And in the shadows other figures appeared, khaki-clad and with automatic weapons in their hands.

One was Horemheb, general of Ptah Regiment. Rameses; right-hand man.

Julius fired, at first blink and right through his jacket pocket, hit the ground and rolled for the cover of the nearest pillars.

To hell with the Beretta. He took the grenade from the left pocket, jerked the ring, waited a little while fire spattered and pinged off the marble—being sure he would not get the grenade back—and flung it.

Thunder broke. So did the columns. So did a considerable portion of the superstructure of that side of the atrium; and a cloud of dust went up in the light of the single brazier and the glowing eyes of brazen Drusus, where Tiberius had taken refuge, climbing into its lap as the plaster kept falling, where Horemheb and his crew had been standing.

Work for the Undertaker.

"*Cai! Valesne?*"

"*Valeo!*" he answered Antonius' shout from amongst the further columns.

As the front doors blew half off their hinges and sent smoke and marble-dust and the stench of explosives wafting through the shattered hall.

"*Damn you!*" Tiberius screamed. "*Damn you!*"

"*Antoni!*" Julius yelled; and ran for the doors, outside, where a shadowy figure waited with an Uzi in its hands. He heard Antonius, hard on his heels, stop, and whirled, ran back and grabbed a fistful of tunic, dragging Antonius on. "It's Mouse, dammit, move!"

Antonius ran. Someone else must have, because Mouse cut loose with a burst of fire as they pelted down the

steps for the jeep parked at the bottom, as Drusus'
mechanical voice thundered:

"*Murder, murder, murder—*"

"He won't forgive this!" Antonius yelled.

"Neither will I!" Julius yelled back as he reached the
bottom of the steps and vaulted into the jeep, which sat
there with its motor running. He threw the hand-brake
off. "*Mouse! Back off and get out of there!*"

Mouse backed, firing another burst, and a third.
Julius reached and pulled the Galil out of the holster.
"*I've got you covered! Run for it!*"

Mouse spun about and ran. Julius aimed a burst up at
the doorway, hearing shots from inside, and the rumble
of more masonry in collapse.

A bullet spanged off the hood. He swung the Galil up
and fired at the roofline, as Mouse stumbled on the
steps and recovered himself, still running, still able to
vault the side and throw himself into the back, reloading
and firing as Julius gunned the motor and burned rubber
on the turn.

"Is he all right?" he yelled at Antonius. "Is he all
right back there?"

"He's taken a bad one," Mouse yelled into his ear.
"I've got my hand on it! Keep going!"

"*Antonius?*"

"Antonius," Mouse said.

"*Marie—*" Napoleon murmured, with his fingers
wound into soft curls, his lips quite, quite close to
Marie Walewska's own, in Napoleon's floral-print sheets,
in the soft glow of the nightlight.

The phone rang.

And rang.

"*Excuse-moi.*" Napoleon murmured, trying not to lean
on Marie as he reached across to the bedside table. Or

to let temper get the better of him. *"Mon Dieu, quelle espèce de idiot etes-vous? Qu'est-ce que vous voulez?"*

"Is Felix there?"

The air of the bedroom was suddenly cold. *"Non,"* he said. *"Je ne le connais pas."*

"Sorry."

Click.

He shivered, leaning there on his arm, put the receiver back, and stared off into the dark.

"Mon amour—"

"Marie, mon Dieu, pardonez-moi—" He shifted his weight and shifted back across and kissed her. On his way out of bed.

"Napoleon—"

He leaned down and took her face between his hands. *"Marie—je n'y ai pas de choix. Je t'aime. Je t'aime—"*

No damned time. Hell had broken loose. And Marie sat up in bed, threw her feet off the edge, intending to come with him.

"Non," he said, and grabbed his clothes.

Brutus' side hurt. He had run and run, and now he came to streets again, streets where cars came and went, and the lights of the city shone on the other side of the greenbelt.

Dammit, not the straight course, he heard Sargon saying.

And he thought of jeeps and searchlights and remembered that they might be watching the street, this being the only street he had yet come to, and that in a straight line from the villa.

He limped along in the dark, among the rhododendrons and the pines, and pressed a hand to his side, which hurt with a consuming pain. He began to despair. He had done things terribly amiss. He wished himself back in his safe bed, in his room, with the door locked—

—without the guards.

He wiped sweat from his face and staggered in his

steps, blinked and nearly ran right on into his sycophant,
which had come to a stop and swerved suddenly left,
toward a lump of granite amid several trees. One old
pine was recently blasted, white wood glaring jagged
spikes in Hell's night.

But then, there had been a lot of confused shots
landing in this region during the Viet Cong affair, and
he had seen more than one shell-hole, larger than
anything the rose garden had suffered, in his course
across the greenbelt.

The sycophant meant that he should rest. It counseled
him to take cover. He was relieved. He staggered in
among the rocks, next to the shattered pine.

Suddenly a live weight hit him and threw him rolling,
tangled with him and went for his throat.

"Ai!" he yelled, and broke the hold and rolled and
had it perfect, just the way Scaevola had taught him,
except he was so damned tired he staggered as he came
up, facing a tee-shirt-clad adversary. "Brother?"

"Bastard!" Caesarion hissed in Greek.

He straightened back, offended, offended and too out
of breath to defend himself, in any sense.

"*He* send you?" Caesarion demanded.

"I came myself," Brutus said between breaths, and
went and sat down on a downed branch of the shattered
tree. "I came—to find you. To find you." He swallowed
down the other reasons. He was afraid to blurt them
out. "I want—want to talk with you. I want you to go
back—with me—to Julius. To our father."

"To our *father!*"

"He *is* our father. —I've met your mother. She's—"

"Leave my mother out of this!"

"I like her. I'm not sure she likes me. Did you get to
see her?"

There was long silence. Angry silence. No, he thought,
Caesarion had not seen Klea. Or Klea had not seen
him. It was dangerous territory.

"He didn't let you?" Brutus ventured.

"You damn fool."

"Maybe I am. I don't know. I don't know a lot of things. That's why I came to find you."

Caesarion made a spitting sound, tucked his hands to his back and slouched over to sit on a rock. "*Sure* you did. What do you get for it?"

"I get in a lot of trouble. They're looking for me, same as you. I wanted to find you—to ask you—ask you— Is it me you hate? Am I the reason you ran away?"

Caesarion stared at him a long time. "What in hell are you doing there, that's what I want to know."

"They say—they say Mithridates sent me. Because somehow I could be useful to him. I guess I have been. I've made enough trouble." Brutus leaned his arms along his legs, favoring his aching gut, and felt for a moment like he was going to throw up. "O gods."

"Mithridates, is it?"

He looked up at the cold tone. "That's what they think. I don't know."

"That's what they *think?* You don't *know?*"

Brutus shook his head. "I just woke up here. I fell off a horse. Then the Undertaker's table. And I walked down a hall and I was here. There." He indicated what he thought was the direction of home. "In the villa. Julius says it's two thousand years back in Rome. Hatshepsut says it's nearly three. I don't know. All I know is, everything's changed. I didn't know about you. I didn't know about Klea. I didn't know about Augustus. I just walked into all of this, and I'm not your enemy, I'm not anybody's that I know of. I don't want to be. I don't want anybody to get hurt. Look, if you're afraid of Julius, tell *me* what's going on, and *I'll* go talk to him— I can. I'd do that."

Caesarion stared at him a long time, as if he were looking at something he had never seen before.

"You're not my enemy," Caesarion repeated. "Not my enemy. Bloody hell. *What do you mean, you didn't know about me?*"

"I didn't. I don't. I'm sorry." He had dealt with egos before. Gods knew, the villa was well-supplied with royalty. "I know you're a pharaoh. And my half-brother."

Caesarion was still looking at him in that strange way, with his mouth slightly open.

"Don't know."

"I'm sorry," Brutus said again. "Julius told me a little of it. I mean, I know who you are. But not enough to know what's going on."

Prolonged silence. Caesarion raked a hand through his hair and it fell back again. And still the stare. "Off a horse."

"I don't kn-kn—" He shut his eyes a moment and tried again. Gods, he was not about to start that. He was suddenly sweating. He did not want to get into that. "—know. That's the last I remember."

Not the fall. The riding. That was all. How did a healthy life end, just sitting on a walking horse?

Did somebody shoot me? Can you die and not feel it? Killed instantly, that's what the television calls it.

Caesarion set his hands on his knees and stood up. "Come on."

"Where?" In sudden apprehension. He had *found* Caesarion. Trusting Caesarion was not what he had intended; and Caesarion was standing there holding out his hand.

"A place I know. *Scared?*"

There was a world of scorn in that word. Brutus' face went hot. He gathered himself up without the offered hand.

"Where is it?"

"Just come with me—brother."

V

Julius paced. There was damned little else to do, banished as he was to the hall, outside the room where Augustus' personal physician labored to save Antonius from the bullet that had made a mess of his gut. He had had a catalog of the damage. It did not sound good.

Mouse—was washing up. Most of Antonius' blood was all over Mouse, all over the jeep, all over the medics, all down the hall, before the sycophants had gotten to work. There was not little on Julius.

They dared not have Antonius in the Undertaker's hands now, tonight, when it was possible that Mithridates was moving pieces of his own. Reassignments, which had reliably dropped Antonius back into Tiberius' domain no matter how often he died in Hell, might glitch and lose him—forever. Might send him to a deeper Hell.

Or the Undertaker might take his time and ask Antonius questions while he worked, which could last and last and last.

And a man would talk. A man would talk, sooner or later, still conscious, while his guts lay beside him on a table, or knives took the skin off him to try a different arrangement. *That* was what they could do.

So they had come roaring back along the back roads to get Antonius to the fastest help they could get, not—

O gods, *not* New Hell General's emergency room, to which no one should take a flattened dog, and where Pentagram agents could get at him; none of their people would go to that pesthole for a hangnail, let alone a bullet wound. They had brought him here, as fast as the jeep could move, radioed ahead to have the help ready, and pulled up in back while there was still enough blood left in Antonius to keep his heart going.

It meant, of course, that another trail was cold, at least as far as they were concerned. Julius listened to reports that came in from the desk; he paced, he longed to go out again, and knew damned well that there were enough competent people out there still searching; and that Out There was a dangerous place for any of them tonight. More, all the reports get here; and here was the center of operations, the best place for the head of operations to hold tight and direct the search.

Even when the head of operations was also a father, and everytime he shut his eyes he saw the same sight, a scared kid huddled under a hedge somewhere out there, hiding from the soldiers which were his hope of rescue.

Or the same kid, none so scared, finally finding the chance to contract one of Mithridates' agents and line up the next phase of his operation: Mettius Curtius— cavalry commander Mettius Curtius—hardly *looked* the eighteen he had died, but there was near three thousand years in Hell behind those eyes, and if Brutus had lacked that example to remind him, there was the face in his mirror in the morning. Hell was wide. And they might have been deceived.

But, dammit, he did not believe it. It was the kid under the hedge that he kept seeing, it was the remembrance of his son's arms around him, of the frightened voice that stammered on the bad questions, the flicker of understanding in the young eyes when he would apprehend some new curiosity of the modern world— *"What's a bomb, father?"*

Gods.

Gods.

He leaned his head against his arm, against the wall, and wished for once in hell there were someone he could go to with the questions.

His own father he had never found. Nor his mother. No one. Relegated to some different end of Hell. In another level. In Paradise, who knew? Events in Rome had cast him early into the role of *paterfamilias* of a decimated and impoverished clan; and it was much the same in Hell. He had found so few of his kin. And those few were mostly in the North Shore, and held him too modern, too changed, too foreign to suit them.

The stubborn ones wandered the open fields mostly, convinced it was Elysium; they built little, cared for less, waiting for rebirth that never came, praying to gods that never heard.

Or they built their little domains like shepherd's cottages and tended vines that gave them good wine, cut their wheat with bronze scythes, herded goats— there were, gods knew, plenty of goats in Hell—and fed the Roman West. Not a telephone among the lot, and not interested—like the old Romans of the Republic, not interested in any war that did not threaten their vineyards, their flocks, their domains.

And if not for the Villa, he thought, they would go out like a candle in a hurricane, absorbed, overwhelmed. He, Augustus, and their strangely-asorted allies, were the bulwark that made Hell into Paradise for their ancestors.

For them, for the rest of Rome perhaps, it *was* the Elysian Fields. Perhaps it was Hell's punishment of his ambition, that that ambition would not let him believe in Elysium, or settle to rest with his people, or wait with hands folded while the tide rolled over them.

Gods. Venus Genetrix, give me my son. Give me my one true son. Is that too much, for the service I do you?

But Her, too, he doubted.

He had ben content, well content in Hell, secure in

the knowledge he could protect his own, because nothing could get through his own armor—he loved only Rome, and those he lost, when he lost them, he had hope of finding again, even so.

Until his enemy sent him Brutus, and a seventeen-year-old boy wrapped his arms about him, all perilous and fragile and, unlike the rest of Hell, subject to drastic and irrevocable change.

Every moment he lives, he changes. And I am jealous for those changes I do not govern. And terrified of those changes I do not know.

I could kill the men who lost him. And yet everything they did, they did at my orders, devotedly. And they suffer—knowing that.

I have never loved anything but masses of men. And the City. And a girl-queen. O Gods, the foolishness of loving something entirely finite, something I can truly lose.

He heard someone running. No soldier, not with that clatter of loose heels, that slight weight.

He knew, before he turned to see. And knew, suddenly, there was another love that Hell could take from him.

"Klea—"

As she arrived, in pink nightrobe and mules. "Where is my son?" Klea cried.

And meant the other one. The one to blame for this.

"What's going on?" Klea shouted at him. "Niccolo drugged me! It was your doing! It was, wasn't it?"

"It wasn't my order. I swear to you."

"*WHAT HAVE YOU DONE WITH MY SON?*"

Our son, he should object. He could not bring himself to do that. He only stood there staring at her, and resenting Caesarion's very existence.

They laid him at my feet when he was born. Like a damned fool I picked him up. I wanted a son that much.

And Rome killed me for it.

"Klea," he said and tried to take her by the shoulders. She thrust his hands off. "I didn't do a damned thing with the boy. *The boy* accounted for a Praxiteles original and the whole damned dining room window and ran for the hedge. *The boy* outran us, that was what he did. *Brutus* ran after him. *Antonius* is lying in there gut-shot by an Egyptian sniper, and Tiberius' atrium is a shambles. *The boy* wasn't there."

Smart woman, Klea. She stood there with her mouth open, rage still in every line of her petite body, and her eyes reacted to every detail he handed her, reacted as the brain added the total up and came out with chaos.

"What in *hell* have you *done* in six hours?"

In that immaculately sane, indignant tone of voice that a man with fault on his hands had most to dread.

"Antonius is hurt," she said, in that same terrible voice.

"He's in there." He caught her arm as she headed that way. "Galen is with him. He's doing all he can. I've got the troops out searching—"

"Oh, *fine*, fine, you have the whole 10th on his track! You send that American after him and chain him in the basement and now you send the army after him!"

"We're not playing kids' games, Klea! Caesarion's *friends* go right to the top of the Pentagram! His *friends* play with sniper bullets and Reassignment computers. If we lose Antonius in there, we may *lose* him, do you hear me? With every damn thing he knows—in Mithridates' hands. And Rameses'."

Klea stood still for a long moment. She stopped pulling to be free and he let go her arm. Her eyes flickered with thoughts like Hell's own lightnings, and her mouth was firm and decisive.

"You will take me into your confidence," she said, "and *listen* to my advice, or by Zeus and by Ammon, by Isis and by Bast, I will go on my own and with what resources *I* can find. It is absolute lunacy to work opposite each other. But I will—if that is the position

you put me in. I want my son unhurt. I want him
gently treated. I want that other boy back here, intact."

He opened his mouth.

Klea held up her index finger. "I'm not through. You
listen to me, *Cai*. You made a mistake with Brutus in
life. You made a mistake with Caesarion. I told you, did
I not, you ought to have taken Brutus in hand and told
him the truth long before this. *You ask too damned
much*, that's what you do. No boy can live up to it."

"I never asked a damned thing!"

"You ask. Oh, yes, you *ask*. You asked it of Antonius,
you asked it of Brutus, you asked it of Caesarion, of
Octavianus, of—"

"*Octavianus* didn't go defect to the enemy!"

"*Octavianus* is a bloody genius, dammit! Antonius
isn't, Brutus isn't, Caesarion isn't! They're smart, they're
just damned smart, they're really *smart*, but they're not
geniuses, *they're not in your class*, do you understand
what you've done to them?"

"*Done* to them, *pro di immortales!* They're damned
smart enough! They get along damned well—"

"—on their own?"

He clamped his jaw and stared at her, mad and
gnawed at from all directions.

"It's the gods' own wonder," Klea said, "why a smart
man can figure everything in the whole damn world
except how smart he is."

"I use my head! If that son of yours thought half he
did halfway through—"

"Are you saying you're as smart as Caesarion? As
Brutus? Are you saying they could stand where you
stand, on their own, *on their own?* Dammit, that was
what you did to Antonius. Antonius had the guts to try
when you were gone. And he wouldn't take my advice,
and he was facing *Octavianus*, for the gods' sake.
Antonius was *almost* man enough. But Caesarion—
Caesarion wasn't in your class. He never was. Do you
think his mother wants to say that? It's the truth, *Cai*.

It's true. Your genes and mine—threw back to my father and gods know who on your side, but Caesarion's no genius. He walked right into Octavianus' trap. He can't *do* better. That's all. I just want my son out of this, I want him—" Klea's eyes brimmed and her lips trembled. "Dammit, I want him out of your shadow. I want him *free* and I want him out of Tiberius' hellhole and I want him to have a little peace—that's all. That's all."

Klea crying and trying not to—was too much. Julius put his hands in his belt and tried to think what promise he could give her. But there was none, if the things she had said were true, and there was an uneasy feeling at his stomach, making him, dammit, angry—angry that it might be true, that he might have no equal among his friends as he sincerely wanted to have none among his enemies.

That was loneliness, loneliness that rang true with his whole life. And his whole life was not what he wanted to deal with at the moment: he wanted his sons, he wanted Antonius alive, he wanted the damned mess solved and the villa intact.

He had damaged a Roman Seat of Power with that grenade, he, himself, one of the Powers of Hell. By the rules he suspected in Hell, such as rules were, resonances were at work. *He* had been able to do it. None of his agents might have succeeded so far against a place like that; but it was *Roman*, dammit, it was Rome's malady he had tried to set in order, and he feared with a dreadful fatalism that it had set other resonances ringing through Hell. The Luck had come down harshly on Antonius, a mere bystander. He tried to think of it as random and senseless, but the intelligence Klea threw in his face had another penalty: that he could not turn loose a set of facts which had begun to show a pattern.

Egyptians and Romans.

He had brought Egypt within Rome's orbit in his mortal lifetime. He had gotten an heir half Roman and

half Egyptian. And lifted up his friends to rule the
world after him—to destroy each other; to break each
other as Klea said he had broken his sons, only by
existing.

It was that, perhaps, to be a god. Not to be able to
act without consequence. Not to be able to love without
shattering the object of that love.

It had taken death and Hell to sort out the few souls
that could withstand him—if what Klea said was true; if
what Klea had said was true, then the cruel move that
had brought ordinary and weaker souls—souls he cared
for—into the Game of Powers here about New Hell—
was bound to win.

He did not want to believe that, most of all.

"Imperator," the sycophant whispered, and Publius
Hadrianus heard the measured tread of soldiers at his
door, heard the rattle of the lock in the next room, and
lay frozen in terror and indignation—terror because
they could do whatever they pleased, and indignation
because that lock and that key were *theirs,* access to his
room was theirs, whenever he was out of it *or* in it—

—and it was another damned middle-of-the-night
visitation, the last of which he had endured drugged
out of his mind by Rameses' agents, the latest of which
he endured in heart-thumping terror, because life had
gotten comfortable, and he had known, dammit, he had
known that that comfort was not going to last—

The door in the living room opened; light flared
under the bedroom door. "Majesty?" a voice said. A
knock came at the bedroom door.

Perhaps, he thought, they would kill him again.

His teeth chattered. He sat up in bed and blinked as
the door opened and a dark figure, khaki-edged, flipped
a switch and blinded him with the room lights.

The sycophant wailed and popped out of presence.

"Imperator," the Roman voice said—and the fuzzy
shape saluted. That was better. Hadrianus rubbed his

eyes and blinked again. "Caesar's compliments, *imperator,* sorry to wake you. There's a car downstairs. We'll help you pack."

"Pack. Pack?" Hadrianus felt for the edge of the bed with his foot and groped after his nightrobe. *"Where's my damned robe?"*

The sycophant winked into existence and chittered out again. The robe floated onto the bed.

Hadrianus snatched it and put it on. He had taken to sleeping in a nightgown. Gods *knew* who would come barging in.

And there were legionaries invading his closet, his bureau, his dresser, carrying in suitcases, laying his clothes into them.

As Atilius Regulus walked all the way in and waved a soldier with a suitcase on out the door. "Quickly, quickly. —Majesty, you'll want to get dressed. Very sorry about the hour. Events are moving. So are we."

"Moving *where?"*

"Majesty," Regulus said with—could it be?—courtesy. "Caesar has sent a car for you. Your baggage will follow. Kindly hurry. We don't want to give our adversaries time to put a tail on us."

"Where?"

"Caesar asks your *help,* majesty. You will have a briefing. Hurry."

"My *help.* After keeping me in this—"

"After rescuing you from traitors, majesty. Rameses occupies your office. Your enemies are firmly in power. Your majesty knows the game. Kidnapping you from the East and taking you back within Roman keeping was an affair of honor. Establishing you in a rival center of power would have declared open hostilities, not to our advantage. We are working on your return, majesty. We have always been. Now Caesar thinks it advantageous that you disappear from the place Rameses' agents know you are . . . and go underground."

"Underground."

The least wicked humor lifted Regulus' eyebrow. "Figuratively, of course."

Julius walked quietly into Antonius' room, Klea at his heels—Antonius was awake, Galen had said; but he showed no sign of it, laying still in his bed, the fine Roman face pale under the curling mop of dark hair, the traces of dissolution purged away so that it might have been some wax image lying there, some sarcophageal saint among the tubes and the stands.

But Antonius' eyes slitted open as Julius and Klea reached his bed.

"Damn mess," Julius said, and laid a hand on his shoulder. "I'm sorry, *Antoni.*"

"Sorry myself," Antonius mumbled. "Damn, got it in the gut again. Hurts."

"*Antoni*—" Klea said, and took his hand in both her small ones.

"I don't know where he is, Klea. Don't know. *Unnnhhh.*" An injudicious attempt to draw a leg up. "Oh, damn, that hurts."

He seemed to go away for a moment, then, his eyes rolled up.

"Easy," Julius said. "Don't move, *Antoni.* Listen to me. You've hunted Caesarion out of his escapades before this one. He's missing. Where would you look? Do you hear me?"

The eyes centered and focused. "De Sade. De Sade and Ashtoreth—*The Pit.*"

It was an address. One hoped.

"He's got friends—friends there." Antonius seemed to drift off again, eyes closed. "Damn, they've drugged me."

"*Antoni,*" Klea said, and held his hand tight. "*Antoni,* hold on. Please. What friends? Names, *Antoni.*"

"I don'—don't know . . . names. Never knew . . . names. Ashtoreth. De Sade. Room there."

"*Antoni,*" Julius said in a hard voice, deliberately

hard. "You're not going to die. That's an order. You hear me? We can't swear to where you'd end up. In their hands, if they glitch the computers—*hear me?* You don't die. You hang on, *Antoni*. This isn't pain, compared to what they'll give you, if you come back in Mithridates' keeping. Galen will keep you drugged. Much as he can. You understand me?"

"Y-Yes."

"We've got all our contacts occupied. We can't go into those computers now, not without getting caught at it. Horemheb's going to tell them enough as it is; and they'll have a pickup out on Caesarion, damn sure they will, if he doesn't get to them first. They'll *know* we'll make a move. And we can't afford to have you going through their hands. They'll trump up charges. That's all they need. Hear me?"

"I hear," Antonius whispered. "O gods, *Iuli*, give me something, make them give me something, it's starting to hurt."

"Galen's outside. I'll get him."

The greenbelt gave out on the city edge and a last few of the trails met inside a stand of aged oaks, where three jeeps met nose to tail and nose to nose among the hedgerows.

It was a place made for muggers.

Or to conceal the goings-on of fugitives and searchers.

"No sign of him," Sargon said, standing at the roadside with Scaevola and Horatius. "Dammit, no sign of him."

"There's been a disturbance at Tiberius' villa," Horatius said, Augustus' lank security chief, in plain legion khaki tonight; but the eye-patch made him remarkable in any company—Augustus' security chief and occasional decoy, since his hawk-nosed, black-patched self did not lend itself to clandestine operations: one never knew whether Horatius was the real matter or the false when things came down, but the man who had stood holding the bridge against the Etruscans while they cut it from under him—had an unflappable calm in crisis . . . even tonight, when affairs between the factions of Hell were rolling downhill toward a blowup.

And Scaevola, who had been both spy and assassin in the Etruscan wars, had no questions; he only folded his arms and waited for Horatius to lay things out for them.

"Tiberius has filed a protest," Horatius said in his unhurrying way. "We believe Horemheb is in Reassignments. We don't rule out the possibility that Brutus is a plant. We don't assume it, either."

"Damned sure you don't assume it," Sargon said in a low voice. "Damn wives of mine, damned kids, I've seen *kids,* understand, rotten ones and good ones, and I know kids. That boy is no plant."

"I don't think so either," Scaevola said.

"We don't assume," Horatius said, "anything. We don't assume this sequence of events is chance. Caesar had the call from the American—*urging* him to action, handing him the chance to extricate Caesarion from among the Dissidents. And the *American* suggested the move that brought Caesarion back and simultaneously involved Brutus. We don't assume this was coincidence. We're trying to find where Welch's strings run."

It was not the kind of information Horatius would drop on a chance encounter in the backroads of the greenbelt—even to two men high up in the security hierarchy. It was a need-to-know situation. Sargon smelled it coming—that Roman security was about to ask a little favor of the king of Akkad—who just happened to look like the enemy.

"In which connection," Horatius said, "we're more than tracking two runaways. We've got to know what the East is up to, and we've got to start calling in old debts—all the Eastern contacts we can trust; maybe some we can't. This could be the push we've been expecting. It might be happenstance that could trigger it. In either case—"

                              *   *   *

They crossed the street at a run, midway along, alley to alley beckoned. The streetlight at the corner was dim against a dawning sky, and what light there was showed a desolate region of boarded windows and barred doors, filthy streets and filthier alleys, through which repulsive and odorous streams wound toward sewers clogged with old papers and worse.

It was nothing like the city Brutus knew. He kept up with Caesarion, panting as he went, with the advantage of tennis shoes, where Caesarion went on bare feet, leaving—Brutus saw it on the cobbles and on the pavement—a splotch of blood from his left foot. Caesarion was not limping, but he was flagging; and halfway down the alley he stumbled and caught himself against a graffiti-written wall.

"Got to rest," Caesarion gasped. "Got to rest."

Brutus leaned against the wall beside him, holding his side. "It's daylight," he breathed.

"Not far now. Don't come into a place panting and blowing. Just stroll in, natural." Caesarion rolled his head against the bricks to look sidelong at him, and jabbed him with an elbow. "You do all right. All right."

It was unexpected, that Caesarion found a kind word for him. He was a fool, he thought, to have come with his half-brother, and to have followed him into a place like this. But he was bound to be a fool no matter what he did, because a fool would go home again and lie low and wait for calamity to fall on the house, on everything he loved, because he was a fool and ignorant. Since he was damned to be a fool he could at least try to educate himself—

Think, Niccolo was wont to tell him, when that sinister man offered him advice. *Learn everything. That, boy, is the only way to know what you dare discard. Even to know that a thing is useless, is to know the value of everything.*

He knew things. And they all jumbled together, unsortable, like the memory of the chopper ride and the fall out of the plane, and this same face, Caesarion's, lying drug-tranquilized near him, with his father's features duskier and whipped by windblown hair, eyes dark-lashed and mostly closed—both wrists chained—he remembered the fight, remembered Caesarion struggling with Welch—

"Come on," Caesarion said, and grasped him by the shoulder, drawing him away from the wall.

"Where—where are we going?"

"Friends," Caesarion said. Caesarion was limping now, finally. The hand which held Brutus' arm was easy, or strengthless. Caesarion dislodged an empty bottle that went spinning away and hit the alley wall.

Something small and black spat at them and fled. It was not a cat.

It was the kind of place that Brutus would have instinctively known to avoid the way he avoided them in Rome. It was the kind of place where accidents happened, because there was no one going to report them, and there was no one in earshot who particularly cared.

But Caesarion drew him onto the street after that last alley, and down it past confusing shops with huge painted signs that said FIRE SALE and BARGAIN, up to the battered red door of a place that called itself (on a weathered metal sign with sputtering neon) THE PIT.

Caesarion knocked, loud and long.

"Everyone's asleep," Brutus said.

Footsteps came to the door inside. The door opened, and a wizened man with a broom in hand peered around the corner. His eyes widened, and he moved to slam the door.

Caesarion hit it and shoved it back. "'Cool it, Charlie." He walked in with an expansive swagger and Brutus walked after him, into a wretched sort of *taberna* with all the chairs upside down on the tables and the place smelling of old drink and the decay of its floors and its plumbing.

It was not Augustus' villa, that was sure.

The custodian closed the door and shot the bolt, and advanced on them with a vengeance. "You shouldn't be here," Charlie said. "You shouldn't come here now!"

"Cool it, I said," Caesarion snarled at him. "I'm here, I want my room, and I want a change of clothes for me and my brother."

"Brother," Charlie echoed stupidly.

Brother? Brutus thought, at once affected by the word and feeling cornered. He was not sure he wanted that part known. He was not sure how Caesarion meant it, or what Caesarion meant to demand of him in the name of a kinship he had himself invoked, in deciding to coming with him.

"My *half-brother*," Caesarion said. "On my *father's* side. Understand me, *your majesty?*"

"He's a *king?*" Brutus whispered, aghast and taking a second up and down look at this wretched and dusty man, while the janitor clamped his mouth and clutched his broom the tighter.

"Charles VII." Caesarion said, sliding past the defense, snagging Brutus by an arm and drawing him after. "*King* of France. Louis threw him out of court, —didn't he, Charlie? Seems some holy woman put old Charlie here on the throne, and damned if he didn't let her enemies burn her at the stake, —didn't you, Charlie? Nice man. Real nice man. Just like our father."

"Don't say that!" Brutus cried, and Caesarion pulled him hard, toward the back of the room.

"Come on. —Charlie, my man, one king to another, tell Muballit we're here and papa's legions are hot after us."

"What?" Charles exclaimed. And: "wait!"

Brutus stopped. Caesarion jerked him onward, toward the back of the room and through a doorway to a hall and another door.

"Where are we going?" Brutus asked, trying to shake his arm free. He thought that perhaps he should fight, that things were going rapidly beyond what he could deal with.

But perhaps they already had. Perhaps King Charles was dangerous. Perhaps King Charles had a gun. Everyone Brutus knew had a gun. He could get into a fight with his half-brother and break away and get himself shot, that was what would happen.

Caesarion opened the door on a dirty hallway and held him, his grip painfully hard, while he shut the door behind them.

And walked him down the hall. It smelled of rot and age. A large rat scurried down the steps at the end, and vanished into a heap of old paper boxes.

Caesarion led him up that flight of steps and up again, around the corner and into a narrow hall worse than the last. "Where are we going?" Brutus asked again, without hope of an answer; no one *ever* answered him.

But: "Here," Caesarion said, and took a key off a nail. "Honest as they come. *Nothing* gets molested in *The Pit*."

He fitted the key in the lock.

Something passed them, cold and green and glowing, and Brutus flinched against the wall, shuddering under a gelid, loathsome touch that went right through his clothes.

"*Di!*" he gasped.

"That's the security guard," Caesarion said, and turned the key and pushed the door open. He yanked Brutus around the doorframe and into the room with him; and shoved the door shut with his hip. "*There* we are, brother."

It was a bedroom to match the rest of the building, musty and dingy. There was a toilet in the corner, and a rusty sink. There was a sagging bed with a stained white spread with burns in it. There was a fat chair with the stuffing coming out of it, and maybe it had been green once, or maybe it had always been that color.

There was a bureau the wood of which was cracked and split; and a door in the same condition, that might be a closet. There was a window clouded with dirt and showing mostly the big metal sign outside that said THE PIT.

Brutus stared. He could not help it. And Caesarion turned him around by the arm that was getting numb and shoved him gently free, against the wall.

"Never seen anything like this—*have* you?"

He had not. He had seen poverty on the streets of Rome and Brundisium, he had rubbed shoulders with the poor, but he had never been *in* a tenement, had never smelled the bad plumbing and rot of boards and plaster. He would no more have gone into one than he would have walked into a quarry or a slave pen or any of the other terrible places he knew existed in the world, where an aristocrat was the enemy, where the prevailing rules were not the rules he knew, where he was automatically suspect of things he did not understand, and where no one would protect him, even with a warning. He was afraid of poor people.

If he took to the hall and tried to escape now—if he could get past the terrible *thing* out there, he was still in a strange place, and lost, and perhaps in worse trouble out there than in here, where he was at least dealing with someone he ought to be able to understand, and who understood him.

He hoped.

"No," he said quietly. "No, I never have."

" 'Never have' covers a lot of it, doesn't it . . . brother."

He blinked and heard that through twice in his head before he was sure it was a gibe at his virginity; but by that time Caesarion had clapped him roughly on the shoulder and gone off to start rummaging through a bureau drawer.

"Maybe you're wrong," Brutus said, nettled. "I've been around. I just never saw a room like this."

Caesarion looked around from his search, a dark look

and then a dark grin. "Oh, you are the little prig, aren't you?"

"*You're* a pharaoh," Brutus said, folding his arms. "Don't say you were born to this."

"No, I was born to palaces, I was born to nurses and courtiers and people to taste your food and people to find you any damn thing you want, *anything* you want, if you'll give them what they want— You want to know what gets bought and sold in Tiberius' palace, pretty brother? You want to know what you can trade in?"

Brutus decided he did not want to know. Caesarion found a half-packet of cigarettes and a lighter, tapped one out into his mouth and lit it with shaking hands. Brutus stared at the procedure, amazed by it, disturbed by the violence trembling in Caesarion's movements.

"Damn," Caesarion said, and exhaled a cloud of smoke. "I've wanted that. Damn soldiers wouldn't give me a cigarette. Damn prig father doesn't *approve*." He extended the pack toward Brutus. "You?"

"N-no." He had not the least idea how to do it the way Caesarion did, and the smoke stung his eyes even from where he stood.

"*Zeus*." Caesarion walked over to the window, where the smoke made a haze about him, several puffs, his face sober and very like their father's in that wan ruddy light as he looked down on the street.

Brutus just watched, thinking that it might be soldiers Caesarion was waiting for, and it might be something else. Caesarion drew a few more rapid puffs on the cigarette and seemed calmer then. He let ash fall on the floor, before he flipped the cigarette into the toilet and rolled the rest of the pack and the lighter into the sleeve of his tee-shirt.

Then he went to the closet and tossed a pair of tennies toward the bed, and sat down and put his shoes on, with a piece of toilet paper folded under the cut on his foot.

Brutus settled carefully onto the arm of the worn-out

chair and watched, thinking it was a foolish way to treat an injury and likely to get infected, but he had figured this half-brother enough to know that Caesarion would yell at him if he offered advice. And yelling was not what he wanted.

"Something the matter?" Caesarion asked then, argumentatively.

"No," Brutus said as agreeably, as pleasantly as he could.

"Brother, you'd be a real prize in Tiberius' house. Gods. They'd have you for main course." Caesarion tied his right shoe and went for the left, and Brutus still stared, disturbed and amazed by this young pharaoh who looked, at some angles, so much like the boy their father might have been, except the duskiness of the skin. Strong, yes: muscle moved in ridges in Caesarion's arms, stood out in the hollow of his cheek— Caesarion generally had his jaw clenched, often enough his shoulders tight: there was tension in him even when he ought to be relaxed; he moved to unheard drumbeats, little tensions that made it seem there was music going on in Caesarion's head that no one ever heard; and a gnawing suspicion of the whole world around him, that it was about to attack him, and he was ready to take it on hand to hand.

Brutus had never met anyone like Caesarion. He slumped down of the arm and into the chair and just watched him, wondering why Caesarion had not fought *him*, and what all this meant. A rival trying to get a reaction out of him: that, yes. Caesarion was wondering just where the line was with him, and planning to sit on him when he found it— That was it, Brutus thought suddenly. Caesarion had to provoke him to a fight and then beat him, because Caesarion would not feel safe until he had tested him and won. Brutus had met the type in his meager seventeen years. Rome had its street gangs. He had seen them here on the television. And Caesarion he could suddenly see in some alley in

Brundisium, with about five or six flunkies to back him;
and himself as the rich boy Caesarion had targeted.

So here he was in the circle and Caesarion had
something to prove.

Something to learn, maybe. He had had good teachers.
The best.

But Caesarion had been in Hell—thousands of years.
Thousands of years, to learn every nasty trick there
was.

Attacking Caesarion was foolhardy. Best to walk the
narrow line, keep him guessing and keep him just a
little contemptuous of the rich boy half-brother, enough
to keep him happy.

Caesarion is stuck at seventeen. Julius had said to
him. *Never gets older. Never any wiser. Seventeen is all
his understanding, just those years he had and who
killed him.*

Seventeen, seventeen, seventeen—

His heart thudded against his ribs. And he did not
know why, except he heard his father say: *I distrust
coincidences.*

Caesarion set both feet on the floor and went to the
closet, pulled out a black leather jacket and put it on.

"Where are we going?" Brutus asked.

Caesarion zipped the bottom of the jacket and pulled
a weathered brown one out of the closet. He threw it at
Brutus.

Brutus caught it, and turned it over enough to stick
his fingers into one of the slashes, with the uncomfortable
feeling of what did that kind of thing to a jacket.

"Put it on," Caesarion said. "It'll fit."

Brutus put it on, this shabby advertisement that here
was a knife-fighter, and one who had not come off
unscathed: there was bloodstain on the cheap satin
lining. "'Where are we going?" he asked again. It was
morning of a sleepless night, and he would as soon fling
himself down on the bed and shut his eyes for an hour
or so till the room stopped vibrating, even if he was

sure he was too disturbed to sleep, even if he had to do it beside this brother of his.

"Out," Caesarion said. "Just out." Caesarion grabbed him by one side of the coat and pulled him close, a challenge. "You trust me, brother. You *trust* me. I'm your friend. Hear?"

"I'll h-h—" *Oh, damn, damn—* "—b-believe it when I s-s-*see* it."

Caesarion grinned at him, flash of white, perfect teeth in an olive-skinned face. "Papa's son." Caesarion shoved him free.

"I thought we were w-w-waiting for s-someone."

"Oh, Muballit knows. Damn sure. Message'll get there." Caesarion went to the bureau, dug to the back of a drawer, and pulled out a gun and a box of shells.

He turned around and slipped both into his pockets.

Brutus earnestly wished he had a gun. He did not think Caesarion wanted him to have one. "Have you got a knife?" he asked.

That surprised Caesarion. The dark brows lifted a little, and Caesarion gave a hostile little smile and fished something else out of the drawer, black and slim and glittering at either end.

He tossed it.

Brutus made a fast judgement: there was no blade; and there were limits to how much fool he dared act without tempting attack—best to surprise Caesarion now and again. He reached up in the kind of slow-motion clarity Sargon had drilled into him and closed his hand about it in mid-air, neatly and without effort.

And watched Caesarion's eyebrows lift again, the eyes lock with his in the surprise he had wanted.

"Push the button on the side," Caesarion said. "Blade springs out."

Brutus pushed it, felt the blade spring against his fingers, reclosed it and pushed it again, this time so that the blade flicked out.

"Nice," he said. It was not even a machine, not like

other weapons he had found in Hell. This was a simple thing, an elegantly simple thing with a spring someone should have thought of thousands of years ago, and it had a good, comfortable balance. He figured out the blade release on his own, because there was a way such things had to work, and he had learned about spring devices. "Nice." A damn lot better than the stick-sword which was all the villa would give him. He *liked* this little weapon. It had enough blade to mean business, and it tucked right into his pocket, so his rich-boy innocence provided the shield and the means to get close enough, and this was exactly right for infighting.

Caesarion gave him a different kind of look, from the time he had picked the knife out of the air. Not hostility. Just perhaps the suspicion that he ought not to push his Roman brother too far.

VI

"Majesty," Niccolo Machiavelli said, so, so quietly, and by the look Hadrian gave him, the two of them in the spare little Armory office, with legionary guards outside—Hadrian remembered him. Hadrian would.

"Bird of ill omen," Hadrian said. "Whose side are you working this hour?"

"Majesty." Niccolo made a depreciating movement of his hands and settled against the edge of the desk, while the emperor sat facing him—toga-clad and very Roman. "I served well one Caesar who served me ill and in Hell serve one who serves me very well and provides me a haven safe from all but a few masters. There is one none of us can evade. But of *him* we shall not speak, except to remind ourselves he hates sedition, being himself the father of rebellions—all monarchs must fear overthrow, thrones being such narrow seats, are they not, majesty?"

"Whose are you, raven?"

"Why, Caesar's, *magnifico*." He made a little bow. Insults. Everyone took the same tack with him, thinking to throw him off his balance; but few outside Caesar's company could scathe him. This popinjay emperor was *not* one of them, and Niccolo looked up with a sweet and not at all killing smile, while imagining where he would like to dispose this man. "He is a very wise man. His friends fare very well. And he is *not* ambitious, *magnifico*. He has not the least desire to rule—nor even has the divine Augustus. Augustus ruled Rome: he *tolerated* the Empire and tried to stabilize it, but so like his uncle, *Roma* was his great love and his true mistress. To take on your burden, *magnifico*, to take on the ministry of all of Hell—that takes a true and special devotion, beyond any nationality; but, then, the salt in one's blood and the iron in one's bones—that comes from the soil, always from the native soil. You are still Roman, *magnifico*. While the usurper Rameses is not."

Hadrian had such an expressive face. He hid his mouth with a beard and a mustache and it still gave him away, like the eyes, which opened wide as pansies when one started talking about possibilities of advantage and darkened with anger when one mentioned Rameses.

"Are you speaking for Caesar, raven, —or for yourself?"

"I am telling you things which a wise monarch would believe, and he would understand—are very delicate matters. Cesare, for instance, is very keenly aware that the Supreme Commander must not be factional—must maintain himself independent of the petty divisions of lesser princes. He has worked constantly to avoid any— entanglement. But he has made contacts among your old and faithful staff—your *Roman* staff, majesty, from whom he has personally . . . removed the wavering and the unreliable. He has suggested to these men that they may enjoy a change of fortunes—soon, majesty, very soon."

"*How* soon?"

"Very soon. And your assistance will be very valuable. Of course the numbers and accesses you know have passed out of date. But file names, *magnifico*, and such things as your successors may think under lock and key— You understand, your successors have advanced certain factional interests. Our self-defense is, to a large extent, merely a restoration of, hmn, balances, in an hour in which Rameses and his minions intend our banishment to the lower planes. And not only ours, *magnifico*. You understand these things. You may be aware of the case of Marcus Brutus. It *may* have crossed your notice, hmn, among other actions the Ramesid faction must have taken. We are sure it goes beyond private malice, toward a most calculated purpose. *Do* you recall that case? Surely, in the Pentagram's secret files, there must be dossiers on those whose personal histories make them a threat—not only to individuals, but to the Powers of hell. Are there not, *Magnifico?*"

"There are," Hadrian said in a small, tight voice.

"Have you never wondered—where Marcus Brutus was? Or has it been known, in the Pentagram?"

"You're asking classified information."

"Has it been known, majesty? This is a most vital question."

A long pause. A minute break in eye-contact. "There are rules in Hell. You understand them, Machiavelli. And I wonder for which agency you are truly working. Or whether you are Caesar's at all."

"If I were working for Administration, you might hope the more, *magnifico*. If I were doing this for Administration, I would not need to ask you about the existence of that file. About the current purity of its information, yes, but not about its existence. I trust I would have seen it. And I would recommend Rameses be consigned to the nether planes which, yes, I do know, and have visited, *magnifico*. But, alas, it pleases Administration to ignore this present struggle. We are on our own. You were on your own until Cesare risked considerable to free you. Now he is prepared to risk more on your behalf—if he may be assured of your good will, majesty."

"He will have it—if I am reinstated. We will not forget who is loyal."

Niccolo restrained himself even from a sizeable intake of breath. In Hell, one had so much practice, and one saw so many asses. He smiled his most benign. "And the case of Marcus Brutus, *magnifico*."

"The law of Ascendencies—"

"Yes, yes, —relegates such destabilizing influences to the nether planes, by the very degree to which the affected Power is risen in the hierarchies of Hell. I am knowledgeable of the rules, *magnifico;* in my service to Administration, you may take for granted that I know very many of them. So Cesare is aware of this one, in general terms. Perhaps the arrival of Brutus on this plane, coinciding as it does with your fall from power— has ominous significance for yourself as well, since it bids fair to disturb Roman power which is, of course, friendly to you . . ."

Hadrian's eyes flickered, completely readable, and predictably alarmed.

". . . Or perhaps it is simply Cesare's problem. You returned to the Pentagram briefly after your latest, pardon me, assassination, before Rameses usurped the office. Perhaps the file crossed your desk. Perhaps it came to your attention."

A dull flush colored Hadrian's face. Embarrassment. dismay. "There were other matters pressing. I asked for the file. I do not recall receiving it."

"Ah." *Ass!* "But there is a file and someone is in charge of it. *Must* I pursue the details one by one, *magnifico*, when I am, after all, working in your interests? Brutus arrived ostensibly without memory beyond his seventeenth year. Cesare, who predates you in Hell, who has seen the administration of two of your predecessors, does not lay it at your door: Xerxes was in office when he arrived, after all. And then the lamentable Wang. Yourself, and Rameses, yourself, and Rameses, and, we hope, yourself again, most triumphantly. *Where* was Brutus, *magnifico*? Who was in charge of him?"

Again the light flush of embarrassment. *Dio! It is possible he does not know!*

"Have you ever seen that file, majesty?"

"Not personally."

"Who originated it? Who added to it? Who had access?"

"There—was no occasion to open it. One assumed—he was in the nether planes. There are so many, you understand."

"*Help* me, majesty. Who would you suspect?"

Hadrian gnawed at his lip. "Mithridates of course. He was in Xerxes' staff. One kept him on. We were magnanimous. We saw no need to purge the entire staff and he was quite minor. He repaid us with treachery."

"He hasn't the weight in history to achieve a Seat of Power for himself. But he is absolutely ruthless and he has Rameses—*has* Rameses, majesty, to an amazing extent. We concur, then. And we want that file, majesty. Have you any idea how to obtain it?"

"You say yourself, access codes will have changed . . ."

"Assume we can provide access."

Hadrian's eyes widened. "This is treason."

"But, majesty—" *Give me patience!* "—you are on the outside needing in. Is it treason to assist you in penetrating the defenses of your enemies? We will give you a list of names and you will identify the ones you wish to contact. We will help you make that contact. You will extricate the information which may help us restore you. Is this treason?"

Thought proceeded in Hadrian's skull. It went like syrup, sticking at all the rough edges, falling into all the gaps of logic and flowing around all the prominences of self-indulgence, but it proceeded.

"Provide us," Hadrian said, becoming imperialy plural, "this list."

"You can't come in here!" the janitor yelled. Charles VII, the file said. King of France. Sargon of Akkad was underwhelmed, and the door of *The Pit* was the worse for wear as Horatius and his aide took up guard inside. "We're closed! Closed! The owner—"

Sargon gathered up a handful of Charles' shirt and

dragged him close. "In my land we knew how to deal with corrupters of the young. We impaled them. Where's Caesarion?"

"Left, left, he left!"

"*Show* us the room." He opened his hand and pushed the king of France into motion. "Fast."

Charles scurried for the stairs.

"Scaevola," Sargon said, and the two of them followed, himself with his rifle, Scaevola with a modest sidearm, up into the maze of corridors.

"*Foeda,*" Scaevola muttered. "I've seen cleaner stys."

"Damn—*Ai!*" Something objectionable grazed past and it was all Sargon could do *not* to pull the trigger. It wailed about them, and buffeted them with insubstance that still managed to feel like cold jelly. "Dammit!" He snatched Charles a second time by the shirt and slammed him against the wall. "Call it off! Now!"

It left. Sargon shook the king and slammed him back again, thump, into the wall.

"Easy," Scaevola said, interposing his handless arm. "Easy."

Which was just as well, since bashing the fool with the rifle was what he wanted to do. He contented himself with a third slam. "Open the door, *mushkinu.*"

Charles gathered himself away from the wall and slithered sideways to the door nearest, reached up for the key on the bent nail and did as he was told.

Nothing. Nothing but a few bloody spots on the bare wood floor, the same as on the concrete outside. Charles looked positively triumphant.

Sargon walked in and opened the closet door, carefully, and tested it with a pass of his dagger within, looking for wires. Nothing. Nothing but empty hangers, a few magazines, a few cigarette wrappers and a few empty beer cans.

The dresser had a wadded-up mess of jeans in one drawer, underwear in another, tee-shirts and polo shirts in still a third. And various mixes of the same in the rest, along with a carton of cigarettes and a book of matches that said *Oasis Bar and Grill*.

That stirred nasty memories. Merc hangout. Eastern. Very.

"We'll be opening all the doors," Scaevola said coldly, addressing the king of France. "*All* of them, from bottom to top of this place."

"See here, fellow—"

Scaevola took out his pistol and held it in front of Charles' nose. "We can do it with or without a guide. Take your pick. And hereafter, *you* open the doors."

Acid rock and bazoukis in combination were an acquired taste. So was tobacco smoke, hash, and the smell of garlic that came up in waves from the fish that was breakfast fare at the Oasis Bar and Grill.

Jean-Pierre de Vauban was not born to it: Rouen was his home city, and somewhere on the road from Moskva the place of his death, by drowning or by freezing, he was not sure which and had not been sure at the moment he died, having slipped while pushing the wheel of a supply cart that had broken through the ice on some unpronounceable river near some unpronounceable town in Russia with Napoleon's *Grande Armée*. He had not been sure where he was when he died, and after talking to Russians here and there in his service with the disbanded *Armée*—for le Petit Corporal had renounced ambition and retired and bidden them all rest in peace—he was still not damned well sure where he had died. There had been a cursed lot of little rivers and little towns and one hump of snow looked like the last.

So he had done a stint with Richard Coeur de Lion in his disastrous attack on Crazy Horse, and died again; and a turn with Lawrence in the Rommel affair: same result; and with Harry Lee in a go at Moustapha's lads: dead again; but hence the taste for moussaka and ouzo— the bazoukis he only tolerated. And it had seemed a change in his fortunes when, panhandling on a street-

corner, he had seen a white Cadillac come to a screeching
halt, all but rear-ended by an irate cabbie, and lo, it
was the Little Corporal himself, who leaned from the
window and yelled: *"De Vauban? C'est de Vauban?"*

He had been embarrassed, truly embarrassed. The
Caddy had gotten to the curb, l'empereur Napoleon
himself had climbed out—and had to borrow a ten
from, of all people, the Duc de Wellington, who was
the driver. A meal, a bath, a room, and a job with an
old friend of Wellington's—it was so damned hard for
anybody but a modern to *get* a job with the new tech;
but monsieur le duc had pull, and lo, Jean-Pierre de
Vauban became a very fine stablemaster to a very lovely
English lady, whose damning sins, ah! included a
fondness for her staff.

And la belle afforded him a handsome salary—which
was not in jeopardy, le Petit Corporal had assured him
in urging him, some time ago, to continue his old
associations and frequent his old haunts—against the
day le Petit Corporal might want him to use his eyes.
By which de Vauban understood *l'empereur* was not so
retired as he might seem and by which he was not at all
startled when a phone call in the night suggested he
take a little leave from *la belle dame Anglaise*, and meet
an English gentleman who handed him two photographs
and suggested he enjoy a glass or two downtown.

Bien. He was not dull-witted. He burned the photos
and took to bar-hopping, keeping his eyes open, between
the *Oasis* and the *Mephistopheles*, and the *Cairo* and
the places along the row where the Eastern mercs tended
to gather. Mostly the *Oasis* and the *Mephistopheles*,
and now the *Oasis*, because it served food, and it was
the only one where there was a sort of life at this
ungodly hour—if one counted men sleeping at their
tables and along the wall and sagging into their garlicky
fish and eggs.

One did not expect—at this hour—any action. De
Vauban dreamed into his coffee and tried to stay awake,

having thought briefly when he had been thus summoned, that it was what he had long hoped for, that the *Armée* would be reborn, that the Little Corporal would reveal whatever plan he had been following that had necessitated this ruse of retirement, and that her, *he*, Jean de Vauban, who had won *l'empereur*'s personal gratitude for succeeding tonight, would find his way to *l'empereur*'s personal service.

But, things being as usual in Hell, it was someone else would get the glory, and Jean de Vauban would end up again at some horse's rear end.

Someone came in. He looked up.

Mon dieur, it was the boys. Both of them. He dared not more than glance. He dared not move. He started to take a drink of the coffee and his hands were shaking.

He got up. He reached into his pants pocket and found the requisite coin. He went over to the phone on the well-graffitti'd wall, dropped his coin and dialed his number. "*Allo, mon vieux, bonjour*—"

"*Jean?*"

"*Oui, oui, qu'est-ce que vous pensez? Je suis à l'Oasis. Je vous attends.*"

"*D'accord. Bientôt.*"

"*Oui. Oui. Bientôt. Merde.*"

He put the phone back in the cradle and carefully turned his face to the room. The two boys had gone up to the bar to order, and likely, if they knew they were apt to be followed, they were going to get a plate and head to the *Oasis*' back room, where they were less in view of the door. There were the two boys, ancestry uncertain, and a pair of Assyrians and a modern Lebanese, assorted Palestinians, a Turk, a European of some ancestry all sitting at the tables; and a small clutch of Iranians sleeping over against the wall. Who had the back room currently, de Vauban did not know, but he had advised his contact, who would advise le Petit Corporal, one supposed, and there was someone coming, as the man had said, Real Soon Now.

So it was keep a string on the boys till help arrived.

And what that help should look like or what the hell two boys had done that required all this set-to, de Vauban had not the least notion. He only slipped his hand inside the duty-worn jacket from his service under Lawrence (it was less conspicuous, than, say, the uniform off the *Armée* in this bar, being khaki like most everything Modern) and took account of the gun he had there in a neat small shoulder-holster.

No few present in the room likely had weapons, if push came to shove; and he was vitally interested that push did not.

He waked over to the bar and leaned there as the lads gave their order for breakfast.

" 'Allo," he said.

"Hello," the fair one said, all nervous; but the dark one frowned and gave de Vauban a look that said Mind Your Business.

"Don't see many occidentals in here. Me, I was with Lawrence. You?"

"That's our business," the dark one said, and pulled money from his pocket and paid the barkeep who ladled out the garlic-fish mess onto two plates and slammed it down. "Coffee."

"Moderns," the barkeep grumbled.

"Just give us the effin' coffee."

"They don't understand Europeans here." De Vauban tried another tack. "You *are* from Europe."

"Come on," the dark one said, and took his plate, leading the way for his fair companion, who looked back with a vulnerable and apologetic stare.

It was the back room they chose. De Vauban followed them.

And stopped cold just at the door, finding the room well-occupied with drowsing Hittites and Assyrians.

One of the Assyrians lifted his head, and nudged his partner, who lifted his head from the table. The Hittites stirred, one and another of them.

Merde. De Vauban had a decidedly isolated feeling. Perhaps the boys did, who hesitated with their plates and cups in hand.

"*Mes amis,*" de Vauban said, inserting himself between boys and unwelcome attention with as engaging and cheerful a look as he could manage while turning his back on a roomful of armed men. "I think the tables here are engaged. *Venez.* I have a little proposition for you— Business, *eh bien?*"

The dark one gave him a sullen, worried look—a worried look for something behind his shoulder.

"*Kaisarion,*" the other boy said, the one with the honest face. "*F-f-fe-fellimus. Abeamus.*"

Dark-hair reacted with a twitch, as if he had not liked something in what his friend had said, but he moved, turned, all tolerably natural, as if he had found the room too full or no table to his liking, let de Vauban shepherd him and his friend back to the comparative safety of the other room.

"*Voila.*" De Vauban passed a table and grabbed a chair, offering it, and Dark-hair shot a look at him, at the room from which they had retreated, then prudently took the place and set his plate and his cup down. De Vauban pulled out another chair for the second boy, and set himself down, snapped his fingers for the bar and mimed an order for coffee, all before something could develop from the interest suddenly roused in the *Oasis.*

He was sweating. And what language the boys had been using between themselves, he was not sure—not Italian, but the accent was damned close. And in the same split-second he ran that *Kaisarion* through his mind again and the sweat went cold.

"*Romains,*" he muttered. "*N'est-ce pas?*"

"Bright man," Dark-hair said, and made a jab at the fish on his plate without even looking at it. His eyes were on de Vauban. "You just nosy or you got something in mind?"

"My English is not so good. *Vous parlez français?*"

"Keep to the English. What's your game?"

"Maybe I don't like to see a couple of young boys walk in back there."

"Come off it, you were on us before that."

Sharp boy. "My name is Jean-Pierre de Vauban. You call me Jean."

"I'd rather not call you anything. I'd rather us have our breakfast in peace. Name Muballit mean anything to you?"

It did. It was one nasty bastard of an Assyrian recruiter. Any merc knew. De Vauban reassessed the boy, the very young-looking boy.

But boys were not boys, who were Roman, and centuries old in Hell. Old Dead, *very* old, and not some lost Modern brat. The sweat on him felt colder and colder.

It was the other boy had decived him—the one with the so-naive face.

"Oui. I know Muballit. I fought with *Coeur de Lion." Never mind that I had been dead for ten years.*

The coffee arrived. Thank the good God. It banged down on the table in a large fist (just the fist: the *Oasis* had a surly and overworked sycophant) and spilled all around, and de Vauban flicked the moisture from scalded fingers and took it up and drank. "Damned creature. I met Muballit, oh, in the Rommel affair. Impatient man. You are tied up with him, eh?"

"Never mind our business. Never mind the history. What do you want?"

"You have such American English. It was that which deceived me. Such young faces, such modernisms. Perhaps I am a fool. Surely you *have* employment, perhaps we should talk no further. We have the breakfast, we have the pleasant company, so, well, we need not ask each other what we might not want to answer, *eh?*"

"Who do you work for?" Dark-hair asked.

De Vauban shrugged with deliberate coyness and

smiled, widely. "For those who pay me, *monsieur*, for which one is grateful, *n'est-ce pas?* You work for Mulballit, *eh?* Or perhaps for Jules César." In one half breath. Dark-hair's muscles tensed; and de Vauban never stopped. "—in which case, *messieurs*, I counsel you not to use the Latin, in this place, which perhaps is an act, *eh*, to seem very young and foolish? No? Your pardon, then. Perhaps you have other reasons to—"

Merde!

Assyrians came in the front door. And there was other movement from the back room: de Vauban saw the one and heard the other, and felt his heart thump and thump, so that he was very glad of the little pistol in his shoulder holster—if he could dare draw it.

"—don't look. The Assyrians who have just come in are the same that were in the back room. I think there are others behind. Are they your friends?"

The honest-looking boy *started* to look, and stopped himself. Dark-hair did not flinch. His eyes shadowed under thick lashes, and doubtless his hand beneath the table had found something in his pocket long since. "No," Dark-hair said. "But not my enemies. Maybe they're yours, huh? Fuck you, you drag us into your trouble, man, I'll blow your head off."

The rest of the hangers-on in the room were beginning to move aside. *They* knew trouble. De Vauban thought fast, what to do, whether to do anything except keep his head down. But he was, alas, it was true—a mere himself, *un des âmes perdues*, not for hire since le Petit Corporal had rescued him from the streets, true, but the fortunes of war shifted and likewise the fortunes of kings and emperors rose and fell, and a man must be practical: it would never do for Jean de Vauban to duck his head or fall down and play wounded when men with him were challenged. The story would follow him through Hell, forever and ever, amen.

Non. One must stand up to the trouble. Bad enough

they would say of Jean de Vauban that he was a fool.
That, he could not help.

"Go for the door," de Vauban muttered, before the
trouble was quite on them; and hoped to hell there was
some honor in his tablemates. Three on nine was bad
odds, but it was better than one.

"Who are you working for?" Dark-hair asked.

But there was no time for it.

One of the Hittites came close and leaned on the
back of the other boy's chair. The boy shifted forward,
looking scared.

Young. Yes. Truly. De Vauban's heart hammered in
his chest as he considered Dark-hair, who, he was sure
had a gun, and who had that look about him that wanted
a fight—*sacre*, wanted blood. He had met such men,
whom Hell itself did not teach prudence.

And he hated like hell to have one near him.

"This man bothering you?" the Hittite asked, and
rested his hand right on the boy's shoulder. "No?"

The boy shrugged the hand off, wide-eyed with fright
and offense.

"You come with us," the Hittite said. "That's our
officer back there. He likes the look of you."

The boy froze like a rabbit. Or a boy—appealing to
de Vauban with a frantic look, boy looking to the man
who tried to cue him, one split-second of *Am I doing
what you want? Is he saying what I think he's saying?*

"Sit still," de Vauban said, taking it all on himself,
and shoving back his chair with a gut-sick resignation—
merde, here I go. *Use* the chance, you damned young
fools.

The one is only a boy.

The Hittite backed off, attention now all for the man
who offered him argument. And there was a lot of
movement around the edges of de Vauban's sight, a
creak of boards and edging of noisy chairs.

Dark-hair stood up, reached out sideways quick as a
snake, grabbed the Hittite and hit him, whereupon the

boy grabbed the table and upended it on his way up—de Vauban jumped to save his feet, and everyone in the room moved, men closing from all sides as the boys ran for the door and the damned table was in de Vauban's way.

Men cut them off—and Dark-hair veered suddenly from the door, grabbed the boy and headed for the back.

It was something like an Assyrian had arrived in the daylight of the front door, but the one-handed man beside him was not, and neither was the eye-patched one who came behind them, de Vauban saw that much, as he followed Dark-hair and the boy, diving for the back room and drawing his pistol all at the same time.

But it was Dark-hair who cleared a path, blowing two men right out of his way, leaping over the bodies as they ran for daylight at the door to the alley—already *someone's* escape route.

De Vauban followed, through the alley door, where the sound of close pursuit brought him about to fire— damnable reflex, he thought, finding himself standing rear guard against all comers while the boys ran—

Find them, his orders had said. Nothing about killing them. He did not assume that was what le Petit Corporal wanted. *Non.* He did what he had to do, blasted the Assyrian surge that came out the door at him, spun on his heel and ran for it, the way Dark-hair and the boy were going, down the alley and for the safety of a solid brick corner; but he was not going to make it without slowing up those behind.

He turned and fired again, once, twice, three times, three bodies, and grunted in surprise as a hammer-blow on the shoulder spun him and sent him flying like a rag doll, legs twisted when he landed, his brain rattled from impact on the cobbles, and a whole barrage of fire ricocheting off the brick walls on either side with a hellish racket as Assyrians fell about him.

Merde, where was the damned gun, was it in his

hand? He was lying there like a pig for the slaughter, and he did not know which way the gun had fallen. He rolled onto his side and grimaced and saw it a body-length out of reach, heaving himself along the filthy cobbles to reach it.

A booted foot kicked it out of his reach.

He looked up at the one-handed man whose left hand aimed a gun right for his face as running steps came back.

"*Per viam fugiunt,*" a harsh voice panted. "*Curtius sequitur. Veni!*"

"*Sit fors'an hic de Vauban.*" One-hand said, and de Vauban, staring up the barrel of One-hand's Uzi:

"*Oui.*" Quickly and passionately. "*Oui, je suis de Vauban.*" Silence seemed no choice at all.

And when One-hand lowered the gun and One-eye bent down to help him up, de Vauban found hardly the strength to cooperate. Another tried to lift him from behind. They did not *look* like Romans, this motley, scruffy group with them. He was not sure what he had fallen into—except they were Roman boys who had fled and they were Romans who had him now; and de Vauban had no wish to find out what Romans could do who wanted information he did not even have.

Mon dieu, what *Romans* could do. He remembered, and nearly lost his breakfast then and there.

"Move," someone said in English. "Dammit, we've got to get our wounded out of here before the cops show up. *Careful* with him, dammit! He's one of ours!"

Ah.

He was very, very glad to know that.

Down another alley and out onto the street again, and there were still men pounding after them. It was only the tennies and the speed of youth-scared-spitless that kept them ahead of whatever was behind them, and Brutus was very glad Caesarion was in no mood to stop and trade shots with them. He ran, and Caesarion and he were sometimes one in front and sometimes the other, dodging passersby and once leaping over a man on the sidewalk.

It was *Sargon* back there, it was *Scaevola* and Horatius, and there was a great lump in Brutus' throat had nothing to do with the panic. It was his teachers, that he loved most in all the world, next his father—who had come in there after them; and there had been shots going off and people had been killed. He had no idea who was behind them now. He was afraid it was people from the bar, maybe it was the man called Jean who might have been one of their father's men, who could know?—and the lump in his throat was half fear that his teachers were hurt or killed back there and half fear that some of the shots coming after them had come from legionaries' rifles. He did not know anything any more. He had run off from his father and into a world he did not know, with a brother who was Julius' enemy—and he knew his father had men to think of, the villa to protect— Even a father had to think of the Family first, and had a first duty to the people who depended on him; a son who went against that, had become his father's enemy. *Caesarion* had. Maybe his father thought that both of them had. Maybe Caesarion was so dangerous his father had no choice but stop him, and if a fool of a son he loved was in the way, that was the way it had to be, and Julius would hope to get him back from the Undertaker—

Terrible things were afoot, and sons had to come second to Family.

Had not Julius given him to the American—to get his hands on Caesarion?

And would not his teachers risk a great deal to pull him out of this, even slighting his father's strict and proper orders, if only they could have laid hands on him, if only he could have reached them, but Caesarion had pulled him violently back and he had been so confused at the instant that he had reacted as if Caesarion were the friend and Sargon the enemy, and let Caesarion face him the other way.

Then he had been blind to what was behind him and with enemies coming at them and a door to reach—he had run, that was all, he had let fear take over, just panicked and run, with Caesarion shooting and everyone shooting, and maybe even Sargon and Scaevola firing after them of necessity—he had thought so in that few seconds. He did not want to die and that had been all his thinking.

And now Sargon and Scaevola were probably back there with guns because they had to be, for the Family, and if he stopped they would probably shoot Caesarion— having a clear target.

O gods, gods!

"Come *on!*" Caesarion seized him by the arm and jerked him down a stairway that led down and down under the street.

"*What are you doing?*" he yelled, following faster than he had ever taken stairs in his life, but Caesarion was faster, down and down into this dead-end place where their enemies could hunt them down.

But there was a huge lighted and tiled place, there were passages to either side, echoing with machine-noise and voices, and a kind of many-windowed car parked with a great many people in it, which some were boarding and some were leaving, while other men and women shambling about here with their bags and sleeping on the concrete paid no apparent attention to the strange many-windowed thing.

"*Zeus!*" Caesarion yelled, "we've got a train! Go! Go!"

He followed Caesarion. He was not going to wait for the men who were surely coming down those stairs. Caesarion vaulted a metal rail, he vaulted it just after, and pelted after Caesarion, through the crowd and up the steps into the lighted interior of a train, *pro di immortales*, a thing he had only seen on the television.

There was a dreadful racket of machinery. The car started to move with them, and he followed Caesarion, staggering and catching for balance, until they were safe in this filthy, paint-sprayed vehicle.

There were not so many people in this end of the thing. There were a couple of lumpish men who looked crazy. There were about eight or nine boys their own age, dressed like them, all standing down near the end of the car.

Boys like them, Brutus thought, tee-shirts, tennies, black leather jackets and a lot of dangly colored animal feet hanging from their zipper-pulls—maybe that was the fashion, Brutus thought. He was instantly insecure, seeing he had a *brown* jacket and that Caesarion's black jacket had no such decorations; and he suddenly knew, as he would have known in the streets of Rome, first that it was a gang and second that he did not like the odds.

VII

"YOU LOST HIM?" Klea cried, hands on the corner of the desk. "ZEUS! YOU HAD HIM AND YOU LOST HIM?"

Yelling women reached a pitch that grated right on Julius' nerves. Ordinarily it got temper out of him. But in this case it just hit all the sore spots—like the helplessness of a damned fine army trying to catch two teenaged boys in a metropolis . . . quietly.

"Maps," he said, striding across the room, where aides labored in a sea of charts and city maps. "Where can we intercept? *Answers*, dammit."

"We've had too damn many calls going back and forth," Augustus said. "We're compromising networks we've had for years. We *have* to use couriers."

"Dammit, we have to find them!" Klea cried. "Mithridates will move! They'll be targets! *Zeus*! You've got corpses landing in the Undertaker's office thick as flies, and you worry about *radio* silence!"

They had not, thank the gods, lost one of their own side. Yet.

"Here," an aide said, laying a finger on a map. "Here. Highgate Station. B Team can make it if they don't get off at Torquemada."

"If!"

"It's too fine a neighborhood," Mouse said. "Caesarion—would choose Highgate."

"Damn, damn—*get B Team over there, what are you waiting for!*"

An aide started making the call. Julius wiped his face and felt stubble, blinking dully at the ruddy daylight out the windows. Morning. And there was another order he could give—Armageddon. Preemptive strike on Mithridates' forces, before Mithridates either finished this move, if he had orchestrated it—before Mithridates took advantage of it, if it was all a surprise to him.

But Mithridates had agents *in* the Reassignments Office. Mithridates could send his dead back to the field wholesale.

The villa could only, delicately, carefully, thanks to Dante's considerable talents, play small games with the accesses and tweak the often-glitching computers to the kind of persistent lunacies ordinary in Hell—

—that landed their own men back, one at a time and by unprovable coincidence that probably located a half-dozen traffic victims right back where they had just died, by the same Dante-induced hiccup in the program.

Not a match for Mithridates.

And if the attack should come, from the Cong in the park, from missiles on some traveling launcher, from some suicide squad at the front door—

If the villa should be weakened—

"Mouse," he said. "I've got a job for you."

Muballit sweated and *smelled* the brimstone . . . which accompanied the cops, particularly the tall one in the trenchcoat, who had an aura about him—a sort of a darkness beyond the darkness of the hair and the eyes, so black one both wanted and did not want ever to look at them; if one ever could—because no matter how hard you tried to look at him, he was in shadow, a kind of perpetual corner of the room shadow, that never, ever, got better even in the daylit alley—or one just could not look at him except when shadow was on him—

And Muballit answered the questions: Yes, no, yes, and no, sir, he had absolutely no idea why a dozen armed Romans had come crashing through his property; and no, everyone had run when the shooting started, so there were only the dead, which had gone to the Undertaker and of course he had called the cops as soon as he could.

"Mmmmmnnn," the Fallen Angel said, and consulted with one of his men who had been up and down the alley.

Then he left, just walked to the black sedan at the end of the alley, and left Muballit still smelling the brimstone.

That was Authority. That was from the Exec's office; and Muballit lifted his eyes nervously to the thing which, even here in the alley among other tall buildings, was still all too visible: the Hall of Injustice, which towered up and up and up unthinkably high into the roiling clouds—nearly to Paradise, perhaps.

But not quite. Satan had his own private torments.

So Muballit understood. In point of fact, *that*, which got in the black sedan and drove away, was as close as Muballit ever wanted to come to Administration or the Authority that extended through (rumor whispered) more than one plane of Hell: Asmodeus, no name, no rank, just Asmodeus, because there was only one—but that was enough.

Mithridates put the phone down, leaned his elbows on his desk and clenched his hands in front of his mouth till the pencil snapped. And snapped again.

Asmodeus.

The Pentagram sat in the shadow of Administration—in all senses. And Mithridates, with the map of New Hell's subway system in front of him on the desk, stared at lines and colors that seemed to writhe and move with the shifting of forces all along battle lines drawn through New Hell—his forces, the Romans, all clandestine, all quiet—

—because none of them could gain by attracting the Devil's notice.

But by Ahriman, if the Devil's notice was coming down on the affair, he certainly had his choice who should be standing in the strike zone.

He punched the intercom button. "Message," he said, "to Kadashman-enlil."

The crazy people just sat there, except one, who made a tent of his newspaper and put it over his head. The noise of the moving train overrode almost all sounds people might make, and the car rocked and rattled alarmingly as it picked up speed.

And the boys at the end just stood there staring a long while, till one sauntered closer and the rest of the gang drifted along behind him.

"Hey," the leader hailed them, "where's your tickets, huh?"

"Free ride, man," Caesarion said. "We don't pay."

It was a challenge, involving money and the right to be here, *mostly* the right to be here, and the gang was trying to decide what it was dealing with, whether it returned the right signals. Brutus followed that with no difficulty at all. He felt the flutter of nerves, he was not fool enough immediately to go for the knife in his pocket: Caesarion knew his way and he was willing to let Caesarion do the talking; but, *pro di*, much as he had rather have been in no trouble at all, it was a profound relief to meet one he knew what to do about.

"This is *Knight's* turf."

"Yeah, well," Caesarion said, "that's nice. We're just riding the train, man, don't want any hassle."

There was a little silence. Then, from out of the ranks of the gang, and loudly: "Ask him if that's his sister there."

That was twice in one day. Brutus drew in his breath and sighted on the fool with the mouth, but: *Temper's a weapon.* Scaevola would say. *Which side are you going to let hold the hilt?*

The gang leader looked momentarily indecisive, upstaged by one of his gang and set off his balance, between fear of his own gang and maybe a better measure of the opposition than the rest had taken. And, gods, he had just lost his timing and his control of the situation: Brutus saw it coming, saw the panic follow that hesitation—lose the gang or risk the fight: this was a leader in trouble.

Brutus moved his hand for his pocket while the leader was thinking what to do, and Caesarion was putting an arm in front of him, all in the strangest slow motion, as if he was thinking faster or events were going slower than real life.

He still had the knife in his hand, and the gangleader was backing up his lads the same way—leader on leader, Caesarion wanted it: fair fight, gang honor.

Caesarion had a knife of his own out, so did the gangleader, and they went into fighters' stance in the aisle, while the crazy people scuttled, but the man with the newspaper just sat there.

Pass one, pass two: Caesarion got them some room. *"Door!"* Caesarion yelled at him. "Get out of here!"

Brutus drew his knife, instinctively wanting forward; but it was a matter of honor, it was one on one, and his team-leader wanted the door open—then, dammit, move it, he heard Sargon yelling at him: he backed up and got the door open, in that place where the plates of the car met and jostled back and forth and the noise was deafening: two doors to hold, and of a sudden he had the strategy in his head—that Caesarion thought him helpless, that Caesarion was going to use the narrow passage, and they were going to make fast retreat.

Horatii and Curiatii. The string-them-out tactic, older than Rome itself.

He held the doors; and Caesarion dived backward—the gangleader suddenly fallen back into the arms of his gang, a hellish lot of shouting and a sudden rush forward as Brutus let the door shut and held it as soon as Caesarion was clear.

Other passengers were scrambling up and yelling; and Caesarion had not expected him to stop: he turned back and held the door too, while the gang rattled and battered at it.

And a bullet smashed right through the glass between their faces. A second followed.

"*Get down!*" Caesarion screamed, still holding, while passengers dived behind seats and some of them crawled down the aisle to get to the far door—Brutus jumped back behind the cover of the wall as another shot blasted through, and Caesarion sent one back. "*Get out of here!*"

"*No!*" Brutus yelled and flicked the knife out. "Let them through!"

Caesarion let go the door and sprang back as the rush came in—blasted one of them and another, as the black-leather mass bore down on him and he backed up fast, still firing; and Brutus came in at their flank, fast and hard, one down and screaming and another in short order, which left two on their feet, one of whom bowled past Caesarion, the other of which met the knife in Caesarion's left hand. Caesarion turned and fired; and that one sprawled, flat in the aisle.

The last few passengers screamed and tried to be invisible, as Brutus stood up, shaking, his feet enveloped in a black-clad pile of bodies— *Never stand on a dead man*, he could hear Scaevola say, who had learned that the hard way. *Sometimes they aren't.*

And he staggered his way out of there, trampling them, on legs that felt like water, and joined his sweating, hard-breathing brother, who looked at him as if he had just met him for the first time.

"Not bad, brother."

Brutus gasped for air and managed to nod, satisfied, though his knees were water and his hands were shaking and his right hand, O gods, was sticky with blood and his feet were slipping in it if he did not hold onto the back of the seat.

The bodies suddenly glowed and vanished, the way he had seen dead people do here: going to the Undertaker, Klea had told him. That left two moaning on the floor, but they were out of it, and *that* left them in sole possession of the battlefield as the whole machine squealed terribly and rocked to a stop.

"Torquemada," Caesarion said, as the signs passed the window. "Damn, this is no place to get out; wipe the blood off—under your jacket, dammit, here—" He pulled out a bandanna and wiped his face and hands and the spatters on his jacket, while the outside doors opened and the shadowy people out there on the platform began moving toward them—he gave the bandanna to Brutus; and Brutus wiped furiously, face and hands and jacket-leather and knife.

But thank the gods no one got into their car or the one back there. Several looked up at the windows, and shied off and went back; and a moment later the whole machine began to move again.

"Highgate's next," Caesarion said, and walked on up the aisle where a puddle of blood was all that was left of the gang member he had shot. And suddenly he whirled and aimed his gun between the seats.

It was, Brutus saw, a gray-haired little man, a passenger, who held up his hands in front of his face as if that could stop a bullet and sat there on the floor with his teeth chattering. "Don't!" Brutus exclaimed, and Caesarion turned the gun aside.

"Don't, don't," the old man echoed—but not really an old man, Brutus thought; just a kind of a gray man, a man no one would ever see, a man no one ever *wanted* to see, as if the eyes could not keep tracked on him;

and he got up now, all dithery, and wanted out, but Caesarion aimed the gun again.

"Just stay put, man. We don't need any alarms. Just stay put and you're fine."

"F-F-F-Fine," the gray man said, nodding furiously. He was in 20th-century dress, a gray business coat, a rumpled white shirt, an egg-stained dark tie. He had a newspaper, a briefcase—he looked like some clerical worker, until you looked in his eyes and saw the gray there too, and the kind of desperate need that made a body earnestly want not to notice him. "I m-m-missed the station."

"That's all right," Caesarion said. "You can catch it next time round. We're getting off at the next stop. Just stay put."

"C-C-Catch it next time. Yes. Yes." The gray man bobbed his head up and down, clinging to the seat back with Caesarion's gun on him. And then the gray in his eyes got grayer and paler and more desperate. "You're going to get *off*. *I* want off. *Get me out of here!*"

"Mister, you just stay out of our way. *Hear?*"

A fervent nod. An enthusiastic nod, staring at the gun muzzle. The train went through a lighted spot and into the dark again, passing black figures on the platform.

And someone came near the front door and went away again, as if what that someone had seen through the door window convinced him he did not want to come in here.

"Just sit down," Caesarion told the gray man. "Sit! Read your paper! Hear?"

"I *r-r-read* the paper," the gray man said. "I *r-r-read* the damn paper." Tears welled up. "I g-got on this train in Boston. I t-t-try to get off—I keep trying to get off—I don't care what stop, anymore. I don't think this is Boston anyway."

"He's crazy," Brutus whispered, tugging at Caesarion's sleeve. "Let him alone, he's just a crazy old man—"

The brakes squealed hard, an iron-on-iron sound, and the floor went out from under all of them. Brutus grabbed for a seat as he went flying and ended up tangled with Caesarion at the door, bruised and shaken.

"*Damn!*" Caesarion yelled, fighting to get up, and Brutus struggled one way and the other missing his brother's arms and legs as he and Caesarion staggered upright. "We're stopped," Caesarion said. "We're stopped!"

It was all dark outside the windows. They were not, Brutus thought, stopped where they were supposed to.

The gray man's head rose above the seats, just about to the nose. His hair all stood on end and his gray eyes were hell itself. "It's not supposed to do this," he said in the immemorial way of people in disasters.

Caesarion leaned against the wall, slid down into a seat and took an ammunition clip from his pocket, patiently loaded it, in the echoey silences, while people shouted some few cars up, while the wounded gang members at the back of the car moaned and pleaded for help. "Get down," he said then, and slid down to the floor.

So did Brutus. It came to him that if anyone was outside they were in here with the lights on, and there were all those windows.

"Could they have stopped the train?" Brutus asked.

"Our *father* can damn well do anything," Caesarion said bitterly.

"Are you sure it's him?" Brutus asked. There was a lot riding on that answer. He shivered when he asked it, hoped for truth, and maybe Caesarion knew. His brother looked him straight in the face and hesitated before his mouth got its accustomed scowl.

"No," Caesarion admitted, "I don't know. It could be a breakdown, body on the tracks, a wreck up ahead— It happens. But we can't take that for granted. Not with Julius. Hell." He slammed his fist onto his knee in front of him. "Bloody hell!"

"Where are we *trying* to go?"

Caesarion was silent a moment, in which things seemed to have gotten quieter up ahead. "I have friends."

"Who?"

"Our father set you to ask that?"

Brutus flinched and stared at him wide-eyed, remembering Caesarion had the gun.

"With the Dissidents," Caesarion said finally, answering his question.

"Julius s-s-says—" Brutus hesitated figuring any objection was likely to provoke another outburst from his Egyptian brother; but he was more scared of the uncertainties around them—and the chance that those were friends who had stopped the train, and Caesarion had the gun ready for anyone who came in range. "Julius says the Dissidents' leader doesn't know what he's doing—that he can't w-w-win—"

"We're fighting for something better," Caesarion said between his teeth. "Our old man—he just sits there playing fox and hounds with Administration, century after century. He never *gets* anywhere— *Never!* Just staying alive. Just playing the game. And trying to stop the Movement! The only thing that ever *will* make any difference in Hell, is to turn it over, overthrow the whole damn Administration—put the People in charge!"

Brutus just stared at him with his mouth open a moment. "You mean like, overthrow Satan?" And in the absence of an answer, just the set of Caesarion's face that meant just that, and with a chill down his back: "He's pretty tough, isn't he—I mean, he's not just like a king—he's—"

"A damned lousy tyrant who doesn't *care* what happens. Just plays games, plays off one power against the other, with the most incredible, the most unbelievable damn nest of self-seeking administrators—" Caesarion waved a hand about them, at the whole situation. "Damn computers foul up every time you turn around, probably a damn computer got this train all fouled up—poor sod

falls onto the tracks, damn computer's going to screw
up his records and drop him who knows where? Water
system's fouled up, the damn computers can't find the
bills, the streets are gone to hell because nobody's got a
work order, people living ten to a room because the
assignments computer can't remember it just put nine
other poor sods in the same apartment— It puts *Antonius*
back with Tiberius every damn time he dies and he
hates it, he *hates* Tiberius—even Julius can't fix that
glitch-up. And what happens to the People? I'm telling
you, there's too many damn bureaucrats around here
just sitting on their ass, don't give a damn about *solving*
anybody's problem, they just want their perks. And
until we have power to the People, it won't get fixed!
That's what we fight for."

"You sound like Julius."

"Fuck off!" Caesarion's eyes went wide and for a
second Brutus thought Caesarion would hit him in the
face. "Julius *talks* that game. He doesn't do a damn
thing."

"How would you know? *You're* not there."

"You damn little fool."

"I know what I've s-s—" Oh, *damn*! Try to say
anything really important and the stutter was back. He
had not stammered when people were shooting at them.
And now he choked up when he was trying most to
make sense. "They're g-g-*good people, dammit!*"

"They're living on the backs of the whole Empire,
are you blind?"

"Wh-wh-where's—y-y-ours?"

He had not meant to hit a sore spot. He had honestly
wanted to know where the Egyptians were and if they
were helping Caesarion. Perhaps Caesarion sensed that;
perhaps that was all that kept Caesarion from hitting
him.

"I m-m-mean, where do the E-E-gyp-tians—live? Why
do you l-live with T-Tiber—"

"Because the fucking computer dropped me into the

West!" Caesarion cried. "Because when I try to straighten it out down at Administration that's what they tell me I am! I'm registered *Roman*, dammit! Under *Augustus'* thumb. *And* Julius'. And my mother *lives* with them!"

He was not so old as Caesarion. Not by centuries and centuries. *Never gets any older*, Julius had said of Caesarion. And for all he was seventeen, he knew pain when he heard it.

And shut up and stared at the dirty floor between his feet.

Which Caesarion seemed to take with some gratitude. After a moment of silence: "They got us both screwed up," he said. "Augustus killed me. He ever mention that?"

"No," Brutus said. And plunged in again, chipping away at the matter. "You know him? I mean—did you know him when he was alive?"

"If I'd *known* him, I wouldn't have taken his safe-conduct."

"He died old. Older than Julius. I think he changed a lot. Klea thinks so."

"My mother—my dear mother—wants her comforts, that's what."

"Augustus—really didn't like me at first. But he—I don't know, he's just—like he's all for the villa, that's all, and he didn't trust me at all and he was afraid I was going to make trouble. But I didn't, and then he—just sort of warmed up, in his own way."

"*Sure* he did. That's what I thought. Before he had me assassinated."

"Julius says—he just sort of covered up what a soldier did."

"Oh, yeah. Yeah, *sure*. It was his letter, older brother. It was his letter got me to that meeting. I figured it was arrest. I figured I was going to be one of those poor sods like that Aeduan king they sort of invited in and kept. That was all right. I'd have been alive. My tutor would have been. Figured I could trust Octavianus that

far, and politic my way out of it later— Ha! *Damn* him.
He knew. He knew I'd make him trouble."

"But maybe he didn't plan it."

Caesarion looked daggers at him. "You got a dumb
habit, brother. A real dumb habit. You make excuses
for your enemies that they don't even bother to make
for themselves. *I'll* tell you Augustus would have cut
your throat. Somebody in that house stopped him. Or
all of them did."

"My father. Our father."

Caesarion's mouth made a nervous, hard line, as if
there was something he was keeping behind his teeth
with the greatest difficulty. There was panic in his eyes,
that darted desperately over his. "You damn—*fool*," he
said at last. "You—"

Someone opened the exit of the car next to them,
more than one someone, coming across the intervening
plates; and Caesarion scrambled for his feet as the gray
man scuttled for better cover at the other end of the car
and Brutus clawed his way up with his heart thumping,
knife in hand.

"Come on!" Caesarion yelled, running for the back of
the car, and Brutus ran all-out after him, ricochetting
off seat edges and colliding with the gray man, who
tried every which way to avoid him and who tangled
with him and went down in the aisle.

"You!" someone yelled, and Brutus looked back at a
man in a mechanic's uniform, the while he desperately
disengaged the gray man's hands from his coat and tried
to get past him after Caesarion. "Hey, you! Wait!"

He had no such intention. He broke free, trod on the
gray man and ran, through into the space between the
cars, where he overtook Caesarion at the door and saw
through the window that the man in the green uniform
had friends back there, storming toward them down the
aisle. "They look like maintenance men!" he yelled, hoping
that made a difference.

"The hell!" Caesarion yelled back, and grabbed him

by the arm as they headed through the last doors, with the maintenance men in hot pursuit.

In the last car, then, and nowhere left to go—except Caesarion waved him to keep going, and gestured at the window.

No questions then. Brutus dived for it and managed to get out it feet first and drop into the dark, a fall that sent his heart into his throat; but he hit gravelly ground and lost his balance as he heard shots over his head and saw Caesarion coming out the lighted window, ready to drop right in the middle of him.

He rolled out of the way and scrambled to his feet to steady Caesarion.

"Let me go!" the gray man was yelling, trying to follow them out a window, but someone had him, pulling him backward. "Let me go! I don't care where it is! I want off!"

"Run!" Caesarion yelled, grabbing his arm and pulling him about; and they pelted down the tracks in the diminishing light of the stopped train. "Don't touch the rails, and run!"

"What—" he panted between gasps "if—a t-t-t—train comes?" There were walls close on their left. They were running into a black near absolute. And of a sudden the dark behind them erupted in gunfire.

He looked around as he ran, jogging awkwardly, seeing the blaze of searchlights and the smaller flash of gunfire.

"Someone's s-shooting," he yelled, and stumbled and recovered himself, because Caesarion was not stopping: Caesarion was going to run the whole way back to the last stop, and they could get out there— He had sudden hope that Caesarion was going to get them out of this.

But it might have been one of their father's men, back there. It might have been one of the soldiers he knew. People were being killed, and *killed* hurt, he knew that it did: he remembered Scaevola, and how Scaevola had suffered in his death, and how it was a miracle Dantillus had snatched him back to them by the computers—risking arrest: he understood that, from bits that had fallen to his ears.

What ought I to do? he wondered; and imagined himself simply hitting Caesarion from behind when they got where they were going, and tying him up and getting to a pay phone.

That their father would not listen to him then—he could not imagine that. Julius would talk to him, would talk to Caesarion, everything would be straightened out—he *knew* that it would; Caesarion would forgive him; everything would be all right then—

Light flashed into their faces, blinding bright. "*Hold it!*" a voice yelled at them, and Brutus skidded to a stop, brought up against Caesarion, the two of them pinned there in the light, in front of silhouetted figures that blurred and ran in his watering vision.

"Back!" Caesarion yelled, and jerked him around and they ran that way, back toward the train, back toward the distant lights where fire was still popping and echoing.

More lights burst into their faces. They were bracketed between. "*Halt!*" a second voice yelled; and he grabbed Caesarion's arm as Caesarion had grabbed his, the two of them pinned blind in the lights before and behind, as dark figures closed in on them.

"What do we do?" he asked; but this time he did not reckon Caesarion had an answer left.

Out of bed in the middle of the night and into a taxi— *Roman*-provided, *bien sur*, one need have no fear of that: so the instructions which, some time ago, had given Napoleon the name *Felix* had assured him. The taxi driver would have a shamrock sticker on the windshield and a rabbit's foot hanging from the mirror— *Otherwise*, Horatius had said with Roman equanimity, *shoot him and run*.

The taxi driver had had both. The taxi driver had driven him to an obscure warehouse in downtown New

Hell, and delivered him to the custody of two ruffians who looked as if they would cut throats for a *sou*.

But so did a lot of Horatius' finest.

Reliable fellows. Part of the Family.

And no bribe, no pleas, no logic could sway them—against the Patron's orders.

One felt quite safe—if one were *inside* their protection.

There was a phone—a safe line, one of them assured him: Lucius, the one who did all the talking . . . just Lucius, no other name. It was understood that Napoleon had resources: he must use them, and get in touch with his chain of intelligence, and find certain two young boys—

One did not argue with such men, or such seriousness, or with the pictures they laid on the table, and which they intended Napoleon pass along to his own contacts: the taxi driver would run courier via a certain passenger who could not be traced, to bring identical pictures to the man who would send them to appropriate people in Napoleon's chain of command—quickly, they said. And named the district.

Such fine young men had stared up at him from the tabletop—candids, both shots, of teenaged boys. Napoleon had had a moment's reluctance, a moment's dreadful suspicion of terrible things intended—dynastic murders, or some dire doings, escapees from Tiberius' villa. But there was a familiar cast to the young features that cried out Roman, and aristocrat, and one of them—*one* of them jarred at his memory. Hell was so long, and one saw so many faces.

"Who are they?" he had asked.

"Augustus wants them found," Lucius had repeated, as if he would repeat that till the last judgement. "Before morning."

Felix, the man had said.

Covert action of the highest importance. This was not a small matter. He had been given a command post. He might, at his discretion, summon whatever contacts he

wished. *Felix*—meant that Augustus was mobilizing.
The whole Roman West was on maximum alert.

And there were these two young faces staring up at
him from the bare formica table, jarring his sense of
recognition and telling him nothing at all. Important—ah,
oui, important enough to risk war with the East.

Find them. Mon dieu.

One tried, that was all. Napoleon had made one
discreet phone call with a handful of codewords, set up
the drop, and sat there and sweated through the hours,
thinking of Marie, reassuring himelf that Roman security
was watching her, that by now Wellington had been
alerted to trouble, that his peaceful suburban neighborhood was safe as ever, the milkman making his rounds,
Attila's kids drawing disgusting things on the driveways—
such things assumed an importance outweighing the
affairs of kings.

Until a motorcycle pulled up outside, and the guards
took a careful look before they opened the side door to
the warehouse and let the man in, cycle and all.

Napoleon stood away from the barrels which had
been his temporary hiding, and lowered the Uzi pistol
he had, himself, liberated from Roman supply. The
visitor, a silhouette in shadows, got off the big black
Suzuki, and lifted off the visored helmet.

Flash of fire and golden eagles. Legion-shrine.

Le Souris.

Mouse.

Napoleon drew a slow breath and walked forward. It
was bad, then, it was very bad.

"*M'sieur le souris?*"

"Your operative found them," Mouse said, in Mouse's
Roman way, sans preface. "They escaped. We have
damage. It is widening."

"And my man—"

"De Vauban is still in the field, with our people. His
knowledge of the district is valuable—"

Mon dieu, usurp one of mine and appropriate him,

*will you? I have spent a good man on your behalf, and
you have compromised him—*

"—but it is not enough."

"We are neutrals!"

Mouse pulled off a ring and held it out to him.

"Non!" Napoleon exclaimed.

Mouse held out the ring. And held it. "You know,"
Mouse said, his lean face half in shadow, "whose this is.
And what you owe him."

"*I* owe him. *I*, personally. Not my friends."

"Perhaps that is the way modern men reckon. *We* did
not. We do not weigh things in market scales, *imperator*,
nor haggle about matters of honor."

"Damn you!"

Still the outheld hand.

Napoleon reached and opened his, and the signet of
clan *Iulia* fell into it, heavy gold, authority of the head
of house. Not Augustus, as title formally lay. It was
Julius who wore that ring. And Napoleon knew the
meaning of it, and the true state of affairs within the
villa, and which ring of the two, so very alike, had
absolute precedence. He turned the face to the light,
the intaglio of Venus Genetrix, identical to the other;
but this one had a dove in the upheld hand.

"We are near to war," Mouse said. "And there will
be no neutrals. Caesar needs access to the East, by
uncompromised agencies. He wants Lawrence."

"*Dieu*. He *believes* that defection."

"You do not?"

"I distrust any man who changes coats, *monsieur,*
especially once the moves are on the board. How much
must we commit to this man?"

Mouse lifted an eyebrow, as if Mouse were not that
far from his own thinking. "More than any of us wish, if
we have to call on him. There are large-scale troop
movements, about New Hell's perimeters. A mission
against the Dissidents—of course, which happens to
take them past the lake shore. *We* are under alert—a

mere exercise, of course. We have picked up movement in the Park. Mostly we are worried about the lake shore. You understand. We want Lawrence. Quickly."

"Hands against the wall," the order had been, there in the dark, between armed men and the floodlights—in English.

"*Qui estis?*" Brutus had shouted at the faceless men, in Latin, hoping for a Latin answer.

But: "Up against the wall and spread 'em," the answer had come back. "Police."

"Oh, shit," Caesarion had murmured.

"What d-do we *d-d-do*?" Brutus had asked.

"Do what they tell you," Caesarion had said then, and dropped his gun and put his hands on the wall.

So Brutus had, and shadowy men came up still shining the lights on them, and kicked his legs back and apart and searched him in a detail that made him flinch and wish he knew what to do about this. But they were the law. What was there left to appeal to?

They would surely take them to the police station: he had seen it all on the television. They had the right to one phone call, did they not?

He would call home then. Julius would think of something. Julius would not abandon him, and for his sake, would not abandon Caesarion. Julius could call friends downtown and get everything fixed—

But men had been killed back at the *Oasis*. They had killed people on the train. It had seemed the only thing to do at the time. It had seemed it was the way things were in this terrible part of town—that people tried to kill you and you killed them first, and no one cared, like on some battlefield.

Except there *was* a law and it had shined the light on them and shoved them up against a wall and, gods, dragged their hands back and put chains on them, like the most dangerous of criminals.

If they were in Rome, the watch would take them

home to Julius and ask clan *Iulia* to stand good for them; and to defend them before the magistrates; and, if it looked as if matters were going against them, clan *Iulia* would get them out of Rome or out of Italy or out of Roman territories, depending on what they had done; and see them settled in safety till matters blew over.

Except in the terrible days of the Civil War, there were too many cases where the accused had accidents and where people just disappeared; and police frightened him. What he had seen on television frightened him. He did not like it when they did not go back to the train to confront witnesses and answer questions, but down the gravelly side of the tracks in the light of the lamps; and to a metal door which opened on a grim concrete stairs, and to a long dingy hallway. He liked it less and less. It seemed the kind of place in which terrible things could happen; and he looked at his half-brother and wished he could understand what was going to happen to them.

Up more stairs, up and up; and the police held his arms so tightly it hurt, and shoved him against a wall while they unlocked a door.

Brutus flinched and turned his eyes from the light inside, and blinked as they hauled him roughly through the doorway, into an untidy office with wooden furniture—

And men in khaki who waited for them.

"Shit!" Caesarion cried. "These aren't any cops!" He gave a great heave to free himself, and Brutus jerked at the hands that held him, panicked, not knowing what Caesarion hoped to do, both of them with their hands chained.

Nothing. The trench-coated men who had brought them upstairs flung Caersarion face-forward against a wall, turned him about and hit him in the face, while Brutus tried with all his might to reach the man who was hitting his brother. *"Nolite!"* he shouted. *"Desiste!"*

It was one of the men in khaki who stopped it, just

held up a hand, and they let Caesarion slide down as far as he wanted to—which was not to the floor: Caesarion braced his feet and stayed upright, bleeding from the mouth and the nose.

Brutus caght his breath, staring at the men in khaki, looking in outrage for their legion insignia, whether they could possibly be men of the 10th or whether they might be some other legion, maybe—gods help them— Tiberius' men.

But there was no legion number. The insignia were not anything he had ever seen, and the gold pins that ought to be a Roman numeral were simple discs.

They spoke a language Brutus could not identify. And whatever they had said, the men in trenchcoats began to drag them toward another door.

Brutus looked back wildly, afraid that they might be separated; but they were bringing Caesarion too, hauling him along dazed as he was— Outside, then, under a moment of open sky, with two military staff cars waiting outside the cinder-block that was the office they had climbed into.

Caesarion balked, and Brutus planted his feet to resist the men who were hauling him along by both arms.

But then one of them hit Caesarion hard enough to stun him, and Brutus let go his brace and let them haul him along: *No way*, he thought. *No way to do a thing. Wait—wait and play dumb. Dammit. Caesarion, don't let them beat you up— What chance have we got if you can't walk? Dammit, dammit, dammit—*

Caesarion was still fighting them, if weakly. And, predictably, they bent him back against the car and hit him; and hit him again when he tried to get a knee up.

"Stop it!" Brutus yelled at them, because their officer didn't. And maybe he had learned what Julius called the Right Voice, because they stopped and looked at him—too intently. He had not wanted that.

"What is *this*?" one asked.

Two men shoved Caesarion into the car, flat, onto

the floor. The ones holding Brutus pushed him in after, down on top of Caesarion; and the men got in after, trampling them, all but kneeling on them.

"I'm sorry," Brutus said, partly because he could not help how he was lying, Caesarion giving helpless and miserable heaves to get his breath, and getting nowhere, with his hands cuffed and Brutus' weight on him; and partly because he truly wished he could have thought of something to get them out of this.

But, *pro di*, for all Caesarion knew a lot about the city, he had *not* reckoned on them being smart enough and powerful enough to stop the train.

Brutus did not know much, and knew that he did not know, except what he had seen on the television. But it seemed to him that it was no easy matter to stop subway trains—that it took moving a lot of men very fast; and that meant a large organization—which could be their father. He earnestly hoped so.

But it could also be their father's enemies.

The Cong, he thought in a wash of terror. And: *Rameses. The Pentagram.*

Ra. Hatshepsut's Ra. The god of the Sun.

Remembering the plain gold disc that was the emblem of the officers.

Mithridates.

He had fallen off a horse on the Baiae road. He had somehow jumped across all the years between, while people invented great machines and electric lights and flew to the moon, and landed in a hallway in Augustus' house in Hell—*that* was the way he thought of that time lapse.

Surely he had not *been* anywhere during those lost years. Surely those years were just lost, never lived; and he had never *been* anywhere, and not *been* in Mithridates' hands, in some prison somewhere—his memory had no trace of such a thing, no trace of Mithridates, except as he had known of him when he was alive, as a terrible, terrible man—

But he did not remember why he had left the villa
and jumped out of an airplane either, or why Welch
had tied him to a tree, or what someone had said to him
which had left him with nightmares, people talking to
him and their mouths moving and no sound coming out
and the lips unreadable, impossible to look at when he
tried, as if somewhere in that nightmarish journey (it
was real, surely it was real, and he had not dreamed it)
someone had said a *nefas* thing to him, a thing forbidden
by the laws of this place, which even his sleeping mind
could not recall—

There were holes in his memory even since coming to
the villa. There were dreadful holes. He remembered
the gathering he had first walked into, and how people
had said strange things. . . .

"*You,*" *Augustus had said.* "*What's your name?*"

He: B-B-B-Brutus, if it please you, sir.

*Augustus: Di immortales. Which? Lucius, Decimus,
or the Assassin?*

Himself: A-A-A-Assass-in?

*Niccolo Machiavelli, from the side: S-S-S-sounds like
the First Lucius.*

*Augustus, again, sternly: Shut up, dammit, Niccolo.
Which are you, boy? Uterque?*

*Himself, more and more confused: M-Marcus. Marcus
Junius Brutus.*

Kleopatra, from the side: Ye gods.

*(Sargon rising with his hand on his sword. Everyone
frozen.)*

*Himself, desperately: What's wrong? What's the matter?
Which are you, which are you, which are you . . .?*

Sargon, hand on his sword. . . .

*But I'm not of their time. How should Sargon know
me? Did Julius miss me that much, that he explained me
to them?*

Who was the kinsman of mine who killed someone?

*—Kinsman of Junius Brutus, dammit, I'm not his
son, I'm Julian: the blood in my veins is Julian. . . .*

"So," Julius had said, the hour of their meeting. "Honest with you. You stand here less than twenty. And you don't remember anything. That might be a benefit."

Himself: Why? What happened? Where did I—?

Julius:—die? That's a potent question. What if I asked you not to ask yet?

Himself: I—

Julius: Yes. Hell *of a question to hold in check, isn't it? You can die in Hell too, you die down here and you can come back right away or a long time later. When do you think you came?"*

Himself: Did I fall? Did my horse throw me?

Julius: You weren't to ask, remember. For a while.

Himself: It was something awful! It was something—

Julius: Can't let go of it, can you? Whatever time it's been, you're not the boy who was riding down that road outside Baiae, now, are you? Death is a profoundly lonely experience. It changes everyone. But— You don't have that, do you?"

Himself: I don't! *I* haven't, *I* can't *remember—*

Julius (surprised): Without that perspective. Gods. Poor boy, you can't well understand, can you? You just—

Himself: —blinked. I blinked and I was here, on that table, with that nasty old man, that—creature. I—

Julius: Can you trust me?

Himself: (silence)

Julius: Can you trust me? I've told you that the dead change. You don't know what direction I've changed. . . . You're late. I've been waiting for you—thousands of years. Now do you see what you're into? You're a lost soul, son. One of the long wanderers, maybe. This is Hell. *Not Elysium. Not Tartarus. Just—Hell. And it rarely makes any sense. Do you trust me yet?*

The car bounced over something, maybe a curb, and turned right and sped off over cobbles. Caesarion groaned and tried to shift his legs. Brutus tensed muscles and tried to give him some relief, but a man's heel shoved his head down, hard.

Gods, gods, what are we going to?

I'm Mithridates' creature—something he gave my father.

Maybe they're taking me back to him—before they're supposed to. I'm going to meet this man who killed fifty thousand of us, even little babies, and maybe he'll tell me why he did all this and what he has to do with Caesarion and what he wanted with me.

O gods, I don't want to know.

VIII

The elevator let out on the fortieth floor of the Savronarola Building, a clean, 19th-century sort of place, travertine and Italian marble, Victorian British aping the Renaissance aping the Romans aping the Greeks kind of place, meaning rich, and conservative, and cloyingly baroque, right down to the cupid-faces smirking fatly out of the cornices; and Niccolo Machiavelli would have been right at home here in his usual scholar's black, doublet and all—no difference between the bad taste of his age and the bad taste of a later one—but he had no desire to be seen here, and came in gray pinstripe, with briefcase and umbrella, no matter that rain in Hell was rare; gloves and, *dio*, a ridiculous top-hat.

He looked, in short, like someone who *belonged* in this building, in this small district, like the horde of starch-shirted fools who came and went hereabouts, preferring collars that could slice a throat and underwear de Sade could love—it was the collars and the corsets, he surmised, which drove most Victorian British to Roaring 20's or to 1960's Beat, and thinned out the population of Victoria's stuffy court.

But there were some sharp minds in the lot; and one of them was not even British, and did not observe the

Forms. And the Victorians tolerated him and Victoria
had him at court.

Which indicated that money, even in Hell, did talk
. . . and that a man who managed to create and hold a
financial empire in an environment where flux was the
rule, was either mad as the proverbial march hare and
luckier than a five-time lottery winner—or had, ummm-
nnnn, inside information.

Dangerous man.

Hadrian said he was trustworthy; and swore it
repeatedly. "No matter what advantages he has, they are
precarious under the present situation. He can*not* support
the East. He has enemies who are their friends. I
would rely on this man for my life."

"You have died repeatedly," Machiavelli had said
coldly. "Forgive me, majesty, if I reserve some doubt
about this gentleman. He is Byzantine. That is *not*
quite Roman."

"Nor a friend of the East. He is not in their camp."

"Majesty, he is *Byzantine*. He will be everywhere."

But this was, Hadrian swore yet again, an absolutely
reliable man—who had profited very greatly in his prior
administrations, an Easterner with a pipeline to information in the West; and who stood to lose heavily if the
East came to power with the help of his rivals.

Hence the ludicrous costume—foppish, Machiavelli
admitted to himelf, would have been bearable, but *not*
the hat, which he had gratefully whisked under his arm
as soon as it was proper to have done so.

Hence his stroll past the huge burl doors where an
elaborately incised brass plaque proclaimed the offices
of Leonidas Agathodemas, Broker.

He deposited his card with the secretary, a young
man with a bright, thinking look to the eyes, who took
one look at it, and at him, and immediately betook
himself to the inner sanctum, as if the Devil himself
had come calling.

Some did, Niccolo reflected wryly, confuse the two.

*   *   *

The Ferrari purred imto the villa's garage and a door opened and slammed. Hatshepsut was back; and Kleopatra flew down the gray garage stairs, past the legionaries on duty there, a clatter of heels and a precarious descent on the slick concrete into the meticulously ordered and unusually equipped mechanics shop, as Hatshepsut came up the steps from the garage entrance.

"Nothing," Klea read the look on Hatshepsut's face. The pharaoh of a more orthodox Egypt looked both weary and uncomfortable, at this meeting in the backstairs of the villa . . . her usually meticulous bob windblown, the electronics not visible, but probably there, up the collar of her quiet and very modest green jumpsuit. Hatshepsut had been out most of the night. And surely meeting Klea and dashing another hope was hard, between friends; meeting Klea whom she had helped drug and betray—was harder.

"I'm sorry, Klea. I'm truly sorry."

Klea just stood there and looked at her, and Hatshepsut looked embarrassed even to have come back for rest. "I'm going out again," Hatshepsut said, hoarse as she was, and with eyes shadowed by want of rest. "I just thought I'd check in, wash, pick up some equipment, and see if there was any news."

"They've lost them *again*," Klea cried. Composure cracked. "Dammit, they can't hang onto them! They got there too late— "

"I heard," Hatshepsut said. "No word on where they've taken them?"

"We don't know whether *anyone*'s taken them! We know we've exchanged shots twice with Mithridates' men! We know we've left corpses all over town! We know my son's out there in the middle of it and no one's able to *do* anything. Someone's got to *do* something, dammit! You're all the hope I've got. Get me out of here!"

Hatshepsut stood still another long moment, only

looking at her. Perhaps it occurred to her that what Kleopatra wanted was counter to what Augustus and Julius wanted. But they were old friends, often enough under fire together—or in it; and Klea stared at her until Hatshepsut must know that the wrong answer now would never be forgotten.

"What in hell do you think we can do," Hatshepsut asked, "where the whole damn army's helpless?"

"I'm his mother," Klea said, ultimate logic, and Hatshepsut looked as if she had run into an unexpected wall—looked tired, and desperate. "*Find* him, that's all I want, take me where I can talk to him!"

Hatshepsut listened; and suddenly acquired a little cold light in her eye that meant Hatshepsut's brain was working.

And Klea, who had run out of one hope after the other, suddenly found reason for a new one: her partner-in-plots was back; her partner was thinking; her partner had that look that meant direct action, and that was the best news she had had since her husband captured her son and her best friends drugged her.

"Last chance," Klea said on a small, tightly held breath. "Last chance, my old friend. You owe me for what you did to me. No grudges. Just make it good. Whatever you think of—let's try it."

"I should do this alone."

"The *hell* you will! *What* will you do?"

Hatshepsut snapped her fingers and a veritable cloud of sycophants appeared. "Court dress," she said. "Mine and Klea's. *Fast*, you sons of dogs, and if you gossip I'll see you roast in the Pit. Hear?"

"Where are we going?" Klea asked, as the sycophants vanished and Hatshepsut seized her by the arm and drew her down the garage stairs.

"Going? We are going, my dear friend, to have my bath with the hose in the garage, since we do not want to draw attention to ourselves in the house; we are going to dress and go for a drive."

"Don't play games with me! What have you got in mind, dammit?"

"Secrecy." Hatshepsut stopped at the bottom of the steps and faced her, looking down the difference in their stature, for all that Hatshepsut was far older Dead. *"Nuk Ra maket su t'asef, nuk Ra, nuk Amon, nuk neb khut. Hotep'k nai, nebt seshep. Aihai airek."*

A chill went down Klea's back, then. It was the old language. It was incantation. It was Egyptian, the half of her that was not rational, and knew it: I am Ra, Amon, lord of the horizon. Peace, lady of light, and come with me.

Which like everything in the Old Language meant a damned obscure lot more.

Lady of light. Fair-haired queen. Interloper, foreigner in my land, we are still allies.

It took Hatshepsut to insult a friend she was risking her sanity to help; Hatshepsut or any other of Egypt's god-kings. Pharaoh owned everything. Could one take offense at such generosity?

The olive-burl doors opened and Niccolo walked in, relieved, *grazie a Dio*, of the ridiculous hat, which hung on a stand in the secretary's office, and offered his hand to Leonidas Agathodemas' birdlike claw.

It was something, he supposed, that Agathodemas had bestirred himself from behind the monstrous desk, with its oil-lamp and its incredibly ornate ink stand, a wraith-thin, not at all English gentleman with eyes black as unreported sin and very, very guarded.

"A pleasure, sir," Agathodemas said, and offered a chair—leather, of course, as he took his own, and the secretary fussed about the sideboard. "An honor. Of course I have read your work. Most, most, excellent."

After so many centuries, that statement as often out of the mouths of fools as sages, lost its enchantment. Even considering the source. "I am flattered, sir. You do me too much honor." There was liquid forthcoming,

tea, in the hands of the secretary, on a silver tray; and
Niccolo was far more concerned about that, and about
the safety of it. But this was not altogether a Victorian.
Agathodemas had Established in the Eastern enclave
once and long ago, and the tea was a very delicate
matter, a prerequisite.

It arrived, steaming hot; was poured with Eastern
ceremony, which made the provenance of the dark-
eyed, olive-skinned young secretary less and less in
doubt.

Eastern too, that flourish of Agathodemas' hand which
dismissed their sole audience, and the placidity with
which Agathodemas approached the initial sip.

A flurry of sycophants showed up in the garage, cases
and cartons hailed down into a pile, and Hatshepsut,
whose going out and coming in had been attended by a
servant for every imaginable function, whose person
must not be touched, whose very shadow must not be
crossed, else the offender die screaming on hooks—
hopped on one foot, pulling off one boot and the other,
unzipped and peeled out of the jumpsuit and swore like
a legionary as she doused herself with cold water and
mechanics's soap.

"Dress!" Hatshepsut snapped at her, between chatter-
ings of her teeth. "Set take it, *towel*, useless wretch!"—
The latter was for the sycophant, who as a towel
whisked off the rack nearby. "*Perfume*, fools! Roses and
myrrh! Lily and lotus! oh, *damn*, that's cold!"

Klea stripped and dressed, dousing herself with the
cloying-sweet perfumes that brought back the Nile for
her—peeling off the French lace and the nylons—
wrapped about her the starched linen and the beaten
gold that were the damnably uncomfortable regalia of a
god-king, in what was surely the shortest time that a
pharaoh had ever taken about the process, with the
half-substantial hands of two-score sycophants to tug
and fuss things to rights.

"Zeus," she said, trying to get herself and her starched pleats into the Ferrari's passenger-seat, trying to sit without the gilt belt pinching or the damned wig and vulture crown tilting when she leaned back on it—and a cloud of sycophants hovered desperately, plying paint-pots and brushes, applying the precise shape to the eyes and brows, the blush to fingertips and sandaled toes.

There was a good deal less to Hatshepsut's official regalia—a *great* deal less, which let her partner slip behind the wheel with a good deal less to encumber her: kilt and gilt *atef* and apron and sandals, nothing at all above the waist except a wide collar of carnelian and gold. Hatshepsut shifted into reverse and sent them out of the garage and about with a spin of the wheel. "Not wearing the damn beard while I'm driving," she said, tossing the braided human hair into Klea's lap. "Hold onto that." They shot out of the driveway, turned with tires squealing, and Hatshepsut shifted again as they hit the street and accelerated.

Klea clutched the braid in one hand, the handhold in the other, as Hatshepsut went through the gears and the street rushed at them and the trees of Decentral Park rushed past them ungodly fast.

"Cong are out there," Hatshepsut said, tight-jawed. "Not moving—yet. Whole damned street is a deathtrap."

"*Where are we going?*" As the Ferrari kept accelerating. "Dammit—"

The tea diminished, interminably, and there was still feeling in the fingers and the toes, which was a good sign. Niccolo smiled his most engaging smile and talked of (*perdio*) the lack of weather in Hell lately, the unpredictability of the traffic, the welfare of the Queen, and (at last) the state of the markets—which, with a trader of the ancient school, was the polite means of ascertaining, department by department, the area in which the negotiations might be opened. It might have gone two more rounds, from trade to tax to politics, but Niccolo saw his opening and went for it with a slow smile and a melting earnestness.

"Ah, yes, *difficult* times. And certain ones have made it so."

That was a directness which got a rise out of Agathodemas, whose cinder-dark eyes almost met his and did not, immediately. Here would follow frosty silence, if the guest and applicant did not care to risk his neck with explication.

"I must be direct," Niccolo said, empty cup in hand. "And impose on your courtesy through a mutual friend, *signore*, because a life is at stake, indeed, your own welfare is at stake. Therefore I have come to you, I must be plain, because a friend declared you a man eminently wise and one he would trust to act for him."

"I am of course honored to be so well thought of by this unnamed friend, but naturally I cannot speak in generalities—"

The frost began to form, in clipped words, in stiffening of the spine, shielding of the eyes.

"*Signore*." Machiavelli lifted his hands, both. "I speak for a Caesar."

"*Which* Caesar?"

"One who is still your friend. And another who may become your friend. Are we now talking business?"

The Byzantine's eyelids half-lowered, a little glance down at the tea-glass. And lifted again, on interested darkness. "I am a businessman."

"Do we speak now on coinfidence?"

Agathodemas reached to a drawer of his desk and Niccolo observed the moves and the sounds with some anxiety. But it was the soft whirr of a tape resetting itself.

"Now we do," Agathodemos said. "Name names."

"An old friend who may see better times—is in Roman custody."

"Names."

"The Supreme Commander. Hadrianus."

The stare was ophidian. One fine, bony finger traced the rim of the tea-glass beneath the oil-lamp. "Ah."

"I will be frank," Machiavelli said, "which is not my wont, but time is critical, *signore*. A move of the current command has brought us very close to war—not with the Dissidents, *signore*, which is another and complex affair; but a war of factions. I shall spare you the details."

Agathodemas nodded, eyes glittering. "*Signore Machiavelli*. I shall be completely reckless and say that I know more than this: that Hadrian has been removed from his house arrest and taken somewhere I do not know. That grievous damage has been done Tiberius' villa. And that there is considerable movement of men and equipment about the city. On such rumors markets rise and fall. You may believe my intelligence network is efficient."

"*Signore*, my compliments. You must understand if I have taken some time approaching a most delicate matter. Not alone for the Supreme Commander,—the *rightful* commander, as all of us must believe who have enjoyed the benefits of his administration— But for older, truly older interests, on which the Roman West in truth depends for its stability. I should not understate the matter to say that all of this could conceivably collapse, indeed, collapse, one timber to the next; and who would be safe, who, indeed, *signore*, whose antecedents are on the Tiber? You see the gravity of the situation."

"Most clearly, Florentine. Most, most clearly. Be plain with me. Is Julius himself your principal in these negotiations?"

"Ostensibly it is Hadrian, *signore*. But who knows? Surely Julius would be most grateful for your assistance."

Agathodemas gazed long and long at him, hollow-cheeked and with those black and burning eyes; and the fingers ceaselessly rotated the tea-glass on the desk.

"I am retired from political affairs, but rumors *will*

come to me, how can I prevent them? What is it you wish?"

"A thing of more risk and more substance, excellency."

"I am merely a merchant, *signore*, ill-suited to the affairs of princes."

"You are a prince among merchants, *signore*, on whom princes depend, and who prefers the solid things in life—as do I. Would I choose a setting sun in preference to the morning?"

"What is this thing of substance?"

"A dossier. A thing of considerable risk. But then— the value is commensurate. We are speaking of survival, *signore*, of all those connections which make life bearable. I have seen the nether planes. I do assure you—they are not rational!"

Perhaps a shudder passed through that thin frame. It was no easier to tell than with a snake.

"Where does this dossier exist?"

"Likely within the Pentagram."

Brows lifted gently. "Copy or original?"

"Original."

The fingers stopped their movement. "The name?"

"Marcus Junius Brutus. Cesare's assassin."

The boys still missing, reports of a third shootout in the garment district of New Hell, and Julius was at the map table shouting at Curtius when the phone went off again. Augustus looked left and right and there was no one else: he grabbed it, in an act of courage—damn, he hated these electrical things next his ear.

"Hello?" he shouted into it—no one ever talked loud enough for a man who did not trust contact with these things, and he did people the courtesy to suppose they likewise held the receiver at respectful distance. "Hello? Hello? Who are you? Speak up!"

"*Who is this?*" the voice came back to him.

"Octavianus Augustus!" he shouted at it. "Who *are* you, man, speak up!"

"Murderer!" the voice on the other end shrieked at him. *"Murderer! Assassin!"*

He slammed the phone back into its cradle, heart pounding. It was *not* the sort of lunatic they needed at the moment. Julius yelling on one side, a madman on the phone—he had always *known* it was not safe to put one's ear to the thing: who knew but what the maniac had wired some sort of device to his end?

The phone rang again. And again. He put his hands over the receiver, pressed it down, hard, attempting to ignore it.

"Answer the damned thing!" Julius yelled at him.

"It's a madman."

"What's a madman?" Julius looked one jump from homicide himself; and crossed the room and snatched up the ringing phone from under Augustus' hands. "Give me that! —*Hello?"*

Augustus reached to take the receiver away quickly if he could. It was, he feared, some ploy of Mithridates', and he was helpless with these modern gadgets.

But Julius listened. And listened. And listened, dourer and dourer, until his face was ghastly as his deathmask. He drew a breath. "Listen, you—" And another, after another few seconds. "Listen." A third breath. *"Termina nostra praeteritos, perfoede canifornicator, infimas ad regiones mittam, te et omnes plagiferentes catamitos tuos tecum! Audisne?"*

Augustus found his mouth open, and shut it, as Julius slammed the receiver down.

Our borders.

Of a sudden he recognized the voice.

"That was Tiberius," Augustus ventured.

Julius just stood there and smouldered a good long moment, then drew a breath and got quiet, very quiet. "That damned fool," he said. And then: "I shouldn't have said that. *Damn,* I shouldn't have said that."

"What did he say?"

"He's threatening lawsuit." Julius ran his hand through

his hair and drew a rumbling breath. "He says I damaged his damn statue. He's mobilizing."

There was sober, instant attention over at the map tables.

"He's a fool!" Augustus exclaimed.

"He's also got the Praetorians, right the other side of the tennis courts." Julius walked back to the map tables. "And, dammit, we can't afford it."

"The Praetorians," Mettius Curtius said in his archaic accent, and with his Republican directness, "are dogmeat. Five *cohorts* of the 10th could handle that lot."

"We can't afford to beat him," Julius said. "Resonances, *Curti*. Civil war is a fight we can't win. We daren't lose a base here. Even his."

The car swerved, tires squealed, and suddenly there was gravel under the wheels. It was not a comforting sound. It meant no more city, no more streets.

It meant a place where two boys could be shot and dumped, for all they knew, or asked questions at length; and in spite of more complex and more exotic worries, having an assassin's heel resting on the small of one's back and the cold barrrel of a gun jostling against the back of one's head did not make the gravel-sound a welcome one.

And how Caesarion fared, Brutus did not know and dared not ask—dared not do anything, even shift his weight when the car's wild turns threw them slightly and wrung a moan from Caesarion.

More of gravel, and another turn, that drew a grunt and an obscenity. His brother was not, at least, overwhelmed; and Brutus took that for comfort, even when the gun jolted painfully against his skull and the heel dug in hard.

The car stopped.

They had arrived somewhere. The door opened behind him, the villain crawled off and out of the seat, and someone grabbed him by the feet and pulled, a second by the chain between his hands as his belly hit the door-rim; they hauled him upright then, and spun him about to face a mansion larger than the villa, a true palace—garish with painted bulls in bas-relief, with horned crenelations, with —*gods*, he had never seen such colors in combination.

They jerked him back by the arms and shoved him on toward the doors. They were taking Caesarion out too, no more gently; and Caesarion kicked a man in the groin.

They hit him. He knew that they would. Doubtless Caesarion knew. But that was Caesarion. He found a vague, frightened admiration for his brother, wishing that he were brave instead of smart, because smart was not going to work here, not surrounded as they were with automtic weapons and with their hands chained.

The only thing smart did for him here was to tell him that they were in deep trouble, and that no one here meant them any good at all; and he reckoned even Caesarion, who did not think overlong about things, had had that figured from the beginning.

The phone went off again. Augustus snatched up the receiver in a blind rage. *"Tiberi? Audisne?"*

"Hello?" the other end said. *"Who is this?"*

Not Tiberius. Augustus expelled a breath he had been saving for his nephew. "Damn this contraption! This is Wolf. What's your authorization?"

"Pythias. The Cubs in the fifth, by ten."

"Cubs in the fifth by ten," he repeated, waving his hand frantically at the map-table, and heard the phone go dead without goodbyes.

They had *found* the boys again.

"Five and ten," Julius said between his teeth, and his face was utterly grim as he looked at the gridded map. *"Damn!"*

Augustus crossed the room to look where Julius' hand rested.

Assurbanipal's villa.

And Tiberius' establishment and five legions—were dead-set in the way.

"We've got Tiberius to—" Augustus began diffidently. There were times to remind Julius of things. There were times not to.

Julius raked a hand through his hair and paced a fast circuit of the table-end. "Call Horatius again. I know, I *know* it's a risk. Tell them they're out of time, dammit. —*Where* the hell is Klea?"

"Left with Hatshepsut," Curtius said.

"*What?*"

"Left with Hatshepsut," Curtius said, very carefully this time. "The pharaoh came in, the watch reported they both left in the car. We supposed—it was authorized—"

"Where?"

Curtius' face was decidedly pale. "I'll try to find out, if you—"

"Dammit, no, we're stretched thin enough. They'll turn up. I want the 10th, the 12th, and the 14th ready to move. The 5th and 6th in reserve. Courier that. We've got too much coming in." Again the hand through the hair. Another few paces. "And get Horatius on the line, dammit, we've got to know what we've got."

"Got them located," the operator said; and Sargon looked up, laid his hand on his rifle—but the operator's face did not herald anything he wanted to hear. "Assurbanipal's villa."

"Damn," Horatius said, who rarely let emotion into a mission.

And: "Damn," Scaevola echoed. Exhausted, all of them. Quarter hour for breakfast and a sit in the mobile command station back in the greenbelt safe-zone to think and regroup, and this came in.

Sargon gathered up the rifle anyway. Horatius was in titular command, while it was a Security operation, but it was a disputable point right now. He only waited for details.

"Two cars," the operator relayed to them. "Our spotter had the boys in sight. They're inside now."

"Damn, damn, and damn," Scaevola said; and gathered up his own rifle.

"We need you," Horatius said. "Majesty. Now, especially."

Sargon turned a jaundiced eye on Horatius. Assurbanipal's palace. "You know what you're asking. All my wives are there. And my sons. I'd rather face liches."

Bulls with the head of a bearded king stood on either side of a gigantic staircase; balconies dripped greenery lighted from above.

And guards were everywhere, khaki-clad ones with automatic weapons and others wearing the fringed kilt of Assyria and carrying broad-bladed spears.

It was not the homey splendor of the white-marble villa, that somehow always seemed large enough no matter how many the Household happened to consist of at the moment, but not too large for the people who lived there. *This* place was a palace indeed, a monstrous thing, cold and huge, that made every human seem small.

"*Di immortales*." Brutus murmured, looking up that stairs they climbed. The immortal gods might live at the top of such stairs. Anything might. *We are going to die*, he thought. *It doesn't matter so much in Hell because you can do it over and over—* The latter he kept telling himself; and he was still scared sick and feeling the breakfast he had almost eaten was going to come up again. *But this is going to be it. We're going to die here. There's no way out of this, and they'll do terrible things to us, or try to make me do things against my father* —O Iuppiter, pater deorum nostrorum, protege nos— *And I won't, and it's going to hurt. It's going to hurt, and nobody can get in here to help us—*

Caesarion was beside him, Caesarion the same as he,
under the rifles of their guards, both of them handcuffed.
Caesarion had the same sullen look he generally had,
despite a cut lip and a knot on his temple and gods
knew how many bruises.

But it was Caesarion lent him courage. If he had not
had Caesarion beside him, he was not sure he could
have climbed those stairs, or presented something like
Caesarion's jaw-clenched temper to the soldiers who
jabbed them with gunbarrels and cursed and shoved
them.

More soldiers with guns waited for them at the top;
and it was clear they were supposed to stop: Brutus
stopped, Caesarion beside him.

"Kadashman-enlil," Caesarion muttered, with a jut
of his jaw toward the man coming up on their left, him
with the brass all over his collar and soldiers behind
him. "Damn."

"Who is he?"

"A rat, looks like. A lousy, stinking rat."

"You can't park there!" the Pentagram guard yelled.

Hatshepsut parked, jerked the emergency brake, and
Klea braced her crown and the heavy wig and caught
herself short of the dashboard.

Then she flung open her door and got out; and
Hatshepsut did the same, which was the evident reason
the man was still in shock as Hatshepsut flung her door
shut and threw the keys at him.

"Then park it!" the pharaoh said. "We have business
with the Supreme Commander."

The keys hit the pavement at the guard's feet. The
guard just stood there with his mouth slightly open.
The insignia of Ptah Regiment was on his collar. A
Hellene pharaoh fluent in half a dozen languages could
pick that out at twenty paces, right along with his
ancestry.

He was a soldier, and an Egyptian. His ilk had

murdered pharaohs, at the behest of priests and with abundant assurances and blessed amulets, on appropriate days which might be safe for him.

Perhaps this was not one of those days, decreed by the Hathors at his birth.

Perhaps he just did not *feel* lucky.

The phone went off again. Tiberius, Julius reckoned, and ignored it. Augustus could field that well enough. He was up to his ears in the best information their reconnaissance had on Assurbanipal's establishment, charts and more charts which their electronics had gotten in spite of Assurbanipal's electronics and which, reciprocally, they could figure Assurbanipal had collected on them over the centuries.

Most of all, Sargon had been useful in the compilation of the data, and Sargon was still the most useful resource they had: *Sargon* had lived thereabouts, till Assurbanipal arrived in Hell and overpowered the more modest Akkadian domain—had not displaced the Sumerians and the Akkadians to another plane, had just come in as ally against the Babylonians and grown and grown in a very short time, allying itself with one and the other of Sargon's troublesome offspring— It was not a matter Sargon spoke of, except to say he had found less and less pleasure in his successors and could not, while they ebbed away first toward the Babylonian power and then with ready disposition to treachery, toward the Assyrians and their allies, keep them from folly.

Therefore Sargon found Augustus' villa much more to his liking. And therefore they at least had one sane source of information, outdated as it was by a millennium or two.

Lunatics, Sargon was wont to say of certain of his successors. And: *That's all right*, Julius had answered him once and long ago. *No family's perfect. We've got Tiberius.*

"It's *him* again," Augustus crossed the room to say in

a low voice. "He absolutely insists to talk to you, or he'll start shelling."

Julius groaned, shoved the charts aside and picked up the phone that was beside the chart table. "Hello, son. What can I do for you?"

"*Do for me, do for me!*" the aged voice on the other end shrieked. "*You damaged my statue!*"

"Would you like a new one?" Julius said most reasonably. "Really, majesty, I *am* sorry. The Egyptians haven't been very reasonable guests, have they? Throwing grenades under your roof—"

"*You threw the grenade!*"

The old bastard had better memory than he had wished. "I'm not sure it was the only one—" Hysterical shouting erupted on the other end. "Yes, yes, but Horemheb was violating your hospitality, absolute disrespect. Could I tolerate that? You've had too many traitors under your roof, son, —as your grandfather, I'm bound to take action when I know your house has been invaded by foreigners and revolutionaries." Trigger-words: Tiberius had psychoses and revolution was one; being dragged through the streets with hooks was another—not surprising, considering that was what had happened to his corpse: a man already unstable grew no saner in Hell, and those who did not cope well with change grew absolutely paranoid facing an eternity of flux. "I absolutely support you in your indignation against these intruders. I'm so very glad they didn't succeed in their ass·· ·nation attempt."

Til······· ad not interrupted him, at least, meaning that h· ···· ·he old lecher off his balance and trying to think, which when one was crazy, was sometimes a chancy process.

"*You're the assassin.*" Tiberius screamed then. "*You walked into my palace! You threw grenades at my guests! You damaged my statue!*"

"How would I be your assassin? I'm your grandfather."

"You're younger than I am, you damned conniver! It's not fair!"

"Hell just isn't fair, grandson, but we try to look out for our own. Beware the Assyrians. We're very worried about you. Have you got any Egyptians in your house?"

Silence a few breaths. Then a nasty, rising chuckle. *"I've got the Devil in my house—asking all sorts of questions. Attack me now, grandfather!" My Praetorians will take care of your legions. My devil will take care of you* and *that traitor Antonius."*

Click. Julius stood there a heartbeat and settled his own handset into the cradle.

"What did he say?" Augustus asked, with a worried look and a pallor under his freckles. "Is he going to attack?"

"A devil," Julius said slowly, with a worse and worse feeling about it all. "He says he's got the Devil in his house."

"Prodi, he thinks he has Jupiter and the nymphs in his house! He mistook Nero for his pastry cook! Why not the Devil for a butler?"

"I don't know," Julius said, rubbing the back of a stiff neck, and looked out beyond the window, where the Administration building towered up and up toward the clouds. "I just don't like it."

There was silence from the other quarter. Likely Augustus did not like that thought either. And Julius paced and fretted his way back to his charts, considering every angle of the building, height of the windows, location of what rooms they knew.

His sons were in there, dammit, and he ached to get them *out* of there, even knowing what he might get back for his pains. Or the hazard of trying.

Let the boys go, reason urged him. *Frustrate the hell out of Mithridates. He needs to get Brutus back here.*

But he kept remembering the boy asleep, the boy running to him down the villa steps when he came back from Troy.

Even Caesarion, damn him, had had his moments;
and Klea loved him, which was good enough—Klea,
who was off with that woman, that Egyptian, that
Bacchantic, weapons-rattling lunatic who believed in
ships to the stars and who, gods knew, he had been
damned glad to see now and again—

Egyptian. Egyptian is a way that Klea was not,
Egyptian down to the oracular fits that, dammit,
sometimes worked, for reasons he could not figure, except
that the woman-king had Connections to Something—
connections like the damned electronics she wore and
which he knew spied on everything around her: electronics which played merry hob with the villa's own
surveillance system and which, in his own way of live
and let live within his command, he had never made
issue of. Hatshepsut was on their side and if she wanted
to carry a personal and unregistered armament sufficient
to take out a tank, if she carried on affairs with Sargon
and had seduced every man in the house except maybe
Dante and Mouse, that was all right: there was a core to
her that no man got to, the same with Sargon, and a
passage with her was like a five-day binge, one of those
things a man enjoyed at the time, enjoyed recollecting
a year later, and had no desire to do any time soon—
less *what* one did than the sensation of waking up in
bed with *that one* staring into one's eyes, untouched,
unaffected, and bright, gods, yes. Like spending the
night with a cobra and waking up in bed with Hannibal.
Gods knew how she affected the legionaries. And no
wonder so few of them talked or joked about the
experience.

He had *never* trusted her. And yet—had a little
twinge both of dread and hope knowing that Klea was
off with her. Klea—

—Klea would do anything to save her son. Anything,
however dangerous. Would not betray the Roman
interests on which her own existence rested— *Dared
not!* he knew his Klea. Her life was too tangled with his

and with Antonius', and dammit, in her way, she loved them both.

But there was Egypt. Egypt could offer her a new base. Could offer her—and Hatshepsut, the renegade, the female king Egypt tried to forget—a refuge in the fall of Rome, salvation for her son Caesarion and for her children by Antonius, for whom not even Hell had found a proper niche. If the two of them were together—

Gods, Hatshepsut had come into the house when Sargon came—right at the beginning. Had been here forever—even before Klea, before Augustus. She had—

—had found him, a bewildered new arrival in a much less prosperous establishment, still with the chill of the marble about him, the theater floor where he had fallen—

—stunned by Brutus' presence with the assassins. Trying to fight, though a damned pen was all he had in hand, until he had seen that face among his murderers, and gone time-wandering back to a day in Massilia, and a meeting with a seventeen-year-old boy—

He blinked and shook his head.

"*Iuli,*" someone was saying at his elbow. "*Iuli*—" And when he looked into Cirtius' young face: "That was the infirmary. They say Antonius is slipping—badly. They don't know how long they can hold him. They ask—if Dante can—"

"Dante can't!" He had that strangely disconnected feeling, the aftermath of one of his attacks. The falling sickness had not bothered him in Hell—except these dazed interludes, in which the whole room seemed to swing round, and his eyes refused to focus on the here and now. Touch of the gods. Mantic sensitivity, as the ancient world had thought it.

Epilepsy, moderns said.

Himself, he blinked his eyes clear and struggled to remember recent data. Everything seemed to have fallen into slots, a little out of immediate reach, but he had it, the location of every piece on the board. And he felt quite calm now, armored in numbness.

A smart man could think too long, want to know too much in a shifting situation.

Mithridates had penetrated the Dissident organization—damned well riddled it with his officers and his own forces and with mercs bought and paid for by Pentagram funds, and with codewords and signals doubtless which could bring them instantly facing whatever direction their group-leaders dictated.

Caesarion had held a lieutenancy with the Dissidents and knew contacts he would have gone to when he escaped. Caesarion was, gods knew, not long on patience or planning.

Mithridates might well have known where to find the boys even *before* they walked into the *Oasis*, might well have had his own man in the *Oasis* who had called some superior about the time Napoleon's man had phoned for help—and Mithridates' men there had not moved, perhaps, because they had expected the boys to go off with some traitor guide meek as limbs, Caesarion secure in the belief they would go to the Dissidents. But the French agent had gotten in the way, instructions for the pickup had suddenly had to change, and in the meanwhile Horatius and his lot had arrived, to the consternation of Mithridates' men—

And two frightened boys just ran like hell—

While Mithridates, with all the shielded communications the Pentagram could offer, spies in the Undertaker's office, men and equipment all over New Hell, and police powers and access that made ordering a train halted a piece of cake, had finessed the subway intercept just a few minutes ahead of his own men, who had managed to get a car over to Highgate—points to Severus and his lads from the 12th, nonetheless, outnumbered and outflanked, who had gotten in the hard way and reacted fast when they knew the train was not going to reach their position.

Got out again too. That was an attitude Julius had

drilled into his men: *Don't send information to the Undertaker.*

Beyond that—beyond that—

Mithridates had to be chewing nails. Had not planned on the thing blowing up like this. Had not *planned* to have two runaways—hell, he could have let Caesarion and Brutus quietly get to the Dissidents and gathered them up there

No, *not* only Mithridates at the *Oasis.* The *Dissidents'* command must have had a pickup order out on Caesarion as a Trojan Horse—untrustable. Infiltrator. One of *his* agents, gods knew. Or the Devil's. *Welch* had lifted Caesarion out of the Dissident camp before it got blown to glory, lifted him out in a damned noisy chopper, to deliver him to his father—but maybe neither Dissidents nor Mithridates had known the realities of that situation. Caesarion—they had pegged as a double agent, a dissembler only pretending to be a feckless lunatic. A man could laugh at such an idea.

Except Caesarion knew too much. Caesarion could blow the whole Dissident operation—to Welch, to whoever his putative controls might be, and leave Mithridates in the spotlight that Mithridates so desperately did not want shined on his operations.

But Brutus had gone askew—had run off down a bedsheet, and five would get ten that no one of the Dissidents or Mithridates' agents had recognized Brutus at all, not some field agent unbriefed in Mithridates' most secret plans. Just haul Caesarion back, grab the Roman kid with him in the theory he *might* be worth questioning, and lo, there they were with one of Mithridates' most cherished projections hot in their hands—if they knew even yet what they had laid hands on or what he meant to Mithridates' plans.

It was not alone the Roman army that was having such a rotten day. *Mithridates* was, and *that* was what made the logic of the thing so damned hard to figure.

"Damn!" he said, and suddenly it was as if time had slowed down, the weight of the centuries had gone off his shoulders. He went over to the rack by the door and gathered up his sidearm and his helmet. "Tell Galen *keep Antonius alive*, just a few more hours. A few more. Aftre that, he rides our chances. Get Dante!"

"*Iuli*," Augustus protested, and Julius turned to the First Citizen and pointed a finger at him:

"*You'll* have Cong in your lap, son of mine! See to it! I've got my hands full."

"Tiberius—"

"Tell that boy-loving grandson of mine Mithridates is coming up his backside. And blast a message through to his guard commander: he and his damned Praetorians are going to be the front line and they can face the legions or face Mithridates, take their pick!"

XI

The Pentagram guards supposedly *had* no factional loyalties; were supposedly drawn from various Principalities and Powers; and it was strange how many of them used to be Roman or Greek and how many of them were Egyptian nowadays.

And Rameses, hating democratic notions and unorthodoxy, had only those men about him who *respected* the pharaonic office and emblems.

Which was a convenient circumstance for two sister pharaohs who had blitzed their way from the downstairs entrance to this place near the Supreme Commander's office, one of them in the starched pleats and vulture crown of a latter-day pharaonic queen, the other quite modestly crowned with the *atef* and serpent, distinguished with beard (no matter that it was fake: *most* of them had been, braided hair twisted and ornamented with gold and carnelian) and ponderous collar, belt and gilt apron and starched white kilt. One might have wondered at first glance just *which* young pharaoh accompanied the Ptolemy: beneath the eye-paint and the braided beard and the gold, identities blurred and one looked much like another.

Until one looked slightly south of the collar and blinked and stared just long enough to realize he was staring at pharaoh in a personal way, and thinking thoughts which were damnation to think about pharaoh, who was god, whose flesh, (and pharaoh was somewhat vain on this point) however conically shaped and interestingly mobile, was divine; and whose spoken curse could damn a soul to the Eater in the nether planes of Hell—so rumor had it.

It had worked this far. But on this floor and by this time, phone calls had doubtless flown every which way; and Hatshepsut walked as fast as she could without unseemly haste, anxiously, since there was little of her weaponry she could hide in this damned rig, and since they were very near now to another pharaoh.

Between whom and themselves the average Ahmose line-soldier had just as soon *not* stand.

Hence the phone calls, delivered probably in the fervent hope that Ahmose the line-soldier would not be ordered to stand between; or that the aforesaid Ahmose would go with the specific blessings of the pharaoh who ordered him there, and that he would have amulets and charms in plenty to hedge his soul about. Some said a soul so cursed simply went, *blink!* away; some said that it happened at next death, that Reassignments would glitch and send one . . Elsewhere. In either case, one wanted to have so many beneficent and blessed amulets and spells about oneself as would make the Eater look about in confusion, seeing the soul, but smelling the holiness of it, which the Eater would avoid.

As for pharaoh herself, she was not sure it worked like that, but it was at least some comfort in the absence of the heavy-duty firepower she had rather trust. There was no chance getting her private arsenal into the Pentagram—not even Klea's little Beretta.

So they went now to the double doors of the office of the Supreme Commander, and hoped to hell they were not locked, and that there would be no barrage of fire the other side which might send *them* back to the Undertaker, or the River of the Dead, or wherever it was dead pharaohs went when they died in Hell.

The doors opened without a protest; and it was the habit of a lifetime on the throne of Egypt that kept Hatshepsut from flinching when she found herself between Klea and a leveled row of AKMs in the hands of kilt-wearing Egyptian elite.

Five of Rameses' guards held that incense-reeking secretarial office, between them and the further door; and doubtless they had the requisite amulets and blessings, or they had their own pharaoh's curse to fear. They clearly meant business.

"I am Horus," Hatshepsut intoned, "descended beneath the earth; with Isis I seek the Osiris Rameses, pure in heart, lest a curse fall on the land, lest darkness rise from the fountains of the deep and blight the servants of the Osiris who is Ra incarnate. A blessing upon the feet swift to obey; a curse upon his enemies, may crocodiles devour their bowels and their hearts, may the Eater smell out their wickedness."

It was in the best classical style: she had paid attention to her tutor-priests, fully intending, even in her girlfriend, to *be* pharaoh and not Great Royal Wife to one of her brothers—she, descended of Ahmose the Conqueror, through *his* daughter, and more royal than her father Thutmose, a provincial than whom a jackal was more royal; and *hyenas* were more royal than her half-brothers and -sisters. Thutmose's get with his other wives— whom she had not found in Hell, and whom she assumed the Eater must indeed have gotten.

The approach at least did not set the guards off. They stood there with their rifles leveled and their orders behind them, but she had said, in pedestrian terms, We're here to see Rameses and curse his enemies, who are endangering all of you. That took a minute or two to sort out of the priestly language and think over for traps and hidden curses and spells, and finally for the senior of them to get the nerve and form a response that would leave him in the clear.

"The words of the Luminance Rising over the Two

Lands: Ra shining in the height of heaven and un-
attainable sheds light impartially on his sons and on the
strangers."

Meaning, No way, pharaoh refuses to Get Involved.

"Look upon Isis his Great Royal Wife." The latter
with a flourish toward Klea. "And upon Horus his Son—"
The latter with clenched fist on her breast, a nice bit of
raising the ante, she thought: she saw the confusion in
their eyes. "—ascending into the heavens to shed light
upon the sons of Ra and to gladden the face of his
Father. I am Horus the Hawk, whose right eye is the
sun and whose left the moon. I am Horus who flies in
the face of Set, blinding the Destroyer, bringing life to
his father."

Freely translated, Let me in through that door, you
bastard, if you value the old goat's life.

The guards' faces showed a pious dismay. The officer
looked indecisive, and finally tucked his AKM aside and
edged through the doors he was guarding, vanishing
totally inside for a very long time.

Hatshepsut stood, Klea up beside her by now, rock-
steady: a lifetime as a god gave one the ability to shut
down the nerves to the legs or the posterior—or the
ears, when it came to that; and any time one thought
oneself suffering, one had only to remember that it was
not the papyrus crown one was wearing which was the
worst; not even the double, which compressed the
vertebrae of the neck and started doing the same for
the spine after an hour or two— One simply fixed one's
eyes somewhere the other side of nowhere and pretended
the guards were cockroaches.

Until the door cracked, and the officer came in with
the glistening of sweat on his face, leaving the doors
open behind him. "Down weapons," that one said in
a muted voice, to his men; and: "Blessed be Horus
and his Divine Mother. One wishes to make wide the
way."

"Blessed is he who opens the way," Hatshepsut

intoned. "May he be written in the rolls, may his name be remembered."

Carrot and stick, the American Welch had called it. And the doors stood wide on the Place of Purification, with its spells and its incense. Destruction to Enemies was written on its walls; and Strength and Life to the Loyal.

Klea's steps faltered. Perhaps she read the spells. Perhaps it was the incense, strong enough to stop the breath. Perhaps a Hellene doubted her safety here, or her son's future. Or it was the presence of two more guards, armed with spears this time.

"Pharaoh is one," Hatshepsut muttered under her breath. "We are all Osiris." And before she need give an order, the guards pulled back the doors.

The office beyond was modern, from its expensive desk to the deep pile carpet with the symbols of life and victory written around its border. But not the man who faced them at the width of the room, standing before a gilt chair, wearing the blue enamel War Crown, and thanks to his vanity, probably seeing them both as a glittering blur: Rameses was notoriously near-sighted.

But he faced them, in his armor of golden vulture's wings and leopard-skin, this slight, myopic man, War Crown and all, by which he at least looked the part of the Supreme Commander of Hell.

That had taken some fast work on the part of his sycophants, the same as theirs.

"Abominations. Profaners of the Crown," he hailed them. "We are not amused."

We are outright pissed, was what Hatshepsut thought, in the soldiers' argot, but that would never do with His Luminance the Prig. She had heard it often enough in life—Egyptians who could not accept a reigning queen. "Ra Shining in Splendor is my father, in his Son's heart is no wickedness, who says: Truth has written my name in the rolls although the liars had laid their hand to my monuments; she has made pure my heart before the

Eater; she has opened my mouth to speak her words in
secret to my father Ra Arising in Splendor."

Ra-Arising set his mouth and scowled, and scowled
the blacker. But he waved a hand and the doors shut,
thump.

"You *presume*, woman. You *presume* on our forbear-
ance, to come here with the emblems you usurped.
This foreigner, this daughter of a corrupt line, at least
has the decency to abjure *your* example: we are grateful,
we suppose, not to have *two* bearded daughters."

"Let the Eater judge me." Hatshepsut lifted a hand
without a qualm, and stared her brother pharaoh hard
in the face. "Luminance, you have nursed the serpent
and warmed him in your favor. Now his fangs are set for
your hand as well as ours. We have our disagreements.
But we do not countenance lies to the majesty of Egypt.
We are indignant, we are *outraged*. Luminance, and
we refuse to be maneuvered into hostilities against the
majesty of Egypt."

"Then the solution is simple. Advise Caesar to disarm.
Advise him we are not pleased." Rameses crossed to his
desk and grabbed up an indiscriminate fistful of papers.
"We do not countenance the kidnapping of our predecessor! We do not countenance the actions of barbarians who invade premises under guard of our
legitimate authority and remove a sick and confused
man from our protection! We do not countenance
adventurism and we do not countenance sloppy accounting!"

"We do not countenance the pursuit of my son!" Klea
cried, before Hatshepsut could stop her. "*He* is pharaoh,
my heir, majesty! *And that jackal tried to kill him!*"

"We are speaking of Ptolemy Caesarion, the ne'er-do-
well, the consorter with rabble, the revolutionary from
Tiberius' polluted house—*this* is the heir you mean."

"You—"

"*Peace!*" Hatshepsut shouted. Fast. Klea and Rameses
looked at each other like two set cats. "We are speaking

of disrespect to the office. We are speaking of *treason*, Luminance, which has aimed at domination, and which has its roots deep in the Pentagram!"

"Meaning Caesar!"

"Caesar has *no* establishment in the Pentagram, Luminance. We are speaking of a reckless and ruthless man who has acted in despite of your interests and who would be well content to see all Egypt sent to the nether planes!"

Rameses' eyes were wide. His mouth and his nostrils drank in a breath.

"We speak of Mithridates," Hatshepsut said, before he could get a word out; and Rameses swallowed down the breath all unprepared. "Who has pursued his own plans and used your office for his own ends—casting aspersions on your name, Luminance, and aiming to let the dust of this affair blow into your eyes, not his, who will claim to have followed orders, as he claimed with your predecessor, and his predecessor before him— We speak of *Mithridates*, Luminance, who aims at the stability of Hell itself, —who usurps your titles, Luminance, and claims the sun; who has the power of your office behind him when he raises troops and moves men and enlists assassins, —who, barring pharaoh's watchfulness, will use Egypt for a bulwark and seek advancement in Egypt's fall, as he rose at each successive commander's accession— Where has he left to climb, Luminance, but to affront your person and your divinity? This is *ambition!*"

Rameses let go the breath. His mouth was still open. Then he shut it. "Lectures, —*lectures*, is it, from the blasphemer? From the polluted and the defiling?"

"*I* have no wish to see Egypt go down!"

"Nor do I!" Klea snapped. "I am Alexander's heir. Mithridates is an upstart, who claims *my* inheritance, —who claims *Asia*, Luminance, and makes common cause with Perians and Assyrians, the destroyers of

Egypt, Luminance! who seek to rise in Egypt's fall.
And you will not hear a warning!"

"Upstart woman! Out of my office!"

"Give me my son!"

"Out!"

"Luminance!" Hatshepsut pursued to the front of the
desk as Rameses passed behind it, and leaned her hands
on it and the disordered papers and stared straight into
pharaoh's myopic eyes. "This man has counseled an
attack on Caesar for his own purposes, and if it brings
war, if it brings chaos—then whose cause does it serve?
Caesar's? Yours? Or the cause of rebellion, of revolution,
of the Persian East, Luminance, the likes of which
slaughtered the divine bull and profaned the shrines,
—claiming the Sun for their own, Luminance! and calling
pharaoh a liar! This man upsets the natural order, sets
son against father, subject against lord, —is *this* the
policy of pharaoh, or is this the whispering of Set
himself?"

"*Out!*"

"Look to your back, Luminance. You have taken
Typhon to your household and believed a foreigner! I
have said!"

"*Out!*"

Hatshepsut turned on her heel and regarded Klea
with a lift of her jaw and a look that said: *We tried*.

While Klea looked as if she would go for Rameses
bare-handed. But she was too wise for that. She turned
on her heel with the smooth precision of a court
processional and the both of them turned their backs on
pharaoh, which no one dared; and walked to the doors
which Hatshepsut struck with the flat of her hand.

If they had lost, Hatshepsut thought as they passed
the doors, they had at least got out no worse than they
had gone in.

And maybe troubled the old vulture's sleep. *Rebellion*
was not a thing the Sun Arising cared to contemplate.
He had nowhere to rise in Hell; he had, though one

dared not remind him, only a great distance to fall—a very great distance for a god-king unused to the sight of a stiffly retreating back, who clung to his ceremonial prerogatives, and who was, by Set, entirely unfitted for any existence without those privileges to shield him.

Guards saluted, having no clearer orders. Doors opened and boomed shut again. They gained the hall.

No word passed between them. There was an excellent chance that the hall itself was bugged, at least in this vicinity.

And whatever dark thoughts Klea was thinking, Hatshepsut reckoned, they were no darker than her own. She drew one breath and another to clear the stink of incense from her nostrils, and recollected not Klea's thankless son, but the other one, the handsome, well-spoken lad who had *not*, she was sure beyond any doubt, *not* acted against Julius or against the house. She did not know why she thought so, except she recollected a talk on the stairs, and the look in his eyes, that here was a lad who tried like hell to *understand* things, and that whatever had brought him to kill Julius back in Rome, selfish hate had had nothing to do with it.

She was sure of it, who had dealt with assassins and connivers aplenty in Egypt, and clung with her fingernails to her dreams of wielding power *well*. And every time she came within the stifling closeness of pharaonic ritual she remembered the walls around her and the betrayals and the stink of incense and of narrow, goal-directed thinkers.

A boy like that was no match for jackals the likes of which occupied that office back there.

Neither was a young hothead like Caesarion.

"Damn you!" Caesarion yelled, and braced his rubber-shod feet on the marble floor, till the soldiers wrestled him into motion again and slammed him into the wall and hit him.

Whereat Brutus hit them, with his shoulder, which was all he could do with his hands chained; and kicked one of them for good and proper, and tried for the other— *No half-measures*. Niccolo had told him. *Do, or don't do. Leave no enemies.*

Unfortunately he was not able to follow that advice: Niccolo had not had a brother up against a wall being beaten by an Assyrian colonel.

And thereafter himself, with at least the knowledge that they had stopped beating Caesarion; but that meant it was him, and it hurt, gods, they were going to kill him. His head hit the wall behind, stars exploded in his vision, and a fist knocked the breath out of him and the legs out from under him.

After that, they could have killed him, but instead they hauled him up, spun him about and made him walk behind his brother, which took everything he had left, just to get air into his lungs.

Down the hall and to a pair of doors that could have let trucks in and out, except they were gold, and covered with bas-reliefs of chariots and dying lions. King-bulls guarded the place, in gold too; and the doors opened on a vast echoing room, on hanging tapestries of gold and silver, columns studded with lapis and ivory and banded with gold, gold, and more gold, that shone in lamplight, golden tables, gold fringes on the men and women who stood and stared at the door; so much glitter it blinded and dazzled; and at the end of the room a huge wall of gold relief-work, in the midst of which a throne, and on that throne a figure wrapped in a cloak of gold that had the sheen of blood, under a diadem that shone like ice. To either hand of that one were other thrones, some empty, most occupied—by a figure all in silver and ice on one hand, by one in pale gold, by one in bronze and sapphire on the right, and one in gold and purple. All of them with diadems, all shining and terrible.

Brutus stared, thinking of the Olympian gods, having

heard of Satan and the fallen angels. Surely these were
the lords of Hell, who had snatched them up, and who
were about to do something terrible to them for having
made trouble and caused all the shooting—sending two
boys to the Pit right along with their enemies, and
perhaps Julius and all the villa as well. His knees were
weak with more than the beating when they hauled him
and Caesarion toward that distant figure, that gained
more and more distinction as a black-bearded man who
looked—

Damn! —more and more Assyrian.

Their guards let them go, and pushed on their
shoulders, about the time that realization hit, and he
knew they were only men—a collection of kings.

Again the shove, which Brutus could not for the
instant understand, until his dazed wits sorted out that
they were actually supposed to kneel down in front of
these—these mortal kings in glittering robes.

Oh, damn, he thought tearfully, *I can't, I can't do
this*— Because whatever Caesarion would do, he could
not even imagine himself on his knees: it was too
ridiculous, too shameful. He was obliged to stand there
on his feet till they killed him, being Roman, and
having all his ancestors to respect.

Neither, it turned out, did Caesarion intend to do
what they wanted. "Fuck you!" he yelled, when they
tried to kick his feet out from under him. "*Send* me to
the Undertaker! *I'll spill everything I know, damn you!*"

And: *Oh, shit,* Brutus thought in profound despair,
borrowing from Caesarion because none of his own oaths
seemed to cover it. *Brother, that wasn't terribly bright.*

The 10th and the 12th came overland, since Administration and the Pentagram could hardly fail to notice
any great number of jeeps and troop trucks pulling up
in front of the villa, and there were, gods knew, enough
of them filling the gravel parking lot that had once been
green lawn.

They came overland, not in parade dress, but in 20th-century combat gear, not with the bright flash of shields and armor, but with precision for all that, and with their eagles and their standards: they were still legionaries, and Julius had told the courier to tell them: Tiberius had called up the Praetorians—the Praetorian Guard, the police of the Empire, who had sold themselves as well as the purple, and been both the Empire's salvation (they had removed Caligula) and its bane (they had bestowed the throne on him and worse).

The Praetorians—the unit Augustus had created of the survivors of the 10th; but *those* men had rejoined old comrades in Hell, *those* men were marching with the 10th, with their honor to avenge, against the time-servers and murderers who had tarnished the Guard through five centuries of misrule: and the 12th was there to back them.

No more than that. There could not be more than that, on the field, in an action which Hell did not sanction, headed first up from the armory and through the private forest and hunting preserve of Louis IV and Maria Theresa, out now into the daylight of Hell's red skies. Six thousand men to a legion—three to four in terms of what a field commander actually got, in the wars of Rome; but in Hell they were more numerous than that. In Hell, all who had ever died following the eagles—belonged.

Julius folded his arms and watched them as they came, with that peculiar relief and dread that a commander had to feel, who had not seen the legions take the field for a pitched battle—in decades.

And who knew that, this time, their dead might be lost to them. That *he* might be, and all the West might well go down.

Not for you, son, not even for you—

They've challenged. That's why I've raised the eagles. That's the only thing that could justify this.

No single life.

Only Rome.

Cohorts of the 14th to occupy the Dissidents, the 6th to guard the villa; and the 20th and 8th on drill at the Armory—in case . . . while others were on alert as far and as fast as couriers could reach them across Hell.

What the Assyrians by rights had, and the armaments they had, was one worry. What underground sources might be supplying them was altogether another. In this much the legions trusted their lives to Machiavelli and to Horatius' lads.

What the Pentagram might decide to do was altogether another question. Therefore the need of speed. It was the best tactic they could manage, while Dante, in his small room, was a fragile warning system.

(*"Cesare,"* Dante had said, shadow-eyed amid the clutter, the scattered papers—gods *knew* how the man found his notes— *"Cesare, prego— Non potest fieri!* Impossible, impossible, I cannot do miracles—they will cut our throats, they will rain down fire and grenades and the Lord God knows—" . . . And he: "Niccolo is relying on you." Gods knew, shame worked when all else failed; and the little scholar was proud. He had cuffed Dantillus on the ear, gently, like a brother, and Dantillus, his face lined with years and studies, had blushed and looked at him with shimmering eyes. "I'm relying on you," Julius had said, which was only truth. "The legions are. You're our hope, *Dantille*, you're our ultimate medevac—you're all we've got.")

It was truth, too. There was no other. Niccolo had not called. He had his hope in the legions. And gods knew what it was going to cost them in blood. He had far rather have finessed this, the easy way.

Brakes squealed, horribly, out toward the street,—two sets of brakes, and he looked out past the drive in time to see a black staff car short the driveway and clip the junipers as it evaded a big silver bus with *IZMIR TURIZM* in peeling paint on the side.

Who in hell—?

But it was Horatius who came up the drive in a spray of gravel, Horatius unmistakable behind the wheel as he whipped around into secure territory—Sargon and Scaevola were with him, and some fourth man, Caesar saw as the car passed and braked; he spared half a glance for that and the rest for the Turkish tour bus that was blocking the drive and opening its doors.

He snatched his Colt from its holster and yelled at the sentries: the guards on the roof likely had already shortened their range from the Park to that bus, out of which one khaki-clad passenger had come while others stayed aboard.

But, damn, he *knew* the blond man; and the tall dark-haired one was his own aide.

"Hold fire!" he yelled, "hold fire!" And ran forward himself, before some overzealous legionary put a hole in T. E. Lawrence or in Mouse. He holstered his pistol and met the offered hand. "Lawrence. Welcome."

"Julius Caesar. A pleasure, sir." Lawrence's eyes darted momentarily beyond his shoulder and back again. "On the move, are we? I've two dozen specials with our own gear, and Attila's bringing in another lot to the north. The bus was what we could liberate: we've got ten of mine and a squad of French. I understand this is a hit and run. Where do you want us?"

Clear and concise. It was a relief, after chaos. "If that thing will take the roads, right through the greenbelt and in, quick and loud."

"Julius." Sargon had come up behind him, out of breath. "Are they going in?"

"Close as they can." Julius looked at him, at Sargon and Scaevola both, hard-breathing and exhausted; and damned well the best he had for what he could not do himself.

Sometimes old friends read minds. "I can get in," Sargon said. "I know where I'm going."

And: "He'll need help," Scaevola said.

"Sargon of Akkad," Julius said. "Mucius Scaevola.

—T. E. Lawrence. Have you got a couple of spare seats? We've got two boys held hostage somewhere inside and we're short on transport."

"A rescue, then?"

"A damned difficult one. Our main objective is to scotch this snake before it breeds. Gods know *what* we can do about the hostages."

Lawrence's frosty gaze flickered back and forth over the several of them. "More than paying the dues, is it?" Meaning his recent defection from the East. "Climb aboard. If we're going in first, we'd best hope we can get that bus over those roads and get in. Then we'll see."

Lawrence turned and ran, and disappeared into the bus. Sargon and Scaevola jogged after him with never a hesitation.

"Go with them?" Mouse asked, and Julius looked bleakly at his aide, slowly—no expression on Mouse's face, except for someone who knew how to read him. Mouse wanted to go.

Which left a father clenching his hands and reminding himself what he had told himself since he knew where his sons had gone: *Not for any one life*.

And he could not send the legions under any subordinate, or detach his best field officer on a personal mission.

Especially not on a personal mission.

"No," he said. "*I* need you." The bus had its doors closed. It squealed into motion and rumbled on down the street as a stray shot rang out from somewhere.

Cong sniper. Fire spattered back from their own snipers on the roof. He grabbed Mouse's arm and the both of them got the hell out of the open.

"Lawrence knows who the hostages are," Mouse said. "I figured he had better. He's got all the maps."

Efficient. As usual.

That had been the flicker in Lawrence's expression. The Englishman might or might not understand a Roman's necessities.

It was damned certain that Brutus did. And it hurt to think of it. And of Caesarion, not alone for Klea's sake. Caesarion had never expected much of him. And was right, in this case.

A handful of men and a distraction. And a damned rattling bus that might or might not make the rough roads in the greenbelt.

The legions were moving steadily—a deceptive pace, that ate up the ground at a rate enemies unaccustomed to face them would not believe.

"Come on," he said to Mouse, and headed for the jeep that substituted for a horse these days.

As the legions began to shift in their precise way from the marching formation to a battle-line.

So the Praetorians would be doing—facing one direction or the other, somewhere the other side of the tennis courts.

"*What* can this person tell us?" the king asked. "What does he claim to know—that we would be unwilling to have known? *Nothing*, perhaps. This half-Egyptian, half-Roman kinglet only wishes to make himself more important than he is—a consorter with rabble. A roisterer and a libertine, useless even to the rabble he claims to defend. Does he think to threaten *us* with his revelations?"

"His majesty Assurbanipal," said a man with a staff, advancing to the edge of the dais, "has generously asked several questions. One will answer thoroughly. His majesty the light of the lands, slayer of lions, is not patient of subterfuges and does not engage in dialogue with persons of no consequence."

"Wha'd he say?" Caesarion asked, jaw hanging, with a casual shrug toward the row of kings in splendor. He was still on his feet and his step had acquired that sense of unheard music, insolent to the extreme, even with his hands chained. "Subter-what? *Wha's* his majesty say?"

"Caesarion," Brutus said, coming up against him to

force his attention, the best that he could do without the use of his hands. "Caesarion, for the gods' sake don't play games with these people!"

"Hey, they're not going to do a damn thing with us." Caesarion danced a step further and pivoted on his heel, full spin about to shout up at the kings: "Not a damned thing."

"They're going to beat us to bloody ribbons," Brutus hissed. "For godssake! Caesarion!"

"That one there's his majesty Assurbanipal." A jut of Caesarion's chin. "The guy next to him is Darius the Great, *the* Darius; and crazy Xerxes; and his imperial lunacy Cambyses. On *that* side is Cyrus, who's got his marbles—"

"Caesarion! —Dammit!" Brutus put himself between him and the kings, holding him with his eyes. "*Are you trying to get us killed?*"

Then he gulped in a breath, looking at Caesarion face to face. He was staring at a crazy man. It was a wild, terrible look that took him and the rest of the world and just threw it aside, and he was momentarily more afraid of the brother he was facing than of the guards closing in around them.

A spear-shaft swung. Caesarion tore loose to counter it and Brutus let him go, evaded another spear in the hands of a guard and lost his balance.

He just did what Sargon had taught him, went down, crossed his leg over in a kick that caught the man's legs, and wrenched hard, sending the guard off *his* balance and down on the polished floor.

All of which was very good, but when he rolled to get his feet a spear-shaft cracked across the side of his head and dropped him flat and blind with a point pressing hard in the middle of his back. He heard Caesarion shouting obscenities, blinked the room halfway clear and saw three guards trying to carry Caesarion to the floor.

They crashed down together and sat on Caesarion

finally. And half the kings were out of their chairs, some of them halfway down the steps as the shouting died away,

Except Xerxes.

"Impale them!" Xerxes yelled in a madman's voice, pounding the marble steps with his staff. He was the one in gold and pale purple. He had a baboon by his chair, on a golden chain. "Impale them!" he shrieked, and the baboon circled and bared its teeth.

"Flay them alive," Cambyses suggested, chin on fist, from his chair. "First."

O gods. Brutus made a try at getting up. The spear-point dug into his spine.

There was quiet as Assurbanipal lifted a jeweled hand and rose from his throne, the man in the image of the king-bulls . . . or they in his. He walked slowly to the edge of the dais. "We will ask his companion," he said, and guards seized Brutus' arms and jerked him to his feet. "Our servants will ask him at length. And have the truth from *him.*"

"Caesarion?" Brutus asked. It came out shakier than it was supposed to. His voice cracked. They were hauling him away, toward the doors, and he tried to plant his feet, having some luck with the rubber-soled tennies, but with his hands chained and a fist gripping his hair and two others his arms, he was losing ground, he was going toward whatever they had in mind to do to him, and the last friendly sight he was likely to see was Caesarion, who struggled wildly to get up despite the guards pinning him.

"Damn you!" Caesarion shouted, waking echoes. "Damn you, let him alone! He's Caesar's *son*, you fools!"

"*Stop!*" the Great King Assurbanipal said, waking as many of his own. And Brutus, braced as the guards froze, all but threw them all off their balance till they got a better grip on him.

"Caesar's son," Assurbanipal said.

"He didn't tell you." Caesarion's mouth curved in a

mocking smile, a grin, as his guards hauled him to his feet. "The *Pentagram* didn't tell you. Your own *staff* didn't tell you—"

"Insolence!" Xerxes cried, pointing a finger. Spittle flew. The baboon screamed and bounded to the arm of his throne and down again. "We know what to do with his like! Give him to us!"

"What am I not told?" Assurbanipal asked, and stamped the floor with his staff. *"What am I not told? Eh?"*

"Ask Kadashman-enlil!" Caesarion said from amongst his guards. "Caesar had an illegitimate son—a son he favors. My half-brother—the center of a whole fucking Pentagram operation—and you've muffed it, majesty! You've blown it wide, screwed up what they didn't tell you, huh? Just didn't want to disturb you. Kadashman-enlil, majesty, *and* the Egyptians on your staff. Ask *them* what you've just happened to gather up—and watch the bastards squirm, you—"

A guard gripped him by the hair and pulled his head back. Steel flashed.

"No!" Brutus yelled.

Assurbanipal made a backhanded wave of his hand.

X

"*Prego*," Dante said, "*prego, signore, magnificio—non lo so—*"

"*Latine!*" Augustus snapped. Dante had vapors. *He* was having his own, by the gods, Antonius was breathing his last downstairs and Dante babbled excuses designed to get himself off the hook if they let Antonius slip— which they were not, by the gods, going to do.

"I must not do this for one man, *magnifico*. I must not be specific—it is too dangerous—"

"I don't care *who* you sweep up in your net, man, just be ready! Galen can't hold him."

The First Citizen slammed the door—suppliant at Dante's shrine, as they all must be; and Julius headed off gods knew to what—

He was left with Antonius. With the man he had disgraced and hounded to a shameful death.

And he fought for Antonius—since Julius was bound to believe the worst. He was no fighter: he had done his share of rattling about in armor during the wars against Antonius, but he had rarely lifted a sword; he had been rackingly seasick during the battle at Actium; he had gotten out of his wars alive because of his advisers and his guards and a devout practice of leaving war to the soldiers and staying out of the lines, unlike

Julius, who, even past forty, had had no hesitation about rushing into battle, with and without his shield, his helmet, gods knew what. Julius had a temper and when it was touched he was the despair of his aides and his shieldmen, even in Hell.

And that temper was touched indeed. Two of his sons had caused this mess and Octavianus Augustus, the third, and his heir, had helped; dammit, it was not *his* fault that the mere sight of him had spooked Caesarion and precipitated the chase that had led to Caesarion's escape. Klea forgave him her death; Antonius—forgave him his death, if not other things too painful and too deeply rooted in Antonius' character to forget; Brutus did not know about his—gods knew what he knew by now; but Caesarion—Caesarion had Julius' temper, that was what, Julius' temper and his headlong recklessness but not Julius' cynical good sense, dammit! which was what had led them to this pass. Everything was simple to Caesarion, no matter how complicated it was, and extenuating circumstances meant nothing.

Augustus was heir, Augustus caught the flak, and if Augustus did well Julius would never remark it, that was the damnable truth. If disaster struck, *then* Julius would notice.

And if the villa took harm, if he lost Antonius, if Antonius *got* lost while Antonius was left in charge, and some enemy glitched things and hurled him into the nether planes—Julius would explode; and settle, and be civil; but by the gods, nothing would be the same. Ever.

Therefore Augustus insisted Galen stay with Antonius, never take his eyes off him—as much to have a witness of good faith as for Antonius' welfare.

Therefore Augustus fretted between Aemilius Paulus, in command of the house defenses, and Dante, and finally back downstairs where a cloud of sycophants flitted in and out the closed doors of the infirmary, highly agitated.

Something's wrong. Augustus thought, and pushed the door open—not wanting *to be at hand if Antonius slipped; but he had to know, he had to do what he could.*

He saw the tubes, the dreadful machines—Galen understood them: he did not; he did not want to. Tubes and buckets and more tubes and Antonius shrouded in clear plastic like a man caught in some monstrous web, with his life displayed in all the arcane lines and blinking lights, which might make sense to the Greek doctor who hovered there, but only seemed pitiful to Augustus —that a man's inexorable decline should be made so public.

He went as far as the bedside, stood uncomfortably by as Galen fussed with the needle in Antonius' arm—an exhausted doctor, shadow-eyed and pale-faced . . . until one looked at his patient and knew how white a face could get.

Then he saw Antonius' eyes slit open, black as death itself, and saw Antonius' hand move and grope toward him.

Gods, he did not want to stay here, did not want anything to do with Antonius in the condition he was in—he was an enemy too close to family; and that Antonius should have no one but him for comfort was shameful. But the fingers strained and trembled, the little that they could lift at all, and Antonius tried to speak past the dreadful tubes, in mortal pain; Augustus moved because he could not stand to see the man hurt himself, took Antonius' hand and sat down there on the chair Galen had used.

"It's all right," he lied. "Everything's nearly under control. All you've got to do is hang on a little longer. Julius' orders. Hear?"

Antonius blinked. Slowly the fingers tightened on his. And would not let go.

The Ferrari spun a close turn off the street and into the drive, and Klea put her head up. There was a bullet

hole in Hatshepsut's door. She did not want to know
where it had gone after that. A Cong sniper had done
it, just as they hit Park, and Hatshepsut had peeled out
of there with all the speed the Ferrari could manage: if
they were shooting on the street, it was bad.

And it was worse when they had come far enough up
the drive to see the villa's parking lot with a good many
empty spaces where trucks and jeeps assigned to the
10th had been parked. "Something's happened," Klea
said. "O gods, something's happened."

For a while Brutus was content to lie where they had
thrown him, on the cold stone floor, in the gray little
room with a single light-bulb overhead. Caesarion was
with him. They were both breathing. That fact and the
ache in his skull and his back was all-absorbing, and he
did not have to think much further than that. He did
not want to.

But he did not hear anything from Caesarion, and
that urged him finally to turn his head and twist over
where he had a view of Caesarion's back, which told
him nothing. He struggled up to sit and nudge Caesarion
with his knee. "Are you all right?"

"Fuck off."

He took in his breath, thought for a moment that
where the Assyrians and the Persians had failed to
break Caesarion's neck, *he* would like to do it. For a
moment he had trouble breathing at all, and meditated
smashing his knee good and hard into Caesarion's skull,
which might at least give some relief to the frustration
welling up in him, that left him a little short of unmanly
tears: dammit, he was snatched up in this, he had never
asked for it, and now Caesarion wanted to treat him like
poison and act like he was born in the gutters.

"Damn you," he said to Caesarion. "You're a *fool*,
hear me?"

Caesarion did not move for a moment more. Then
he got an elbow under him and sat up and twisted

around to stare murder at him. *"I'm* the fool? Bastard brother—" Caesarion caught his breath and shut up in a way that had gotten to grate on Brutus' nerves. *"Hell!* If I hadn't had you to look out for—"

"Dammit, you didn't need to tell them who I was! That was sheer spite! They hadn't figured it out, for the gods' sake!"

"For godssake, they were going to cut you into dogmeat, you dumb shit! I saved your fucking *life!"*

"Saved my life? Good *gods!* you had them if you'd kept your damn mouth shut, they'd have asked us questions, you could have lied to them, told them stuff it'd take them days to check out—and *pro di*, you open your mouth and use language like that to the king— What kind of nut *are* you?"

"Doesn't fucking matter." Caesarion no longer looked at him. He tucked his knee up and his shoulder over against the wall and looked somewhere at the baseboard in the corner.

"What are we going to do?" Brutus asked as reasonably as he could. "Dammit, you got us into this. You know these people. How can we get out of this?"

Caesarion did not even look around. "There isn't any damn way out. And shut up. They'll have this place bugged."

"It doesn't matter, does it? You're going to fold up like a coward, it doesn't matter."

No reaction.

"Is that it?" Brutus goaded him. "No guts?"

Caesarion rolled over again, shoulders both to the wall, and stared somewhere at the ceiling. "You name it, bastard brother. When they come for us we can just beat hell out of 'em, handcuffs and all."

It was more truth than he wanted. He felt sick at his stomach. He edged over close as he could get to Caesarion, got up on his knees and whispered against Caesarion's ear: "You have any friends here?"

Caesarion jerked away from him and looked at the

corner again. Brutus sat down on his heels and stared at him in dull rage.

"Remember the pair on the end," Caesarion said finally, acidly. "Man in gold and brass? —Woman in silver? That's my brother and my sister . . . Alexander Helios and Kleopatra Selene. For what it's worth."

"They won't help you."

"Hell, no. They won't lift a finger. They'll be there—when they crucify us."

"For godssake—"

Caesarion looked at him, a bleak, weary stare. "I'm out of tricks, brother. Damn well out of tricks. And you know what hurts like hell?"

"What's that?" Brutus asked, forcing the words in all that silence.

"Our mutual father—was *right*. Bloody right. I hate that most of all."

"Right—about what?"

Caesarion shut his eyes a moment. "Kadashman-enlil."

"What?— The colonel?"

"Colonel Kadashman-enlil." He drew a long and shaky breath. "Colonel Kadashman-enlil—"

There was silence then. And Caesarion's chin dimpled and trembled, steadied finally as his mouth took on a hard line. Caesarion wept, tears leaking from his tightly shut eyes, and Brutus settled sideways to the floor, confounded.

"I was taking us to the Dissidents," Caesarion said at last. "And here we are. A Pentagram operation. Just like the Old Man said, huh? I believed—dammit, I really believed! But Kadashman-enlil shows up. An Assyrian *colonel*, for godssakes!"

"You knew him."

"Yeah, I knew him. *Know* him. Mere recruiter. In charge of *all* the mercs Guevara bought— *The Pentagram* bought. The Pentagram bought and paid for. All those men. Damn, damn, damn. Julius was right—the whole fucking Movement's a fucking *front*—"

Brutus did not understand all of it; most everything he knew about revolutions and clandestine movements he had gotten from his boyhood in Rome, and from the television and the bits and tags one and the other person had spilled in his hearing. But he got the gist of it: Julius had told him, too. The Pentagram had bought their way in among the very people that thought they were overthrowing the government of Hell. And Caesarion had believed in those people, had latched onto them as true and right—attached to them all the devotion he withheld from Julius, from whom he had long since been bitterly estranged.

Julius was right, was a terrible honesty for him.

And Brutus, who had spent years nerving himself for that ride to Massilia to confront Julius with his existence, who had suffered his own hell on earth and hated Julius before he had known he loved him—just sat there staring with a lump in his throat and a fervent wish he could do something for his brother, who had not been so lucky in what he gave his trust to.

It was that, which made Caesarion so desperate. Even with company in tow, Caesarion was still, always, all alone.

"Damn," Caesarion said finally, quietly, but his chest was still heaving with his breaths, and his chin trembled. "I don't figure it. Assurbanipal didn't know. . . ."

"Didn't know what?" Brutus asked, after Caesarion seemed to have his breath again.

"Didn't know what game Kadashman-enlil was playing. Dammit, they swept us *up*, they brought us *here*— Assurbanipal is all snuggles with the Pentagram ever since Rameses came in— No friend of the Egyptians in general, but damn sure no friend of Rome. Assyrians high up in the Pentagram, Egyptians snuggling up to Tiberius, Horemheb and Ra-hotep and his lot—and a merc captain with the Dissidents turns out to be an Assyrian *colonel*—"

Brutus thought of the bugs and made a worried gesture of the eyes toward the ceiling.

"Hell," Caesarion said, "hell with the bugs. Let 'em listen. If it's Kadashman-enlil in charge, what I know's no news to him. If it's somebody else, I hope he gets an earful. I only wish I knew which of them hauled us in—him on his own, or him for Assurbanipal, or Assurbanipal—with him sweating bullets knowing I'd say too much. Maybe his meeting us out there was supposed to scare me into keeping my mouth shut. I don't know. I don't bloody care. He's not ours. He never was. Bought and paid for. All the guys he hired— They were supposed to have raided this Pentagram weapons cache. That was the story. All these guns. All that equipment *they* got—whole damn story we swallowed—Guevara swallowed."

Caesarion was calmer then, staring off at the far wall. For a long moment more he said nothing, then:

"They'll have sent to the Pentagram. That's why they're just holding onto us. I was scared the Dissidents might be on our case—papa pulls me out in a chopper just before he blows the whole damn camp— *What* in hell were you doing there, brother? *Why* were you standing there tied to a tree?"

Brutus' heart did a lurch, the way it did when he thought of that fall out of the plane, the way it did when he thought of that black gulf he could not pull any memory out of, or when people started to tell him things and suddenly clamped their mouths shut, re-organized and said something else instead. All his life was full of such little pits and drops. And this was a big one. "I don't know. I hurt myself in the jump. I don't remember much about it."

"What were you *doing* there?"

"I don't know. I don't remember. Julius said he had to send me. He said he thought I could help. But I guess I hit the ground pretty hard. I think I was supposed to count in English."

Caesarion gave him a look that said he was incredibly
stupid. And Brutus reckoned that he was, that he had
always been, and he felt that dark spot wider and
wider, and more dangerous.

*What is it that makes me important? As a hostage? Is
that why they're waiting on the Pentagram? Julius can't
give in to them, whatever they want. Money's nothing
to these people. They're already rich. There's nothing
else Julius could trade for me—nothing that wouldn't
hurt the villa and everyone depending on him; and he
won't do that. Can't do it. No matter what they do to
me and Caesarion.*

And some of these people are crazier than Tiberius.

O gods, I don't know how to face this.

Caesarion nudged him with his knee, once, twice,
until he looked him in the face. "Hey," Caesarion said.
"They'll pull you out. You'll be all right. No way they'll
send you to the Undertaker. Me, either. Gods know I
tried. We're both too valuable." And suddenly up on
his knees, his lips close to Brutus' ear. "You want to do
me a favor? Insist you want me along."

Panic shifted focus, that was all. Brutus turned his
head quickly, whispered against his brother's ear: *"Why?
What can I do?"*

Caesarion sat down again, away from him, with that
guarded look on his face people got when they kept
secrets from him.

Brutus shivered, not wanting to; but a terrible chill
came over him, and his knees shook and his teeth would
have chattered if he had not clenched his jaw tight.

He dared not ask further. It was something, among
the other things, Caesarion did not want to discuss in
the Assyrians' hearing.

It was one with all the other questions no one would
answer, all those things Julius had said to keep in
abeyance and not ask, not wonder on, not think of—

—like: *Why don't I remember dying? Why do people
keep secrets from me?*

And: *What use does the Pentagram think I am?*
*Why does Caesarion think I have any influence to
save us?*
Gods, what am I?

The legions moved at their ground-devouring pace, a
battle-line of the old style, experienced in two millennia
of Hell's turbulent politics, and with a good many more
tactics to rely on than this straight-edged, face-on
approach to a problem.

But this was a *Roman* problem, and Julius kept his
jeep to the center of the line, just ahead of them, the
tennis courts left far behind and the hulking mass of
Tiberius' house with its colonnades and porticos and
balconies and tiled roofs rising into clear view beside
the ruddy, sky-reflecting waters of its Lake.

There was also a considerable expanse of manicured
lawn, and another battle-line, of Roman soldiers in a
gods-awful mishmash of Roman armor and 19th- and
20th-century military regalia. Red cloaks, plumes on
the officers' helmets—like some damned salad, Julius
thought, who had always counted dyed horsehair showy
enough to serve; and who right now had the more
protective comfort of a 20th-century helmet on his
head.

Mouse was his driver. Mouse usually was; and Curtius
and Agricola were in charge of the legions behind him.
That would be Mummius Achaicus on the other side,
Commander of the Praetorian Guard and head of
Tiberius' secret service, which in the case of the Guard
branch was little secret and given to knocks on doors at
night and mysterious disappearances— They would do
more of it than they did, except that Horatius and *his*
operation had Disappeared a few of the Guard back in
Tigellinus' administration and made it clear the Julian
establishment took a dim view of midnight arrests and
assassinations. Tigellinus had gotten himself a Pentagram
post, and Mummius had made his ferret's way into

Tiberius' good graces—being, like Tiberius, a man capable of sniffing out gold and secrets at a hundred paces.

Not incompetent as a general. And the Praetorians were full strength: thousands upon thousands of them, all the thieving lot of them that had preyed on Rome from the day Tiberius set them up in a walled camp and gave them special immunities, letting them run rough-shod over Senate and citizenry alike—damned few the emperors who could manage them after that, and no emperor had been powerful enough to disband them. They *could* fight. *They* had had the sole dispensation to carry steel inside the City, and that had given them an unbeatable advantage . . . against a populace whose weapons were cobblestones and awning-props.

But that populace had stiff fought them when it got bad enough.

And Julius, having led that populace as often as he had led armies, felt a damned well in his place facing the Praetorians, with the hard core of his Gallic veterans at his back.

Revenge . . . tempted him.

It damned well tempted the 10th, who had been the Praetorians of Augustus' day, when the term had meant something far different—a commander's personal body-guard. They had far rather, for this encounter, be in their old gear, hand to hand with the bastards.

As it was they kept a businesslike, sensible pace beside the 12th, and when their commanders halted them, they halted with an unasked-for and exaggerated precision.

"Keep driving," Julius said to Mouse. "Right up to the bastards."

Meaning right up to Mummius and his aides, who signalled parley by their position.

"Can't trust them," Mouse commented, shifting gears and picking up speed.

Julius had thought of it—the more than small possibility

that Mummius would signal truce and violate it, attempting with a fusillade of modern weapons to remove the opposition. He and Mouse could go out together.

But the man who killed Mouse—so the legions believed, and it might well be true—had a hot place in the Pit. Likewise those Mouse killed—did not come back again. It was the nature of the curse on him. And the latter was, thus far, true, even for those not Roman.

As bodyguards went, Mouse was the best.

And drew them up with a spin of the wheel that put himself between Julius and the guns.

"Dammit," Julius said under his breath, and stood up, facing Mummius and his aide. "You get my message, *Mummi?* Face this mess the other direction. You've got nothing to gain in this one, and who knows, you might get off with the Assyrians' silverware."

Mummius' face turned colors. "You're about to trespass, *Cai Iuli*, and you damned well know it. The emperor won't countenance this adventurism. We have nothing to gain by this."

"And everything to lose by standing in my way. Listen to me, *Mummi*. I'll put it in simple terms. We're being pushed. *Rome* and its clients are being pushed; and you damn well know what we'll get if we tuck down and wait and see if our enemies reform. Come off it. You've bedded down with Mithridates' pets long enough to know the score. You've got a chance to get the old man out of the trap he's dug himself into *and* save your necks. You value yours. All you have to do is pull this force around and let's not weaken our mutual position, all right?"

"Makes fine sense," Mummius called across from his own jeep. "But it's not Egyptians this time, *Cai Iuli*. It's the Authorities. You do the turning around: that's what makes sense, before you take us all to the nether hells. You pay over the cost of repairs, you get your army off the emperor's lawn, and you keep real quiet awhile, those are the conditions. And maybe, *maybe* we can patch things up with Administration. We're out here on official mandate. *Official*, do you understand me? An Insecurity Agent is at the palace yonder, asking questions. I don't doubt he's coming over to your side in short order. You might as well start thinking of the answers."

It would not be politic or particularly smart to blow Mummius out of his jeep under truce. But it was damned tempting; and Julius clenched his hand on the dash and did not spare a wondering look toward the palace or the skyline of New Hell, in which the Hall of Injustice, Administration, was the most prominent feature.

"*Mummi*," he said, "you always were a pirate. What's the Guard selling for these days? Renting by the pound or by the hour?"

Mummius grinned, in that way of a small man having won.

"Go back to your lines," Julius said.

The grin went a little wooden. "And what?"

"Defend your honor," Julius said with a lift of his brows. "Remember?"

The look was utter dismay as Mouse obeyed his signal and threw the jeep into gear. Then Julius caught his balance wildly as Mouse swerved hard about and snatched his pistol out. There had been a shot behind them. Mouse sent one back, and Julius looked back as Mummius slumped and fell.

"Turn!" Julius yelled, and Mouse spun the wheel hard over and took them straight for the Praetorian lines. Behind them a shout went up: the legions were in motion.

Julius dived and snatched the Galil up from the floorboards as Mummius' driver trenched the lawn getting away.

"Get *down!*" Mouse yelled at him. He got mostly down, as far as gave him some cover, and took the targets Mouse gave him, spraying the Praetorian lines as Mouse took the jeep on a crosswise pass to the Praetorian right.

Fire came back, fire came past them the other direction, and as far as they went there was chaos in the Praetorian lines—

—the more so when Mettius Curtius in a troop truck rigged with steel plate came roaring up from the slope of the lawn and the hedges on the Praetorians' left flank with horn blowing, and a dozen of the cav's best firing over the armored sides, the whole thing banging and rattling like thunder let loose—*hell* of a substitute for the tank they didn't have; but by Venus Mother, it worked well enough for the Praetorians, who took it and that horn-blowing for another major assault coming in out of the bushes.

Julius took the chance to reload as the legions caught up to them, firing as they came, as Mouse turned about and blew the Standards Leftward on the jeep's horn, the hell with the field phone they had not been able to liberate.

By which time the Praetorians had started a disordered retreat, having figured out severally and unit by confused unit that things were coming apart, their signals were gone all to hell, field phones and all, and that the safest place to regroup was somewhere, say, over behind Tiberius' villa, as far as a rapid withdrawal could take them from the disorder of the field and the chaos Curtius' contraption had made of their whole left wing.

They were not even firing at the last, just backing up. And no few of them were outright running.

The 10th sent shots after them, desultory and measured encouragement, as Curtius' truck lumbered and thundered into the chosen line of march, one tire flapping. "Get that thing fixed!" Julius yelled as they passed, and if Curtius could not hear behind his shielding on the cab window, the men in the truck heard and hammered on the cab to get his attention. "Catch us up!"

"Sit down!" Mouse yelled at him.

He slumped down into the seat, feeling no satisfaction in the spectacle of a field littered with Roman shields. He felt more sick at his stomach.

Gods knew the Assyrians were not going to bluff.

And gods knew what fallout there was going to be from this, a pitched battle under the very nose of Administration.

But he could not have gone back. Not once it had gone this far. What the Praetorians had sold, the rest of the legions, the ones who had followed the Eagles into Hell, did not give up for any cost.

He had learned that in his life. A man did not lead the legions. The Eagles did; and their demands were absolute.

A black case materialized and its strap fell into pharaoh's outstretched hand, there by the villa, under the witness of the guardstation and the anxious ward of the commander of the 6th—Antonius hovering between life and death, the legions already gone over the hill toward a confrontation with the Assyrians, where the boys were held hostage; and Kleopatra climbed back into the Ferrari in haste, ignoring the pleas of the legate.

"We don't know what's come down over there," the legate said. "Stay. Wait."

"The hell," Hatshepsut said. "Tell the First Citizen where we've gone. Tell Julius if he checks in."

"You can run straight into a trap!" the legate yelled at her as she dropped into the seat and slammed the door. "We've had no word back yet!"

Hatshepsut started the car and threw it into reverse and about again, *not* toward the tennis courts.

Toward the street.

"Hey!" the legate shouted after them. "Wait!"

"Where are we going?" Klea gasped, as Hatshepsut took the corner and spun them off to the street. "Good *gods!*" She grabbed for the handhold, and took in her breath.

They had gotten *in*to the villa unscathed. Getting out again—Klea stopped asking questions. She took the Beretta out of her purse and held onto it, as the Ferrari screamed around a gentle curve and roared up Park like the proverbial bat.

Pharaoh had motives of her own. She knew that. Rameses himself was in danger, and with him the whole Egyptian establishment. But she and Hatshepsut were too long with each other and too many times at shouting, outright odds and too many times co-conspirators that she could think Hatshepsut would pull a silent, unprovoked double-cross of every old friend she had in Hell. No. Not with that set of her jaw and that reckless fury in her driving. It was not treachery Hatshepsut had in mind; it was overtaking Julius and taking a direct hand—in a situation already out of the Pentagram's control and getting worse by the minute.

The bus with its odd assortment of passengers bounced valiantly along the dirt roads and cycle trails of the greenbelt, lashed and battered with pine branches that slapped against the windshield and scraped along its length; crunching hedges and undergrowth on wild turns, and pitching wildly as it hit dips in a dirt road designed for four-wheel drive and cycles.

No matter. T. E. Lawrence clung with an elbow to the pole by the front exit, keeping his footing while reading a map and yelling Arabic instructions to the driver, one Mahmud, who with his brother had hotwired the vehicle in the heart of New Hell, where driver and passengers had gotten off for a museum tour.

"Yes, Aurens, yes, Aurens," Mahmud said, fighting to make the turns, desperately intent on the road. "Go right, yes, Aurens—"

"What we've got," Sargon of Akkad was telling Lawrence, in his other ear, Sargon occupying the poleside

seat with a khaki-clad knee, down to his undershirt and
clinging to the rail, while a huge Frenchman labored
with a wildly jouncing needle to stitch a patch on his
shirt. "What we've got is a small window to get a force
in there—we're all those boys have got, you understand?
You can get through the doors, can't you? You've still
got your credentials—"

"Leave that to me," Lawrence said, and in Arabic:
"Left! Left!"

The bus took out a sapling that raked all along the
undercarriage and traveled under them along the gravel
till they hit the next washout and nearly lost the right
front wheel.

"Sorry, Aurens, sorry, Aurens!"

"I can get in," Sargon was saying. "Scaevola can
handle the backup. You go in the front, I'll take the
side—go in through the barracks—I *know* the place.
too damned well."

"So do I," Lawrence reminded him. Sargon, being a
king, being Julius' ally, pushed to assume command—
assumed he *was* in command. Well enough: Lawrence
was in this to pay his dues, and it led him right back to
the Assyrians, the ascendency of whom in the councils
of the East was the reason of his defection. There was a
certain justice in that.

More, there were two boys in there, two adolescent
boys for whom there was no rescue if it did not come
from their end of the operation. The Romans had the
whole Assyrian war machine on their hands, or would
have, if something went wrong. It was a diversion and a
strike force they wanted, and if he could have picked
which end of this operation he would have preferred,
he would be precisely where he was, coming up on the
flank, where, beyond a last screen of trees, the fantastical
palace of Assurbanipal would soon be visible on the
shoes of the Lake.

"Stop!" he yelled at Mahmud, who squealed the brakes
grandly in obedience.

Lawrence opened the door. It was still public land. And he knew well enough *where* Assyrian surveillance was concentrated, what sort and where. "*Capitain*," he said to the tall, grim Frenchman in charge of *La Le'igion Étrangère: "D'ici, chacun a son devor."*

"*Bien, d'accord*," the answer came back, the men at the back starting forward as the Arab contingent gathered up their gear and prepared to vacate.

The Lion of Akkad recovered his shirt and followed him: Mucius Scaevola was staying, in the case Latin became a sudden necessity for the Foreign Legion.

"Quite!" Lawrence said shortly, stifling a natural enthusiasm in his followers.

For them as much as himself he had quitted former loyalties. If the Faithful found themselves in the hand of Shaitan, if by some dreadful mistake they had come into this place which was not Paradise, at least they did not have to cooperate with close-fisted and wicked kings who called them barbarians.

Neither, for his part, did T. E. Lawrence, who settled his knife at his belt and waved his men to follow him. The Lion of Akkad had already gone his own way, surprisingly quietly for so solid a man.

Operations continued in the war room, in the third level of the Pentagram, behind successive doors each with their guards and their security systems, and Mithridates issued orders as pieces shifted on the board.

"Get a chopper over there," he said, then keeping his voice down, and speaking to one of his own aides. But old Ass-cars caught it; he could see Rameses' attention shift from across the room, saw the tightening of Rameses' mouth and the characteristic push of the wire-rimmed spectacles up the nose——Rameses was back in his ordinary uniform, the one with the copious battle-ribbons from encounters he had mostly made with pen and ink, if anyone delved into the records——or dared confront a god-king with the facts. He came over with his swagger-stick tucked beneath his arm and flicked it out to stop the aide, an inconsequence; and to face Mithridates with a down-the-nose scowl.

"Why?"

"*Why*, Luminance? Because—" Mithridates mimed ground and trees, a if he was speaking to a child. "—we would prefer to *see* what's going on over there. The minimal necessity—"

"No," Rameses said. "Absolutely not. We have no need to involve heavy equipment. We have no need of choppers to know what our observers perfectly well report."

Mithridates gasped in a breath for one he had just lost. His mouth hung open an instant in shock. There were times Rameses still astonished him. "Luminance, we know what we *can* see. But we are talking about *Julius Caesar*, whose tactics are notorious for flanking—"

"Then post observers! We will not be reckless, King of Pontus. I have said."

A second try after breath. The first seemed insufficient. "We have posted observers, Light of the Two Lands, but if—"

"Are they blind, then?" Pharaoh spun his swagger-stick with a flourish and whipped it back to rest beneath his arm. Flicked it out again to tap at the map. "Here and here are sufficient elevations. Here is the roof. Take advantage of it. Let *someone climb the stairs*. King of Pontus! We see no reason to account for helicopters, when our very point with Administration is Roman waste and misaccounting. We may *have* equipment. There is no need for profligate consumption."

"Yes, Luminance. Climb the stairs." Mithridates grabbed his aide by the arm and jerked him sideways. "Tell them climb the stairs and have a look." He propelled the man to a refuge the other side of the translucent map, faced him so his back was to the Light of the Two Lands and said: "You never heard a thing.

Get the damned chopper up. If they cross that line, hit them with rockets—*you hear me?*"

"Majesty—"

"Reassignments," Mithridates said simply, eloquently, as he was wont to say, in private, to his immediate staff: *Fail me and you'll find out how deep in Hell Reassignments can lose a man. And you will need Reassignments. Hear?*

"Majesty," the man said, sweating, and went.

Fifteen minutes Pharaoh had been down here. Mithridates walked back and found a course that evaded Pharaoh's person and his suggestions, his endless, ill-conceived suggestions, and his irrational interference.

Pharaoh ordered general mobilization the moment the word came in of a legion-against-legion confrontation, hard upon the heels of the intrusion of the two queens into the Pentagram, with what kinds of charges and accusations Mithridates could imagine—damn them and their interference.

Whatever they had said undoubtedly regarded the whereabouts of Caesarion, whose flight from Roman custody had been thus far a windfall for Mithridates' intelligence operations—the Romans, to Mithridates' initial alarm, had acted with uncharacteristic haste and lack of planning . . . to penetrate the dissident organization, had been Mithridates' initial analysis. Possibly Caesar had even suspected his own rebel son as an agent of the agents who took their orders from the Pentagram: Mithridates despised the Romans, but he did not despise their efficiency or forget that Sargon of Akkad had penetrated Kadashman-enlil's operation undercover, whereafter the Romans had raided the Dissident camp, dislodged Alexander in one raid, killed Guevara (again) in another; and in general caused havoc with the whole Dissident operation which it had hitherto ignored as someone else's problem.

Caesar might well suspect how things worked, and might well think that there was some dark purpose in

Caesarion's flight—hence Mithridates" willingness to play this lethal game through New Hell's streets and subways, and hence the shift of tactics—

Not to let the fool Caesarion reach the Dissidents, but to pull him back to Assurbanipal's villa—where Caesar's well-known temper might serve them well: that was the plan, hastily immprovised. Caesar, being Roman, might kill Caesarion with his own hands, might disdain to rescue him, might not, in fact, care if Assurbanipal crucified the fool; but Caesar's own alienation of the madman Tiberius, who had strings on him Mithridates' could pull; and Caesar's having committed so much of Roman resources to this effort—made it little likely he would pull back from a direct challenge once the Assyrians held the prize.

Which Mithridates had seen to it was the case: Kadashman-enlil had had several options, and bringing Caesarion under Assurbanipal's roof, Mithridates had figured, was a sure way to get the reaction they wanted—a perfect inspiration, seeing that the Insecurity Service had launched their own investigation, and was at that hour making official inquiries as to why Roman agents had shot up the *Oasis* and the New Hell subway system, and why they had attacked their Assyrian fellow-citizens.

It was a rare opportunity for the Pentagram—to whisper in certain ears that there were heavier than anticipated expenditures in Julius' accounting of equipment and munitions in certain "training exercises" and "expeditions against the Dissidents." When questioned, certain of Tiberius' staff would certainly lodge that as a reason for Tiberius' apprehensions, even if the old fool forgot what informers had primed him to say.

And Assurbanipal's forces could find ready justification for *their* equipment the same way Caesar had long managed it during Hadrian's tenure as Supreme Commander in Hell: through the Pentagram, and the rumor of Dissident activities near their perimeters—hence the

Assyrians had moved quickly to snatch up the fugitive Caesarion, a known Dissident; hence they had had Pentagram support in the infiltration of Assyriana agents into the Dissident command structure; and official Pentagram sources could leak suspicions of collusion, Caesar *and* his son using the Dissident threat as excuse to maintain the legions under arms. . . .

The situation, with Asmodeus descending on Tiberius' palace in the course of the investigation (thanks to a well-timed phone call) just as Caesar found himself with a serious credibility problem, was the piece of improvisation of which Mithridates was supremely proud. Rameses had been nervous enough when the queens came stamping into the Pentagram's very halls—Rameses had come to Mithridates, in fact, a veritable lump of jelly, quivering with the indignity of an interview with Hatshepsut, whom he despised, and with Kleopatra, whom he refused to acknowledge as Egyptian; and likewise quivering in terror that their drive utterly to replace the Hadrianic influence in New Hell might have just had its cover blown. The Romans, so Rameses had surmised with that interview, might be in possession of information which could destroy them, and everything might come down about their ears.

Which was nonsense. Caesar *had* no knowledge he dared act on. He was doing what he was doing precisely because he had no choice.

It was a magnificent piece of work. Not even Rameses could damp Mithridates' satisfaction in that fact. He had started impromptu, but there was nothing impromtu or haphazard at all about the web of traps he had woven about the Romans, from the infiltration of the Roman Seat of Power, to the maneuvering of units in the field, to the magnification of the Assyrian threat in Roman eyes—even Kadashman-enlil had not seen that coming, that he and his collection of effete kings could be used, Sun in heaven! merely *used* as the pawns they were, in the hands of a man who truly *was* a king divine right, and who had maneuvered the Romans and Administration itself into confrontation.

Ordinarily Pharaoh hated to be Involved in Details. In a very little the Light of the two Lands would decide he had seen enough and done his duty, and retreat upstairs to his office. That would leave Mithridates free to do what had to be done, and if it worked, Pharaoh would rant and rave, but then—there might, shortly be a new Supreme Commander in Hell, and a new Ascendency, one whose Seat of Power occupied all the lakeshore near New Hell. That was the place Mithridates had picked out for himself. That was where his palace would manifest. And he would melt down the Roman Eagles for his tableware.

"Majesty," an aide said, and gave him a written message.

Second boy claims to be M. Junius Brutus, the message said.

Mithridates clenched it in his hand, seeing better and better chances.

He smiled, broadly, so that the aide stared at him "Have them get me a helicopter ready," he said; and ignored Pharaoh, who had doubtless heard that too. "*Move.* Pentagram pad in five minutes."

"King of Pontus," Pharaoh began.

Even at him, Mithridates smiled. "I'm going out there," he said. "It wants a direct observer—Luminance. I leave things here in your capable hands."

Because there's no way you can screw it up, Luminance. I've got him.

The *Daily Hell* was, predictably, bad news, worse news, and disasters—fattened with page after page of supermarket ads and recipes in stultifying profusion, not to mention advice to the lovelorn, the social pages, and the want ads, the latter of which provided the sole interest to an active mind, particularly the personals—

But Niccolo had been three times through the

personals, *and* the sports pages and had begun to consider the advice to the lovelorn, there on the park bench in the shade of the venerable oak, in stately Victoria Park, one of those bizarre little islets which punctuated New Hell's statelier thoroughfares. One saw horse-cabs hereabouts, common as the rattletrap automobiles, and *never* took them if one could help—any animal that had deserved Hell was *not* to be trusted. One saw a dangerous-looking nanny with disheveled hair walking a pram into which one had absolutely no desire to look. One saw a great many things, sitting in Victoria Park, glancing from time to time over the top of one's newspaper and trying not to fidget or get a headache from these abominable, ridiculous glasses—one was a gentleman reading his paper in the park, one was, and one was getting an ulcer, *per dio!* waiting and waiting and waiting on the Byzantines, to whom Niccolo composed elaborate epodes, all alliterated with d's . . . delay, defer, dilatory, dialectic, demented and damned: a sane man had to do something to keep his sanity, while meditating on another chain of thoughts mostly consisting of c's, to wit, Cesare, Cesarion, credibility, calamity and crucify.

And one must sit still, recollecting continually that Cesare had given him this means to recover his good graces, which circumstances had lost him—one had *had* to assassinate a friend of Cesare's friend, not gladly, but when Administration ordered, Administration *ordered,* that was all, *finis,* that was all that could be.

Cesare knew all this; Cesare knew, *per dio,* that he occasionally must answer to other Authority. But Cesare had been mightily piqued, nonetheless, and more than cool toward him, to let him know as far as one dared make such a thing clear—that Cesare expected more of him.

Cesare expected—what? That he should betray the Devil?

No one would dare voice such a thing, in Hell. But,

eccolo, here he was, as close to it as a sane man wanted to contemplate.

Sitting on a park bench reading advice to the lovelorn, because a man had to have something to do with his wits before they fried from the mere exertion of holding oneself immobile and calm.

He calmly, elegantly, readjusted the damned gold-framed glasses which sweated on his nose, and folded the paper to a more manageable dimension.

A portly gentleman rolled his way down the walk, at which Niccolo looked up with hope.

The gentleman kept going with a tip of the hat. Niccolo returned the courtesy with proper English stiffness, and reapplied himself to the want ads.

The bushes behind him rustled. He took in his breath and recollected he must not create a scene.

Rustle again. "Drop your newspaper," a voice said.

Per dio, what is brigandage coming to?

He dropped it and thought of Administration. Of muggers. Of Assyrian agents.

Of the face he had not a single weapon but the umbrella beside him . . . that and the sword inside it.

"No, no, fool! On the ground."

He moved his knees and let it fall. And sat very still as bushes rustled and rustled, and a cane hooked the paper from between his feet.

Another *Daily* nudged its way into the spot the other had occupied.

The brush rustled, rapidly.

Per dio! Lunatics!

He bent and retrieved the folded paper, within which—ah! A forefinger located an un-newspaperly stiffness, the edge of an envelope. Now one behaved very naturally. One waited a little, looked at one's paper, then one's watch—

One put the paper in the briefcase, rose, casually, hooked one's umbrella over one's arm, and strolled back toward the street hoping for a motorcab, which would take one to a warehouse where one could find Horatius—dealing with the Byzantines, there had been no way to set a timetable and a pickup. Then he would get out of this damned collar, trusting Horatius to ferry the prize under armed guard.

One stood, and stood, and waited, and looked at the time; and swated, profusely.

"Maledetto!" Niccolo groaned beneath his breath, in a frenzy of British calm, and lifted a hand, hailing an oncoming horse-cab.

A helicopter had just come in, around back, and lifted again, sound beating off the incised walls with their lion-hunt and processional reliefs, a shadow passing over the neat and rolling lawn of Assurbanipal's palace. Jeeps and soldiers went every which way along the impressive front drive, and the Arab delegation was not an unaccustomed sight, not the sort of thing likely to be questioned, Lawrence earnestly hoped, himself being the most conspicuous of his group in his white and gold. He took a deep breath and headed up the steps between the golden bulls at the head of his entourage, more and more confident, delighting in this walk along the tightrope. He was magnificent. He smiled graciously at a passing Assyrian major, who did the usual blink and recognition of the English officer with his guard of honor, the Englishman who was advisor to the King of Kings, and who, perhaps, had been somewhat scarce about the palace lately, but there had been such times before. It was crisis, the Romans were coming, and was not every loyal subject bound to take his place on the lines?

Lawrence reached the top of the stairs with a brisk intent he did not reckon the guards would challenge.

They did not.

"Spread out," he said to his men. "You know the places. Find them."

'Yes, Aurens," the answer came back, and his entourage scattered to every hallway and up the stairs.

"*Aurens,*" a colder voice said as he took the side hall.

He turned in a casual, confident way, and gave a stare as glacial to the Persian Immortal who had hailed him.

"We've *wondered* where you were."

"Klea," Antonius whispered, tightening his grip feebly, and Augustus endured it in an agony of moral discomfort. Perhaps Antonius thought he was back in Egypt. He had died of a gut wound then, too—fell on his sword in a theatrical act of honor, and the damned thing had skidded with him on a marble floor, doing irreparable and horribly painful damage, but missing the upward thrust it should have had, whereafter some fool had told him he was wrong after all—Klea had *not* killed herself that long ago day the way the report had come to him: Klea was alive and, which Antonius had not learned till later—had already been sending peace overtures to the Roman side. He forgave her. He always did. The fool who could not even manage his own suicide.

No. Be honest. Poor Antonius had tried to do the right thing at the end, the plebeian-made-general had had his army desert him to the disgrace they thought he merited, and Antonius had tried to do the right thing, the ancient and honorable solution, not the gentle way, with a nick at the veins, but the way that might win him the honor his public burlesques had not— gods witness, this was the man who had clowned his way to power, laughed his way into public favor, play-acted his soldierly rank till it landed him in command of a real army, on a real field, facing real steel, and he had not been Julius, that was all, nor had Augustus' advantage of Rome's best tacticians. So Antonius had tried to wipe everything out that day with a soldier's death, with no one to help him; bungled it; and then they told him Klea was alive.

It gave Augustus cold chills to think about it. And he sat there like a fool holding Antonius' hand while he took Augustus for Klea and mumbled personal things that thank gods did not make clear sense.

Truth was, *he* could not have done what Antonius had done. Not then. He had done harder things, made hard decisions, walked a narrow line between assassins and sycophants for a long, long life; but he could not have thrown himself on his own sword. He was not a soldier. He had had generals to front for him. Had had Agrippa, above all. Antonius had been tolerably good at the things he did, even at war, until fate made him a general.

And Octavianus Augustus, born Octavius the commoner, could find some sympathy for Antonius the commoner, who had tried so damned hard.

"Klea!"

"Hold on," August said. "Listen to me." He had tried before to explain their present situation, as much as they dared tell a man a breath away from the Undertaker. He was not sure Antonius heard any of it. He tried again.

Antonius' eyes slitted open, beyond the plastic, and drifted toward him in vague dismay. "Hell you say. I'm getting out of here. Going home."

"We can't get you back! Dammit, *Antoni*, listen to me."

"Dante on the job?"

"Tiberius has an Insecurity agent over there. Julius is fighting his way past the Prætorians on his way to Assurbanipal. For the gods' sake don't complicate things. Julius shot Tiberius' statue to hell and the old man's gone raving mad."

Antonius grinned around the tubing, a grimace, but positively a grin, like a deathshead. "Got the damn statue?"

"Listen to me!"

"Going home," he said then. "Got to go home now. Let go. I'll handle the old goat."

"Galen!" Augustus called out. There was a sudden

laxness in the hand he held. Antonius' eyes had shut
again, down to white-rimmed slits, and the machines all
around gave out cryptic messages he could not read.
"*Galen!*"

XI

Up the outside steps to the barracks entry, that was the brilliant plan. Trojan Horse maneuver. Just walk inside—not much hope of deceiving the sycophants; and no damn chance if things blew up. But Akkadians were common enough hereabouts, ordinary grunts, a handful of them swilling beer and gambling in the barracks as he walked through—just the kind of thing none of them wanted to get caught out at by their Assyrian officers.

"Who's that?" one said, and Sargon earnestly ignored it on his way to the barracks-room door. "Hey, there!"

He turned then. There was nothing for it. And his hawk-nosed, bearded face was well enough known in Akkad and in Hell.

A handful of soldiers got very quiet and stood up. "You didn't see me," Sargon said "I didn't come in this way, and it's Not your Fault. Understand?"

They stood like adoration-statues, eyes about that large, faces about that white. Sargon, his collar and his sleeve decorated with a handful of Assyrian insignia and a unit designation Horatius had come up with, started to go about his business.

But one of the grunts came unglued from where he was standing and hurried to intercept him. "Lord king," that one whispered, an anxious-looking man with a crooked nose and a scar crossing bearded lips and chin. "The Great Kings have the Roman boys."

"Where?"

"Upstairs. Lord king!" A broad, three-fingered hand sealed the door, and terrified eyes stared at him face to face—a man no taller than himself. And speaking the language he had all but given up. "They will kill you here! Go back. Go back. You can't go in there."

There was desperation in the man's face. Terror. And something else Sargon had had no hope of, which drove a common man to put a shoulder between his king and a door and argue with him.

It stopped him, when the shoulder could not have—stopped him to realize after so many centuries it was not Roman territory and it was a man of Akkad risking death at his king's hands—with a look in his eyes like a drowning man seeing the shore just maybe too distant—and maybe, after all, not.

"What's your name, soldier?"

"S-sharri, lord king."

He laid his hand on the man's shoulder. "You're in my way, Sharri. Now, do you want to move, or do you want to help me get those boys out of there?"

Sharri blinked, seemed to run that past several times, then gulped a breath. "Yes, lord king."

"Which?"

There had been a great deal going on outside, a great deal of trucks, and a while ago the sounds of a helicopter, at which Brutus had entertained an irrational hope—and looked up, thinking of Welch the American, and the helicopter had lifted them out of the Dissident camp.

He had dared say nothing, but Caesarion seemed to understand that glance and that look and possibly had the same thought—even Caesarion had looked ceiling-ward with a certain anticipation—had lasted them a little while.

But nothing happened, there was no explosion, there was no shooting in the halls, and non rescue; and hope just faded, quietly, and had its burial when they chanced to look at each other at the same instant, in the same reluctant estimate. "Probably some officer coming in," Brutus said; but he felt sicker and sicker at his stomach, remembering what Caesarion had done and said in the hall of the kings—

Ask Kadashman-enlil! Caesar had an illegitimate son—a son he favors. My half-brother—the center of a whole fucking Pentagram operation—and you've muffed it, majesty! You've blown it wide, screwed up what they didn't tell you, huh? Just didn't want to disturb you. Kadashman-enlil, majesty, and *the Egyptians on your staff. Ask them* what you've just happened to gather up—and watch the bastards squirm—

He shut his eyes, rested his elbows on his knees and dropped his face into his hands, thinking and thinking of Mithridates.

"*Mi frater,*" he said finally, calmly, looking up. "Caesarion. The things no one will tell me. . . . They're going to send someone in here. Maybe they don't want me to know—whatever it is no one will say to me. And my knowing would screw it up and make me useless to them. Maybe they'll tell me themselves. In which case—I'd rather not hear it from an enemy. Do me the favor. *What* will no one tell me?"

Caesarion looked at him a long, long moment, sullenness gone, replaced by a kind of exhaustion, and suddenly a worried, weary look. Then, which shocked him in Caesarion, Caesarion put out his hand and gripped his wrist, held it hard. And said nothing for a long moment, during which Brutus' heart beat like hammer-strokes.

"You—" Caesarion said, and seemed to lose his way.

"For the gods'; sake, brother, *tell me.*"

Caesarion's hand slipped to his and just held it, as if he had been a child. The way everyone treated him.

"You didn't die the way you remember," Caesarion said. "You were a lot older."

Which he had somehow suspected, but not the *lot* older. He clenched his fingers on Caesarion's hand to encourage him; and because he already felt the floor sliding out from under him.

"You—"

There was someone in the hall. Caesarion heard it too, and for the first time Caesarion looked truly panicked.

"Tell me!"

"You—" Caesarion said again. And whoever it was had stopped at their door, and was working with the lock. Caesarion grabbed him by the shoulder and jerked him around face to face with him. "Whatever they tell you, everything you know in Hell is just as true. Just as real. Remember."

As the door opened and guards with guns were there to escort a bearded man with a crown of a king about his wild, long hair; a king in the fine, many-pleated tunic and trousers of the Persians on vases, with gilt sunbursts worked into the fabric, all in expensive purple.

Except he had a khaki webbing belt at his hip, and a holster with a large black gun, not forgetting the guards who were there to back him.

"Bring *him*," the king said, and pointed straight at Brutus.

A kind of blank panic to him, as if it were a dream to which reality had suddenly caught up. He felt a tightening of Caesarion's fingers and expected his brother to do something crazy.

But no, Caesarion was telling him something else, standing as he stood up, still holding to him and laying a hand on his shoulder to steady him. *Remember.*

Remember.

"My b-b-brother—" *Damn!* "—goes w-with me."

"Your brother is a Dissident and a traitor," the king said, "and already condemned. Do you want to join him?"

It was not, he thought, a rhetorical question. In honor, he had to answer it, but his stuttering would overtake him. A nod was all he could manage, to keep their mutual dignity.

"There is a fool," the king said, and came into the room and stood with his arms folded, looking at them a moment, and maybe thinking what to do about them.

A Persian king? Brutus wondered. But he had a barbaric look, a wiry little man with the whites showing often all round his eyes, and a way of looking at people without blinking, like a crazy man.

He liked it least of all when the king smiled, a showing of teeth. "What we will do, dear boy, is talk a while. And if you want, when we are finished, I will *save* your brother the very uncomfortable fate the king intends for him. *I* can get him out of here. *I* can send you home to your father. Would you like that?"

Snake, that was what the king reminded him of, the furious kind, that both slithered and struck with brute force and poison.

"Come along."

"Caesarion g-g-*goes*."

"Don't be foolish. Do you want him shot? I can do that, and hold him in Reassignments indefinitely. Still better than what Assurbanipal purposes for him. Or worse . . . all depending on you. I *don't* want to harm you."

"You're M-M-Mithridates," Brutus said, blushing with shame and hoping no one could see that, the way they could hear the damned stutter.

The king's brows lifted. "For a moment, the smile was all gone. Then it returned. "I'm the king of Pontus. Yes. Mithridates. You see I know all about you. And you, about me, is that so? Come along. We have so much to talk about. A mutual interest."

"What's my f-f-father doing ab-b-bout this?"

He felt Caesarion's hand clench on his shoulder.

"Your f-f-father," Mithridates said, "has acted the

fool. Right now he's taken a couple of legions right under Administration noses, that's what he's done, which is precisely what you'd think he'd do—not to rescue you, dear boy, he's far too Roman for that; so are you, aren't you, all iron and duty, honor and all that, aren't you, boy? You'll understand if he just blows the house down around your ears and hopes to get you back from the Undertaker. Or not, as fate decrees. You see, I do know you. But Caesarion is no Roman. Caesarion is the one who's going to suffer in a moment; and he could have such an easy way out of here. If you're very, very good, we can find a way just to let him go. That's all. Just let him go. All if you're smart, boy."

"Go with him," Caesarion said quietly, pushing him forward. And more quietly still: *"Remember."*

He turned around suddenly and hugged Caesarion, and said against his neck, faintest of whispers: *"Valeas."*

"Not *farewell*, but a different inflexion. *Be well. Hold on.*

Caesarion hugged him close and let him go; and he went with the king and his men, out into the polished stone halls with their bull-reliefs and their giltwork and their echoing expanses.

Julius was going to attack this place? What could ever even reach inside here?

And they were going to let Caesarion go? He did not believe that either. Their father's enemy meant to use both of them somehow; and he wondered, walking along with the soldiers at his back, and staring at Mithridates in front of him, thinking—thinking—whether he dared make a move, whether a strike such as Sargon and Mouse had shown him could break the king's neck.

But *then* where was he, and where were they both, when they already knew what the Assyrians and the Persians were intending to do with them—except their enemy intervened?

And where was an outside door, a window, anything that promised an escape?

And what would they do to Caesarion if he ran?

The latter answer . . . he could imagine too vividly.

There was nothing unusual in an officer and an aide either, walking briskly along the halls—Sargon hoped fervently, and locked his hands behind him and strolled along with his chin tucked down, glancing up from under his brows from time to time as if he and Sharri-the-soldier were engaged in some important and private discussion.

They were. Sharri swore that the boys were in the lower section, over in a hallway he described until Sargon had a very good idea which room and where; Sharri worse *at* the Assyrians and the Egyptians and the Persians and the whole damnable establishment, and in the meanwhile Sharri's friend was going from man to man Sharri swore they could rely on.

It was more noise than he had wished, gods knew, but of a sudden he saw something that made him very glad of any extra help he could get.

That something involved a group in the black and gold of the Persian Immortals, with automatic weapons instead of spear and shield; and walking in their midst, the white-robed figure of T. E. Lawrence, who did not look particularly happy in the association.

"Damn," Sargon muttered, stopped there at the intersection of the corridors. "Damn."

He stood against the wall on the far side, then, out of sight as the Immortals took their prisoner past, and Sharri gave him a worried look.

"Get the boys out," Sargon said, "that's the first job. Luck of the draw. At least he hasn't blown us. He won't. Come on, dammit, faster."

He grabbed Sharri by the arm and looked up to see if the way across was clear.

And looked straight at a bearded man he had not seen in a gratefully long time, at that and a pistol drawn and aimed at his gut.

"Grandfather," said Naram-sin. "Fancy meeting you here."

The chopper made itself heard before it made itself felt, in the rolling landscape—a thumping noise seeming to come from most everywhere at once, and the legions, well-drilled, did not wait for the orders their centurions yelled at them. They scattered for cover and for vantage.

Likewise Mouse, who veered the jeep off for the cover of the trees as the chopper rose above the level of the hill and the trees ahead, raking the ground with its fire.

"Dammit," Julius yelled, "dammit, *Curti, get out of the way!*"

Because the truck was still out there, turned backside to the oncoming chopper and its rocket-fire. Julius let off a burst from the Galil as the camouflage-painted Black Hawk went beating past close enough to whip the tree-tops to froth, no damn good—the thing was bottom-armored; and fire was coming at it from all sides, wherever a legionary could get a clear shot at it.

The ground kicked up around the truck; and in it, fire and smoke billowing out as the truck rocked on its suspension and a rocket came *out* of it.

"*Venus!*" Julius yelled, in the middle of loading another clip. "*Curti,* you *fool!*"

About the time the chopper blew apart and came down in a ball of fire and fragments that flew like shrapnel. Parts of it hit the trees and Julius did not need Mouse yelling at him to get down. He dived for what cover the jeep provided as Mouse came down on top of him and the ball of fire singed the treetops.

"Go!" he yelled when it stopped raining big pieces, and Mouse grabbed the wheel and gunned it, laying on the horn.

Follow.

"Grandson," Sargon said, folding his arms, smiling wide. "How's your mother's fleas?"

Naram-sin did not think it funny. But that was always the brat's failing. He always laughed at the other fellow's expense. "Guards!" he yelled, and never took the pistol from where it was aimed.

"Squandered the whole damn empire," Sargon said. "Sharri, lad, you see this thing? My son thought he whelped it. It's my bet his bitch wife picked it up where she got the fleas and the clap."

"Guards!" Naram-sin yelled.

Sargon stood smiling at him, waved a wrist leftward. "Why don't you go look for them? Or you think you're man enough to move me, grandson?"

"I'll blown your damn—"

Sargon's foot came up between Naram-sin's legs, the shot hit the wall between himself and Sharri, and the gun went flying off sideways.

"That's torn it!" he yelled, and finished his grandson with a two-handed blow to the back of the head as Naram-sin was reeling around doubled over. By which time Sharri had his gun out and was standing in wide-eyed fright against the shattered fresco. *"Lawrence!* Sharri, dammit, which way did he go?"

A moment later removed no doubt as a white-robed figure came skidding across the polished floor from a side hall down the way. *"Sargon!"*

Shots came spattering out after Lawrence. "What the other way!" Sargon yelled at Sharri as T. E. Lawrence scrambled up and ran for them.

An Immortal and a handful of the Egyptian guard ran out to fire at the fleeing Englishman.

Right into Sargon's fire—as a wild yell erupted from somewhere in the maze of halls. *"Aurens! Aurens!"*

Lawrence reached Sargon's position and flung himself past it, sliding. An instant later he was up and beside Sargon with a gun in his hand—Naram-sin's, Sargon reckoned, suddenly baffled as his targets turned sideways to defend themselves, as a yelling handful of Arabs plunged out of the cross-passage the way Lawrence had come. Suddenly it was impossible to find a clear target in the melee: knives flashed, at close quarters with the rifle-carrying Immortals, and already a body was glowing and vanishing the way bodies did in Hell.

"Majesty!" Sharri yelled, and fired into the other direction as he took cover.

Sargon did the same thing, facing a half-score of palace guards who had taken a split-second too long to be sure of two khaki-wearing targets between them and the melee: he dived and rolled into the cover of the hallway as Lawrence found himself a spot behind a column and all hell broke loose, bullets knocking great holes off the stonework and the columns as the Assyrian guard tried to remedy its mistake.

Dammit, they were pinned for a prolonged fight of it, the Arabs having gone to cover at one end, themselves down here—no damn way to get through behind them; he remembered this area of the halls. "No way?" he confirmed it with Sharri, got a despairing look before Sharri sneaked a shot around the corner and nearly lost his head for it.

Then a yell cut loose from the Arabs and T. E. Lawrence streaked past, a white blur with his Arabs behind him.

"Damned fool!" Sargon yelled at him. An Arab fell and died, glowing and vanishing. And there was nothing to do but take advantage of it. He surged to his feet and launched himself after the Arabs.

Fire cut through the middle of them. And somehow missed Lawrence, whose fire did not miss the center of the Assyrians. The Arabs who had armed themselves in the melee up the hall sprayed the Assyrians with their own Pentagram-supplied rounds, as somebody's damn pet baboon went careening loose right through the fracas, screaming its idiot head off and trailing a gold and amethyst chain.

*   *   *

That was gunfire. Deep in the maze, in the halls, Brutus heard it, and he froze half a heartbeat, as suddenly his guards grabbed his arms and held him, and Mithridates looked around wild-eyed, looked at *him*, as if somehow this was his fault.

He grinned at Mithridates, his widest and best. He thought Caesarion would do that in his place.

Come to think of it, so would his father.

He kicked right for the obvious place, Mithridates covered, but he freed one arm in the shock Mithridates' jump backward caused, and rammed his heel into the other guard's kneecap and his elbow into the other guard's gut, one, two, three—before he himself could hardly draw that number of breaths.

Mithridates slammed a blow to his head and blinded him; and at that point he did not know what he did, except he caught his balance, chained as he was, and flung a karate kick at Mithridates' hip, connected and landed with a roll, up to his feet and down the hall with all the speed teenaged legs and a pair of tennies could give him.

Toward the shots.

Someone was yelling behind him in a language he could not understand; he heard the guards running to overtake him as he reached a side stairs and sprang for it, up and up, faster than he had ever taken a stairs in his life or death.

The Assyrian defense was dug in good and solid. Their own reconnaissance and Lawrence's account of it had not mistaken the extent of it, and Julius, seeing the real thing through a pair of field glasses, hissed a slow breath through his teeth and muttered to Mouse:

"We go with it."

Meaning the plan they had formulated over the weeks that they had known some confrontation of this sort was inceasingly likely, the plan that they would *not* have radio or equipment other than what they could liberate by stealth—thank the gods Mettius Curtius and the lads from the cavalry had rigged that rocket launcher or they would have lost the only armored vehicle they had.

Which was right now headed for the enemy's left flank, around the minefield they had been warned about.

Machine-gun nests giving full coverage of the front of the building marksmen on the roof, and themselves with no air support. It was a time when he would have been damned glad to see Archilles Peliades and his chopper, no matter his other shortcomings.

But there was no Achilles, no Welch and his bag of electronic tricks.

Just the two legions, men who had drilled and drilled this operation and who had been under arms and fighting whatever Hell threw at them since they had come here, a long, long service.

Raw experience could make a man a hell of a fighter and no mean tactician after a couple of thousand years, and the 10th and the 12th in particular were not populated by fools. "Over the hill," he had told his men in the briefing which, typically, was short and sweet, and gave a great deal of credit to his men's wits, "once we break the lines, you're on your own, whatever teams you pick, whatever stuff you brought, whatever targets you find. You know where the big stuff is. Take care of anything else on the way. Trust the Italian *magus* to haul your ass out of there if you run into trouble, but remember he might be grabbing your buddy about then, so *don't* confuse the wizard, huh? Go for it."

They went. Julius climbed out of the jeep and unloaded his gear. Mouse did the same on his side.

"If only the damned Practorians don't get themselves organized again," Mouse said, "and come up on our rear."

Julius threw him a sidelong glance. "Let them. They'd make a fine distraction."

Praetorians were only a minor worry. *That*, out there, was a well-equipped line. And they were going to lose men. There was no way they were not.

He struck out through the trees. Mouse kept with him. That was all the team he counted on.

That and a few of the grenades they had listed expended in the Trojan War.

"Hellllppppp!" Brutus yelled, pelting down the upstairs corridor, and yelped as he ran face to face with a hysterical ape trailing a gold chain. It screamed, he screamed, they missed each other dodging side to side, and he kept running, suddenly seeing a lot of toga-clad people—no, not togas, white and brown robes; and soldiers.

He had made a mistake. They were going to shoot him.

"*Fall down!*" Sargon's voice yelled out, echoing quite realistically in the halls, and his body which had learned to respond to that ghostly voice did not even stop to let the brain think about it: it sprawled flat and went skidding, belly-down and helpless on the slick marble floor as the white-robes opened fire right over him.

Aimed behind him. He twisted to look over his shoulder and saw his pursuers on the floor, saw them glowing and burning—*dead;* and aheada of him—

He twisted again, got a knee up to try to lurch for his feet as the robed men came running; and slipped in surprise and exhaustion and banged his chin on the pavings—rolled over as strong hands grabbed him and unceremoniously dragged him for the side of the corridor.

It *was* Sargon with these men, who jabbered something in some outlandish language at the bearded little man with him and at the desert-men, surely that was what they were; and their blond chieftain. Brutus gasped after air and gasped again.

"No damn way to get these cuffs off," Sargon said. "Shooting them's too risky."

Brutus concurred, wordlessly, trying to get his aching knees under him. "M-M-M-M—" he tried to say, tried to point, with his head, his knee, his shoulder, toward the lower hall. "M-M-M—"

Sargon grabbed him up by an arm. "That's all right, lad, come on, your father's out there keeping them busy. . . ."

"M-M-M—"

But Sargon was dragging him along the hall faster than he could take his balance, the desert-men going before and behind him; and suddenly a khaki-clad man was yelling and waving his arms at them up ahead.

The bearded man with Sargon jabbered something and no one shot. Suddenly there were a whole lot more of them coming out and waving rifles and yelling: "Sharrum-kin, Sharrum-kin!" or something like; Brutus caught his balance as Sargon yelled something sobering at them and waved a violent gesture back.

"M-M-M-*Mithridates!*" Brutus yelled out, getting Sargon's sudden attention. He pointed with his chin and a twist of his shoulder, since he had not the use of his hands, back toward the stairway.

"Damn!" Sargon said, then faced him back again. "He'll be to hell and gone by now. We can't chase him down. We've got to get you out of here. Come on, boy, *move it!*"

"M-M-My *brother!*" Brutus yelled, planting his feet, resisting with all that was in him. "C-C-C-*Caesarion!*"

"That wolf-whelp can take care of himself!" Sargon snarled. "He always lands on his feet. Come on!"

"N-N-No, dammit!" Brutus ducked and dived, and ran for the only stairs he knew led that way.

Back down the hall. Back down where he hoped to all the gods Mithridates had done the prudent thing and run the other way.

"Stop him!" Sargon yelled, and the desert-men did, just snagged him by either arm and right off his feet.

And he had not enough left in him to do more than scrabble after his footing and twist to get loose.

"Damn fool," Sargon yelled at him, grabbing him by the front of his tee-shirt. "Is it catching?"

"They'll cr-cr-crucify him! He's n-n-not th-th-th— *not one of th-th-them*—" He gasped for air, and deliberately sat down, collapsed right where he was. "Not g-g-going—"

"Get him out," Sargon said in English. "I'll get Caesarion. Sharri and I know where."

"Done," the blond chieftain said, and the desert-men dragged Brutus with them down the hall, running, till Brutus managed to get his feet under him. The blond chieftain had taken the lead, was up there in his white robes with a pistol in hand, and when a band of Assyrians popped around the corner, they ran right into his fire, Brutus saw that much before the desert-men jerked him to cover and shots started flying.

"Aurens!" they called their chief, who had gone down on one knee there in the center of the hall; and one of them made a sliding tackle getting Aurens to the other side of the corridor as more and more Assyrians shot pieces off the stonework. One cut Brutus's cheek and he ducked his head and lay there a moment before he risked a look back.

Sargon was not there. Thank the gods, Sargon and the rest of them had not gotten caught.

Firing broke out, the steady chatter of machine-guns, punctuated now and again by sharper explosions, all down the hill toward the lake; and Julius caught his breath and made a few fast yards as flat to the ground as he could get, hearing the jeep start up.

Start it and leave it, that was the plan. Mouse had the wheel wired. Mouse aimed the damned thing and got the hell out of there as it came charging up the hill at the gun emplacement that guarded the forest edge.

Machine-gun fire cut loose, spattered the whole front of the jeep, shot the tires and the windshield to hell, and the thing kept coming, grinding along with uncanny persistence—

"*Mouse!*" Julius yelled, forgetting for the moment to duck his head. *that* was how it was steering, one stubborn son-of-a-bitch was tucked down under, still guiding it. "*Mouuuuse, damn you!*"

The jeep kept climbing, lurched over the top as a khaki-brown figure left it and lay still.

Then the jeep blew the way they had rigged it, and there was no time to see to anything but scrambling up and running, pull the pin on the grenade at his belt and lob the thing high and handsome.

It came down right in the nest, and he gave them another to be sure while the shock of that was dying down—rolled on his shoulder right over the sandbags and came down in a bloody mess that was doing the glow-and-burn that made bodies uncomfortable to be around.

Another body came over the wall, flipped and slid down out of breath.

"Dammit!" Julius yelled at Mouse. "That was a damn fool stunt!" While he flung himself over to the machine-gun and swung it down to try a burst at the dirt of the hill. "Hell, it *works!*"

Another explosion.

That might be the truck, punching another hole through the line, letting the 12th through.

As, most improbable of sights, a huge bus marked IZMIR TURIZIM came bursting out of the woods and and straight along behind the Assyrian lines, with rifles blazing from the windows.

"Hang on to this position!" Julius yelled, leaving the machine-gun to the first legionary who came up the rise. He scrambled over the battered sandbags and started to run.

Open a corridor for the rescue team if there was a chance of it—that was what that bus up there was trying to do, with shells hitting the ground around and behind it.

It was running close to the palace itself. It was aiming at those positions up there, too close for the roof emplacements to come to bear on it.

"Go!" he yelled. It was not in the plan.

But there was that bus right where it needed to be. There was a frigging great target ahead of them, and they had momentum with them at the moment: give it up and there were good men dead. He saw Mettius Curtius' truck, incredibly still moving. He saw the 12the pouring over the hill toward the mansion.

And by Jupiter and mother Venus, there was a bright red Ferrari headed in behind the tour bus, with the most improbable pair of invaders since Klea had tried the rug trick.

Hatshepsut and Klea, by the gods—
And Hatshepsut's little black gun—

Not mentioning the arrival of the Hunnish polo team over the lawn at the rear of the palace in combat fatigues and brandishing rifles and swords, a battered Volkswagon bus with gods-knew-who-had-joined-the-party, and a handful of *La Légion Étrangère* who had appeared out of the bushes with grappling hooks and coils of cable.

"Come on!" Julius yelled, prudence to the winds. "Let's get those sons of bitches!"

Straight on against the lines and hand to hand at the end was the way the legions understood war. They had saved something for a charge; and they did it the way they did everything, thorough-going smooth and businesslike.

And wanting this—gods, even more than they had wanted a piece of Praetorians.

Even here, the sound of shelling penetrated the walls; and Caesarion tucked himself down in a corner, head against the concrete wall, shoulders braced. He had no illusions now, of importance.

What would happen, he reckoned, was one of two things: a, the Old Man would get Brutus out, whereafter Caesarion could wait and explain things to the Assyrians; or b, the Old Man would *not* get Brutus out, the Assyrians would win, Mithridates would win, and thereafter Caesarion could wait and explain things to the Assyrians.

In his long stint in Hell he had *seen* an impalement, and men flayed alive, all of which he had absolutely no wish to remember under the best of circumstances, and, gods, Zeus Soter, not now, or his knees would begin to shake and his teeth to chatter, and that was not the way he wanted to be.

It was not the way he wanted to be at all, only he was alone again, and they had taken the kid away—he thought of Brutus like that, though he well knew that Brutus had lived to be twice his age—taken the kid away to turn him into their own creature.

And why he should care he did not know, except for a little while, in Hell, there had been someone who wanted nothing but his good.

He caught himself with a lump in his throat and a stinging in his eyes, and an earnest wish he could have somehow been some help. He had tried, gods knew, had done the best that he knew, except his damned temper, except he had lost his head with the colonel and nothing else had made sense.

Julius was right in more than one thing. Fool, Julius had called him. Mostly, he thought, he had fouled things up. He had believed in lies and followed will of the wisps. As a reward of his folly, it was going to cost him agony to get back to the Undertaker, and, if he was terribly, terribly lucky, home again to Tiberius the Lecher.

If he was not—

If he was not, Mithridates had boasted he could affect Reassignments, and he believed it. There were neither hells: he believed that too, and tried not to think about it the way he tried not to think of the things he had seen done to flesh and bone in Hell.

He heard them outside. He heard someone work with the lock, and knew they were coming for him now; and without Brutus with him, without any sense of what he was fighting for any longer, he found no strength left in him. He was only tired, and wished they would just shoot him.

But a shot outside and the shattering of the lock galvanized him, made his heart turn over and sent him scrambling up with his back against the wall—

Face to face with Sargon of Akkad and a leveled Uzi pistol.

"Come on," Sargon said instead of shooting him. "We're getting out of here. Do we have to carry you?"

"No," he said, and came to them of his own accord, more shaken than he wanted to show. Two of the men with Sargon grabbed him by the arms and hauled him with them, and it hurt like hell with his shoulders stiff from the fixed position and his gut and ribs sore from the Assyrians' tender attentions, but he ran with them as best he could, truly the best he could, hearing the pop and rattle of shots exchanged upstairs as they ran down the hall and started up.

Sargon stopped on the steps, staring upward and gnawing his lip. "Damn, they're into it—" And he said something else to the man around him—Akkadians or Sumerians, Caesarion reckoned suddenly, small men but broad-shouldered and strong as the bulls the walls portrayed so frequently. The man nodded and a couple of them pinned Caesarion back against the wall while Sargon and the others went on upstairs with guns ready.

Then despair came over Caesarion. *We're not going to make it*, he thought with a sick feeling and an impulse toward tears. No way out of the damn handcuffs and no way out of the building; he had let himself hope for about two minutes, wrecked all his carefully-constructed cynicism, and now he just wanted to sit down and hurt

in peace. There was no damn where he was going,
Sargon was only marginally friendlier than Assurbanipal,
and they were not going to get out of here anyway
except to the Undertaker—which Mithridates had made
promises about too.

And upstairs, bullets whined and automatic fire spat
from this end and that, so that he knew Sargon had run
into more than he and his could handle, more than
anyone could, in a head-on attack. If things were going
right they could go to the roof, where a helicopter
would pick them right off; or a tank would come crashing
right up the front steps and occupy the Assyrians'
attention, so that they could make a run for it. He did
not know much about generaling, but he reckoned that
things were going badly for the attackers, and that the
whole thing was running out of juice.

Dead, he thought, *dead, dead, dead.*

And winced when sudden fire broke out behind them
and his two guards started firing the other way, down
the stairs. He tucked down in a ball, and saw one man
sprawl and glow and burn; and the other was down,
holding his leg and writhing in pain, when Assyrian
soldiers charged past and right up the stairs; one paused
to rip the man apart with a burst from his rifle. Caesarion
braced himself to die then and there.

But they went past. The man on that side fired at the
dying and the man on this side was in a hurry and looking
the other way, and no one else bothered—that was the
difference in life and death, that was all that saved him.

Then he knew it was time to get off the stairs and try
to find a door, any door, anywhere. He staggered to his
feet, caught his balance on the blood-slick steps and ran
for it, downwards, along the hall with no idea where he
was going, except it was better than staying there,
where the shots came loudest.

"Klea!" Julius yelled, figuring *she* would pay attention;
and Klea was driving the red Ferrari, Hatshepsut was

riding shotgun—figuratively and not: the tiny weapon in Pharaoh's hands was far and away more powerful, and facing artillery and machine-guns with rifles, Julius found Pharaoh the happiest sight he had seen in recent memory—

"Klea!" Waving his arm and yelling at the top of his lungs, as he and Mouse covered ground already pocked with Assyrian fire. "*Mine! Mines*, for godssakes! Look out!"

Klea veered toward him and the 10th which was in full charge behind him, braked to a halt as he hit the side of the Ferrari and leaned there panting—

—whereupon Hatshepsut took his instant attention and the rest of the breath he had: confronting a half-naked woman in the seat beside his wife on a battlefield was still disconcerting, much as he had seen of Pharaoh on one memorable occasion. He gasped for air, remembered Klea, Caesarion, and the reason two women in a Ferrari were out here, at least why Klea was. "In there," he said pointing up the hill. He wanted Hatshepsut, that was what he wanted, wanted that little black gun of hers, and if she held gods knew what favor as the price for that weapon, then he would pay whatever it took. "The boys are still in there. Hatshepsut, the French Foreign Legion's going for the emplacements on the roof—can you get us those doors up there?"

Hatshepsut flashed him a smile a crocodile might have used. "Damn sure," she said. "Want a lift?"

The Ferrari was a two-seater. He was in full kit. He stepped up on the rear bumper, grabbed the luggage rack and none too soon. "Follow us in!" he yelled back at a much-chagrinned Mouse, left behind with the rest of the legion, as his arm strained with the jounces and bumps the lawn made. Then he looked forward again, and hammered on the seat with the Galil. "*Mines*, Klea, bear right, bear right, bear right—!"

The Ferrari cut divots and headed straight for the

row of Assyrian trucks and mobile artillery that defended
the front of the palace.

A shell landed on their left. It was an increasingly
shortened range and bad news for the artillerymen
who had never yet gotten a good fix on them. The
artillery Hatshepsut's disrupter could not handle, but it
did right well on flesh and blood, blew tires out from
under a couple of the vehicles, and she was a hell of a
shot, even with the car bouncing.

"Haaaaiiiiiii!" she yelled, standing up to brace a knee
in the seat and her arms over the windshield, and
exploding tires and men dying and glowing all up and
down the driveway convinced the Assyrians they had a
serious problem in the red Ferrari.

Which meant sudden attention from the guns, except
the Ferrari was going like a bat, Klea was weaving like a
lunatic and hunting for a hole in their line, and Julius
was hanging on for very life, thrown this way and that
and hoping to hell the luggage rack stayed bolted.

An imprudent squad of Assyrians tried to fill the gap
they were going for in the line of vehicles, and
Hatshepsut swept the whole lot of them, which left
nothing but a clutter of weapons and smoking cloth as
the Ferrari banged over a walk, a flower-garden, the
curb, and right through the Assyrian line. Julius twisted
over on his back like a toy on a string and just opened
up with the Galil in a series of bursts that raked the
troops *behind* the line of trucks and jeeps.

And near broke his arm as Klea spun the car sideways
and braked, giving Hatshepsut a clear sweep at the
Assyrians, who suddenly found more of them were
dying than they wanted to stomach. As many started
running to get to cover as were running forward, and
Julius let go the luggage rack and staggered down to his
feet and over to the shelter of the steps and clipped
bushes to crouch down and reload.

In time. A band of Assyrians tried to sneak through
the shrubbery, and he grinned them a cheerful welcome

and sent them to the Undertaker all in a mass. Which got a startled look from Klea, who was trying to pick off isolated short-range targets with that damn Berretta, aimed over the seat behind Hatshepsut's back—while Pharaoh was creating general havoc.

It wasn't going to last, Julius reckoned. There were too many Assyrians, too much armor, far too good equipment on the other side, and it was going to be a tight window to dive in and do maximum damage, and give Lawrence and Sargon and the boys the chance to get out. *They* had to hold their position until Mouse and Curtius and the legions caught up.

Come on, he kept thinking, to the two men he hoped had made it inside, *do you need a louder invitation? Get out here!*

As suddenly the 10th came charging up through the line of parked trucks, and in an admirable display of initiative, no few of the teams broke off the straight-forward charge to take possession of the abandoned trucks—*and* the guns and the ammunition.

"*Pro di*," Julius cheered them with a wave of his rifle, "*bene, been factum! Io! Io! Roma!*"

They were *through*, through the lines, *they* had the weapons, and of a sudden the whole affair had shifted—never mind what the Assyrians had to draw on. It was no question of Hell's rabble having gotten their hands on equipment they had no idea how to use. The *legions* knew, by gods, knew any damn weapon they had ever had a chance at, and they had used most everything the armory had to offer in the two thousand plus years they had been in business in Hell. Eager eyes and fingers checked over equipment they had lusted after on this affair, it was theirs, by the gods, and the Assyrians who had bedeviled them a century and more were in range.

The guns started opening up one by one, on whatever targets their impromptu crews thought priority, and Julius gleefully pulled the pin on a grenade and lobbed it high and neatly right up by the doors.

"Duck!" he yelled at Klea and Hatshepsut in the car. "Grenade!" And followed his own advice.

Brutus tucked down as shots whined and spat up and down the hall. The blond chief named Aurens had gotten them within *sight* of the door, though some of them had died doing it; they had gotten up a stairway and into a hall that showed daylight from tall barred widows—it was the front door, closed and dark. And very strong.

He was with a youth Aurens called Mamud, a wiry desert-bred lad who had more strength than seemed likely in so small a frame, though Mamud was as scared as he and alternated between incandescent grins when something would go right for Aurens, and shivering like a dog when the fire came close to them, which it was doing, and the shivers were contagious.

"We've got to move," Brutus said in English, of which Mamud seemed to understand a handful of words. "Go! Understand?"

Mamud got it. He patted Brutus on the shoulder, the both of them at the moment trying to fit into the same body-sized niche behind a column, and grabbed him by the shoulder, pointing up ahead—Mamud, gods save him, never backed up; it was always forward, but there did not look to be much forward left, Aurens was pinned down, the enemy had shifted position so that the fire was coming at a worse angle for them out of one hall up the way, and they were all bleeding from masonry shrapnel thrown loose by the bullets. The echoing explosions outside shook the whole building, and gave them hope of rescue, but it was not coming fast enough.

"Go!" Brutus yelled, and tried to get up, but a shot caught Mamud and brought both of them down, himself when Mamud fell against him at the unstable moment of his rising, and there he was trying to get back to his knees, out in the open as fire bracketed them, hovering

over a wounded comrade he did not have his hands free
to help.

"*Go!*" Mamud yelled at him, writhing in pain, and
Brutus thought then that there was cover for one if
Mamud could get to it, but both of them were going to
be dead. He got up and he ran, for the other side of the
hall, trying to reach Aurens and the rest of them that
survived, with shots burning the air around him and
ricocheting off the stone.

Then fire came past him in the other direction, and
he skidded, in one eyeblink between strides knowing
that that other angle had Aurens' position exposed, and
they were done for.

"*Down!*" Sargon yelled at him for the second time
that day, out of that direction, and he dropped and
rolled from the momentum he had, slid right in against
the wall as Sargon of Akkad and a handful of his khaki-
clad men came charging right up the center with guns
blazing, with position on two of the groups that had
been giving them hell.

"*EEeeeyaaaaa!*" Aurens yelled, and charged out in
Sargon's wake, over to the other wall where he could
shoot at the ones that were going, Brutus knew, to put
their heads out and fire from the cross-corridor. They
did. Aurens did.

And the big doors blew inward like thunder and let in
daylight, smoke, and a silhouetted figure in 20th-century
battle gear who swung to his left and opened up the
cross-corridor that had cut them off from that door.

It might have been Jupiter himself intervening. Brutus
just lay bruised and battered and staring until someone
came back to help him and Mamud to their feet and the
god-in-khaki came running toward him.

Then he knew it was Julius. It was his father, who
caught him in his arms rifle and all and hugged the
breath out of him.

"Are you all right?" Julius asked. "Damn, you're
bleeding—"

"All right," Brutus gasped, and then: "My b-b-br—" About the time he recollected Julius was who Caesarion was running from and the last person Caesarion wanted to have find him. "S-sargon—supposed to f-find him— Not here—"

"Where's Caesarion?" Julius yelled at the men forward. "Anyone seen him?"

"Lower hall," Sargon yelled back. "Dammit, *Iuli*, get out of here, take the boy and get out! We've got an Assyrian regiment scattered through this damn maze and we can't hold it—*get out! I'll find him!*"

"Damn, no," Julius muttered, "I've got Klea to live with. Go!" He hugged Brutus against him half a breath and shoved him into the hands of Sargon's men. "Get him out! I'll make it!"

Brutus caught a breath to yell after him, but Julius was already running, Sargon and his men going after him, and he was being pulled backward, dragged along willy-nilly by men who were all too anxious to clear the building and get back to daylight.

It was not manly to cry out a protest, not in the high, cracked way it was apt to come out, or to fight men who had taken wounds trying to help him. He went, he got as far as the doors; but when his group met Klea and Hatshepsut and a handful of legionaries inbound, and he met Klea's burning stare that searched his vicinity for *her* son, he babbled: "Julius is trying to f-f-find him," like a fool, before his rescuers pulled him out the doors and into the daylight and the smoke.

Caesarion ran with all that was in him, darted up a stairs and out into a hall before he sorted out the cadence of marching feet from the hammering of his own steps and the pounding of his pulse in his ears, and came nearly face to face with a troop of black and gold Immortals.

One yelled, the ranks went disordered as men swung guns into line and braced to fire and Caesarion did not run back to the stairs, he *threw* himself, and slipped on the steps and rolled and bartered himself and somehow found his feet again with agility raw terror found in him.

Down and down again and down the corridor, stairs when he could find them, up and down, and wherever he smelled smoke, in the dim hope that smoke meant fire and fire meant invaders and that meant some hole in the building where he could get out and lie in the bushes until dark.

Around another corner, down the hall. There was the taste of blood in his mouth, the cut on his foot had opened up inside the tennies, he ran soaked with sweat and finally blind with red flashes and growing dark in his vision.

That was how he ran into the wall, came careening off a stairway and slipped and saw there was no door where one usually was in the scheme of things, just bang! right into the wall, and wham! right flat on his back, and bone and muscle and brain were just too shocked to get up when he saw himself staring at the muzzles of a couple of rifles quite distinct against the blurry background of Immortal gold and black.

And the white of fierce Persian grins.

"Heiaaaaa!" rang out from down the hall.

The guns swung round, thunder hit, and Caesarion contorted himself without thinking and slammed his legs around with all the force in him, right into the Persians' legs, as they cut loose and blasted stone and plaster down in a stinging rain of dust.

He *was* blind after that, his eyes tearing, but he tried to move, tried to run and was still fighting when a hand like iron closed on his collar and dragged him up and into a sweaty, panting embrace. "Damn fine move," a familiar voice said in Latin, and he knew who it was then, stiffened and tried to protect himself from what was at least going to be a paternal whack across both ears.

Instead it was a paternal shoulder slammed into his

groin, the wind knocked out of him, the blood rushing
to his head, and Julius yelling at Sargon of Akkad to:
"Get those damn stairs clear! I've got him—get the hell
out of here!"

"Hatshepsut's got the main hall secure!" Sargon yelled,
his voice echoing in the emptiness.

It was a damn embarrassing way to exit a palace,
butt-first and upside down, carried by one's father at a
run he would have sworn the Old Man could in no wise
manage, but Caesarion did not fight it. His father was
going to beat him bloody; the Assyrians were gong to
impale him and watch him die for hours; and given a
choice he was damned glad to see the daylight and hear
Latin voices around him.

"Come on, come on," Decius Mus was shouting,
"we've got a jeep—clear that doorways and let's get out
of here!"

"Klea," Caesarion muttered, soundlessly, because he
had no wind. He tried to shout it. "Where's my mother?"
Because he remembered them saying she was in the
doorway. But it sounded like a fool, and he was still
butt-upside until his father threw him off and he landed
in legionaries' arms, picked up again and thrown into a
jeep's back seat, where he slid mostly to the floor and
could not get righted until someone got in and pulled
him upright.

The jeep lurched into motion, bounced over a curb
and roared onto the lawn, and he stared into his father's
sooty, sweating face.

"I didn't—didn't tell him—" was what he thought to
say, after which the daylight went all to gray and he lost
his sense of balance and his sense of most everything,
except he had fallen over and Julius was holding onto
him, saving him from bashing his face on the floor.

It was truce, then. Maybe he wasn't in it so bad.
Maybe Klea could save him. Maybe Brutus could. For
Brutus, Julius cared—in the bizarre way a man tended
toward things that would destroy him.

Himself, he was always smarter than that.

Give or take the Dissidents, in whom he had once believed. In whom he still believed, in most of them, except the leaders who betrayed them.

Meanwhile having Julius' arms shielding him from the jolts and the bumps was not a bad thing, one which made his eyes leak tears—exhaustion, relief, gods knew, pain, too; maybe just a little sense of what he had never had, or what he had long ago remembered.

Dammit, there was something in Brutus that people loved him, that was all; Julius did, Caesarion knew it: Brutus innocently gathered up everything Caesarion had ever wanted, and left him penniless.

Brutus was all right. He knew that much, without anybody saying. Because if Brutus had not been, Julius would have left him with the Assyrians.

XII

Antonius staggered, reeled left and right in a wild try after balance, and sat down, naked as the day he was born, on the cold marble of Tiberius' ravaged atrium.

Home, by the gods. He was home, the little Italian had come through, he was in one piece—he felt himself over to be sure, but there he was, sitting on the polished black stone with his feet cold and his backside cold and his muscles all gone to jelly.

"Where in haiill am I?" a naked fat man screamed, in a voice that went right to the nerve centers. *"This ain't th' Dallas turnpike!"*

There were a whole lot of naked people, disposed around and about—nothing unusual for Tiberius' atrium, gods knew, there at the feet of his dour, disapproving ancestor-statues and the bronze atrocity of Drusus; but some of them Antonius knew, there was the second centurion of the 10th, a couple of men from the 12th, a few big rough-looking men who could be legionaries, except he had never seen them in his life, a few dark bearded ones who looked Middle Eastern, and—gods—a baboon, which sat rocking back and forth and looking decidedly dizzy.

"Antoni?" Rufus of the 10th asked, confused-sounding. *"Quonam sumus?"*

And the big man over by the image of Drusus: "*Òu nous trouvons-nous?*"

Same question as the American, give or take the Dallas freeway. Antonius rubbed his face and made another try at getting his feet. "Tiberius' house," he murmured, with a misgiving look around him. "Gods, gods, the old man's going to have a—"

"*Quidnam videmus?*" a voice rasped out, with an edge of hysteria, an all-too-familiar voice, and Antonius grabbed after the support of a Claudina ancestor and clawed his way to his feet.

"*Imperator,*" he said with all due respect.

O gods, it was one of the bad ones, Tiberius was wearing the damned black toga, reeling out into the middle of potential enemies with no knowing what delusions. He had a spear in hand. He waved it about and legionaries scattered. The baboon screeched and fled up to Drusus' bronze ankle, huddling there in drunken alarm.

"*Petis vitam meam, acies feritis, aedes ruit tonitru sonituque armorum! Luvies saniesque, sanguis ferrumque! Sanguis et ferrum! Vobis sanguinem adferam!*"

"What in hail is he taking on about?" The American staggered up to Tiberius. "Who's in charge here? Who's in charge of this place? Hah?"

Tiberius just stared with his mouth open. Antonius did, clinging to the statue, trying to focus on here and now.

"Sheee-it," the American said, and staggered away, waved his arm to the rest of the room. "Any o' you guys speak English? Habla Espanol? Hey?"

"*Look out!*" Rufus yelled, and give it to the American, he was fast for all his size: he turned as the emperor charged him with the spear, jumped out of the way, and Rufus jumped, and the ape climbed up to Drusus' shoulder, shrieking in falsetto.

"Traitors!" Tiberius yelled, recovering himself and his spear. "Traitors! Assassins! Barbarians!"

"Divinity," Antonius said, holding out his hands in appeal. "It's Antonius! Listen to me!"

"Traitors! Destroyers! Vandals! I'll have you whipped! I'll feed you to eels! I'll fry you in oil! Traitors! Where's my guard? Where's my guard? Traitors!"

"Divinity," Antonius said. "General. We are your soldiers. Order us! Order us against the Assyrians and the barbarians! We will avenge your honor and defend your house!"

Tiberius fixed him with that one-eyed stare he could use, as if the left were in focus and the right was staring into some supernatural gale. "Defend me against what?"

"Assyrians, majesty!"

"The Devil does that!" the emperor snapped, and clamped his jaw tight as a moray. "The Devil does that! The hell with the damned Praetorians! I'll fry Mummius' tripes! The Devil defends the house! *Hear that, brother?*"

He turned and looked up at the brazen Drusus. The baboon had taken refuge on Drusus' head, and, baboon-like, screamed.

So did Tiberius, and flung his spear.

"Ghosts!" he cried. "Die, Caligula!"

"Run for it!" Antonius said, shoving Rufus, waving furiously at the others. Get out of here! Go home!"

The Middle Eastern types banded together and ran for it. Rufus caught his arm, tried to pull him along. Antonius shook him off. The emperor was dangerous. But it was a danger he knew and he stood fast. It was a sure thing that Praetorian Commander Mummius was already in hiding: he usually was, when the emperor got this bad. Mummius would head for a three-day drunk. So would anyone else of sense and taste.

"Traitors!" Tiberius sobbed. "Ghosts and traitors!"

"Anyone speak English?" the American asked, wandering about.

Till the Frenchman grabbed him and rushed him for the door.

Tiberius just went and patted Drusus on the knee.

And leaned there, patting the bronze and mumbling to it. "The Devil," he said. "The Devil's my friend."

"Is he, divinity?" Antonius had to find something to lean on himself, and picked one of the pretty nymphs, and sat down on her marble feet. *Don't set the old bastard off. Easy does sit.* Damn, it was hard to think. "You know where he is now, divinity?"

"Gone to Augustus' house. Arrest everyone! Question them! Treason?" For a moment the old soldier flared up, mad as a Thracian, and the light blazed in his eyes. Then he patted Drusus on the shin and rested his head on Drusus' knee, introspective. "You know you can't trust anyone. What's Caligula doing in my house? I threw him out."

"I'm sure I don't know. Do you want me to find out? I can take the Praetorians."

"You haven't got a stitch on."

Antonius twitched his shoulders, slight shiver. "True. I'll find my clothes. Can I have your ring, divinity? So the Praetorians know it's *you* that orders them?"

"Julius is coming back again." Tiberius' clamped mouth snapped eel-like and trembled. "Coming right back over my property. He can't do that. Trample hell out of my rosebushes." Steadied and spread in a nasty grin, transfiguring the raddled face to something demonic. "I'll invite him to a party. Tell him I want him for dinner. Him and Egypt. *Tell him bring my Germans!*"

"I'll do that, divinity."

"We'll play nymphs."

"Right. Of course."

"Invite the Devil too. You think you can find my cook?"

"I don't know, divinity. Maybe if you ask the Devil he can find your cook." Antonius shivered. The room spun—Tiberius in his black toga, the statue with the burning eyes, the anxious baboon perched atop Drusus' head. *O gods. I can't faint. Not now. Where is Julius?* "I'll go take command." He thrust himself for his feet

and propped himself against the nymph's generous
bosom. "Your ring, divinity, to convince the disbelieving
and the doubtful, to put the fear of your presence into
those who might otherwise say to mere Antonius: Where
is your authority? Give me a token of your power and I
will teach your enemies to dread you."

"Dread me. Ha! Yes! Dread the dead. Iron and blood.
Bring me Egypt, *Antoni.* Bring me Egypt."

"The ring, divinity!" Antonius staggered free of his
support and held out his hand. "Give me the Practorians
and I will discover your enemies and deal with them—
enemies in your house, divinity! Enemies about you! The
ring! And I shall root them out!"

Tiberius' mouth worked, moist at the corners. His
one focussed eye peered through the murk. Feverishly
he tugged off the signet on his forefinger, then clenched
it in a thick, scarred fist as his jaw clamped.

"The ring!" Antonius said hysterically—hysteria
worked with the old lunatic. It made him think he had
been enthusiastic a second ago, and had forgotten again
what he was doing. He had a touching habit—not liking
to quash a going enthusiasm: but, O gods, Antonius
thought, his own knees were going to go, he was going
to tumble down in a heap, he was going to puke up his
gut right here at Drusus' bronze feet— *"Give me the
ring, divinity!"*

Tiberius handed it to him from a sweating fist, and
fumbled at his face and shoulders, tender as a grandfather. "Go. Go, soldier. Bring me honor. *Bring me my
honor!"*

"At once, divinity!" Antonius clenched the ring in his
own hand and gave the old lecher a legionary's salute.
O gods, don't let me puke. He made his withdrawal,
caught the nymph's leg to steady him and dared not
look back, thinking of the spear in Tiberius' hand, feeling
the cold of Tiberius' stare between his shoulders.

Keep walking, keep upright Don't weave.
He'll kill me for this. He'll kill me for sure.

A screech rang off the roof behind him. He flinched and staggered.

"Caligula!" Tiberius screamed, the ape screamed, and the spear fell with a ringing rattle on the pavings. "Let my brother be! Avaunt! Avaunt!"

Antonius gasped for breath and ran for the hall, figuring the god was occupied.

Another shell landed in the rose-garden, and Augustus flinched and held the phone as close to his ear as he dared. "Yes! Yes! I understand! Returning—"

Boom! Glass rattled. Another thump as the men of the 6th returned fire from the roof.

The Viet Cong were making alleged overshots again.

"Hello, hello? *Arri*, tell them—"

Boom!

"—we are doing our absolute best! There is a limit—"

Boom!

"—to our resourcefulness! We have inquiries from Administration—we—"

Crash!

Augustus flinched from the wreckage of the windows and brushed glass powder from his hair and his neck, clinging manfully to the phone. "—have lodged official protests! We request the Park Department *do* something about this—"

"*Thwup-thwup—thwup—crack!*

Augustus looked up at the manifestation of room-wide wings—or was it shadow? Or had that black and red been there at all? Illusion, a trick of eye and ear, as wings wrapped cloaklike about a shadow that became a man, a man in a trenchcoat (never mind the smell of brimstone—or was in the stink of cordite wafting in from outside?)

The man was tall, dark-haired. The face was maybe handsome, but hard to look at—even for the god-emperor of Rome: just the hand made itself clear, extending a wallet, flipping it open to show a badge.

Insecurity Service.
Augustus hung up the phone.

"O my gods," Klea murmured, peering through the bullet-crazed windshield of the Ferrari, as the legions made their orderly retreat from the chaos of Assurbanipal's territory. Their rear ranks were still under fire from a reorganizing and stiffening Assyrian defense, and doubtless outraged calls were going out of Assurbanipal's palace, asking air support. Strike and get out, that was what Julius was doing: get clear and get back to the villa, back under the shield of the villa's defenses, where they could turn and fight with the advantage of tech on *their* side.

Only there was a movement on the hill that fronted Tiberius' land, a long shadow that glittered in Hell's daylight.

"Tiberius' guard," Hatshepsut murmured. "Damn."

The disruptor was out of charge. They were down to Klea's Berretta and six shells—that and an AKM with gods knew what left: Hatshepsut had snatched it up off the pavement in their retreat, and Hatshepsut had taken inventory of it—whatever the answer was.

Hatshepsut gathered it up as the distance narrowed between their own front line of slow-moving stolen trucks that held their wounded, the majority of the legions still to the rear, along with the two half-track howitzers.

"What do we do?" Klea asked, looking desperately left and right.

"Sister, we just consolidate our line as much as we've got a front end and hope to Set we can get enough momentum to go through them," Hatshepsut said. "Or we end up a Tiberian-Assyrian sandwich. Julius sees it. He's got to see it."

Klea drew a ragged breath and looked at the gas gauge. Quarter tank. Look at the advancing lines, and back at their own, which were woefully thin up front.

She slowed down, honked the horn to be sure others were aware of the situation.

Other horns blew, staccato signals, off in the distance.

"What we've got to do is get the wounded through," Hatshepsut said calmly. "I figure Julius will keep us out this far from the woods, keep them from outflanking us . . . damn, if there's no trap in the woods. If they've got artillery set up—"

"Hatshepsut's voice trailed off into alarming silence. Klea threw her a desperate look. Pharaoh was tapping her right ear, where there might well be something under the traditional pharaonic headgear. Pharaoh's kohl-rimmed eyes were wide and alarmed.

"There's a Pentagram force coming in."

Who says? Klea wondered desperately. *Who talks to you through that thing? Whose* are *you, sister?*

"Mithridates," Hatshepsut said, "is leading them. Bast! We've got real trouble."

"We've got to get to the villa! We've got to get the rest of the legions up here! Oh, damn, if you can send, 'Shepsut, *do* it! *Tell* them—"

"Just get over—over!" Hatshepsut waved her hand the way that they should bear, and Klea shifted gears and put a little more speed on it, as the distance closed further.

But there was a strange thing about the legion that barred their way home—that it did not *bar* it, that it was going off toward the flank, paralleling their line of retreat, making a brisk and orderly advance as if it had an utterly different objective.

"What are they doing?" Klea wondered, glancing from that side to the few trucks on their left, and back again. "They're not paying a damn bit of attention to us."

"Moving to flank us," Hatshepsut said. "To join with the Assyrians and the rest of them. Gods know Mummius is no genius."

Klea scanned the lines, biting her lip, thinking of

Julius, of her son back there with him, helpless. Her heart kept wanting to come up in her throat.

And the distance grew less and less.

Until her heart seized up in utter startlement. There was a jeep moving out from the other lines, heading for them at a fast clip; and Hatshepsut lifted the rifle.

"Don't shoot!" she said suddenly, everything uncertain. She *hated* uncertainties. Could not act in them. And Hatshepsut tended to the shoot-first persuasion. Both were wrong. She knew that they were. There was an opposition commander coming over for parley, and it was not a situation she had been in for centuries. Not since Egypt. Not since—

She knew the man riding passenger in the oncoming jeep, knew the hair, black and curling as Pan's, the handsome, strong-boned face that had once corrupted all her judgement—

"*Antoni!*" she cried, easing on the brakes as the jeep veered alongside.

They faced each other over Hatshepsut's rifle—between the legions and the Practorians.

"Where are you going?" Hatshepsut yelled across.

Antonius stood up in the jeep, waved an arm toward Assyrian territory. He had no wound evident. He was terribly pale. And there was no question what Trip he had gone, and where he had come back to, after all. "Going that way," he said. "Did you get the boys out?"

"Got them both!" Klea called across. Her heart was hammering in absolute terror "*Antoni*, there's Pentagram stuff coming in. Coming in on our tails!"

It was a warning. She had to give it. She saw him hesitate, —the man who had turned tail at Actium. The man his own troops had deserted in Egypt. He had run more than once in his life. And the Practorians were treacherous to their commanders.

And he knew—O gods—he knew she thought he might run. It was in his eyes, and in the sudden clenching of his hands, white as death, on the rim of the windshield.

He was not up to this. A man back from the Trip was lucky to be standing at all. He had every reason to run and she shamed him; and did not want to.

"I'd better get you some room, then," he said, and his eye raked the Ferrari over, tires to windshield, in genuine pain. "Gods, Klea, what have you done to my car?"

"I'm sorry!" she cried. "*Antoni*, be careful! *Antoni*, Administration is on us, we don't know if we can get *anyone* back, we can't depend on it—"

He spoke to his driver. The jeep started up and Antonius fell into the seat, and gave them a wave of his hand. "Speed it up!" he yelled at her. "Get home!"

She threw the Ferrari into gear and blew the horn for attention, accelerating as she headed across the hill, signalling the trucks to pick up speed. The landscape blurred in her sight. Hatshepsut was turned backward, leaning over the seat with the rifle in her hands, her eye still on the Praetorians.

Or maybe on Antonius.

The Praetorians passed their position and headed back to the rear, where the fight was; and Julius, riding the back seat of a jeep that maintained a position halfway along their retreat, within reach of the active fighting on the rear or the potential for trouble ahead, watched them go with a mix of emotions he could not sort out.

Dislike, for one. They were Praetorians. And anguish: it was Antonius commanding them, leading them where they were going to get chewed to hell.

Other troops might have questioned the orders that took them to protect the rear of the legions whose advance they had resisted; but being Praetorians, they were pragmatic, and had advanced and retreated more than once on a higher bid or a policy shift in midstream. More, they served Tiberius; and they were used to it, Julius reckoned, when he had gotten the radio message from Antonius that he should allow the Praetorians to pass behind him.

A few things in Hell a man could rely on, and if Marcus Antonius told *him* a thing was so, it was so, never mind that Antonius would lie to his grandmother if the heat were on him. Not to him. "Withdraw," Antonius had ordered him sharply, "in the name of the divine Tiberius. He will not tolerate this traffic on his land! In the name of Tiberius Caesar and the goddess Rome, withdraw your troops!"

"Our respects to Tiberius," Julius had said into the liberated Assyrian radio, which was about all they dared say, reckoning the Authorities were breathing down their collective necks. *The name of Rome* was the codeword: *What I say is true*. "We will clear his land with all speed. Over."

"Got you loud and clear," Antonius had replied. "Out."

"Papa's got his hands full," Caesarion muttered, where he rested against the seat, a miserable and badly-battered Caesarion, whose head nodded with the jolts the jeep made. He meant Antonius, Julius reckoned, his foster-father, and it was the old surly-insolent tone in his voice that ran over his nerves and made him want to grab this son by the front of his jacket and beat the attitude out of him.

"Antonius just took the Trip for your sake," Julius said sharply, with what he considered profound restraint, "or he wouldn't be where he is. He's damn likely to take it twice. Dammit, thanks to you we could all end up in the nether hells—and may yet, —*hear me?*"

Caesarion shut his eyes, shut his mouth and let his head roll aside against the side of the jeep. Just shut him out.

He could hit him. He could beat him senseless. But the boy had the marks of previous beatings all over his face, and had his hands chained with handcuffs they could not get off, and was already in pain enough to fog his wits. Hitting his own son under those circumstances was a shame to which Julius would not descend, no matter now provoked. He only set his jaw and ignored him, wondering how Brutus was faring, in Sargon's care, whether the boy was hurt, whether—

I didn't tell him, Caesarion had said, which at once he had doubted and then believed, and felt the first tenderness for this Egyptian son of his that he had felt since—very long ago.

It was the perverse luck of the draw had put him in the jeep with *this* son, and not the other, when he had his gut tied in knots worrying not over Caesarion (who had done *something* right for once, gods knew, and saved his neck down in Assurbanipal's basement with a typical Caesarion move, without a thought between his foot and the Assyrians' knees) but over the other. Brutus was the vulnerable one. Brutus was the one who could be hurt and broken and turned against him.

Brutus—had run to him without hesitation in that upper hall. Had not flinched in the way a son might who had discovered himself his father's murderer, or recovered those lost thirty years of increasing bitterness. Brutus could *not* be so thorough an actor. He insisted to believe that, and told himself, with the wariness of millenia of Hell's snares and traps, that he had himself become vulnerable.

But one trusted—sometimes. As he knew that Antonius would not play him false. Everyone else—but never him. He knew the people of his household; and Brutus— was of his household.

Damn, he wanted Brutus where he could have sight of his face and watch his reactions and reassure himself that things were as they had been. And instead he had Caesarion, who had never forgiven him—

—for whatever it was. For his existence. For—whatever turned a kid that wild and that deliberately hateful.

He only wished—

And reached out to the side and felt his way to a grip on Caesarion's shoulder, feeling the chill of loneliness as he stared at the roll of the land ahead of them, where Klea and the trucks had already begun to swing toward the hedges that lined the approach to the villa.

Trouble there—he could see the plumes of smoke and dust. But they had expected that. Augustus would have handled it. The 6th would have handled it. "Speed it up," he told the driver—Mouse was taking care of things farther back along the lines. He had no wish for Klea and the wounded to be the first into trouble up there. Hatshepsut was down to conventional weapons, and the legionaries doing the driving and no few of the wounded might be competent to defend themselves, but he had no intention of using them for a leading edge. "Tell them pull back a bit." To the legionary riding shotgun in the front seat.

They had radio to use now and so did most of the trucks up there, but the Ferrari did not, a situation Julius swore to remedy, no matter what the risk of illicit equipment on city streets. He watched, jaw set, as his driver brought them closer to the front; but, dammit, there was a limit to their speed: the exhausted legions could only go so fast, and they had to take it slow enough for them, no matter how he longed to get up there and find out what was going on at the villa, and whether they *had* a home left.

No use getting there with no troops to back him up.

"There's smoke up there" Caesarion mumbled.

"You noticed." *Damn! No need to answer him like that.* He felt the sudden tension in Caesarion's shoulder, and tightened his grip. "Easy. Not so far now."

"Yeah." Caesarion chose English over Latin. Another of his petty annoyances. He did it even at that subconscious level at which his speech slurred and his eyes were glazed. "Just get the damn cuffs off. Oh, damn, I hurt."

Julius said nothing. Anything he said with this son was bound to cause trouble. He just let him alone.

The Praetorians had not stood against the legions.

They *were* going to fight the Assyrians, on their own, when it was damn rough back there. Difficult to admit, they *were* Romans, in their mercenary way—just saw no profit in the one, and the second set of orders, coming from Antonius replacing Mummius, so improbably reasonable that they would rumble, curse, pick up their weapons and march against the foreigners, partly because a change of commanders confounded everything and made it likely Something Big was happening—which they dared not buck until they understood it. That was the psychology of the Praetorians.

And gods knew, it was their necks on the line too, if this thing got messier than it already was.

There were no new clouds over the villa as they advanced. The old ones dispersed on the winds. That was encouraging.

They've ceased fire, the radio report came in from the Assyrian border, Mouse asking for instructions. *The Praetorians insist they'll garrison the line.*

There was something underneath that, the knowledge that Antonius might be in command of the Praetorians now, but that would not speak for an hour from now, or two hours, or tomorrow. There would be furious politicking going on in Tiberius' domicile.

And bidding.

Or the old lecher could just change his mind, which happened about twice an hour, and enabled him to govern the Praetorians, just by keeping their internal factions and those who represented them so damned up-and-down again no one could get a firm grip on power.

Do we rely on them? That was what Mouse did not, diplomatically, ask aloud.

But for Mouse to defy the Praetorians to establish a defense line on Tiberius' land was a provocation Tiberius might not forgive. Even if he had forgotten about the damn statue.

"Withdraw," he ordered. "Let Antonius handle it."

Thinking all the while that Antonius, who had the constitution of a bull, was apt to fall on his face: even Antonius could not shake off a bad Trip that fast. But there was no other choice. Lawrence and the Arabs and the French had gotten themselves and their stolen bus out of there the moment the boys were free: Julius had ordered it, to keep Napoleon's part in this as difficult to trace as possible. If Horatius had done his job, only a couple of men on that bus knew *who* had volunteered them, and maybe not even two. And Attila had taken the polo team out of there in a fair hurry, but by the gods, the lads had done their bit to keep the Assyrians busy at the rear, where they had counted themselves most vulnerable, and vanished again into the trails in the greenbelt, where the Assyrians might have hoped to outflank their advance.

They owed a debt there, that was sure.

But . . .

Julius stiffened and leaned forward, gripping the seat ahead of him. "Damn!" he said, about the same time his driver and the other man saw it—the black Pentagram staff car parked back of the villa. He slapped the seat rim. "Get us up there. Move it."

The driver moved it. The jeep jolted forward, well ahead of the rest, while Julius leaned back in the seat and searched his pockets for incriminating bits of anything.

Nothing. He had been careful.

"What are we doing?" Caesarion asked blurrily, sitting forward in peril of his balance.

"Different front," Julius muttered. "Different weapons. Now we save our ass, is what." He gripped the front of Caesarion's leather jacket and Caesarion flinched and turned his face as if he expected a fist, that was the way things had gotten between them. "Listen," Julius said, and shook at him. "Caesarion. Whatever's between us, do me a favor—do these men a favor. And yourself, *pro di*, yourself. Just keep your mouth shut. Whatever they ask you, keep your mouth shut and don't *do* anything. Hear me?"

"Pentagram," Caesarion said, looking ahead of them, and looked him in the face with a lift of his chin and an insolent, half-lidded stare, give or take a swollen right eye. "Deep shit, huh?"

Julius restrained himself His fist bunched. He did not hit him. The knuckles were white on the hand that held the jacket, and he did not even jerk sense into him. "Real deep shit, son. If you want out of this, if you don't *want* a tour of the nether regions, you play it humble and real, real quiet, hear me? You don't give Authority any cheek. You don't open your mouth. That's all I ask. *It's not bloody much,* son, it's your own ass too, I'd think self-preservation would mean something to you."

"The kid all right?" Caesarion asked, no sneer, no surliness; and took him off-balance. He let go of Caesarion's jacket.

"As far as seems," he said. "As far as I know."

"Caesarion nodded, soberer than he had seen him in centuries. "Yeah, well." He looked forward.

"What did they do to him?"

Muscle jumped in Caesarion's cheek, the clenching of a jaw. And when he looked back again it was the old Caesarion, hateful as ever. "Nothing. Nothing much. Beat hell out of him. Didn't know who he was, can you buy that? Fouled up Mithridates' whole operation."

"You knew about that."

"I wasn't in on it, dammit. Brutus told me."

"Told you *what?*"

"*Wonder* about it," Caesarion said, jaw tight. "Or beat it out of me, who cares?"

"What in hell gets into you?" Julius smothered an impulse to grab him and jerk him sideways. "What in hell makes you tick?"

A flash of dark, sullen eyes. "Mother always said we're too damn much alike."

The hand did move. He stopped it, rested it gently on Caesarion's knee. Patted it wordlessly. There was no time for talking. They were coming up on the villa's lawn, past the recent shell-holes. Not a synophant was stirring to do anything about them.

There was something ominous in that. Usually at least a few of them would try.

But there was that black car sitting there in the beginnings of evening. There were jeeps parked up and down the drive that were not theirs.

And when they pulled up on the pavement and the officer of the 6th met them:

"It's *Mithridates*." Paulus said, his face calm as it could be under the circumstances. "*And* the Insecurity Service."

"Julius took in his breath and stood up, reached down to pull Caesarion up to his feet and help him out.

"What do we do?" Paulus asked.

"Get our wounded taken care of. Form up the lines as they come in." Practical matters. Paulus hoped for more than that. Himself, he helped his rebel son down out of the jeep and steadied him as he stepped down. "I'll take care of it. Get the necessities done."

Paulus took in his breath and saluted and went to do it, that was all. Julius spared a glance sideways as Klea parked the Ferrari and Hatshepsut bailed out with the AKM in hand; as Sargon and Scaevola pulled in, Sargon driving, and Brutus, thank gods! was in the back seat and safe.

"Easy," Julius said to Hatshepsut—gods, even a half-naked woman today had no more interest for him than the necessity of keeping her finger off the trigger. Her damnable enthusiasm for blowing things up was a fine thing when it came over the horizion in a crisis, but having her near a dispute with Insecurity upset his stomach. "For godsake, keep the guns out of sight. We've got enough to explain."

She gave him a look he could not figure, except she

nodded and gave him no argument. And slid her eyes sideways, where, down the steps leading to the parking lot, Augustus was on his way, with a trench-coated stranger who gave Julius a bad feeling even at distance.

And behind *them,* Mithridates, with a handful of aides.

Then it was a good thing the gun was in Hatshepsut's hands, and that his was in holster.

Mithridates, under *his* roof.

But he drew a quiet breath and walked forward to meet Augustus and the visitor, reckoning that in a very little he might be under arrest; and then that gun at his side was going to be more than tempting.

No. Not sensible. What he had done was desperate, but he had had no choice. Actually pulling the boys out—*that* had been next to stupid, to risk to himself and to others, for reasons which had too much personal and too little of policy in them for him to be comfortable with what he had done; but going after Assurbanipal and his lot—

That, he did not have any apology for. And if they arrested him, and if he ended up a smoking spot on the carpet in the Devil's office—

He intended to resign before that. Head it on to Augustus. Disassociate the Roman West. He *knew* then why he had diverted himself after the boys, in that way that his Luck usually operated—a subconscious addition of pro and con until he jumped the right way even when his conscious mind did not know why.

He would simply claim he had gone *for* the boys, if it came to it, giving Augustus the chance to do a public repudiation of him and all his actions; and Rome would be in the clear.

He hoped.

"*Auguste,*" he said, face to face with Augustus and the Insecurity agent. And for Mithridates, standing at the agent's side, a glance diverted when the Insecurity agent showed him a wallet and credentials.

"Asmodeus," the agent said. "We have a series of complaints under investigation. One of which involves trespass. Bombing. Sabotage of city property. Murder. Public endangerment. Public nuisance. High treason."

Disturbing the peace, Julius longed to add, sarcastically. But he folded his arms, took a deep breath, and said: "We'll be glad to testify against him."

"Him?" Asmodeus asked.

"I can see you have the culprit," Julius said with a nod toward Mithridates. "I can get you no end of witnesses."

"Caesar's sense of humor is undiminished," Mithridates said. "*You're* the one answering the questions. Caesar, and you're going to be answering them for a long, long time. Shall I add to the list? Kidnapping. Assassination. Theft of government property. Conspiracy to commit murder. Theft of a bus. Damage to Assyrian property. Injury and wrongful death, on how many counts we still haven't got a tally—"

Julius strode back, grabbed Caesarion by the shoulder of his jacket and hauled him forward. *"This* is my son. *That*—" He pointed across the parking lot where Brutus stood with Sargon and Scaevola. "—is my son. And I damned well have charges of my own." He turned Caesarion's face to the side, where the bruises showed to the Insecurity agent. "Kidnapping, assault, attempted murder— *His imperial majesty Assurbanipal kidnapped my sons, officer. Roman citizens! and damned if I'm bound to stand by and let him threaten their lives.*"

"Damned if you're *permitted* to divert Guard equipment," Mithridates said.

"*That?*" Julius made an extravagant wave of his hand at the vehicles coming in. "Check the serial numbers. They're not ours. Hell if I know whose they *are*, but we got them out of Asurbanipal's front yard! Only thing we took was my personal jeep and a truck for supplies. We were on our way over beyond the Lake to join the 14th, mopping up a Dissident incursion; we had the 6th in here to cover our tail because it usually happens the Cong make overshots about the time *they* think we're busy elsewhere, which is a damned towering coincidence, officer! and one that bears investigation! We were already rigging up to move when my sons here took a night on the town and found Assyrian agents all over their case— found themselves chased and shot at and finally kidnapped off public transport by Assyrian agents, officer, who intervened to stop a train in mid-tunnel, and engaged in a shootout with members of my household who were there in the station to try to get the boys away to safety. This was purely and simply an act of provocation against us—and we refuse to tolerate it! We were ready to march and *pro di*, we just took a side trip off our march to join the 14th and got the boys out, that's the long and the short of it, and when we recovered illicit equipment, we brought it out! There it is! I want a listing of those serial numbers, I want an accounting of who authorized it, and I want the parties responsible to answer for it!"

"That equipment was legitimately checked out," Mithridates said, "since the Dissidents your 14th legion has been waltzing around with and *not* making contact with, were threatening Assurbanipal's land. He has the right to draw weapons from the North Armory, and you'll find his first appeal for police assistance when your agents opened fire on peaceful Assyrian nationals in the *Oasis* bar. We have a complete dossier on your son's clandestine activities, and we have questions to ask. You're under arrest, you *and* your household!"

"The *hell!*"

"*I* have questions to ask," said the Insecurity agent, in a tone that could frost glass. "*Inside*."

Brutus watched, restrained by Sargon's hand on his shoulder, as Julius and Mithridates and the stranger in the trenchcoat and Augustus all turned and went toward the house. Caesarion stayed. The soldiers round about stayed, and the Egyptians barred the way of the legionaries who wanted to follow Julius, leveling rifles at them.

"Easy," Sargon said. "Patience."

"That's Mithridates!" Brutus exclaimed, thinking that perhaps no one understood except himself; but Sargon held his arm and squeezed hard.

"I assume you your father knows," Scaevola said darkly. "We all know. If Julius wanted, we would be up those stairs."

"Are we in t-t-trouble?" Brutus asked.

"A whole lot of trouble," Sargon said.

Klea had crossed the asphalt among the cars to get to Caesarion, who stood where Julius had left him. She put her arms about him. Brutus watched with a lump in his throat, thinking he would not be so ungrateful as Caesarion seemed, jerking away from her and turning his head, if he had a mother anymore who would do what Klea had done to get him out—there was nothing shameful in a boy respecting his mother, even in front of the soldiers, even in the condition Caesarion was in, in chains and with blood all over him.

Only he had not been hateful with Julius. That was something. He had not fought back against his father, had not made a scene in front of the enemy, —no, not even with Augustus standing right there.

Caesarion had brains when he wanted to use them, Brutus thought. And he knew damned well he hurt his mother. Which infuriated Brutus and made him wish not for the first time that day that he could beat some sense into the brother who was, dammit, so much like Julius in so many ways it hurt.

Which was most of the trouble, he thought with an ache in his heart. Caesarion had Julius' looks and Julius' quickness and Julius' pride, and he was legitimate, what was more. Caesarion had everything he ached to have.

And just threw it away.

Caesarion could have gone up those stairs with Julius: likely the soldiers would not have stopped him, he was standing that close. But he had not even tried.

What are they going to do? he thought. *Gods, what are they going to do?*

And hard upon that: *This is my fault.*

At least half of it is.

With a look at Caesarion, and his forlorn mother, the little queen of Egypt so desperate and so beautiful in her golden crown and white linen.

Hatshepsut was a different kind of sight, one that Brutus felt guilty even looking toward, because he would never, ever forget such a sight, —which Egyptians might not blush at, but he was a boy from a strict family, and if he had been in Rome he would have died of embarrassment when Hatshepsut came over and hugged him in one arm. As it was he knew he went red, and tried not to look at—what it was not polite to stare at on a lady.

Hatshepsut kept touching her ear with her other hand and saying: "Hurry up, dammit! Set take you, *hurry!*" as if she was imploring the gods, but this was Hell and there were no gods likely to intervene here, that was what Scaevola had told him, except the ones that no one wanted to hear from.

He was outright scared. He was glad Sargon and Hatshepsut held onto him. He thought he would fall, otherwise, just slump down in a puddle of sheer terror and exhaustion; and he was terribly afraid they were going to die, all of them, or be turned over to the Assyrians, which was worse; and Mithridates might come out of the house and say of him: "Give him to me. That boy is *mine.*"

If it came to that, Brutus thought, trying not to let his teeth chatter or his shivers be felt, if it came to that he would fight them with all he had in him and try to escape, because he was not going anywhere with that man who thought he owned him. He did not belong to him. He did not, he did not, and Mithridates could not just claim custody of him.

Could he?

The damp night air came freely through the library, from shattered windows that showed Hell's sky dimming and the Administration building and the skyline of New Hell turning to silhouette against the red clouds. Paradise was setting. There was fog out; and in the room, curtains hung like wan ghosts next to the broken windows . . . no cheerful sight. The library lights were on, Asmodeus stood in the center of the room in what should have been adequate light, but somehow he seemed more cast in the twilight outside.

Julius regarded him with a straight-on stare, refusing the instinct that made the eyes want to blink or slide away, baffled by what should not happen to them. It *did* happen, *was* happening, and a man who had ventured more than one level of Hell and looked on the impossible did not let himself blink at this one, when it stood under his own roof and threatened his people.

"There's no regulation against lying," Asmodeus said in that silky-smooth voice that cut like a scalpel. "No regulation against treason—as long as it doesn't aim at Administration. Administration makes the rules. Naturally it makes them to favor itself. Any administrator understands that. So let's not talk about the little things. Let's talk about stolen equipment. Let's talk about the New Hell subway system, and shooting in the streets."

"In all of which," Julius said, "you'll find the Assyrians fired first, and you'll find those serial numbers belong to the North Armory."

"I wouldn't depend on that," Mithridates said with a dry, cold smirk that Julius did not like in the least.

"If otherwise," Julius said, "then treason goes very high indeed—right into the Pentagram—and the altering of records."

Asmodeus reached into his pocket and pulled out

a small notebook, flipped it open and consulted his notes.

"There have been numerous incidents," Asmodeus said, "involving the East Armory. We have numerous trespass complaints. Not, in itself, serious—except taken in context. We have, of course, a report from Tiberius Caesar, officially lodged, concerning an assault with explosives."

"Tiberius," Julius said, "is hardly a reliable witness. An Egyptian colonel was attempting to assassinate him. I stopped him."

Asmodeus' brows lifted, the first reaction Julius had seen in him. He made a note. "Also a complaint from one Horemheb, killed in that blast."

"I'll be glad to file one against Horemheb—attempted assassination of a Roman emperor."

"Motive?"

"Ambition. Collusion with Assurbanipal."

"Ridiculous," Mithridates said. "Pentagram records will show that Tiberius requested a bodyguard, since Kleopatra lured away his German Guard. The Supreme Commander granted the request and assigned one of his own squads to the purpose. Surely you aren't impunging the integrity of the Supreme Commander."

"Only of Horemheb," Julius said tightly, "and his relations with the Assyrians—*your* friends, sir."

"I'd be very careful," Mithridates said, and smiled with all his teeth. "Very careful, in your position. The days when you had influence in the Pentagram are done. The days when you could borrow armament at will and falsify records . . . are past. The trouble is, you don't seem to have noticed the change in—"

"Why would I need to," Julius retorted, to shut it off, "if I had *influence* in the Pentagram? It seems to me, general, that an outlying power whose contact in the Pentagram is less than the Supreme Commander has far more reason to falsify records and 'borrow' armament, *some* of which is sitting out there in the parking lot, *some* of which was used to fire at Roman citizens, to kidnap Roman citizens, to hold Roman citizens for ransom—"

"Your own equipment," Mithridates said. "Records will show it. You mounted an assault against a rival Power with armaments and munitions devoted to Pentagram use. You attempted to falsify records, you diverted funds, you aimed, in short, at the overthrow of the Supreme Commander, the appointee of the Supreme Executive, which is *treason,* sir, and you will answer for it."

"Right! Right! Turn right!" Niccolo yelled, clinging to the straps, his teeth snapping together in a jolt as the horse-cab took a turn through the greenbelt and wound itself serpent-like about the metropolis—they had made it that far, after going for hours in the winding backstreets of New Hell, through geography Niccolo swore could not *possibly* be in New Hell, and now the cabby passed the one turn Niccolo was halfway sure of.

"Stop, you blithering fool!" Niccolo screamed, came out of his seat clutching the ridiculous hat, and stuck his head out the window, on a view of careering horse, shadowed, ominous trees, and a fog-bound dirt road of the sort that no one in his right mind would choose for a night drive *"Stop!"*

The driver finally pulled in, in a rattling of harness and wheels, the black, lank horse blowing and snorting and looking back with a blinkered eye as it came to a halt.

"That was the turn!" Niccolo shouted. "Fool! Turn this cab around!"

"Ye're mistaken, guv'nor."

"I am *not* mistaken! Turn this cab!"

"See 'ere, guv'nor, ye give me this address by some bleedin' park—"

"Decentral Park, per dio! Don't tell me you can't find Decentral Park!"

"Well, now, guv'nor, I know Victoria Park, Hyde Park—"

"Park *Avenue!* You call yourself a cabby, *maledetto*, just *turn* where I tell you *turn*, is that so difficult?"

"Maybe if ye spoke *English*, guv'nor—"

"Turn the damned cab!"

"Now, look 'ere, guv'nor, there's only one 'and drives this 'ere 'orse, an' if you think you can do better, maybe you better climb up 'ere and drive this 'ere cab, eh? Otherwise—"

"Damn you!" Niccolo flung the door open, jumped out onto the step, grabbed the window edge and scrambled for the driver's seat as the driver shoved at the brake and set the cab in motion.

" 'Ere, 'ere! Get off! Get off there!"

"*You* get off!" Niccolo shouted, achieving the edge of the seat, ignoring the blows of the whip and the lashing of branches as the cab passed under trees. "Give me those reins!"

" 'Elp! 'Elp! Robbery an' murder!"

"*I'll;* give you murder, miscreant!" Niccolo seized the whip in one hand and tugged it hard, cracked his fist across an undefended jaw, gave him the knee and the boot as the cab swayed wildly around a turn and branches raked them both. "Let go!"

The man screamed, losing his balance as he swung outward holding the rail.

Niccolo helped him with a foot in the midriff and snatched up the reins before they went over the edge of the footrest, reining back at the driver and a branch made close acquaintance.

"Aiii!" the driver yelled.

Thump.

Niccolo reined back and searched after the fallen whip, as the horse the its head and fought the bit. It slowed, finally, it turned, no easy matter, threatening the fragile wheels with the ruts and the shafts with the narrow space of the roadway.

"Gi' me back me cab!" came out of the gathering dark.

"Haiiiiiiiii!" Niccolo yelled, let free the reins and cracked the whip

"Aiiiiiiii!" the driver yelled, turning up in the roadway with arms wide.

The horse was a thorough ingrate. It saved itself from stumbling, striking the driver with its shoulder, which threw the driver beneath the right wheel, where he made a kind of gentle bounce, and another, sharper: aaiiiiiii!

"Buona note!" Niccolo wished him, and seeing the turn loom up, hauled hard right.

The horse fought it all the way. The whip convinced it.

Then it lit out running, and the cab jolted along over the ruts, tilting this way and that, threatening ruin at every instant till the trees opened up and pavement showed in front of him.

"Hyyyyyyyyyaaaaaaaa!" Niccolo yelled, cracked the whip, and the creature leapt forward. Perhaps it was a trick of the gathering dark and the streetlights by the Park, perhaps it was the fog that hung about the sodium vapor lights, and the steaming sweat that rose from the horse's back: but the steam that came from the horse's nostrils seemed tinged with red, and the sparks the flying hooves struck from the paving seemed to send up the scent of brimstone.

It might have been cordite. *That* was heavy on the winds too, with the smell of turned earth and bitter burning.

"Hyyyyyyyyyyyyyyaaaaaaaaaaaaa!"

The horse stretched itself into a careening run, avoiding potholes and shellpocks in the concrete, the glow about its nostrils more and more pronounced. It no longer fought for the bit.

Until the villa came up on the right, and Niccolo began to pull in. Then it fought, threw its head and fought as he jammed on the brake with his foot. Sparks flew from the iron rims on the pavement; he braced himself and leaned his whole weight into it as he hauled in the reins and plied the whip.

Bang! Right rim over the curb by the junipers, the whole cab tilting madly as it made the turn. Niccolo jammed the brake down again, hauling in with all his might as armed soldiers ran in the porchlight to threaten the cab with rifles.

"Fools!" he yelled, as the cab nearly ran them down. "Fools!"

A mass of soldiers were sufficient finally to stop the horse, and Niccolo clambered down from the driver's seat, ignoring questions. He flung open the cab door and snatched his briefcase and his hat, slapped the top-hat onto his head and touched its brim to the arriving officer—*not,* he saw, a Roman.

Egyptian.

"Who are you?" the Egyptian asked.

"I?" Niccolo raked the scene with a quick eye and a wild estimate of the situation, with staff cars and Pentagram personnel everywhere. "*I,* sir, am a solicitor. *Lawyer,* if you please. I'll thank you to conduct me to your commanding officer."

It was going very badly—*very* badly. One could see that, from the way that soldiers were coming and going downstairs, and now, now, they had started through the rooms of the villa on a general search.

Dante Alighieri settled himself stark naked before the little Buddha incense burner and stoked it with more patchouli. His hair was frizzed. The air was thick with marijuana. The thick red drapes were drawn on the night, and there were black-light psychedelic posters everywhere about the walls, along with a construction-paper peace symbol.

On the computer screen, the *Commedia Divina* glowed in green letters, halted in mid-reconstruction.

"Ommmmmmmmmmmm," the poet chanted. "Om-
mmmmmmm."

As footsteps neared and the dreaded knock came at
the door.

He heard a foreign voice raised in a staccato order,
and there was a terrible crack.

"Ommmmmmmmmm—"

As the door splintered inward and banged against the
wall of an amazingly neat room, admitting a horde of
Egyptians to his sanctum.

"What is this?" the officer shouted.

Dante Alighieri, truly blissed, grinned and held up
two fingers in the peace sign as rifles aimed toward
him, while the Egyptians swore at the stench and waved
hands to clear the air.

"Set! Who are you?"

"Dante Alighieri," Dante said, holding up a cigarette
and smiling benignly. "Have one?"

"It's the Italian," one soldier said. "The poet."

"Debauchery," said the Egyptian.

"I court the muse," said Dante, waving the cigarette
and grinning beatifically. "It's where we poets get our
ideas. May I show you, *signore*, the font of knowledge?
May I impart to you the true wisdom, which I have
discovered, marvelously, *signore*, in the chant which
was taught me by the magnificent, the learned Lao
Tzu? *Ommmmmmmmmmmm.* . . ."

One of the Egyptians muttered, made a sign and
backed away.

"A faker!" the officer snarled in English. "Examine
that machine! Confiscate the files!"

"True wisdom lies in the mind," Dante said, smiling.
"Not in the works of machines. Lay down your weapons,
ye men of war, and I will show you the benefits of
peace. A great wise man showed me a chant. Shall I tell
it to you? *Ommmmmmmmmm.* Ommmmm is the way to
truth. Ommmmm is the jewel in the mind."

"No phone," the officer said, stooping to examine the

wall, the plugs. "Search the walls!" He set the monitor off the CPU and a soldier produced a screwdriver and began rapidly to take the cover off.

"Ommmm is without parallel. It goes trapezoidally inverse to the universe."

"No modem," the officer muttered. "Damn! Take everything. It's confiscated."

"Ommmm is without paradigm. Generally it confounds the statisticians."

The soldiers grabbed up papers and books and program discs and disk file, uprooted the CPU and the keyboard and hauled it away.

The last one slammed the door.

Dante fell over backward, hands over his heart.

No one had smelled the paint or detected the recent patches which the legionaries had made with quick-set plaster, which covered the phone connections. No one had discovered the contents of the little space in the floor, beneath the tiles which were now firmly cemented back in place, which held the terribly damning disk-files, as well as the backup copies of *La Commedia Divina*. Marijuana and patchouli could cover about any stink.

And madness was the best defense against questions.

But Dante was beginning to have a terrible headache, and the room was doing very strange things.

"Ommmmmm," he muttered, finding the light-fixture of unexpectedly cosmic significance.

Niccolo climbed the stairs to the level of the library, walked down the corridor with briefcase in hand, the ridiculous hat left behind with a soldier at the desk, petty vengeance.

A pair of soldiers stood guard at the door, and barred his way with the expected: "No admittance. Where's your pass?"

Niccolo smiled and reached delicately for his coat pocket, drew out his wallet and flashed what gave him cold chills to use, what he never carried, unless the cause was dire.

Administration credentials.

Backs stiffened, rifles went up respectfully. "Yes, sir. But the general said no admittance, sir."

"I'm sure the general wouldn't want a phone call from—ahem, my superior. I'll take responsibility." He reached for the door. One soldier twitched, and the twitch stopped as Niccolo fixed him with a stare and smiled. "Or you can."

He opened the door and walked into a room fervid with sweat and questions, despite the broken window and the moths that circled the lights.

"Machiavelli!" Mithridates exclaimed; and to his men at Niccolo's back, pointing: "Get him out of here! He's under arrest with the rest of them!"

"I don't think so," Niccolo said, and gave a nod to Asmodeus. "Good evening, captain. Pleasure."

"You have information to contribute?"

"Cesare did ask me to bring some affidavits—" He laid his briefcase on the library table and opened it as the soldiers confusedly withdrew and shut the door at a wave of Asmodeus' hand and no contradiction from Mithridates. He spared a glance at Julius, who stood there by Augustus' desk, Augustus behind the desk, looking pale under his freckles, Julius' face smeared with soot and blood and showing a decided five o'clock shadow, his whole stance showing exhaustion; but there was a dark and desperate interest in Julius' eyes, a tightness about his mouth that meant bloodyminded stubbornness had set in.

"The business this morning," Niccolo said blandly, "did come to some further difficulty? I fear I've been somewhat buried in my work."

Mithridates came to stand over his shoulder and investigate the contents of the briefcase without quite laying hands on it.

Niccolo lifted certain of the files on Assyrian activity,

which he had brought to one Agathodemas, and left another one lying in the briefcase.

TOP SECRET, the stencil on that one said. And the tab said: *Brutus, Marcus Junius*.

He lifted his face with the gentlest, kindest of smiles for Mithridates. "You see," he said, "these records make it quite clear there's been a string of provocations, and they do quite well document that there's a connection between one Kadashman-enlil, resident within Assurbanipal's domicile, and the Dissident operations. Now, there are certain files within the Pentagram which will document this, I am sure. I fear Cesare's activities may not have been communicated to all branches, certainly in the interests of security—when the Pentagram is engaged in an internal investigation: after all, the colonel *is* seen in the halls of the Pentagram. Perhaps you would care to examine the files more closely, general, to assure yourself of their authenticity. But I fear you have made a mistake, which of course, the emperor Augustus *will* forgive, but I do hope you will make the necessary phone calls and try to ascertain the truth of this before it harms certain reputations."

Mithridates' face had gone an astonishing shade of white.

Venom. There was that. And terror, when he looked toward Asmodeus

"I fear there has been some confusion," Mithridates said in a strangled voice.

"Ah," said Julius cheerfully. "Well." He drew a long breath and folded his arms, smiling at Asmodeus. "Suppose, then, we try to get these civil matters attended to. Of course the Pentagram would rather not give an accounting in court. It's a delicate matter. But if you want a desposition against Kadashman-enlil, in any civil matter, I can find certain of my people who would be glad to cooperate. In many cases, they can name names."

Asmodeus lifted a brow and made a note. "General?"

Mithridates cleared his throat. "I think, officer, that this falls within military jurisdiction."

"You wish to take responsibility."

"I'll consult with the Supreme Commander. I'm sure—" Another clearing of his throat. "I'm sure we would appreciate the cooperation of the Insecurity Service. Both of us, after all—have the interests of the Executive at heart."

"There will be a report at that level," Asmodeus said. "We may ask for certain files."

"The Pentagram has its privileges, sir."

The air in the room grew decidedly cold.

There was a shock of air, an impression of wings unfurled, and the curtains flew out the shattered windows on a gust of wind. Asmodeus had vanished.

Mithridates went for the door, flung it open. "Take them!" he yelled, and faced about white-faced at the sight of the gun in the emperor Augustus' hand.

"I'd think that over," Julius said.

Niccolo just folded up the briefcase and hugged it against him.

"You can be very dead," Augustus said, "or you can take that damned lot of pirates out of my house!"

"Remembering," said Niccolo, "what must surely come to light otherwise. We not only have the original—there are copies elsewhere."

The soldiers came down the stairs, a very angry Mithridates came down the stairs, people got into cars and drove them away, while a very surly horse with a carriage attached cropped the lawn and wandered at will.

Brutus watched in bewilderment, where he and Caesarion, Sargon, Scaevola, Hatshepsut, Kleopatra, and finally a most distressed Mouse and Mettius Curtius and Marcus Agrippa (who had come in with the rear guard of the 10th and 12th) stood and sat according to disposition, under the rifles of twoscore Egyptians.

Scaevola and Sargon and Caesarion who had been sitting down stood up when that started.

"What's happening?" Brutus whispered.

"I don't know," Sargon muttered in reply. "*Something's* going on."

Someone had come in with the horse. None of them were in a position to see who, except Hatshepsut had said then: "Things are looking up."

But now Brutus felt a decided chill as a courier ran over to the Egyptians who held the rifles on them.

They're going to shoot us, he thought. *They've arrested everyone inside, and they're going to shoot us.*

He was afraid to ask if anyone else thought so. He would stutter or his voice would go up and he would sound like a coward. Already his teeth were chattering. But he did not reach toward anyone for comfort, just stared at the Egyptians.

And drew a huge, shaken breath when suddenly the Egyptians lowered their rifles and slung them to their shoulders and formed up and marched away.

Brutus looked at the others then, in the dim light from the porch and the windows. He saw relief elsewhere, saw Mouse start for the house in a hurry, Curtius with him.

Sargon laid his hand on Brutus' shoulder. "Come on, let's get you inside."

"What's happened?" His voice did break. "Why are they leaving?"

No one answered him.

But Sargon shoved him toward the house, toward the warmth of the porchlight and the safety of their own soldiers, who were moving in, thousands of them, the men of the 6th and the 10th and the 12th, who were cheering the Egyptians and the Assyrians off with a rattling of gear and helmets and a hammering of rifle-butts on fenders of captured trucks and jeeps. "Haaaaaa-

iiiii," they yelled. "Hai, hai, hai, hai!" And: *"Cae-sar!*
Cae-sar! Cae-sar!"

Someone pointed, and others did, and men lifted
their faces. It was Julius, standing at the library window.

Epilogue

The dawn came chill and foggy, the more so that they had not yet been able to get the windows replaced, but the villa was secure: thorough searches had determined that much, and Julius stood looking out over a lawn full of tents and Assyrian trucks on the dewy, misty green.

He watched Mouse escort the two boys toward the house— "Don't take chances," had been Mouse's advice this morning, sharp and worried.

And: "What do you expect me to do?" he had asked. "How will I *ever* know?"

Mouse had had no answer for that. Mouse had trekked out himself to bring the boys in, from where they had spent the night with the 10th, out under canvas where they knew there were no bombs, no assassins, no hazards beyond a Cong overshot, and they had pitched their tents beyond the usual range the Cong achieved.

It had been quiet all night, a kind of wrung-out, exhausted quiet, as if truce were called in the underground warfare. Antonius had phoned in, to say the emperor Tiberius had determined it was the fault of Assyrian agents that his statue had been damaged, and that Caligula had shown up incarnate as a baboon . . . all of which meant that Antonius was in one piece, currently

377

in favor, and tolerably in good humor with the emperor's latest fancy.

Mummius . . . gods knew what Mummius had come to or if Tiberius had gotten him back.

They still had a horse-cab wandering about the lawn. And Dante was sound asleep, after approaching the duty officer with the news that he had understood the paradox of time in Hell and that it was related to triangles.

Dante, gods knew, was beloved of the legions. Deservedly. A hero, after his own fashion.

There had been a great many heroes, of them, that brought them through to this morning, with nothing lost but glass and plaster. And with things gained they could not explain, chiefly a strange and bewildered American who kept insisting he had to phone his office in Tulsa.

Julius heard the downstairs door, measured the time it took Mouse and the boys to climb the stairs, listened for the knock and snapped his fingers.

A sycophant hastened to open the door.

"*Marce*," he said, summoning Brutus inside, and: "Caesarion."

Brutus came in on his own. Then Caesarion did, and managed not quite to look at him. That left Mouse standing there.

"It's all right," Julius said to Mouse. "Go get breakfast."

Mouse closed the door. And would not leave. He knew Mouse's ways.

He looked at his sons, one and the other. Saw Brutus look at him with terrible anxiety, and gnaw at his lip. Caesarion's stare was dark and elsewhere, sullen as ever.

"I'm sorry," Brutus said.

"Are you?" Julius asked. "It was a damn fool thing to do. Bedsheets, *pro di*."

Brutus looked at the floor. "I'm s-s-sorry."

"Helping your brother, was it? You know how wide a path you cut?"

"I kn-kn-know, sir, I'm s-s-s—"

"Did you learn anything?"

Brutus looked up at him. There was slight surprise, bewilderment. Nothing furtive, just a quick, embarrassed flush. "T-t-that t-th—"

"Calm down, son."

"I was a f-f-fool," Brutus said. His chin trembled and steadied. "And I c-cost t-too m-m-m—*much*. Sir."

"I won't lecture you," Julius said. "You're old enough. You know the score. It's those men out there you owe your apology to. But you can't make it up in words. You understand. *I* couldn't help you. Do you know why?"

"Yes, sir," Brutus said faintly.

"Good," Julius said, and did what he had wanted to do, which was to embrace his son, and to look him in the eyes. "Now go on, get some breakfast, and for godssake stay out of trouble. Hear?"

"I'm n-n-not a k-kid."

He looked soberly at the boy who stood holding him at arms' length. And it was, at least in some measure, true. "You're not a kid," he said, and brushed his knuckle along Brutus' slightly bearded jawline. "You go upstairs and get cleaned up. You put yourself under Mouse's orders."

"Yes, sir."

"Go."

Brutus went, not without a backward look.

Which left his other son, who gave him his back when the door closed—standing staring out the windows toward the city. Toward Administration. And power in Hell.

"Well?" Julius asked.

"Well," Caesarion echoed coldly. "What do I get?"

"What do you want?"

"I want the hell out of here."

"Use the stairs. You're on the second floor."

Caesarion turned around with a furious look. "Funny. Real funny."

"I'm glad you've figured it out. Did you get the rest of it? How do you like your Assyrian allies?"

"Damn you."

"You didn't tell him," Julius said. "That surprises hell out of me."

"*You* didn't," Caesarion said. "What are you setting him up for?"

There was no good answer for that. Julius turned his back and walked to the desk and sat down on the edge of it. "Maybe I don't find it easy. Same as you. *I* don't know how to tell him. And you think he doesn't know."

"I think you'd better tell him," Caesarion said. "It had better come from you."

"I will. When he's gotten through this. He's had enough."

"Yeah," Caesarion said, and shrugged and looked at the windows, hands in pockets. "So. What do I get? Back to the basement?"

"You get a place in this house if you want it."

Caesarion gave him a sudden, wary look. "Upstairs, you mean, instead of the basement. No, thanks. Call your soldier-boys. I'll take the basement. At least I know where I stand."

"Or there's the door."

"Huh."

"You're free. I won't stop you. Go to the Dissidents if you like."

"Bloody hell!"

"Or back to Tiberius. Or stay here. You've got your choice."

Caesarion stared at him. Then walked for the door and opened it.

Mouse was there.

"Let him go," Julius said. "He's free."

Mouse's expression never changed. He only stepped out of the way. And Caesarion started through the door, with a misgiving look toward Mouse.

He got all the way out into the hall, and then he

stopped facing the wall, stood there a moment, with his head bowed.

Then he turned and came back again, with one of those furious scowls on his face, and held out his hand. The scowl looked somehow frightened.

Julius took the offered hand wrist to wrist, Roman style, not modern. Caesarion did not look up, not once. He broke the grip and turned and walked away, took the stairs quickly.

"Go behind him," Julius said to Mouse. "Make sure no one stops him."

"Shall I have him followed?"

"No," Julius said. And called out after his son: "Tell your mother you're leaving, dammit! You owe her some courtesy!"

Brutus ventured the halls again, scrubbed, shaved, aching in every bone and muscle, but free.

So was Caesarion. Scaevola had told him so. And he was sorry to know Caesarion had left, and glad too, that Julius and he had come to some kind of peace.

He found Dante sitting out, wincing at the light and moving cautiously. And he met Hatshepsut, resplendent in pale, pale green, with her jewelry blinking and winking busily; he did *not* blush. Last night seemed like a dream—and the green jumpsuit, transparent here and there, seemed amazingly modest.

Niccolo and Sargon, she said, were down having a swim, and Julius was closeted with Niccolo and Augustus and Klea, which was ordinary enough, and reassuring, especially when Hatshepsut gave him one of her brightest smiles and . . . not quite chucked him under the chin: she sort of touched him lightly under the chin with her finger, grinned at him and called him kitten again in a low voice that left the whole world quivering.

Hammering had started, the repair of windows and plaster. The villa was putting itself back to rights.

And Brutus found himself taking the stairs on his

heels, the way he was accustomed to do, found himself even cheerful, because whatever he was responsible for, somehow everything he loved had survived it.

Suddenly, without so much as a whisper to announce itself, a point of green light popped into existence and bobbed anxiously ahead of him down the hall.

His sycophant was back, brighter and more definite than before.

They knew, somehow, when a body's fortunes were on the rise.

APPENDIX

On Roman Names and Civil Rights

A roman patrician (noble) has three names: the personal name, of which each clan, or *gens*, has only two or three (the Julian clan used Caius and Lucius), which are used in alternation through the inheriting males. Sons other than the heir are known by number-names such as Tertius, Quintus (three, five, etc.) which were, however, given for their pleasing sound or possibly to commemorate some relative, and without much regard for sequence; or by names such as Ruus ("red") or Postumus ("son born after the death of his father") or whatever nickname attached to them in the family—some of which stuck, and were bequeathed to sons in their own lines.

Women had no such personal name, or *praenomen (lit. forename)*, which was in any case used mostly by intimates and family members, and which seems to have been hedged about by rules or religious significance, the same as Senate membership and other privileges reserved for senior males. This is not to say that women were without rights or identity in Rome: the operative word is *senior* as well as *males*, meaning that seniority counted for more than gender, in a back-and-forth weave of rights—elder females outranked younger males, and so on, and any woman of a clan would convoke a clan meeting and compel the clan to defend her rights against a husband, the state, or another individual. A woman when she married did not change her name, and actually acquired rights in *two* clans, which her husband did not. A wife could convoke her husband's clan if she had children, and in some instances if she did not; or she could repudiate that clan and return to her own at any time with full rights—but the father kept the children, since they were indisputably of his clan. She could not vote in the Senate, but she could give certain instructions to the senior male clan member who had the family senate seat—and expect to have her opinion regarded according to her seniority and the respect accorded her in the clan. Certainly such women as Caesar's redoubtable Aunt Julia held profound influence within their clans, and Antonius' wife, outraged by Antonius' bigamy with Kleopatra, raised and led legions in civil war—with no better success than Antonius later had in the same cause.

All Romans had a *gens:* name, or clan name, which in the case of males usually ends in -ius and females in -ia, and this is the name by which a person is called for courtesy. Women used this name throughout their lives and never changed it. The surname is a name attached to the particular family of the clan to which one belongs, and when such a tag is added, it becomes inheritable. No one knows, for instance, the ancestor who added the name *Caesar (lit. long-hair):* to clan Julia.

Plebeians usually had only two names, as for instance, Marcus Antonius; and even Gaius Octavius who became Augustus . . . who was a commoner by birth, and ennobled only by his adoption by his patrician great-uncle Julius Caesar.

On adoption, a name such as Octavius changed to Octavi*anus*, and he acquired the full name of his adoptive father, becoming instead Caius Iulius Caesar Octavinus. The Augustus ("Noble") was added as an honor by senatorial decree.

A name may be diminished affectionately or sarcastically by the insertion of the particle -ll-, as *Augustullus,* meaning "Little Augustus."

It is quite rude to use a person's name first in a sentence: you always begin your statement and then state the name of the person you are addressing.

There are also special spellings of Roman names ending in -us when they are used in calling the person: -ius words become -i and -us become -e. Hence the shifts in spelling.

In general, to explain Roman names is to explain Roman identity. In some sense, a Roman was extremely individualistic: personal eccentricity was tolerated, personal freedom was highly valued, and Romans had a very humane system of law which protected the rights of the individual against others and against the state. The necessity for trial by jury, the right of appeal, the concept of bail (far more liberal than our own), and pardon, are all Roman institutions which passed into modern law. But in a certain sense, a Roman did not *own* his name. Young Caius Julius Caesar would have been led by his father Lucius into the presence of the deathmasks of his ancestors and there he would be shown a succession of seven hundred years of Caius Julius Caesars, and he would be told that he, at the latest to bear the name, was responsible for handing it on with honor: he was in effect *carrying* the name, without owning it. The male heirs in one sense had a burden equal to their privilege, and had no more *personal* name than whatever personal nickname they might acquire in their life, the same as their sisters and younger brothers. Marcus Junius Brutus, the first of the name, was a hero of the Roman revolution which expelled the kings in the 500's B.C. Marcus Junius Brutus of the 40's B.C., the Brutus of our story, was the last of the name: when he died, the Junius clan refused to honor him among its ancestor-spirits, thus damning his souls (a Roman had several) to fade, and struck the name Marcus

from its rolls in dishonor so that no son of the house
would ever carry it again.

General Glossary

adsum   *Latin:* I'm here.

Acduan   *English;* belonging to the Aedui tribe,
modern Burgundy.

Aelius   *Latin:* clan name of Hadrian.

Agamemnon   *Greek:* king of Mycenae in Greece,
attacker of Troy in the Trojan war.

Agathodemas   *Greek:* (lit. Goodpeople) a Byzantine

Agrippa   *Latin:* a general who served Augustus and
who was chosen by him as heir: he died before Augustus.

Agrippina   *Latin:* daughter of Agrippa, mother of
Caligula; also Agrippina the Younger, daughter of
Agrippina, who was the mother of Nero, murdered by
him when he had to take power away from her.

Ahmose   *Egyptian:* a very common name roughly
equivalent to John in frequency, probably the original
of Moses. Also the pharaoh Ahmose, the liberator of
Egypt from the foreigners: grandfather of Hatshepsut.

Ahriman   *Middle Eastern:* Zoroastrian power of
darkness

Akkad   *Middle Eastern:* variant spelling of Agade, the
kingdom of Sargon, between the Tigris and Euphrates.

Dante Alighieri   *English:* poet, author of the *Inferno*.

Americane   *Latin:* American, in the calling-form.

amis   *French:* friends.

Ammon   *Egyptian:* late spelling of Amon, *Egyptian:* god of the wind.

Amon   *Egyptian:* god of the wind, often paired with Ra, the sungod.

Anglaise   *French:* Englishwoman

Marcus Antonius   *Latin:* Julius Caesar's lifelong associate, co-ruler of Rome with Augustus for a while, husband to Augustus' sister Octavia, later husband to Kleopatra, committed suicide rather than be captured by Augustus when Antonius broke with Augustus, divorced Octavia, and plunged the Empire into civil war. Antonius' children with Kleopatra were reared by Octavia along with her own, although she had been publicly rebuffed by him in her attempt to help him in Egypt. The one of Antonius' children she did not rear, however, was his adopted son Caesarion, Caesar's son by Kleopatra, who was entrapped and murdered after Antonius' own suicide.

Archimedes   *Greek:* mathematician and inventor.

Aristotle   *Greek:* philosopher.

Arrius   *Latin:* Roman clan name.

Astoreth   *Middle Eastern:* variant of Ishtar, goddess of fertility and war; also a street in New Hell.

Asmodeus   *Middle Eastern:* a Fallen Angel.

Assurbanipal   *Middle Eastern:* king of Assyria, noted for his library.

Assyria *Middle Eastern:* a nation of the ancient Middle East, roughly where modern Syria is.

atef *Egyptian:* the head-dress.

Atilius Regulus *Latin:* a noted Roman general proverbial for keeping his word. When he and his whole garrison were captured by the Carthaginians and held hostage, he delivered the terms to Rome in person, then requested the Senate reject them and fight; he then returned to Carthage to die with his men.

Attila (the Hun) *English:* famous conqueror.

audisne? *Latin:* do you hear?

audi, pl. audite! *Latin:* listen!

Augustus *Latin:* Caius Julius Caesar Octavianus Augustus, born Gaius Octavius, Julius Caesar's adopted son (actually his grand-nephew). He was the first Emperor of Rome.

Aurens *Middle Eastern:* local pronunciation of T. E. Lawrence's name.

Babylon *Middle Eastern:* a city of the ancient Middle East, conquered by Assyria and often in rebellion.

Bacchante *English:* via *Greek:* a celebrant of the spring rites of the ancient Greeks, which involved a great deal of wine, dancing, and in some instances, human sacrifice. The term is usually female.

Baiae *Latin:* coastal resort community south of Rome famous for the number of political exiles who lived there just outside the 100th milestone, the legal limit for their arrest.

Bastet *Egyptian:* variant for Bast, feline goddess of love.

bella *Italian:* beautiful.

bellissima *Italian:* very beautiful.

bien *French:* well! Fine!

bien sur *French:* to be sure!

bientot *French:* soon.

Bithynia *Latin:* ancient Asia Minor kingdom which figured in a scandal in which Julius Caesar was involved.

Napoleon Bonaparte *French:* famous French general.

Cesare Borgia *Italian:* Italian nobleman once served by Niccolo Machiavelli.

Brundisium *Latin:* modern Brindisi, a port city at the heel of Italy.

Marcus Junius Brutus *Latin:* name of both the liberator of Rome from the Kings, early in Rome's history; and the assassin of Julius Caesar, rumored during his lifetime to be his illegitimate son. Julius' reputation, let it be said, was not sterling in his youth.

c'est *French:* it is.

Caesarion *Greek:* son of Julius Caesar and Kleopatra, foster son of Antonius, murdered along with his tutor after the collapse of Antonius' civil war against Octavianus Augustus.

Caius Julius Caesar *Latin:* dictator of Rome but never was emperor. He was assassinated on the Ides of

March (March 15) 44 B.C. by a faction of the nobility who
ostensibly feared he would establish a monarchy, but
diminution of aristocratic privilege may have been an
equal motive: Julius was more noted for his revolutionary
activities on behalf of commons' rights than for his
assumption of monarchial powers. He had had a long
history of activism on behalf of the Italians and the
commons who were not at the time equal in privileges
or voting power; and had inherited the mantle of his
uncle Marius, a commoner who was married to the
aristocratic Julia, who went to war with Sulla and the
senatorial party over the selfsame issue. The 10th legion
was actually a disgraced unit when Julius assumed
command of it: it was heavily Italian, had been stationed
up in Gaul to keep it out of Italy, because it had been
recruited by Marius and had been heavily involved in
the civil war. It had been given securely aristrocratic
officers and keep on border patrol—when Julius unexpectedly got the right to choose a military appointment.
He picked Gaul, fought his early campaigns weeding
out the senatorial appointees from the 10th and the
other legions, and after a number of years' service in
that province as virtual warlord, was called home forcibly
by the Senate to face arrest: this was not the wisest
move the Senate ever made. Theoretically he should
have come back alone . . . but the 10th refused to
leave him, and so did the rest of the legions. That meant
civil war . . . and the ultimate fall of the aristocrats who
opposed him. It should be noted that not only was he
never an emperor, the very term has little meaning in
the early Empire: *imperator* is a title that meant, at
that time, only "commander," and was a military honor.
When Augustus "assumed the throne" there was no
throne, *Imperium* did not mean "Empire" but rather
"god-given right to command," and Augustus, a commoner, held conjointy the presidency (the consulate)
and the power of Tribune of the People, the latter of
which gave him the right of veto and the right of special

protection against assassination, but nothing else: he insisted to be called *Princeps,* "first citizen," from which we get the word "prince," but ruled in theory as the common people's representative co-equal with the aristrocatic legislature, the Senate—which mainly represented the wealthy and the old blood-lines. So the so-called emperorship was founded as a democratic reform. But Augustus' insistence on choosing his successor in effect founded a dynasty, although his preference was to choose a non-relative bound to his family by marriage (a custom with deep roots in Roman society, in which marriages frequently cemented political and financial alliances), and although his successors did follow somewhat the same principle, it became more and more dynastic, more and more convolute, and more and more a true emperorship in the later meaning of the word.

Caligula *Latin:* "Little Boots," Tiberius' successor and likely murderer. Regarded by the Roman as of great promise as a leader, he suffered a high fever and reputedly was not sane thereafter. Certainly his was one of the worst reigns, and he was, by all reports, far madder than Nero.

Capitolinus *Latin:* the double-humped sacred hill which is at the heart of Rome. It draws lightnings and is sacred to Jupiter. There is alleged to be an iron deposit there. In thunderstorms the metal-roofed temple of Jupiter which stood on its left summit was frequently struck by lightning, which is why so many Roman legends refer to that particular omen. In any given rainy season it had a fair chance of being hit.

Carthage *English:* via *Latin:* the city and empire roughly where modern Libya is, arch-enemies of early Rome.

Cassandra   *Greek:* the prophetess of Troy, doomed by the gods always to foretell the truth and never to be believed.

Cenabum   *Latin:* modern Orleans, France, scene of a dreadful massacre of Roman traders by the Gauls and later of a Roman siege; also famous in association with Joan of Arc.

Cesare   *Italian:* Caesar.

Tiberius Claudius Caesar   *Latin:* Augustus' adopted son and successor, who brought the Claudian line into the Julio-Claudians. Tiberius was a good general, but he and Augustus disagreed violently on the stabilizing of the northern border, up by Germany. When Tiberius' brother Drusus was killed on that frontier, Tiberius walked all the way back to Rome with the body and was accounted never quite right after. (Actually Augustus meeting him at the funeral with the news that he was supposed to marry the notorious Julia, whom Tiberius hated, did not improve matters.) Augustus lost all chance of winning the north when a general named Varus lost the northern army on a tactical blunder, and the great grief of Augustus' life was the knowledge that he must surrender the empire to a successor who would not finish his work. This defeat and this division of opinion laid down the boundaries of modern Europe and affected modern history profoundly.

ciel   *French;* heaven

cloacina   *Latin:* of the sewers. Venus Cloacina, the patron goddess of whores.

Horatius Cocles   *Latin:* "One-eye": an ancient Roman warrior who stood on the Tiber bridge to hold it while it was cut out from under him, to prevent the Etruscans from crossing in a surprise attack. He had his two comrades run back before it went. When it did go, he jumped to the Etruscan side, fought himself a clear spot, hurled his shield into the river to save it from dishonor and swam the Tiber in his armor, under fire. As he reached the far side, nearly out of range anyway, and was hauled up by his own side, it is reported even the enemy cheered him.

Cocytus *Latin:* the river of sand in Hell.

Richard Coeur de Lion *French:* Richard the Lion-hearted.

Mettius Curtius *Latin:* an ancient Roman hero. When Rome was threatened by earthquake and a spreading fault line in the Forum, and a prophecy demanded the most valuable thing in Rome, citizens threw in everything they could think of and it only grew worse. At last one of the youngest cavalrymen saddled up and rode into the chasm, casting himself and all he had into the gap. The quakes ceased. The gift accepted was simple courage.

d'accord *French:* OK.

Dantillus *Latin:* diminutive of Dante.

de *French:* of.

Decimus *Latin:* "10," a common first name.

Decius Mus *Latin:* a Roman general who, when faced with an impossible battle, vowed himself (according to an old ritual of human sacrifice) to the infernal gods, along with whoever he killed and whoever killed him. He then charged the enemy line singlehanded and opened a hole the Roman army under the other consul (Rome in those days sometimes took the field with both

presidents) then used to defeat the enemy. Mus actually
does mean Mouse.

déjà   *French:* already.

desiste, pl. desistite   *Latin:* stop!

di   *Latin:* gods; *Italian:* of.

dictator   *Latin:* (lit. "Speaker"): an emergency office
appointed by the Roman Senate for six months or the
duration of the emergency, whichever comes first.
Assisted by the Magister Equitum, whom the Dictator
appoints, the Dictator's appointment is tantamount to
what we call a declaration of martial law, in which
normal civil rights are abridged for the sake of public
safety. The dictator was immune from prosecution and
absolute in power until his term expired, but then must
stand civil trial for any act he has committed, if indicted.
The appointment was extremely rare, being granted
only every few centuries of Roman history. Julius Caesar
held it, and was given the highly irregular appointment
of Dictator for Life, which many Romans found more
than alarming. It should at least be noted that he was in
his sixties and, by Roman standards, approaching the
end of his lifespan, which surely affected the willingness
of the rather pragmatic Senate (which was also somewhat
stacked, since all his enemies were in flight) to vote
such an office. It gave Julius extraordinary powers, and
certainly contributed to the resentment which led to his
assassination, but Rome was in profound crisis, and he
had brought peace to the streets after a near century of
unrest and civil violence, a peace for which many average
citizens were grateful. In his day, *dictator* was an office
of very high honor, since only the most honorable and
trustworthy individuals were appointed to such an office.
It had always been a point of pride with particular dictators
to complete their task as rapidly as possible and resign.

Julius may or may not have intended to resign, but though he was a still-vigorous sixty, capable of physical feats that would have daunted some younger men, he was stricken with epilepsy and beginning to feel the press of time and events. It had taken him a decade to bring Gaul under Roman rule. Rome's problems were more far-reaching and the tangle of politics went right into the heart of Roman society: it is likely he himself added up the job and his remaining years and came up with himself in his seventies, which a Roman figured as the decade of his death—so there may have been indeed some justification for his having asked for and received such an unprecedented office. It could be questioned, however, whether he intended Octavianus as his succesor. Certainly he would have sent for Octavianus to return to Italy as the land grew more peaceful and his position grew safer—they had not seen each other in a long time—to second him and move gradually toward public acceptability, in a role which Marcus Antonius was then filling. Marcus Antonius was highly resentful of Octavianus when the young man moved into the void after Julius' death and grabbed power with both fists: Antonius may have known about Octavianus and may have understood Julius' intentions—may even have altered some of those intentions, since Antonius was the custodian of Julius' will. Certainly Antonius must have planned on directing the young man and teaching him in a kind of regency—but the desertion of the 10th legion from him to Octavianus, and Octavianus' immediate insistence on equal power, with the hint of more demands to come, alienated Antonius and led Antonius to a great mistake—as Antonius sought to establish a rival power base in Egypt with Kleopatra as his ally. In fact Antonius was not a brilliant strategist, and always needed someone of first-class intellect to do the planing: if it was not Julius, it was Kleopatra, who, a scholar as well as a pharaoh, had the intellect—but she did not well understand Romans, and did not always

prevail in her advice. Moreover, the position of Antonius and Kleopatra was politically and militarily at
disadvantage: the most seasoned troops were with
Octavianus, and so were the best field officers. Antonius' popularity waned and hit bottom at Actium, when
he fled the battle—Octavianus was there, but incapacitated by seasickness, a fact not generally known,
which only shows to what extent the winners write the
histories.

Thereafter Antonius' troops refused to fight Romans
for his sake, and the Egyptians resented him for the
very habit which had once made him popular with the
Romans—his fraternization with the troops, which they
did not appreciate. Neither army would serve him
faithfully, remembering Actium. Kleopatra attempted
to distance herself from him too late. She had become a
hated if romantic figure to the Romans, who feared her
capacity for intrigue, and she committed suicide rather
than face the Roman mobs, when Octavianus spurned
her peace mission. Antonius died just before her,
mistakenly believing she had killed herself, attempting
a Roman soldier's kind of suicide: he botched it, and
lived long enough to be hauled into her fortress—her
tomb, as it happened, but it was also the strongest
building available to her. She would not or could not
unseal the doors to admit him, as the story goes, and
when he was dead, when she knew that she had no
more troops standing between herself and the enemy,
she took her own life.

Dieu   *French:* God.

Dio   *Italian:* God.

Drusus   *Latin:* see Tiberius.

dux   *Latin:* general.

The Eater of Souls *Egyptian:* waited by the throne of Osiris in the netherworld. When a soul came to be judged, its spiritual heart had to balance the feather of the goddess Ma'at (Truth) on the scales. If not, the Eater of Souls leapt forth and gobbled up the unfortunate and that was the end of him forever.

ecce *Latin:* Look!

eccolo *Italian:* Look!

edepol *Latin:* by Pollux! A fairly strong Latin oath.

equitum *Latin:* of the cavalry.

est *Latin:* is *French:* is.

estis *Latin:* you are.

Etruria *Latin:* ancient Italian kingdom which tried to make Rome one of its cities.

excuse-moi *French:* pardon me.

Felix *Latin:* "Lucky," a Roman surname.

Fulminata *Latin:* "Thunderer," name of one of the legions.

Galen *Greek:* a physician.

Gaul *English:* ancient France.

genetrix *Latin:* mother (formal, religious, female equivalent of sire)

Graece *Latin:* in Greek.

grammaticus *Latin:* scholar; sometimes, magician.

Hadrianus *Latin:* Roman emperor.

Hannibal *Latin:* Carthaginian general who invaded Italy with elephants and nearly defeated Rome in what was called the Second Punic War (from the adjective meaning Phoenician, *punicus*, since Carthage was alleged to be a Phoenician colony.) Phoenicia was where the modern Lebanon is. Rome eventually defeated Hannibal in that and in a second bid for power. Hannibal's father Hamilcar Barca fought Rome in the First Punic War and rejected the peace treaty, taking Spain for his base and handing the war on to his son when he died at the hands of a Spanish assassin. It was, incidentally, the First Punic War in which Regulus died, executed by the Carthaginians when he urged Rome not to make peace for the sake of hostages the Carthaginians held, but to go on fighting until they won.

Hathor *Egyptian:* cow-headed goddess of maternity and fertility. Usually singular, although the Egyptians seem to have pluralized their gods in a number of instances, as they believed that an assortment of Hathors attended a birth and brought the newborn his luck: from birth, the child had a sort of horoscope decreed by the goddesses who proclaimed certain days and symbols lucky for him and certain others unlucky and even fatal.

Alexander Helios *Greek:* "Alexander the Sun": a son of Antonius and Kleopatra.

Hatshepsut *Egyptian:* woman who was pharaoh of Egypt.

Hellas *Greek:* Greece.

Hittite *Middle Eastern:* ancient people of the Near East.

Horemheb *Egyptian:* general and pharaoh of Egypt.

Horus *Egyptian:* hawk-headed god of sun and moon, son of Osiris and Isis.

Ilium *Latin:* Troy.

imperator *Latin:* commander, commandant; a term of honor award by the soldiers to a favorite general.

immortales *Latin:* immortal; the immortals.

Isis *Egyptian:* mother goddess of Egypt, queen of the gods, wife of Osiris, sister to Set and Osiris, mother of Horus. When Osiris was murdered by Set she restored him to life.

Italia *Latin:* Italy.

Iulius *Latin:* Latin spelling of Julius.

Iuppiter *Latin:* Latin spelling of Jupiter. It actually means Dayfather.

iuvent *Latin:* may they help.

je *French:* I.

Junii *Latin:* members of clan Junius, the clan of Brutus' father-in-name.

Junius *Latin:* Brutus' father.

Kadashman-enlil *Middle Eastern:* an Assyrian.

Kadesh *Middle Eastern:* a battle Rameses falsely claimed to have won, on his monuments. Other kings' monuments say they won. The press had its problems seven in those days.

Kaisarion *Greek:* Greek spelling of Caesarion.

Kleopatra *Greek:* Greek spelling of Cleopatra: Greek was actually her native tongue.

l'empereur *French:* the emperor.

Lethe *Greek:* river of forgetfulness in Hell.

Livia *Latin:* later wife of Augustus, mother of Tiberius and Drusus, said to have poisoned him, although there is some doubt of this. Certainly she had a great deal of power in Rome during Augustus' latter years.

Lucius *Latin:* common Roman first name.

Macedonia *Latin:* homeland of Alexander the Great, roughly where modern Turkey is, and part of Greece.

Niccolo Machiavelli *Italian:* author of *The Prince* supporter of Cesare Borgia.

madonna *Italian:* m'lady.

magister *Latin:* teacher; academic master; also *Magister Equitum*, Master of Horse, cavalry commander, which was the legal title of the aide to a Dictator, q.v.

magus *Latin:* pl. magi: wizard.

maledetto *Italian:* damned.

Marcus *Latin:* common Roman first name.

Marius   *Latin:* Julius Caesar's uncle; a democratic revolutionary, bitter opponent of Sulla.

Massilia   *Latin:* modern Marseilles.

mastigia   *Latin:* scum.

merde   *French:* shit.

Mithridates   *Latin:* arch-enemy of Rome during the time of Marius and Sulla, attempted to restore a Persian-style government in Asia Minor.

mon dieu   *French:* my God!

m'sieur   *French:* sir.

Mucius Scaevola   *Latin:* attempted spy and assassin: caught by the Etruscans when he killed the wrong man and threatened with torture to make him collaborate, he held his own hand in the fire and so overawed the Etruscan soldiery, the king he had tried to kill had no choice but to return him to his people. The name Scaevola means "Lefty."

Mummius Arhaicus   *Latin:* (Achaicus, lit. "conqueror of Achaia, or Greece") a Roman general notorious for spending more time plundering the artworks of Greece than generaling. When his treasure ships sank in the harbor at Corinth, they actually saved the only great collection of Greek bronzes that came through to the modern day; they now reside in the museum at Athens.

mushkinu   *Akkadian:* freeman.

Mycenae   *Latin:* city of Agamemnon, and of Helen when she was kidnapped to Troy.

Naram-sin   *Middle Eastern:* Sargon's grandson, whose ambition led to the downfall of the dynasty.

nefas   *Latin:* cursed; that which must not be uttered; damned.

numen   *Latin:* the aura of divine force which accompanies a god or one possessed by a god.

Nero   *Latin:* a Roman emperor notorious as a madman, more likely the unbalanced result of an incredibly abusive mother, who did everything possible to retain control of him until he assassinated her. He had illusions of bringing culture to Rome. Unfortunately he also viewed himself as a musician and was very touchy about criticism, hence the story that he once locked stadium gates and forced people to listen to him on pain of death. People actually climbed over walls to escape. Considering some of Nero's excesses when his artistry was called into question, this may have been only prudent action on the part of the escapees.

nolo, pl. nolite   *Latin:* don't.

numen   *Latin:* the aura of divine force which accompanies a god or one possessed by a god.

Octavia   *Latin:* sister of Augustus and wife of Antonius, foster-mother of Caligula, Agrippina, and the whole brood which gave Rome so much trouble.

Odysseus   *Greek:* Ulysses, the wandering seaman of Greek legend.

Osiris   *Egyptian:* god of agriculture and the dead, slain by his brother Set and resurrected by his faithful wife Isis. Egyptian dead may be referred to as The Osiris.

oui *French:* yes.

Parthia *Latin:* ancient land of the Middle East noted for its arrow-shooting horsemen, who are credited with teaching Romans about stirrups and generally making eastern advance impossible for Rome.

pater *Latin:* father.

patriae *Latin:* of the country.

pax *Latin:* peace.

Achilles Peliadès *Greek:* "lit. Achilles son of Peleus" hero of the Trojan War. Alexander the Great thought he was Achilles reincarnated. Julius Caesar entertained similar notions about himself and Alexander.

pensez *French:* you think.

perdio *Italian:* by God.

perpetuum *Latin:* perpetuity; forever.

pharaonic crowns: *Egyptian:* were several, the Blue or War Crown; the White, the Red, symbolizing Upper and Lower Egypt; the double, symbolizing the Union of Egypt; the Papyrus Crown, an incredibly complex towering crown worn only on one state occasion. There were others of similarly limited use.

plebis *Latin:* of the Commons; of the common people.

Pompeii *Latin:* Roman city destroyed suddenly by Mt. Vesuvius.

Pontus *Latin:* kingdom in Asia Minor ruled by Mithridates.

Lars Porsena   *Latin:* king of the Etruscans who tried to force Rome into the Etruscan union. Rome threw out its kings and set up a republic. Scaevola and Horatius both fought in this war.

Praxiteles   *Greek:* a famous sculptor. Julius' bronze is more recent work than that in the Greek museums.

prego   *Italian:* please.

Priamus   *Latin:* king of Troy.

princeps   *Latin:* First Citizen; number one; (title actually preferred by Augustus to most of his others.)

prodi   *Latin:* by the gods, for godssake.

prosit   *Latin:* be it to you! Your health!

Ptah   *Egyptian:* god of wisdom; also division name of a unit Ramesses led to disaster by Kadesh.

Ptolemaios   *Greek:* dynastic name of the pharaohs who followed Alexander the Great in Egypt.

Ptolemaidês   *Greek:* son or daughter of Ptolemy: Kleopatra's last name.

Publius   *Latin:* common Latin first name.

quam insaniam petis   *Latin:* are you crazy? (lit. "what crazy notion are you following?")

qu' est-ce que   *French:* what's?

quomodo   *Latin:* how?

qui   *Latin:* and *French:* and *Italian:* who.

qui estis   *Latin:* who are you?

Ra   *Egyptian:* sungod of Egypt, sometimes combined with the wind-god of Thebes, Amon, as supreme deity. This seems to have been a bit of political pragmatism on the part of the priests who had to come to a decision about who was supreme god—and Egypt was actually a fusion of two separate kingdoms, Upper (upNile, or southern Egypt) and Lower (downNile, or northern Egypt), hence the double crowns (the red and the white, which can be worn separately) and the combined vulture-serpent symbol which also symbolizes the union of Egypt.

Rameses   *Egyptian:* one of the best-known Egyptian pharaohs, ruled Egypt at its height.

Romains   *French:* Romans.

Pax Romana   *Latin:* the Roman Peace. A period of Augustus' reign in which there were no wars anywhere in the known world. It was the first time in Rome's history the doors of the Temple of Janus (always open when any of Rome's soldiers were on the march) were shut. It was something of which Augustus was very proud.

rudus   *Latin:* "rough." A stick sword presented to gladiators on retirement as a symbol. It was actually used in fencing practice.

SPQR   *Latin:* Roman nationala motto: "Senatus Populusque Romanus: the Senate and the Roman People," which has a significance similar to the meaning of the Gettysburg Address: that Rome is a government not only of the aristocrats (the Senate) but also of the commons.

salve, pl. salvete   *Latin:* hello! hi! also, more rarely, aha!

Sargon *Middle Eastern:* also Sharrum-kin, king of Akkad.

Scamander *Greek:* river at Troy, which clogged with the dead Achilles threw into it.

scellerati *Italian:* cursed.

Kleopatra Selene *Greek:* "Cleopatra the Moon," daughter of Antonius and Kleopatra.

Sharri *Middle Eastern:* an Akkadian soldier.

signora *Italian:* madam.

signore *Italian:* sir.

sivis *Latin:* if you will; please, would you be so kind as to.

souris *French:* mouse.

Lucius Cornelius Sulla *Latin:* the dictator; general on the side of the aristocrats in the Civil War of Rome; tried to kill Julius Caesar as a boy, but was talked out of it.

Styx *Latin:* river of death.

Sumer *Middle Eastern:* a kingdom overcome by Akkad, in the Tigris Euphrates valley, called the "cradle of civilization."

Tartarus *Latin:* realm of the wicked in the afterlife.

ter *Latin:* three times; thoroughly.

Thutmose *Egyptian:* pharaoh of Egypt, name of Hatshepsut's father and her long-absent and probably fugitive husband.

Tiber   *Latin:* the river that flows past Rome.

Tigellinus   *Latin:* head of the secret police.

tribunus   *Latin:* tribune; office about equivalent to lieutenant.

tunica   *Latin:* tunic; Roman casual wear.

Typhon   *Egyptian:* monster of the desert.

venez   *French:* come!

Vergil   *Latin:* wrote the *Aeneid*, court poet to Augustus.

vieux   *French:* old man; old friend.

voila   *French:* there!

vraiment   *French:* truly!

vu   *French:* seen.

Marie Walewska   *French:* lover of Napoleon.

Xerxes   *Middle Eastern:* king of Persia, reputed to have ordered the ocean flogged for disobedience. Actually, some of the early Persian kings seem to have been given to graphic illustrations for the benefit of their followers.

Zeus   *Greek:* same as Roman Jupiter: king of the gods.

Events contemporaneous with *Legions of Hell* are told in *Angels in Hell,* coming from Baen Books in October 1987. Events directly following both *Legions of Hell* and *Angels in Hell* will appear in *Masters of Hell,* which is currently scheduled for December 1987, also from Baen Books.

C'MON DOWN!!

Is the real world getting to be too much? Feel like you're on somebody's cosmic hit list? Well, how about a vacation in the hottest spot you'll ever visit . . . HELL!

We call our "Heroes in Hell" shared-universe series the Damned Saga. In it the greatest names in history—Julius Caesar, Napoleon, Machiavelli, Gilgamesh and many more—meet the greatest names in science fiction: Gregory Benford, Martin Caidin, C.J. Cherryh, David Drake, Janet Morris, Robert Silverberg. They all turn up the heat—in the most original milieu since a Connecticut Yankee was tossed into King Arthur's Court. We've saved you a seat by the fire . . .

TRAVIS SHELTON LIKES BAEN BOOKS BECAUSE THEY TASTE GOOD

Recently we received this letter from Travis Shelton of Dayton, Texas:

> *I have come to associate Baen Books with Del Monte. Now what is that supposed to mean? Well, if you're in a strange store with a lot of different labels, you pick Del Monte because the product will be consistent and will not disappoint.*
>
> *Something I have noticed about Baen Books is that the stories are always fast-paced, exciting, action-filled and seem to be published because of content instead of who wrote the book. I now find myself glancing to see who published the book instead of reading the back or intro. If it's a Baen Book it's going to be good and exciting and will capture your spare reading moments.*
>
> *Another discovery I have recently made is that I don't have any Baen Books in my unread stacks—and I read four to seven books a week, so that in itself is a meaningful statistic.*

Why do you like Baen Books? Drop us a letter like Travis did. The person who best tells us what we're doing right—and where we could do better—will receive a Baen Books gift certificate worth $100. Entries must be received by December 31, 1987. Send to Baen Books, 260 Fifth Avenue, New York, N.Y. 10001. And ask for our free catalog!

AUGUSTUS SNATCHED UP
THE RECEIVER

"Pythias. The Cubs in the fifth, by ten."

"Cubs in the fifth by ten," he repeated, waving his hand frantically at the map-table, and heard the phone go dead without goodbyes.

They had found the boys.

"Five and ten," Julius said between his teeth, and his face was utterly grim as he looked at the gridded map. *"Damn!"*

Augustus crossed the room to look where Julius' hand rested.

Assurbanipal's villa.

And Tiberius' establishment and five legions —were dead-set in the way.

Julius raked a hand through his hair and paced a fast circuit of the table-end. "Call Horatius again. I know, I *know* it's a risk. Tell them they're out of time, dammit. —*Where* the hell is Kleopatra?"

"Left with Hatshepsut," Curtius said.

"What?"

"Left with Hatshepsut," Curtius said, very carefully this time. "The pharaoh came in, the watch reported they both left in the car. We supposed—it was authorized—"

"Where?"

Curtius' face was decidedly pale. "I'll try to find out, if you—"

"Dammit, no, we're stretched thin enough. They'll turn up. I want the 10th, the 12th, and the 14th ready to move. The 5th and 6th in reserve."